# Bleeding ir

### A novel by
# Colin Cotterill

Bleeding in Black and White
Copyright © Colin Cotterill, 2015
First Published 2015

Published by DCO Books
Proglen Trading Co., Ltd.
Bangkok Thailand
http://www.dco.co.th

ISBN 978-1511671293

## *Also by Colin Cotterill*

### Dr. Siri Paiboun series
*The Coroner's Lunch (2004)*
*Thirty-Three Teeth (August 2005)*
*Disco For the Departed (August 2006*
*Anarchy and Old Dogs (August 2007)*
*Curse of the Pogo Stick (August 2008)*
*The Merry Misogynist (August 2009)*
*Love Songs from a Shallow Grave (August 2010)*
*Slash and Burn (October 2011)*
*The Woman Who Wouldn't Die (January 2013)*
*Six and a Half Deadly Sins (May 2015)*

### Jimm Juree series
*Killed at the Whim of a Hat (July 2011)*
*Grandad, There's a Head on the Beach (June 2012)*
*The Axe Factor (April 2014)*

### Other publications
*Evil in the Land Without (2003)*
*Ethel and Joan Go to Phuket (2004)*
*Pool and its Role in Asian Communism (2005)*
*Cyclelogical (2006)*
*Ageing Disgracefully (October 2009)*

# 1

## Ban Methuot - Vietnam

It was one hell of mess. The wife they'd given him, or what was left of her, was wrapped in tobacco leaves and bamboo matting and stored in a shed out back of the Administrator's place. The rainy season had set in early so the bridges were out and the road was impassable for the next five months. There was only one way of getting word in and out and that was through the telegraph at Dupré's. And now here was that same Monsieur Dupré's pretty young wife lying naked on the missionary's bed. Reverend Robert 'Bodge' Rodgers could see her skinny legs through the doorway. He drained the glass and put it down on the antique table beside the Holy Book. As if things weren't bad enough already, that was the last of the bourbon.

Probably the Viet Minh should have counted up there at the top of his worries but he'd somehow managed to push them on to the back burner. When the possibility of being butchered in your bed hangs over you every night and there isn't a thing you can do about it, you tend to blank a lot out -pretend it isn't there.

Beneath the din of the relentless pounding of rain on the slate roof, he heard another sleepy groan from his bed. He could see those skinny legs cycle in slow motion on the silk sheets. He shook his head. How had he gotten himself into such a hell-fired, Satan-sponsored, God-forbidden mess? It took him several uncoordinated attempts with a delicate brass trumpet to kill the flame in the table oil lamp. The only illumination in the house now came from one last pale light on the bedroom wall. Its glass cover had been smashed to smithereens during the tragedy, so the flame danced in the warm drafts.

Bodge stood on drunken legs that didn't feel at all like his own and let himself sway for a while. The dizziness cleared some but he still walked into the table, the footstool and the wall desk before he found the bedroom doorway. He looked at Monique's tightly luscious curves shuddering in the lamplight. Even in sleep she flirted. Every mound and valley of her told him to get himself over there beside her. A year ago he wouldn't have needed asking twice. But things had changed over the last six months. He'd changed. His priorities and loyalties were tangled. He wasn't sure what he believed in any more.

He held on to the door frame with his left hand to keep himself up and reached behind him with his right to the sliding lid of the French bureau. It came down without effort the way expensive, finely crafted furniture was supposed to. Even the click of the secret compartment was no more than a lizard's tut. The German revolver was heavy and warm and had enough power to blow Monique's sweet head all the way back to Marseilles.

He took a few unsteady paces to the edge of the bed and filled his lungs with air and classy perfume. It was time to show her exactly how he felt.

# 2

**January 1952 - Three months earlier**

"Time, Bodge?"

"Gee, Lou. You haven't asked me for an hour. I thought you'd croaked over there.

"I just want the time. If I needed sarcasm, I'd specifically say, 'Give me some sarcasm, Bodge'."

Bodge pulled back the cuff of his laundered shirt. He wore a reinforced John Bull he'd won from a squaddy in an arm wrestle at an English pub. It was camouflage green and dented, but he wouldn't ever think of replacing it. It was his link to life. "Two."

"Two? Damn. I was sure it was four." Lou yawned again and rasped air through his lips. He held an Italian government report by its corner and swung it like a pendulum. "Why do you suppose it's always rectangular?"

"What's that?"

"Paper."

Lou Vistarini sat at a desk facing Bodge's on the fourth floor of the modest Adams Center in New York City. Down in the lobby was a sign saying this was the Trans-National Insurance Company. That might have fooled one or two mailmen but nobody else on that block of East 23<sup>rd.</sup> and Third believed it for a second. They just had to look at the intense people turning up there each morning to know something was going on and it had nothing to do with insurance.

"It has some connection with the British Imperial system of measures, if I'm not mistaken," Bodge answered without looking up from his own report. Lou clawed his black-rimmed glasses half way down his nose and looked over at Robert 'Bodge' Leon, his office mate. Nice enough guy. Average looking but solid, like he could be the next in line at Mount Rushmore. Built big, six foot five, but getting soft of late like John L Sullivan after he got stuck into the booze. He was smart, really smart; not the type to rile easily, but he tended to take life a little too seriously at times. He was a careful talker — he thought before he spoke and that confused some people into figuring he was a slow thinker. That was Lou's appraisal at least and he'd sat opposite the man for the past seven years. They drank together once or twice a week, spent birthdays together, even double-dated on the odd occasion. So he was probably in a good position to say.

Lou was a lesser version of Bodge: two sizes smaller in white button-collar shirts, five inches off the leg in standard charcoal gray slacks. But he was from a similar mould. Like most of the males at Trans-Continental they wore crew cuts so sheer on the back and sides there was no hairline. They both had a knack of making neckties look like bitten-through lasso ropes — the kind you'd find on escaped cattle. On their nights out they weren't unused to hearing,

"I didn't think you guys was allowed booze." So there must have been something about the two of them together that reminded people of Mormons.

"Yeah. I know all that," Lou persisted. "But it's all random. Some royal guy just sits down one day and makes up all these random numbers just to make schooling impossible: twenty four shillings in a yard, sixteen ounces in a pint. But what was it that made old King What's-his-Lord decide on rectangles for paper?"

"As opposed to?"

"Squares. There's no reason on this earth why paper shouldn't be square."

Bodge looked up for the first time, but not at Lou. He stared into that reservoir high on the wall that contained all the answers to unnecessary questions. With someone like Lou in your office you needed to dip into it any number of times a day. It occurred to Bodge that Lou had reached that 'meaning of life' stage and he felt obliged to help him through it.

"Well, Lou, I guess it has something to do with man's uncontrollable desire to fold things in half. Every square's destined to become a rectangle."

That was Bodge. He wasn't the type of man who could settle unless he had an answer to every question. That was the quirk that got him into the agency in the first place and what got him into most of the trouble he'd ever had in his life. But these days he was finding very little he could be bothered to put thought into.

He signed his name in the box at the bottom of the report to say he'd read it. There was no box that asked whether he'd given it any thought so he hadn't bothered to. He took the next paper off the IN tray pile and scanned the heading. 'Communist Affiliations in the Danish Peerage'. It wouldn't have been any less inspiring had it been square.

Lou wasn't about to let up. "Only the first time."

"Say what?"

"If you fold it a second time, it's square again, right?"

"I guess."

"Then if them royals had been a little more inclined to order and neatness, they could very well have made the standard measure a foot by a foot. Just think how packable everything could of been: square books, envelopes, playing cards."

Bodge was trapped again, lost in another of Lou's foolish sidetracks. They got him every time. It was what happened when two intelligent men are stuck in an office without inspiration. Neither of them was pushed intellectually. Any ape with a degree could have done the work that passed over their desks. Bodge took up the challenge of square.

"A rectangle is more of a natural shape to man."

"Oh, yeah? You got rectangular mountains and trees in Tennessee?"

"I didn't say 'natural to nature'. I said 'natural to man'. Think about it. What shape is most congruous to our needs? We're tall, thin beings."

"You're not."

"Compared to a tortoise I am and tortoises have no need for rectangles. A child grows perpendicularly and you want him to always look out on the world, so what shape are our windows? Rectangular. We have to pass from one room to the next, so what shape do doors have to be to accommodate our bodies? Rectangular. We have an arm on either side of us, so what shape of desk allows us to reach to the left and to the right? What shape of bed best allows us rest? And when I pass on do they roll me into a ball and bury me in a pit? No sir. They bury me in a…"

"Rectangular prism. I get it."

"In fact, there is nothing about our lives that lends itself to square."

"You're right."

"I know."

The OSS had recruited Bodge directly from the mud of France as World War II in Europe edged towards its conclusion. He'd made quite a hero out of himself in his first conflict even though his heroism had come about quite by chance. He hadn't been the type of boy who headed off to battle in the hope of getting medals pinned to his chest. He wasn't a coward but he wouldn't have objected to seeing out the war in some office in London.

He'd been a college wrestler so there was a time he'd been in good shape, and he was smart enough, but there was no mistaking the fact that he'd been appointed combat aide to General Osgood merely on his ability to speak French. Much to the disappointment of his parents, the language had been his major at school. It was largely their fault. When he was little he was brought up by a nanny from New Orleans. At least, she was the one who stayed longest. The pidgin they spoke together was a perfect grounding for formal French at school. His well-to-do mother and father saw him as more of an investment than a loved one. They wanted him in politics, or theology, but their only child chose humanities.

All through his teens he'd dreamed of living in Europe. England was his first choice but he already spoke passable English and he decided French would round him out — make him more saleable to international corporations. It hadn't occurred to him that Europe already had more than its share of unemployed young men and they didn't really need to import others. But luck was on his side. Hitler invaded France and Japan bombed Pearl Harbor and suddenly Bodge had something his government needed: French.

He was almost twenty-one and still six months from graduating when the notice went up on the school careers board. *TRAVEL. Learn a Trade and get paid for using your foreign language. UNCLE SAM NEEDS YOU.'* At the recruitment office the cheerful captain with angles ironed into his uniform assured Bodge he could get credits for his degree and complete it as a member of the United States Marine Corps.

So he joined up and two months after putting his pen to paper he found himself on a troop carrier on his way to the country he'd always dreamed of seeing. His two years in the service turned him into a man and tangled him up in a lie he couldn't get out of. He was glad when demobilization came in '45 and he worked his way home with his Medal of Honor hidden quietly at the bottom of his kit bag.

The war in Europe was won, Bodge was a celebrity and people were asking about him. When the guy in Berlin had first recruited him for the Office of Strategic Services, the subject of paperwork never came up. There was a lot of talk of covert missions to exotic places, parachuting into jungles and sailing down unspoiled rivers, but not a word about paperwork. And that was odd because for seven years, that's all he'd done.

Of course there was no end of excuses for it. For the early months the world had been at peace for the first time anyone could remember. Once the Pacific was won, there was no immediate call for espionage in foreign countries. Any action that came along was handed out to the guys with broken noses and tattoos. Bodge was a nice, soft guy. His superiors had problems with a giant of a man who apparently never lost his temper. What message would that send to the world? So, agent Leon settled down to writing and translating reports on the American war effort. Then on

October 1, 1945 under President Harry S. Truman's Executive Order 9621, the OSS was disbanded. It was a pity, but Bodge guessed it would allow him to find himself a real job someplace. He still had his dream to do business in Europe.

The director of the disbanded organization had other things in mind. He wasn't about to lose this band of handpicked heroes just because there was nowhere for them to work. So, Bodge and 150 other valuable but positionless "agents" were all placed on what was officially termed "speculative hold". They filed, they went on retreats and seminar courses, they processed unimportant "code green" documents left over from the war and they played a lot of backgammon. They were paid well for their somnolence but like most of them it wasn't the money Bodge had signed up for. He wanted to serve his country and if there was a little excitement in the bargain he wouldn't say no.

There was a certain buzz of anticipation when, in 1946, the President established the National Intelligence Authority and the Central Intelligence Group. There was a serious pay rise. All the agents began to work for one or the other organization but as far as Bodge could tell, the same goddamned files were coming over their desks and the same goddamned "you'll have to be patient" met his polite requests for missions. They were reminded that this was the clerical section and a more stable infrastructure had to be established before they could apply for a transfer to *operations*. It was round about here that Lou Vistarini and Bodge found themselves in the same office. Bodge handled French, Lou Italian. Neither of them remembered volunteering for the clerical section in the first place. Lou and Bodge complemented each other. Lou was the hare to Bodge's tortoise, the Costello to his Abbott.

But, despite working for an exciting new organization, the boys did a lot of sitting. When you spend too long on your backside, you tend to get sloppy. Bodge was no exception to that rule. He'd had it in his mind for some time that he'd be a good husband. He wasn't enamored with living by himself and he could picture one of the new Levittown Homes with his pretty wife standing at the door with a freshly baked tuna casserole in her oven mitts. His only problem was recruiting someone he cared enough about to fill the role. It was his mid-twenties crisis. He was starting to abandon all hope of passion.

Shelly LeTissier was a secretary at Curtis and Simon across the street. She and her buddies from the typing pool ate at Max's. That's where Bodge and Lou spent most of their long lunch hours. Bodge couldn't help but notice the pale girl with good teeth. But he was fascinated more by her tall blond beehive hairdo than her face. He could never understand what kept it up. He liked to watch the flies circle around her hairspray. She noticed this not-so-bad-looking guy staring at her and started to stare back. When he found out her name he figured it was an omen; the French connection. Six months later and before Bodge really knew what hit him, they were engaged. Another three months and they were married.

Bodge had followed all the rules when it came to women. He'd had girlfriends, plenty of them. He got on to all the bases he was recommended to be on and never (in his mother's words) messed around in diners when he had his own roast in the oven at home. But it was all so ordinary. He'd heard about love, seen it in movies, read about it. But despite all the affairs, not one ever had him singing in the rain, dancing on the street or hiring mariachi musicians to serenade at his table. He arrived at the firm belief that it was an advertising ploy conjured up to sell chocolates.

His marriage wasn't a passionate thing, but by then, Bodge was so dulled by his job, it was colorful by comparison. He'd come to believe women weren't supposed to be stimulating. Those weren't the days when girls were encouraged to have ambition. He'd never hung out with any he honestly believed weren't in training for house-wifing and motherhood. Thankfully he and Shelly had held off having children. Thankfully for Shelly because she needed all the spare time she could find to be spending her new husband's salary. Thankfully for Bodge because he kind of knew, even before the church bells had stopped ringing in his eardrums, that they wouldn't be together long enough to watch kids grow up.

He didn't actually classify the marriage as a failure. They gave it two years to see if it would turn into a love match all by itself, but neither of them was sad to see the other leave. He probably didn't give her a thought after it was over. It was an experience, negative perhaps but an experience never the less.

His job certainly wasn't adding to his collection of experiences. In July of 1947, President Truman had signed a brand new National Security Act which entered into force on September 19, and the Central Intelligence Agency came into being as a statutory body the next day. This was what they'd all been waiting for, a slick, humanitarian agency with the mandate to rescue the world from tyranny and oppression. Bodge and Lou knew in their hearts that this would be the turning point in their careers. They were given very specific training in infiltration and antiterrorism techniques, had several large volumes of information to take home and memorize, and before the year was out, lined up to receive a certificate, a multi-use penknife, and a very smart personalized CIA identification badge and card. This was the real thing.

Bodge and Lou had been shown their newly renovated office on the fourth floor, their nicely veneered desks, and the stationery sets with *CIA* stamped on each pen. And here they still were, four years later, processing files, and discussing the shape of paper.

"Brother," Lou decided, "You and I are going to head out at lunch time and have ourselves a good old fashioned rectangular meal at Max's,".

"Eating's all we seem to do."

"Get out of here. What about booze?"

"You boys having a good time?"

They looked up to see Supervisor Mooney in the doorway, the perennial cigarette dangling from the corner of his mouth. "I hope those reports aren't doing too much damage to your theoretical discussions."

"Mooney how long have you been standing there spying?" Lou asked. "Go annoy someone else, why don't you?"

Supervisor Mooney had been with these two since the beginning. They'd sunk beers together, been on fishing trips. Then, for reasons none of them could work out, especially Stanley Mooney himself, they'd called him into the top office and told him he was going to be promoted to supervisor at another fifty dollars a month. They didn't ask him if he wanted the job or give him any choice.

"A little respect if you don't mind, gentlemen."

"Go screw yourself."

"Lou!" Mooney looked back into the hallway. "What if anyone had heard that?"

"They'd be impressed at the warm and caring relationship you have with your underlings."

"*Screw yourself* is warm and caring?"

"I got worse than that."

"I don't want to hear it. Hey, Bodge."

Bodge dragged himself away from the Danish royal family. "Yes, Stan?"

"There's some guy here from Washington. He wants to talk to you."

"Yeah sure, Stan." He looked back down.

"No I'm serious."

Lou hooted. "Come on, Mooney. How many times you gonna pull that one, and how many times is it gonna not be funny?"

"I'm not kidding, guys." Mooney did see the ironic side of it and smiled.

"OK, Mooney."

"Listen, Bodge. This guy…"

"I've got work to do, Stan."

Mooney was starting to understand how the boy who cried "wolf" must have felt till he remembered the card in his top pocket. He took it out and dropped it on Bodge's desk.

"See?"

Bodge looked up into the supervisor's eyes and back down at the card. He picked it up and read aloud from it,

"A. Palmer, CIA Department of Special Operations."

Lou let out one of his rude laughs. "Stan, you have got to be kidding me. Just how stupid do you take us for?"

"Oh, I already know how stupid you are. This doesn't change that any."

"So, you want us to believe this guy up on the hill, working in special ops, goes around giving out name cards. Come on."

"I think it's real, Lou," Bodge said at last. He could feel the quality of the shiny card and the expense of the raised lettering under his fingers. Lou laughed again.

"Well, hell. If that's what it takes to get into operations, I'm taking out an ad in the Yellow Pages. I guess we've been too discreet about things all these years. What's he want with my brother, Stan?"

"Didn't say. But I tell you what…"

"What?"

"He's wearing a two-hundred-buck suit."

# 3

"Agent Leon?"

"Yes sir."

The man in the two-hundred-buck suit stood politely and held out his hand. Bodge walked over and shook it. He felt its authority and confidence. The man's hand had established who was in charge. All Bodge's own hand could ever do was grab and shake. It didn't establish anything, except that he was sweating.

"Take a seat, son."

They were alone in a director's office that had been vacated so this meeting could take place. Bodge sat on the sofa across the room from the desk and sank lower than he wanted. He knew the seat was deliberately made soft so guests would feel inferior. It worked.

Palmer was pouring them both coffee at the cocktail counter. There was nothing physically distinguished about the man. He was somewhere in his late fifties, slim, gray-haired, and not particularly tall. If you took him out of his suit and his hair cream he might be the kind of wiry guy you'd meet at weekends in the hardware store. But he did have one of those presences Bodge had read about. He hadn't asked whether his guest wanted coffee or how he took it. But it arrived perfect. Bodge was impressed.

On his walk up the stairwell to the fifth floor a number of things had reeled through Bodge's mind. He had two scenarios worked out even before he'd heaved open the fire door. Both of them scared him. In the first case they were about to throw him out on his ear. They'd invited some impartial executive from another division to do the dirty work because at the Adams Center all the long-term people knew each other. This was his last day at work, and, although he wasn't fond of the job, he wasn't sure what else he could do. That was the first theory.

But the second theory was even more terrifying. After all these years of putting in for transfers and missions and overseas duties — they were finally going to give him one. They were going to send him on an operation. He'd halved his pace along the silent hall carpet as that possibility sank in. It suddenly occurred to him he wasn't ready any more. After seven years he'd gone soft; the muscle behind his heroism had atrophied along with all the others. All this applying and lobbying he did was no longer a result of that urge, it was just what he'd always done. It was expected. Some while back he'd given up hope. He couldn't put his finger on when that happened. It just crawled up on him one day.

He wasn't sure he really wanted a mission any more. He had a season ticket for Giants games at the Polo Grounds and membership of a couple of exclusive supper clubs. He had a nice apartment now with a state of the art hi-fi system, a Frigidaire, and a TV with a color receiver. That TV stuck there in his mind for a second and he stood still on the high pile carpet. Perhaps if he hadn't invested in that latest folly he might have been more prepared to thrust himself into danger.

Five months earlier, RCA had made the first color television broadcast, from New York's Empire State Building. The following month, CBS followed suit. Department stores attracted huge crowds that came to view one more miracle from an already prodigious media. The CBS executives could imagine nothing but awe from a population in love with Technicolor at the cinema. Now Americans could witness living color in their very own homes. What could go wrong?

It only took a month before the company was facing accusations of Satanism. In a pervading atmosphere of communist dread that hung over the country, who but a communist-funded station would do anything so barbaric, so tasteless? The CBS liaison desk was inundated with calls and letters from disgusted viewers. What pornography were they decrying? Nothing less than *The Evening News Hour*. The executives were astounded by the reaction.

For months, news footage had been arriving from Korea. It had become a familiar if sometimes annoying feature of the prime time bulletins. And, indeed, nothing had changed in the presentation or in the selected items. It was agreed that nobody would have even noticed had it not been for the experimentation with color and CBS's race to one-up its rivals. But what, in black and white, could have been oil patches or mud from a rainy season foxhole, had in fact turned out to be glowingly crimson blood.

In those early days TV red was brighter than a Florida sunset. At the cinema, whole legions of Roman warriors could be slain in battle and audiences would see nothing more than a dull red speck of paint artistically daubed on the armor. And that, of course, was paint. Everyone in the movie house knew it was paint. It even looked like paint. It never spurted from a severed vein or spread beneath a slain centurion, because — it was paint. But what they were seeing on the news was blood; the real thing. In black and white it had been easy to ignore. But here was a television station with the audacity to send pictures of real red blood into everyone's home. Our boys in the field were bleeding in color. It just wasn't good enough.

So, after a week of colored news from Korea, everything went back to black and white and the complaints stopped. But although the blood was gray again, it still registered as red in the minds of those who'd seen it. For people like Bodge, who'd been on battlefields where bodies lay like veal in fresh blood sauce, nightmares were rekindled. He had no desire to watch men die slowly or watch blood ooze from their wounds. He had no desire to be one of them. If anyone were to ask, he'd tell them. He was afraid of death and all the unnecessary violence that led to it. CBS had reminded him he was a coward.

At that moment, on the soft sofa with his perfect cup of coffee, he was silently hoping to get fired. Palmer sat on the armchair with his head a good eighteen inches above Bodge's. He tasted his own coffee and smiled warmly like a cocktail host before speaking. Bodge noticed that the man's fingernails were impeccably neat.

"You know who I am and where I'm from?"

"Yes sir."

"This visit is what we call an appraisal."

"Of?"

"Of you, Bodge." He used the nickname comfortably as if it were the most natural thing in the world for a perfect stranger to know all your secrets.

"I'm here to see what you're made of. Do you mind if I ask you one or two questions?"

"Go ahead."

"If you had to select three adjectives to describe yourself, what would they be?"

Bodge kept his smile to himself. It was going to be one of *those* interviews: psychological tests devised by agency shrinks to find the real man inside the man. He pushed his luck a little.

"Do you want all three of them right away?"

Palmer didn't hold back his own smile. "It's up to you."

"Then, if you don't mind, I'd prefer to give them to you as they come to me."

"May I ask you why?"

"I'd hate to say something just to be smart and wind up regretting it. So, okay, here's the first one; *Careful.*"

"You're happy with that?"

"Yes."

Palmer noted it down on a pad that had been strategically placed on the coffee table in front of him. He then scribbled down some notes that kept Bodge hanging. He started to believe the whole interview would be a barrage of IQ and personality tests he could probably manipulate to get himself ousted. But the next question shook him out of that theory.

"Your parents…"

The interviewer waited for some reaction but there was none.

"…are devout Baptists. They raised you very strictly by the good book. Would you say that's true?"

"I would."

"Did any of it rub off?"

"Do you mean, am I a good Christian?"

"Not really. I suppose I mean, could you convince someone else that you were?"

Bodge looked up for his reservoir of flippant answers but realized the question was serious.

"My parents, particularly my father, hammered the scriptures into me from the first day I could recognize words. I had a theological lecture every evening until I was old enough to get away from home. By then I had no feeling for religion. I can't say whether the messages rubbed off but the advertising certainly stuck. I guess I could recite the Bible verbatim if I were pushed."

"Good." Bodge couldn't imagine what was good about it. He watched the man scribble down more notes in a shorthand Bodge didn't recognize before continuing.

"How's your French these days?"

"I haven't had much chance to speak it down there in my cubby hole over the past seven years." He didn't bother to catch Palmer' gaze although he noticed the man look up from his notepad. Bodge continued to speak in the direction of the notations on the pad. "*Observant.*"

"I beg your pardon?"

"I'd like *observant* to be my second adjective."

"Certainly. What have you observed?"

"That you're using your note-taking as a distraction device, probably to give you time to think about your next question or to let me trip over my own feet. You aren't really writing anything I'm telling you."

"What makes you think that?" Palmer smiled again.

"From the number of characters you've scribbled down there, I should by now have noticed some repetitions. Even if I don't know your shorthand, there'd logically be symbols that repeat from time to time. What you have there is just a chain of decorations."

Bodge hoped this was all getting him black marks. Palmer put down his pencil.

"We were talking about your French."

"It's been several years since I last had to open a dictionary. And every document in French that comes into this building passes over my desk."

"And how is that desk?"

"How is the desk?"

"You must be on quite intimate terms with it after seven years."

"Five years. I had a different one when I first started."

"They tend to be pretty much alike. You want to get away from it?"

There. That was the moment. That was the exit. A second of hesitation, a straightforward, "No" and it would all be over. It was that easy. Bodge would be filing for another thirty years. Despite the anxiety he'd brought with him to the Director's office, he suddenly understood exactly what it was he needed. The answer rose up through the murky doubts, ignoring his whiney subconscious cowardice. He looked into Palmer' pale blue eyes and said, very firmly,

"Yes. I do."

The operations man smiled and was about to make another note until he realized there was no longer a point. There were other questions but Bodge got the feeling they were no longer appraising him. They'd turned to orientation. *Do you know anything about the situation in Indochina? Would you be prepared to learn a third language? Do you have any health issues which might preclude you from staying in a hot climate?* They were all asked matter-of-factly as if a decision had already been made. There was only one question where Palmer might have noticed a hesitation, but he'd probably expected it. *Do you have any familial or social attachments that would preclude your accepting a two-year assignment away from the United States?*

It hadn't been the *attachments* part of the question that caused Bodge to think carefully. Operations had done its homework. They knew Leon was divorced and, even including the overnight pickups from clubs: the pretty showgirls, aspiring actresses, for almost two years he hadn't been intimate with anyone he liked. He visited his parents at Christmas and on birthdays without fail, but there was no emotional attachment and he didn't stay there longer than was absolutely necessary. He had no brothers or sisters, so Agent Robert Leon was what they called in the division, 'unhooked'. Nobody would miss him.

What concerned Bodge about the question was the period of time. Two years sounded like infinity to him. He'd always imagined skipping into a country, photographing a secret file, skipping out, and taking a month of emotional leave to recover from the trauma. He'd never imagined a mission being a long drawn-out affair. But he answered 'No' anyway.

With all the formalities out of the way, Palmer apologized for being unable to give Bodge details just yet, but said he'd go ahead with arrangements for a formal and thorough briefing. He welcomed Bodge to what he called 'the team', shook his hand once more and walked him to the door. Palmer had a way of speaking that pumped pride into a man like air into an inner tube. Bodge stood in the doorway puffed up with glory and honor and patriotism. He had a strong urge to salute till Palmer let a little of the air out.

"Oh, Bodge."

"Yes sir?"

"It may be a good time to do something about your shape."

"My shape sir?" The word 'rectangle' leapt to his mind.

"Yes agent. You're a mess. Get fit."

"Yes sir."

Bodge walked off down the hall.

"And don't forget you owe me an adjective," Palmer called after him.

"Sir."

# 4

## Vietnam

Her Highness Mademoiselle Nguyen Von Hong, second consort to the sometimes esteemed Emperor of Vietnam, was on her knees at the new porcelain toilet bowl. She'd thrown up successfully twice. The third attempt was an empty dredging.

The French gin had negated the effects of the first three pipes of opium so she'd taken an ill-advised fourth. When Lan came running into the bed chamber with the message, the room was already in flight; rolling through the air like a Chinese dragon.

"He's back and he wants you — immediately,"

"What for?" she'd asked, although there was no mystery. Her tongue had expanded to muffle her question.

"What for? To nip at your sweet, boyish nipples," her maid servant giggled. "To caress your firm buttocks."

That was the image that had sent Hong into the marble bathroom and her dinner into the palace sewer. Still she knelt in homage to the god of ill-matching substances. She could hear Lan blithering on behind the locked teak door.

"Hong, really. He's waiting and he's had a few drinks. You know what he gets like. He's in a mighty hurry to place his ardor."

"Let him wait," Hong thought. "Let him wait till his ardor builds and fills him from toe to top-knot: till he explodes into two thousand randy pieces." She called out to Lan, "You go. You go in my place. I'm not well."

"Oh, that he'd accept me," Lan lamented. "Oh, that he were a man with an appreciation of ripe swaying bosoms and hips with handles. But, sadly he favors the chopstick over the ladle. Come on. Hurry. It'll be me he punishes, not you. Wash out your mouth and we'll set about making you fit for the table."

Hong looked at herself in the ornate mirror. She looked for the once-pretty child, the once-brilliant student, the one-time Miss Mekhong Delta who'd wobbled on pointed heels to collect her ribbon. But all she saw was an abused woman nearing twenty-five, ravaged by excesses, and painted over to hide the mistakes. She knew if she were able to step out from inside the makeup and the lacquered hair and the antique pajamas, any woman could move in to take her place. She was just a piece of common fruit in this elaborate rind. But it was her he'd chosen. To her the honor, the most awful, unwanted honor, had been bestowed. So, unless she wished her family to vanish like the others, she had no choice.

She dabbed carefully at her paint-work with a damp flannel, gargled with a mint and jasmine mouthwash, and unlocked the door so that Lan could, in five miraculous minutes, turn her once more into the 'embodiment of southern perfection' with whom the Saigon newspapers had fallen in love.

# 5

Bodge and Lou were somewhat stymied when it came to a location for toasting the news that night. They'd developed a habit of celebrating non-events; the arrival of a new batch of stationery, the passing away of an office silverfish, a haircut. For such memorable moments they had several favorite bars and restaurants. But, apart from Bodge's divorce, there had been no really happy events to drink to. None of their regular haunts seemed appropriate for this life-changer. So they didn't even try to match the splendor of the event.

Twenty minutes from the office was a neighborhood bar. It wasn't seedy enough to call a dive, but it wouldn't have made it into the state *Good Drinking and Dining Guide* either. It did, however, have ice-cold Schaeffer's on tap and that was how they decided to christen the end of their era. With another flurry of snow blowing sideways outside the window, they found a spot near the radiator and settled. The barman had instructions to keep the jugs coming until Bodge and Lou fell off their stools.

"So what are you gonna do without me?" Bodge asked. He was expecting another smart-assed answer, but his office mate was in one of his philosophical moods.

"I been thinking about that, buddy. I can't see me sticking around the office for long. It was only having you in there with me reminding me how much worse my life could have been — only kidding ya. You're the only thing that makes it bearable. What would you have done if it had been me?"

"Called on a mission?"

"Yeah. Stretch your imagination."

"I'm not sure. Put in for a transfer to somewhere different? Quit? It would have dynamited me out of the rut, that's for sure. I couldn't imagine that office without you, either."

"Ain't this romantic? But that's just it. You and me, we were headed along that road to long service and a gold watch. They'd have these two white-haired old guys up on a stage talking to the young recruits saying things like, "Yes, it was different when we started out." And they'd all be sitting there with their mouths open and their tongues dribbling, waiting for old-timer stories about spying and near-death experiences…"

"And we'd tell them about how tough it was before the days of the ball point, when we had to use fountain pens and fill them up ourselves out of bottles."

"Exactly. What's the most exciting thing you've got to tell your grandkids about your days with the agency?"

"Me?" He looked up at the reservoir. "The Christmas party of 48?"

"That's what I mean. Mind you, it was one hell of a party. But now it's different. I've got this friend who's off risking life and limb…"

"Wait. They didn't say anything about that."

"…risking life and limb in a dangerous far off land, getting tortured by crazed war mongers."

"Hell. Maybe I'll call in sick."

"Making love to beautiful exotic women, seeing the way things really are in the world and making a difference. I don't suppose they'll let you send me weekly postcards?"

"Unlikely."

"But at least I can imagine all that stuff while I'm doing…what I'm doing."

"And what is that?"

"What?"

"What you're doing."

"Oh, you know. I've got something planned."

"You didn't tell me that. What is it?"

"It's a secret."

"I thought we didn't have any secrets."

"No, the way it works is that you don't have any secrets from me. But you don't know shit about my secrets. You'd be amazed at what I'll be doing while you're off vacationing in Asia."

It was just one exchange in a night of friendly talk, but it was one Bodge would come to think back on. It stuck for some reason. Those coherent moments eventually gave way to slurrings and fictional reminiscences, and loud, badly sung songs. But the nice thing about the bar they'd chosen was that you'd probably have to set light to the place to get thrown out. At around midnight, as they'd predicted, they fell off their stools and the barman stopped serving them draft beer.

Bodge's last few days at the Adams Center felt entirely different. He and Lou agreed that the best way to deal with Thursday's hangovers was to suffer work, go for a meal, then have an early night. On the Friday morning a young guy came into the office and handed Bodge a letter already removed from its envelope. He stuck around while Bodge read it.

It was from Palmer telling him his orientation proper was to begin the following Tuesday. It announced Bodge's position would be taken over by Mr. Edward Gladstein and asked Bodge, if he had time, to go through the procedures with Edward at some stage to ensure a smooth hand-over. Bodge read the letter aloud to Lou. Young Gladstein insisted they both call him Eddy. Bodge was more than happy to oblige. The boy spoke French like a native. His mother was the real thing and he'd been raised bilingual somewhere out in California. He and Bodge yapped away in French for the whole afternoon apart from when they were parrying the odd insult from left-out Lou in Italian.

Then the three of them went out and got stewed in a procession of bars and nightclubs. It was a final goodbye for Bodge, an office welcome for young Eddy, and a farewell to a tradition. Bodge came-round in the back of a Yellow Cab with Lou asleep on his shoulder and the boy nowhere to be seen. Only the driver seemed to have any grasp on sobriety.

"Hey mister?" Bodge slurred. He felt like he was in a sack of flour. "You got any idea where you're going?"

Bodge saw the skinny driver smile into the mirror. Most of his face was nose.

"Yeah pal. Don't you worry. I got both your addresses writ down here. You're getting out just up ahead."

The cab stopped in front of a four-story brownstone that Bodge recognized as his own. He somehow found the car door handle and the sidewalk and used the side of the cab to hold himself up while he felt around for his wallet. The driver laughed again.

"No need pal. It's all paid for. You wanna shut that door?"

Bodge looked inside at Lou. His office mate had dropped down onto the seat and was sleeping like a baby.

"Sweet dreams, Lou."

There was no response. Bodge was reluctant to let the cab out from under him as he wasn't certain he'd be able to stay upright of his own volition. But he slammed the door shut and waved as the yellow blur shot off into the night. It took him a long while to get to his apartment. There were waves on the sidewalk — big Japanese-style waves. The front door, the elevator, the apartment key, they all found ways to complicate what should have been an easy enough journey. Bodge had never felt so numb or so stupidly ill. Even the kitchen-dinette was waltzing. Whatever he'd drunk that night was evil. If he could remember what the hell it was, he'd give it up.

He drank two cups of black coffee so strong he had to chew. It was always a mistake to go to bed drunk. That much he remembered. He didn't want to feel like the devil had set up the satanic quintet in his head when he woke up. He'd had the taste of vomit on his lips when he got home although he couldn't remember throwing up. He wanted to get himself to the state where he could get to the bathroom, shower, relieve himself and clean his teeth before he passed out.

But the third cup of coffee turned out to be more than he could take. There was a current passing through him like a badly wired tenement. He found himself in his boxer shorts, shoes and socks laying on the top bedcover, staring at the lampshade above his head. A siren was going off somewhere far outside his window. His clock was ticking — loudly, and his heart was throbbing like the pump on an oil rig. He was horribly awake, thinking in vivid confused colors.

Somehow his mission to Indochina got into his head. He saw himself in a rickshaw dressed in a white suit and a Panama hat heading off to baffle the enemy. And the foe had to look like Japs because they were the only Asians he was vaguely familiar with. And Japanese and fighting naturally took his mind to Germany and the day that changed his life. It wouldn't be the first time he'd gone over the events. It didn't ever alter things and no amount of thought ever gave him a handle on how he could have done anything differently.

General Osgood had handpicked Bodge from the flock of French-speaking aides gathered at Command on the south coast of England. He hadn't bothered with interviews, just walked into the room, looked around and pointed at Captain Leon.

"You'll do, son. Come with me."

That day, Osgood had explained to Bodge he'd been chosen because German snipers were renowned for picking off ranking officers in the field. Whenever possible, he liked to have heavy-set adjutants around him so the riflemen couldn't get in a shot. Naturally, Bodge believed that story because he wasn't too well attuned to war humor. It wasn't till two months later when he and the general had gotten to know each other pretty well that he discovered the man had been through Bodge's files with a microscope. He was relieved to learn he'd been picked on merit, not size.

After a seemingly endless wait in England, going over tactics again and again, word finally came from Ike that D Day was on. Bodge and Osgood went in following the main invasion forces at Normandy. They had a coordinating role. Once the main body of troops was on the march across France, their job was to travel from one resistance group to the next, show them the ground plan for a coordinated effort and gather intelligence that was too sensitive to radio back and forth. There were four in Osgood's team; a driver, a radio operator, an interpreter (Bodge) and the General himself. They traveled light and fast in a souped up Willys jeep.

Things went well. The push had been held up for a brief spell but now four divisions were on their way to Orleans. Osgood and Bodge had been able to contact over twenty cells of the underground and coordinate acts of sabotage that scuttled German defense plans. As they were technically traveling along the periphery of enemy occupied territory, going into villages that had been vacated by retreating German divisions, their job was classified "low risk". In fact, while many of his countrymen were under fire on the front line, Bodge was accepting garlands and kisses on their behalf miles away from the fighting. His was invariably the first allied unit the villagers had seen and the French wanted to show their gratitude and relief that the occupation was almost over.

Bodge felt bad that he was getting the credit for other men's bravery. When he caught up with the aftermath of a battle, he apologized in his mind to the corpses of his countrymen. But he appreciated that his team played an important role in the overall offensive. He still hadn't been under fire. The war had been just dispatches and distant sound effects until one small miscalculation changed everything. It was his first day of action that earned him his reputation as a hero.

They were traveling through Mousin on their way to a small town recently vacated by German administrators. The resistance group had gathered and was waiting for a briefing from Osgood. But, although the clerical officers had moved on, it turned out that a battalion of German combat troops was still amassed in the neighboring countryside awaiting orders for a counter offensive from the flanks. Thanks largely to Osgood's resistance efforts, the word hadn't reached these men that the offensive had been called off or that they were supposed to retreat. So, still following the original orders, they'd waited for two weeks for the promised reinforcements. Their rations were low and their morale was even lower. Radio signals had been blocked so they were deaf and blind as to the real situation of the war.

It was the forward sentries that opened fire on Bodge's jeep with machine guns. The bullets burst through the heads of the two men in front and ripped into Osgood's chest. By some miracle, Bodge wasn't touched. But he was stunned into inaction by the horror of what just happened. The jeep skidded to a halt and the gunfire stopped. The silence was more frightening than the noise. As Bodge sat frozen in the back seat, the sentries assumed he'd been hit and they ran crouching toward the idling jeep. Bodge saw them as shadows emerging from the tree line but his eyes focused on the blood that gushed like crimson oil from the stub of the driver's neck in front of him. His own uniform was soaked in other men's blood.

A groan from Osgood brought him back to some kind of reality. The General's eyes were open but glazed like those of a market fish. The sentries approached the jeep one from each side, certain they'd wiped out the Americans. Their overconfidence showed when they lowered their weapons and straightened to their full height perhaps with pride. Bodge's reaction was unemotional but instant. He took the General's side arm from its holster, raised it, and fired. It took two shots to fell the first man, but before the second could raise his heavy weapon, he too was dead.

Still Bodge sat in his place. He noticed the hooting of a wood pigeon, then the shouting of men. A shot rang out from the same patch of woodland. It whistled over his head so close he thought he could have reached up and caught it. His thoughts of survival were not only for himself at that moment. He knew it was his duty to keep his general safe. He climbed between the front seats and pushed the two corpses out of the jeep on either side. He lowered himself into the pool of blood that filled the driver's seat.

In his hurry to drive away he stalled the engine. His hand began to shake on the key. He stalled it again. Two, perhaps three shots from the woods. More shouting. The sound of a truck on the road ahead. The engine engaged. He threw the jeep into first. The road was just wide enough to swing one broad U-turn. His front wheels caught the edge of a ditch but the vehicle didn't drop into it. It bumped back onto the road and was facing away from the woods.

But coming along the road towards him was an armored car. A swastika flapped above the hood. It was thirty yards, twenty away. The Germans had closed him in like a steer trapped in a corral. With the ditches on either side of the road he couldn't run. He was dead. He knew it. The thought that came to him at that moment was illogical, but logic perhaps isn't worth too much when you're about to run out of luck. He could have thrown up his hands and had a fifty-fifty chance of not losing his life. But, instead, he slammed his foot on the gas, pointed the jeep at the armored car, and ducked under the dash.

The collision smashed him against the metal plating but the engine took most of the impact. Osgood's body was thrown onto the floor and Bodge could see him smiling between the seats. Now was the time to concede defeat. He raised his hands so they'd be seen before he emerged from beneath the smashed windshield, and painfully eased himself up onto the seat. The front of the armored car looked undamaged but smoke billowed from its engine. Yet it was the sight of the men inside the car that registered as odd in his mind. He sat on the bloody seat of his jeep with his hands up, and four German officers sat in the armored car with their hands in the air also.

Back along the road, a truck full of French resistance fighters pulled to a halt and watched astounded as a battalion of German infantrymen walked from the woods, threw their weapons onto the ground and their hands into the air. Ahead they saw a lone US soldier with a pistol unloading a group of officers from their vehicle.

So that, simply, was what happened. Bodge saw nothing heroic in the deed itself. In fact it was probably tiredness and fear that caused him to act rashly. The rest was coincidence. The Germans were tired too, and downhearted, and a decision had already been made to surrender. The sentries hadn't yet learned of that decision. But at a juncture in the invasion when the public relations people needed heroes for the papers back home, Bodge was ready made. The French told of the brave marine who'd fought off a company of soldiers single handed and rammed a staff car full of German officers, causing their surrender.

Osgood himself didn't help matters. When he recovered enough to describe the ambush, in his delirium he apparently saw a completely different scene. He remembered Bodge in a hand to hand battle with the sentries and his bold attack on the armored car. And it was from Osgood's recommendation that Bodge was awarded his Medal of Honor. In the General's absence, he continued in his role as liaison with the French and there were other more genuine acts of heroism that also found their way into dispatches. Finally, he moved into Germany with the victorious allied forces. But wherever he went, his reputation preceded him. Other men who fought campaign after campaign had died unknown, face down in the mud, but Bodge had become an unwitting celebrity.

Bodge turned on the bedside lamp and looked at the alarm clock. It was four AM. and he hadn't slept a second. He felt incredibly ill. His body lay on top of the bedcover like a range of rolling hills. It was certainly a different body from the one that had run with resistance units for hours across muddy fields along the Somme. The Bodge Leon that had collected since then wouldn't make it down to the street and back without a breather. He'd never be trim, he knew that. He didn't have the build of a Brooks Brothers store mannequin, but at least he could lighten his load. Starting tomorrow he'd dig out his old sweat suit and see what he could do about finding the old Bodge.

# 6

But Saturday was one of those days that doesn't even count as a day. He'd never had such a hangover. It wrung him out. He could neither rest nor work. He even considered going to see a doctor. His head was too heavy to allow him to read and his stomach would have nothing to do with food. The doorbell rang several times but he was in no mood for talking. All he could do was loll in his easy chair, think about how ill he felt, and look around at the end of his showy but empty lifestyle.

By Monday he still hadn't the strength to exercise so he ate a stodgy breakfast and vowed that Tuesday morning in DC would mark the beginning of his health regime. He packed an overnight bag and took a checkered taxi to Penn where he caught the 8:20 to Washington's Union Station. It was a leisurely five-and-a-quarter hour journey and he felt a pang of southern guilt that he was being paid for train travel and sight-seeing. The briefing wouldn't begin until the following day so Monday had been put aside for getting to the capital and moving into his lodgings.

The Sunrise Guesthouse was a converted dormitory left over from the WWII operations center that had been based at Howard University. It stood just outside the university's back gate and was now exclusively used by the CIA. Bodge left his bag on his bed and went for a walk around the campus to build up an appetite. Although he knew of Howard's reputation, it still surprised him, given that his own university in the south had been so white, to see so many Negroes on campus. Howard was what they called an institution for the people. That meant that even in a racially segregated city like DC, blacks and Latinos could attend mixed classes and expect equal attention. Some of the local kids who'd only ever been to Negro high schools suddenly found themselves studying alongside whites. Of course many conservatives believed those whites would have to be radical liberals or foreigners without an appreciation of American history to want to attend voluntarily. Laws were being passed all over the north that banned racial prejudice. It wouldn't be long, they said, despite all the senatorial objections, before the District of Columbia became an integrated city. Then, as people like Senator O'Learman publicly stated, "God help the future".

The Sunrise had a dining room and when he got back Bodge asked the motherly receptionist what time they served supper.

"Any time after six, honey," she said. "And you had a phone call while you were out."

"I did?"

She unskewered a square of paper from the spike beside the telephone and read the name.

"A Mr. Mooney. You know him?"

"Yes."

"He'd like you to call him back. You have the number?" He tapped his forehead to show her where he kept it. She handed him a stack of dimes and pointed to the public phone booth across the reception area.

"Stan? It's Bodge."

"Hey, Bodge. How's the orientation going?"

"Doesn't start till tomorrow. What's up?"

"You don't have Lou down there with you by any chance?"

"Lou? What do you mean?"

"He decided not to come into the office today and didn't feel like calling in sick either. I was ringing his number all morning but he's not answering."

"Well, he's got plenty of sick days in hand, but that sure doesn't sound like Lou not to let you know."

"I was thinking maybe you two had one of your drinking orgies last night."

"No. We tied one on Friday night. Last time I saw him he was passed out in the back of a cab. Does Eddy know anything?"

"Who in hell's Eddy?"

"The boy who's moving into my desk."

"Gladstein? Some boy he is. He won't be starting till Wednesday."

"You've got me worried, now, Stan," Bodge confessed. "You have anyone who can go down to Lou's place?"

"I called his landlady. She said she hadn't heard him clunking around like he normally does, but she said she'd been in and out all weekend. She let herself into his apartment in case he'd knocked himself out in the bath or something. Then she called me back. No Lou. Everything seemed neat enough. The bed wasn't slept in."

"This is all odd Stan. He would have told me if he was going away."

"Did he find himself a woman on Friday?"

"To be honest, I can't rightly recall much of what happened that night."

"You remember where you went?"

"Sure, in the beginning. We started off in a couple of familiar bars, then we went to the Black Cat for a meal. Then I guess we moved on to some place Eddy recommended."

"What Eddy?"

"You're gonna have to pay attention, Stan. That's twice you've asked me. Eddy. Eddy Gladstein."

There was a moment of silence on the line.

"Bodge, Eddy Gladstein wasn't with you on Friday night."

"Sure he was. We all three of us left the office together to celebrate my move and his first posting."

"Bodge, listen to me. Eddy Gladstein had his first posting twenty years ago."

"You're crazy. He's just a kid."

"I worked with Eddy in Japan. I've got his file on my desk here. He's fifty something years old."

"What?"

"And he wasn't even in the country last Friday. He gets back from Korea tomorrow night."

# 7

Agents Jansen and Tuck sat on the bed in Bodge's room at the Sunrise. It wasn't the ideal interview room but at short notice there wasn't a lot of choice. Bodge sat on a hard-backed chair by the TV and Palmer was upright with his backside perched on the narrow window ledge and his arms folded. At 8 PM he had things he'd sooner be doing, but this he agreed, was serious. Jansen and Tuck were an ill matching pair; the former was overweight and sweaty, the latter thin as a rail. They were taking very detailed notes on matching clipboards but it was Jansen who asked all the questions.

"But, is it normal for you to black out on these drinking sprees?" The older guy was starting to annoy Bodge. He reminded him of his father.

"No."

"Has it ever happened before?"

"That I can't recall where I was or what I did?"

"Yes."

"No. Never."

"So you either consumed an obscene amount of alcohol or your drinks were interfered with in some way."

"Yes."

"…Well, which do you think it was?"

"As we've managed to consume 'obscene' amounts of alcohol in the past without too many serious side-effects, I'd have to assume the latter. Lou has an incredible capacity for booze. I've never seen him out of it before. But he was sleeping like a baby in the cab."

"Is there any possibility you may have divulged classified information as a result of this …moment of weakness?"

Bodge laughed. He couldn't help himself.

"Did I say something that tickled you, agent Leon?"

"I doubt anything Lou and I have handled in the past year would be worth going to all that trouble for."

"It's for the agency to decide what is or isn't important. You put yourself into a situation where you may very well have compromised agency confidentiality. In my view, that makes you and your friend potential security risks."

Bodge managed not to laugh again. "With all due respect, Agent Jansen, if you allow unauthorized personnel to *a*, get hold of classified internal mail and *b*, stroll around our offices as free as a Texas stray, I'd say you're more of a security risk than I am."

Jansen shot him a look that left Bodge in no doubt what he'd like to do to him.

Palmer had no jurisdiction over security matters but he was getting tired of the line of questioning too. "Gentlemen, I too believe that is the key issue here. It concerns me greatly that any fool may walk around our offices unchallenged."

"Of course," Jansen snapped back. "Which is why we're attempting to glean as much information from this interview as we can, sir. We aren't even sure where the letter was intercepted."

"I understand. Then let us focus on the letter itself for a brief moment," Palmer said calmly. "I was able to reach my secretary at home. She assures me she caught the inter-departmental pouch on Thursday afternoon, just before it was sealed. That action should be recorded in the courier's log. We can double-check tomorrow. But if she's right, the courier would have delivered the pouch, still sealed, to the Adams Center on Friday morning. The pouch would be signed for and handed over to the building security who have a duplicate pouch key."

"Agent Leon," Tuck asked his first question. "Do you know how the mailing system works inside your building?"

"You'll have to check with Mooney… Supervisor Mooney to be certain, but as far as I know all the mail and courier documents go to the sorting office."

"Where they're sorted and distributed to the respective sections?"

"That's right."

"So," Jansen cut back in. "The sorting room would be a likely place to intercept and read mail."

"I imagine."

"And, if your young Eddy person was smart enough, he could take advantage of the situation and claim to be your replacement."

"Right. Until I got the letter, I had no idea who'd be taking over. Can't say I'd thought about it much. But he'd have to be one hell of a ballsy little guy to get away with that. He was cool as November. We didn't suspect for a second he was anyone *but* who he claimed to be. If he only had from the mail room to our office to put together a cover story, he must have been some kind of genius. I'm impressed."

Jansen wasn't.

"Either that or his audience was, shall I say, naïve." He was talking to his notes so he missed both Bodge and Palmer glaring in his direction. Tuck came to the rescue again.

"Robert, we'll be sending an artist over a little later tonight to put together a sketch of what young Eddy looked like."

"Really? I'd always assumed there'd be some sort of camera in reception taking snaps of everyone coming in and going out," Bodge thought aloud.

"And so there should be," Palmer agreed. It was turning into them and us in that little room. "But there's an inborn arrogance at the Agency, Bodge. They think because we're the good guys we're somehow invincible. It doesn't surprise me at all that our flimsy security system was tested and breached. Perhaps now someone will sit up and take notice."

Bodge was impressed by the senior agent's candor. But the two men on the bed suddenly looked at him as if he'd become a security risk himself. Bodge spotted Jansen make a note in the margin of his paper.

"Yeah," Bodge said to Agent Tuck. "I can give you a pretty good description."

"Assuming you can remember anything through the alcohol blur," Jansen said in a whisper loud enough to be heard.

When all the questions had been asked, the two security men put their pens in their top pockets, folded their clipboards under their arms and shook hands with Bodge and Palmer as if they were acquaintances in a train carriage and had arrived at their destination. Bodge wasn't at all surprised that Jansen's shake was soft and clammy.

Once they'd gone, Palmer went over and sat on the bed.

"You must be concerned about your friend."

It was the first humane comment anyone had made.

"It isn't like him to go off without saying a word. We aren't joined at the hip or anything. He has his private life, I have mine. But we usually go for drinks at the end of the week and he tells me if he's met someone or if he's about to split up. You know?"

"Do you think something might have happened to him?"

Bodge bowed his head in thought, "I don't get it. It's weird. I've been thinking about it a lot. If young Eddy has something to do with this, I mean with Lou not being at the office today, I should have known about it. There were the two of us in the cab at the end of the evening, and no sign of the boy. I guess he even paid the cabby and gave directions to our homes."

"Yes. I admit that doesn't sound very Mata Hari. But one could ask how he just happened to have your home addresses."

"Do you suppose our security agents are up to this?"

"An investigation? Laurel might be. I don't put much faith in Hardy." Bodge laughed for the first time since he'd heard from New York. "Look, as far as Lou's concerned, there may be no connection with this Eddy Gladstein mess. He may just turn up at work tomorrow with a hangover and a good excuse. Let's wait and see what happens. Your briefing starts in the morning. If by Wednesday we still don't have any news I don't think it would do any harm if we took a trip to New York in the afternoon and poked around a little ourselves."

"You wouldn't mind?"

"Life's dull for an old field operative who finds himself stuck behind a desk. I would honestly love to be involved. But I admit, I'd be just as happy if your friend turned up in one piece."

# 8

## Ban Methuot

Monsieur Dupré, the latest in a long line of administrators of Ban Methuot, was settling in to his new post. He was a dull, overweight forty-year-old bureaucrat. He'd never been to Vietnam before, nor to Asia, nor Europe beyond the boundaries of his own France.

After a long, loyal undistinguished career in French local government service, he'd reached the level of P6. He was then offered a difficult choice. He could either spend another five years at his present place of employment but with an incremental rise of fifty francs per month, or, for sixty more francs plus a living allowance, he could volunteer to perform colonial service. After great deliberation, and perhaps to escape his mother, he opted for the latter.

He could apply for either West Africa or Indochina. He wasn't partial to men with dark complexions, and, being of short stature, he was certain he'd feel threatened by towering African natives. So he filled in the requisite form and was awarded a posting in Vietnam in a town he had to look up on an atlas.

On his first day of orientation he was introduced to Gallas, a government trainer with decades of experience in heathen countries. Gallas advised him that life in the remote tropics could be a very lonely experience for a single man. Inevitably, one was left with nothing but native women upon which to vent one's natural animal desires. They were, he told Dupré, a very poor substitute for "real" women. From experience, Gallas was of the opinion that administrators fared much better in the colonies if they took along a wife.

Although Dupré had no objection to such a suggestion, he had no wife, and had never been in a relationship that was likely to yield one. So, the following day he put an advertisement in three of the rural newspapers around Amiens. To his amazement he received thirty-three positive replies. Even after sending his photograph, seventeen women still seemed interested in this man with "an established future in government service". He'd mentioned his posting to the Far East and his position as governor and his mother had no doubts that most, if not all, of these respondents were gold diggers.

Even so over the following month he'd been able to visit all of them. Eight cut off communication immediately after meeting him. Four were so unpleasant he had no doubt they'd be spinsters for life. But five remained who had some endearing qualities and seemed not to mind him. One was a very fine musician, another a minor authority in southeast Asian flora. One more was fluent in English and Chinese and had already begun to study Vietnamese. It was a hard decision to make.

But, like most men with little experience of women forced into a corner, he settled on one applicant from Marseilles who'd performed fellatio on him in the back seat of his Renault at the end of their first date. It had been an experience like no other in his sheltered life, and he couldn't erase from his mind the thought of this attractive hairstylist giving him a lifetime of blowjobs. As Monique fitted all the characteristics of a gold-digger as described by his mother, Dupré didn't invite his only living relative to the registry wedding. In fact, it wasn't till the eve of his departure that he bothered to mention to her that he had a wife. She was inconsolable.

For her part, Monique seemed unconcerned at not meeting her mother-in-law. Neither did she introduce or mention her own parents to Dupré. The closer they got to the wedding date, the more his back-seat servicing began to, as it were, taper off. To the dismay of both parties, the wedding night consummation lasted some thirty seconds. Following that unforgettable night, Monique claimed a month of abstinence for "the tearing", as she put it, "to heal". He apologized profusely for his brutishness. Two days after that she began her first affair and had engaged in two more brief flings before L'Oceanique set sail for Singapore.

To their amazement, their arrival in Ban Methuot was met with real pomp and ceremony. The town itself was a cesspool, a typical third-world pigsty, but their importance in it was unquestioned. There was a band, and speeches from the incumbent, and a cocktail reception and the odd bout of ethnic nonsense with loud noises and peculiar dances. Montagnard tribesmen in ill-fitting guards' uniforms saluted them, and servants fawned around them. Even French expatriate tradesmen and plantation owners treated them with deference.

As is the case when ignorant people are suddenly elevated beyond their rightful station in life, M. and Mme. Dupré became a different breed of ignorant people. They were now VIPs and they had to act in a way they expected important people to act in the colonies. Overnight they became arrogant. They had a district to play with for three years and, in their own ways, they intended to make the most of it.

# 9

The office of the operations unit was housed above a carpeting company in the only three-story building on that section of Rhode Island Avenue. There were plans for a real CIA headquarters some eight miles out of town but that was a year or so off. Meanwhile the agency slummed at a number of discreet locations around the city.

On Tuesday morning Bodge arrived holding his four-by-four-inch map with Casually Yours Carpeting marked with an arrow. The entrance had double doors leading into the discount emporium to the right and an unmarked staircase to the left. On the first floor he was met by a not surprisingly laid-back Casually Yours receptionist who was obviously placed there to divert non-CIA guests. She clicked an electronic lock on the door behind her and told him to have a nice day.

Beyond the door was a much more serious reception area where they went through his paperwork, searched his bag, and fingerprinted him. Eddy Gladstein wouldn't have made it into this building without a parachute. They directed Bodge towards Meeting Room D where his orientation had been slated to begin at nine. He walked along an aisle of squeaky linoleum. In front of each office there was a small desk with a black telephone and, invariably, a smartly turned out girl in her mid 20s.

In front of Meeting Room D was an identical desk but its minder was nearer to forty. She was built like a large burlap sack of yams, and turned out in a frock that could only have come directly from an upholsterer of garden furniture. She wore spectacles with frame wings you could hang your hat on. Bodge stood in front the desk waiting for her phone conversation to come to an end. She had a voice that could scrape scum off a toilet bowl.

Although he couldn't really believe she hadn't seen him, he coughed. A look of annoyance dropped across her face. He coughed again. She told her interlocutor to hang on, put her hand over the mouthpiece and glared up at him.

"You can see I'm on the telephone?"

"I can."

"Then surely you can also see how rude it is to be leaning over me coughing up phlegm all over the desk."

He took a deep breath.

"I'm supposed to be reporting to Meeting Room D."

"So?"

"Okay. Thanks." He walked past her and knocked on the meeting room door. There was no answer so, mainly to be away from the obelisk at the desk, he opened the door and put himself on the other side of it. The room was set up for some serious briefing. There was a movie screen on a tripod on one side and an 8mm projector on a table in the middle of the room. Desks were piled high with folders that burst with ill-matching papers. Along the walls was a gallery of pin boards covered in black and white photos, and graphs and maps. Bodge felt an honest to goodness buzz.

He was up at a board studying aerial photos when the door flew open and Palmer strode in with even more files and boxes in his arms.

"Bodge, how you feeling?"

"A little tired sir."

"Any news?" He offloaded the files onto the only empty desk.

"I called Lou's apartment before I left the lodgings."

"Nothing, eh?"

"No."

"He'll turn up."

"I assume they..."

"Yes?"

"I assume the security people will check the hospitals... the morgue."

"I'm sure they were on that first thing this morning. Coffee?"

Bodge said "yes" before he remembered the sour-faced secretary. She'd probably inflict a curse on him if they forced her to work. But Palmer had apparently come up against her before. He left the room and came back ten minutes later with two steaming mugs on a tray. He'd made it himself. There seemed to be no end to his diplomatic skills. He went back to the door and poked out his head. Bodge heard him call very politely, "Stephanie — when you're ready."

Bodge didn't see her as a Stephanie. More a Helga or a Daisy. She came into the room with her notepad and pen. She too had a mug of coffee. Bodge knew Palmer had made it for her.

"Have you two met yet?" the boss asked.

"Yes," said Stephanie. She sat on the opposite side of the room to the two men and put her industrial-sized handbag on the desk in front of her.

"Yes," said Bodge looking for an opportunity to smile at her but not getting one.

"Good then. Let's begin. The mission is a long-term covert placement in Vietnam under assumed identities." The word identities twanged a string in Bodge's mind and he wrote down; 'Switching ID? Ask later.'

He looked up when Palmer said, "Bodge, I believe you know pretty much all there is to know about the French presence in Indochina."

"Pretty much."

"Then perhaps I could trouble you for a brief historical overview."

"Sure. How far back would you like me to go?"

"From their first involvement."

"All right."

He started a little further back than they really needed to go, with the Jesuits in the 1600s and the opportunist traders that hung on to their robes. He described succinctly how the French came to colonize the region, how the Japanese invasion temporarily gave the Vietnamese dominion over their own lands, and how the French returned to lay claim to the region's vast natural resources until the communist Viet Minh engaged them in a protracted guerrilla war.

"And that war continues," he concluded. "France controls about a fifth of the country, mostly Saigon, Hanoi and the areas around their plantations. But they don't have the resources to regain old territory. That," said Bodge, "is presumably where we Americans come in. It's our aid that keeps their army fighting and essential services running. That's as much as I know."

Palmer applauded which caused Stephanie to look up for the first time from her notes.

"Very nicely summarized from the French point of view. Later on I'll let you know how we believe the Vietnamese communists see things. But I think we have a good enough understanding of where we are today in the Vietnam you're both heading off into."

Bodge's jaw dropped. "Both?"

Stephanie gazed across at him with a look of angry resignation. She obviously knew something he didn't.

"Oh sorry. I assumed you'd talked to agent Delainy already."

"No. I thought…"

"What *did* you think, agent?" the woman asked dryly.

"No offence, but I thought you were a secretary."

"Because I'm a woman?"

"Because you were sitting at a reception desk, answering the telephone, and taking shorthand."

"Well, let's pray the French are as easy to fool as you."

Palmer laughed to himself. He'd obviously already imagined the splinters this relationship would leave. "You are both to be placed in situ in a small…"

Bodge was devastated. His heart churned in his chest. This wasn't what he'd dreamed of. She wasn't the type of person he could spend an hour with, let alone two years.

"I was lead to believe," he interrupted, "that I'd be working alone."

"As I'm the only person in a position to lead you anywhere," the older man said, "I know for a fact that isn't true. We didn't discuss the situation."

"You're right, but…"

"Bodge, this is the first day of a very long program. You aren't going to make life hard for me, are you?"

"No… sorry." He sunk back on his chair and began a sulk that was to last most of the day. He felt as empty as the Polo Grounds off season.

"Then, perhaps I may continue." Palmer drained the last of his coffee, pulled his hand-written notes in front of him, but spoke without referring to them. "You are to be placed in situ in a small town called Ban Methuot. It's in the Western Highlands some three-hundred miles from Saigon. I've included details and photographs in a dossier I'll be letting you have later. It seems like a very…interesting part of the country." He reached for his mug and proceeded to take a sip from it even though Bodge knew it was already empty. Palmer liked to use silent pauses for emphasis. They weren't ever likely to forget that Ban Methuot was "interesting", synonymous perhaps with "complicated".

The boss smiled and continued. "You are to work under cover as Baptist missionaries — husband and wife. You will be replacing the incumbent couple who have prematurely come to the end of their tenure. That, very broadly, is the situation. Could I have your initial reactions and questions?"

Bodge could neither speak nor breathe. Stephanie could, apparently, do both.

"How would our backgrounds check out if anyone took the trouble to go into things?"

Palmer seemed impatient with the question. "Naturally, that's all been thoroughly taken care of. You don't need to worry about logistics. The comment I was hoping for at this juncture was more your feelings."

"My feelings?" She smirked. "Since when did the agency care about my feelings?"

Bodge didn't carry a gun but he hoped the other man did.

"Let's assume we started to as from this morning," Palmer replied without a break in rhythm or a crack in his icy cool demeanor. "And let's assume also that I'm the senior agent here and that when I ask you to say or do something, you say and do it without question…or sarcasm."

Stephanie stiffened, but Bodge recognized something, perhaps excitement, on her face. She switched instantly to "respectful subordinate" role.

"I'm sorry, sir. I feel very proud to have been selected for this mission. I'm excited to contribute to our Government's efforts in…"

"Stephanie!"

"Sir?"

Palmer shook his head. "I helped write the manuals about how you're *supposed* to feel. What I'd really like to hear is how you *actually* feel, particularly about your cover and about working with Agent Leon."

"I don't think this is the place to…"

"It is exactly the place, and the time."

Bodge watched it all like a corpse whose relatives were discussing the handiwork of the embalmer. Agent Delainy shrugged away a slight blush before putting down her pen and unleashing her thoughts.

"Sir, as you know, I was uncomfortable when I learned I'd be working with an agent with no field experience. One never knows how a new operative is likely to react under difficult circumstances. But I was prepared to give him the benefit of the doubt. There was a possibility he could be a quick learner. Some agents are naturally sharp, good at assessing a situation and reacting appropriately. But…"

"But what?" Bodge heard himself ask at the same time as Palmer.

"But, I have a very strong instinct about these things. It's an instinct that's been honed by my years of fieldwork overseas. It grew from the desire to survive, knowing whom to trust my life with and whom to avoid. I'm certain Agent Leon would be a poor undercover agent."

It occurred to Bodge he'd suddenly become so small he could barely see over the edge of the desk.

"In fact," she went in for the kill, "he strikes me as a buffoon."

To Bodge's intense annoyance, Palmer gave one of his wry smiles.

"Well, thank you for your candor, Agent Delainy." He turned to Bodge. "Agent Leon. Your turn."

Bodge felt like some timid domestic animal on his first day home from the pet shop, curled quivering in the corner of his cage behind the wood shavings.

"I…I don't really have anything to say."

"I don't believe you."

"Then, I don't think there's anything I *should* say, given the circumstances."

"Bodge, I didn't have you down as a person who was afraid to speak his mind. If you aren't honest with us today, I can't see any hope for this project."

Palmer seemed to be enjoying himself. Bodge, certainly, was not. It appeared he had no choice. He puffed out one or two steadying breaths before he spoke.

"In that case, I wasn't given the forewarning that I'd be working with an agent with such a vast… set of experiences. Or, indeed, with anyone at all. I'd assumed, quite naively, that I'd be out there on my own. So I didn't arrive here today with any preconceptions about a fellow agent.

"I guess I wasn't blessed with an acute instinct. I tend to rely on the senses you can account for on a medical chart. But, from what I've seen and heard of Agent Delainy in the very short time we've been acquainted, I have been able to formulate an opinion. Here goes. I can honestly say that I can't recall having met a more unpleasant woman. The thought of spending two years with her fills me with dread."

"Likewise," came a muffled voice from across the room.

"Excellent, excellent," he said. "Now isn't it better to have dragged all that out into the open? Get it out of the system?"

"You surely aren't still proposing we work together?" Stephanie asked. She'd already reached for her handbag and seemed poised to head home.

"My dear Stephanie, you two are going to be perfect together. Tough no nonsense missionaries soured from years of marriage. All the internal conflicts of couples wed more to the church than to one-another. I don't want you to lose this animosity. It's marvelous. I'm afraid over the next few months you may learn to respect, perhaps, heaven forbid, even like each other."

Stephanie blew hard through her nostril, expanding a small bubble of mucous that she didn't hurry to clear away with her handkerchief. Bodge looked on in disgust. Palmer continued,

"Bodge, I want you never to forget the way you're feeling right now. It will come in useful. Trust me."

Agent Leon knew for certain he would never forget the way he felt at that moment because he was positive he would never recover from the feeling. If the woman had redeeming features, indeed if she had a personality at all, he wasn't about to chip away at her to look for them.

The day progressed with logistical information about the posting and the CIA role in Vietnam. Although the US was providing aid to the French, it did not legally have the right to place observers in the field to monitor the progress of the Viet Minh war against French occupation. It was supposed to rely on French intelligence, eighty-percent of which was fictionalized in an office in Hanoi.

That wasn't good enough for the Americans. They needed their own intelligence provided by their own operatives. So, the decision had been taken to place undercover agents around the country in French-held regions where they could send back reports as to how they saw the war. Many of the agents would be going in as missionary couples as were Bodge and Stephanie. They would be getting together with the others the following week.

Palmer explained, "Ban Methuot is a small town and in itself it isn't particularly interesting to us. So, why are you going there? There are two reasons. Firstly, the French garrison is only five miles out of town. It's run by a guy named General LePenn. He and his senior officers naturally get invited to social events in the town. You'll no doubt meet them and, we hope, become very good friends. The general doesn't have his wife with him so I'm sure he'd appreciate a little home cooking from time to time."

Bodge rued the fact that he couldn't cook.

"Yours is a particularly sensitive posting due to the fact that all the cross-border operations in Laos are coordinated from Ban Methuot. The other reason," Palmer continued, "is that the mission has a waterfront house out at Lac Lake. The only neighbour up there is the emperor's hunting lodge. A little neighborliness with his highness could get us some very valuable information. Primarily you'd be reporting back on troop movements but we'll take all the gossip and rumors as well. Any snippets from the royal household about overseas trips — that kind of thing."

Although he'd taken copious notes, by four, Bodge realized he hadn't actually absorbed a great deal of the information. He hadn't been wholly there. Prime in the forefront of his mind was the process he'd need to go through to put in his resignation and set about establishing a new life outside the agency. He should have said something when they brought in the lunch trays and the three of them had eaten in silence. He should have interrupted Palmer's spiel and prevented this enormous waste of time. Instead he waited for the day's orientation to be over, for that woman to leave the room like a heifer swaying out of a barn, and to be alone with his supervisor. He knew Palmer would be angry but he had no choice.

"Sir."

"Yes, Bodge?"

Palmer was gathering papers and stuffing them into files with no apparent rhyme or reason.

"Sir, I appreciate your faith in me."

"I feel a 'but' coming on."

"Yes, sir. I feel it would be better if you could find someone else for this mission." Another wry smile. "I don't believe I have what it takes to undertake such a project. The woman was right."

"You want to go back to your desk?"

"No, I doubt I could do that. I believe it's time for me to get out of the agency."

"Goodness. Such a major decision because of a woman, Bodge?"

"It isn't because of her," he lied.

"Then what is it? This morning you were gung-ho about the whole thing."

Bodge could see Palmer wasn't taking this resignation nearly as seriously as he did himself. He found his supervisor's levity irritating.

"All right. I admit she's helped me decide."

"Your first run in with a little difficulty and you collapse?"

"Yes. Better it happens in Washington than out there in the field."

"Point taken."

"I'll put it in writing for you and the agency in the morning."

"Well, you could do that, I suppose."

"But?"

"Do you recall a few years ago, all the hoopla with the establishment of the new agency?"

"Yes."

"And you had to sign a number of confidentiality and national security contracts?"

"Yes."

"Well, one of those documents states that you're obliged to give six months notice before terminating your contract with us. I'm afraid the agency holds its operatives to that stipulation under penalty of arrest."

"In other words I spend those six months in Indochina or I go to jail?"

"Something like that. Except the jail term would be a little longer."

"And you'd hold me to this mission even though you knew my objections?"

"Come, Bodge. I'm no more in control of the system than you. Your name's already in the mill. Hard to get in, even harder to get out."

"Right."

"I tell you what, are you still up for our little private investigation in New York tomorrow?"

With all his sulking and brooding, Bodge had totally forgotten Lou and the matter with the Gladstein boy.

"Damn right."

"Me too. That little adventure would be even more against regulations if you resigned beforehand. Forget the letter. Come in tomorrow and withstand a morning more of orientation. At noon we'll go see what we can find out in the Apple. And you never know, you may see things differently after a good night's sleep."

"I can't see myself getting one."

"I think tomorrow will be a very different day as far as you're concerned, Bodge."

"Right."

They shook hands. Bodge still had the impression the older man didn't believe his threat to resign. But perhaps this was his inscrutable way of dealing with disaster. He could see the man pegged out in the desert, covered in honey and carnivorous ants, still smiling his thoroughly annoying wry smile.

Bodge was looking forward to some fresh cold air and distance from the Casually Yours building. It wasn't till he hit the sidewalk and was on his way back to the rooming house that he remembered his bag. The thought of going through the reception and security one more time frustrated him, but he planned to call around to people who knew Lou, and his address book in the bag had all the numbers. He figured he'd ask one of the security guys to run up and grab the bag from the meeting room, but they weren't allowed to leave their station. So they frisked him one more time before he could get inside.

He walked along to the meeting room. The door was pushed to. He was glad they hadn't locked it. He'd probably need a signed permission slip from Truman himself to get hold of a key. He was about to walk straight in when he heard the voices. He stopped and listened. Palmer was in there talking and from the high-pitched laughter that met his comments Bodge could tell who was in there with him.

"…scared the life out of him." (Palmer)

Laughter.

"So he's handing in his resignation?" (Delainy)

Laughter.

"He wanted to put it in writing."

"I don't get it. How did you know he would?"

"I know his type only too well."

The voices were getting louder, approaching the door. Bodge hightailed behind the reception desks to the bathroom door where he cut inside just as Palmer and Delainy came out of the meeting room. The last thing he heard was the most disconcerting.

"You don't think he suspects anything?"

"I doubt it."

# 10

Bodge sat in one of the stalls with the door locked, running over the conversation he'd heard, again and again in his head. Why would they want him out? Hell, he was hardly in. Palmer could have turned him down right there at the first interview. Weird. Damned weird. It was one of those mysteries that Bodge agonized over; questions without answers.

He sat for another ten minutes before leaving the bathroom. He collected his bag and headed out of the building. It seemed the place cleared before four-thirty as there were only the security guys and the receptionist still on. She wished him yet another good day. This time when he arrived at street level a feeling of escape came over him. He walked slowly along the sidewalk with his nose pointed at the paving slabs and his mind ticking over like a cab meter. He hadn't given a thought to which direction he was headed. It wasn't till he heard his own name that he looked up for the first time. A motorcycle approached, crawling along the far side of the street. The rider wore an old padded leather helmet and aviator goggles. Beneath them was a bright, full-toothed smile.

"Hey, Bodge!" The rider raised his arm in salute. As one does when recognized by a stranger, Bodge smiled, waved tentatively and called, "Hi." He had no idea whom he was greeting. Probably someone who'd passed through the agency office in New York? Someone from baseball? It didn't really matter. He expected the motorcycle to stop and himself be forced into a conversation. But, instead, the bike continued a hundred yards down the street and stopped at a call box. Bodge could have doubled back and asked the guy who he was, but he wasn't that interested. He just wanted to get back to his room and think.

DC was the nation's capital. It boasted all the buildings they put on bank notes and taught about in schools, but you didn't have to travel too far from the impressive white pillars to find yourself in some hick suburb or other. The city had a downtown of cluttered alleyways and an inner city where opulence mingled with degradation. If you headed north along the old Washington canal you'd see dirty congested slums of packing case hovels. Yet only two miles from there you could visit the mansions they took color prints of for House and Garden.

As Bodge got closer to Howard, some of the streets were positively rural; grass on the sidewalks, chickens in the yards, screen doors hanging off a single hinge. There was no growl of big city traffic or buzz of neon. It was like a city that closed before sundown.

He walked the last few blocks along the roadway to avoid stomping through damp weeds and tripping over abandoned tricycles. Heaven knew where all the people were. But maybe a big white man in an overcoat strolling through a Negro neighborhood was a bad omen. It was a peaceful moment none-the-less. Some birds were bickering, but apart from the sound of one noisy truck engine from somewhere behind him, he could have been in small town Tennessee walking home from the fields — albeit twenty degrees colder.

He reached the back wall of the university and the incident at Casually Yours might have slowly erased itself from his mind if it hadn't been for the damned truck. It needed an oil change. The driver was gunning his engine, either checking the rhythm of his pistons or showing off for a girlfriend. It was coming his way but Bodge imagined most folks around there walk in the road. He was big enough to spot. It was the faint squeal of rubber on road that caused him to look back over his shoulder.

The truck was a beaten-up brick-red Diamond T flat back, and it was rolling along about half a block behind him. It was on his side of the road with two wheels in the gutter and had built up a good head of speed in a short space of time. Bodge stepped onto the sidewalk to give the fool all the gutter he wanted, but the driver wasn't even satisfied with that. His left wheels bumped up over the curbstones and the heap flew along at an angle, half on the road, half off. It was heading straight for Bodge, accelerating all the while.

Bodge had reached the worst possible spot on the street. To his left the back wall of the university reached up eight feet and was topped with barbed wire set in cement. He only had a second to gather his wits. If he'd headed for the road the truck would only have to swerve to run him over, and there was no doubt in Bodge's mind that was the intent of the guy behind the greasy windshield.

He had no choice. The front fender was at his legs. He threw himself up at the wall, grabbed for the jagged top and heaved his knees up beside him. He could feel the wire dig into his fingers. The truck scraped along the wall with a metallic screech they probably heard in China. It kicked up sparks and chunks of brickwork. With an almighty effort for an out-of-shape man, Bodge yanked himself above the cab of the truck which thumped his rear end as it passed. Something yanked off one of his shoes and a wedge of wall masonry flew up and hit him in the cheek. But the bed of the truck passed safely underneath him and kept on going. Bodge hung there like a heavy bunch of bananas until the truck was out of sight.

When he finally dropped to the ground, his legs buckled and he lay on the ground shaking.

It was half an hour before he could get his muscles working. Some of the locals had come out to take a look at him. They gave him a cup of sweet tea and bandaged up his bloody fingers. But even by the time he made it back to the guest house, he hadn't been able to put more than three words together. He nodded at the receptionist, collected his key, and went straight to his room. It wasn't until then, laid out on the solid bed, that he could start to work out what had just happened to him and why. He looked at the uneven patches of white and cream paint on the ceiling, and tried to weigh things up. There were more questions for his list. Was there a connection between this and what had taken place in New York? Could it all be related to the new mission? A life that had been singularly grounded before he met Palmer had taken flight. Which led him to the ten grand bonus question; how did it all fit together with what he'd heard at the carpet store?

And like a perfect stage direction, Palmer made his entrance. Bodge hadn't shut the door to his room and the boss was standing there like a royal portrait in the door frame. He smiled and strode into the room. Bodge did a quick juggle of what and what not to say first. Palmer beat him to it.

"Agent Leon, have you been planted into my life to make it more intriguing?"

"I was just thinking mine used to be dull too," Bodge confessed. "I assumed this must all be part of signing up for operations."

Palmer smiled down at Bodge from the edge of the bed.

"Are you in the mood to tell me what happened?"

"How could you possibly know anything...?"

Palmer held up Bodge's bag and pulled the Casually Yours map from the front flap with its phone number. "You left this behind. Someone gave us a call. What do you remember?"

One thing Bodge remembered was that the street he was in didn't appear to have a telephone line running to the shacks. He wasn't even sure they had electricity. A call?

"Some drunk in a truck," Bodge said. "He ran off the road and I happened to be in the way."

"You're sure it was an accident?"

"Why wouldn't it be?"

"There's a witness who swears the driver was idling till you reached the wall of the university, then he sped up. He was of the opinion the man was aiming for you."

Under an hour and they'd interviewed witnesses already?

"Perhaps he was one of those short people who have grievances against everyone over six feet. I was just a random tall guy."

"Did you get a look at him?" He sat on the edge of the bed by Bodge's leg.

"No, I was too busy bouncing off his windshield." It was odd how quickly his respect for Palmer had vanished. He studied the senior agent for signs of insincerity, began to read other meanings into his questions. He decided now was a good time to change the subject.

"Have you had any news from New York?"

"Nothing new. Naturally we'll postpone tomorrow's trip."

"Oh, no. If you don't mind. It's been nagging at me since yesterday. I'd rather not put it off."

"Are you sure you'll be up to it?"

"Just a few cuts and bruises It would help if I could be excused tomorrow morning's briefing."

"I think it's only fair given the circumstances. Bodge, I have to ask. I'm sure it's gone through your mind already."

"What's that?"

"Do you think there could be any connection between this "accident" and what happened in New York?"

"How could there be? It hadn't occurred to me."

"No? You surprise me. Has anything else out of the ordinary happened that you can recall? Anything else here in Washington?"

Bodge's mind sped immediately to the overheard conversation, then the motorcyclist who called his name.

"No. Nothing."

"Well, you sleep on it. I'm afraid you may find yourself confronted by Stan and Ollie again in the morning. They're sure to hear about this."

"Heaven help me."

"I'll send a car around noon to pick you up. I think incognito casual will be the dress code for the day. Just let me know if you don't feel up to it."

"Sure. Thanks for coming in."

Palmer left, shutting the door behind him, and Bodge still wasn't sure what he knew. The puzzle was too soon out of the box to have any pieces that fit and there certainly was no picture. He called reception for a half pint bottle of gin and finished the lot. When he woke up in the morning, the TV was still on and his backside hurt like hell.

# 11

It was exactly noon when Bodge emerged from the Sunset Lodge in his casual clothes. CIA casual would have been church wear for anyone else. He'd decided on a dark suit, white shirt and wool muffler. The driver was sitting out front in a pre-war Buick Cabriolet. He waved at Bodge as if he recognised him from a description and leaned across to open the passenger door, but Bodge opted for the rear. Physically the driver wasn't unlike Jimmy Stewart. He had that same gangly awkwardness. He wore his hair greased flat and the lines around his eyes and mouth smiled even when he wasn't. He stooped over the wheel and drove as if he were watching the white lines on the road disappear under the front bumper. Either the seat or the vocation was uncomfortable for him. But he was friendly enough. He kept up the small talk all the way to their destination. He had a deep voice that twanged through his skinny body like a note from a double base string.

"This is the place," he said slowing down to a crawl. He drove them down a dead-end street full of lock-up garages and sounded his horn. Palmer emerged from a side gate and walked jauntily to the car. Bodge expected him to climb in the back beside him, but instead he waved and opened the driver's door. The wiry man stepped out, smiled at Palmer and climbed into the passenger seat. Palmer eased his way behind the wheel and slid the seat forward on its ratchets so he could reach the pedals.

"How are you feeling today, Agent Leon?"

"A few aches." Bodge held up his bandaged fingers. "Nothing serious."

"Good."

Palmer engaged the gear and set off smoothly.

"You're driving us there?" Bodge asked.

"Why not? It's my car."

"I thought…"

"He thought I was the driver," Jimmy Stewart said, smiling at Bodge.

"See?" Palmer said, adjusting the rear view mirror. "I said you have that chauffeur look about you."

"I'm a master of disguise."

"Gee, look. I'm sorry," Bodge said. "I didn't…"

"My friend, Denholm here is with the police, Bodge. More importantly, he's a New York City detective."

"Denholm Deets," the detective said and held out his hand to Bodge who shook it gingerly.

"Why didn't you tell me?"

"Oh, I figured once you climbed in the back seat you'd already pegged me as menial staff."

"Don't embarrass him any more than he already is," Palmer laughed.

"Don't worry about it, Bodge," Denholm said. "I've been taken for a lot worse over the years."

Being told this man was a New York cop didn't make Bodge believe it any better. He'd seen a lot of cops over the years and this tall streak of lard didn't look like any one of them. He was too...too neat, too gently spoken. Working cases in the city usually beat the niceness out of a guy and left a lot of rough edges. But he could hardly ask to look at his badge.

"For what we're about to do," Palmer said. "I figured we'd need Denholm here on the team."

"What brings you to DC?" Bodge asked. He noticed a slight hesitation, a brief look down at the dashboard before the cop answered.

"I'm on leave," he replied. Smiling at the road ahead through the windshield. "It's been good. I haven't had a real break in ten years. I'm starting to wonder if I should make it permanent."

They took Interstate 95. It wasn't busy. The three men discussed the new Studebaker, the imbecile who'd just brained himself going over Niagara Falls in a truck inner tube, and Doris Day's figure. Bodge didn't get enthusiastic for the conversation until they got onto how the Giants had gone from the cellar in April to a half game behind leading the National League.

It was a guy drive and Bodge momentarily forgot that Palmer was a question mark on his list. He even got to the stage where he forgot he was his boss. It was time to find out something about him — give himself some background of a potential enemy. He started with a question that had been puzzling him. He felt the ice had broken enough to bring it up. He wanted to know how someone with the old man's sophistication could get involved in all this agency cloak and daggery. Of course he couldn't ask it that straight.

"What brought you into the organization, Mr. Palmer?"

Palmer looked to his right. "He asks a lot of questions, this boy."

"It's like driving with a *Times*' reporter," Denholm smiled watching the suburbs get thicker as they neared the city.

"I'm sorry," Bodge said.

"Oh, it isn't a criticism," Palmer assured him. "As long as you remember to temper all the information you get out of me with the fact I'm a spy."

"I'll bear it in mind."

"My father had a factory that made baseballs up in Massachusetts. He fell in love with one of the Boston bankers' girls."

"Banks and baseballs. It doesn't sound like you'd be in a hurry to work for the government."

"See why I picked him, Denholm? Rude bastard. Direct as hell."

Bodge looked at his fists. "I'm sorry if I overstepped—"

"Jesus, boy. Will you stop saying you're sorry? Those that don't ask don't learn. The fact is I was put into Yale with precise instructions to come out a banker. But I guess I did a little too well in the exams and the IQ tests. One day a man in a rain coat sidled up to me and asked me if I'd be interested in joining the secret service. He hit me with that old "national pride" routine."

"That used to get us every time," Denholm said.

"Unfortunately I loved my country more than life, so it worked," Palmer went on. "I never did get to finish a degree. Never saw the inside of a bank vault. And I couldn't tell you the first thing about how they make baseballs. Suddenly I belonged exclusively to the United States. They've owned me ever since."

"How does that work with things like family — kids?"

"Family? You mean my own?"

"Yes."

"Hell, Bodge. You'll soon understand how this life precludes all that. You have to take your pleasures where you can, when you can. You might start off thinking about a home and nine to five, but pretty soon the energy of the work takes you over. Even men who enter ops with that special gal waiting back home soon get seduced by the mistress we know as excitement. You hate much of what you're doing, but even hate becomes an aphrodisiac."

"You don't ever get a need to watch your own kids grow up?"

Palmer laughed. "A curiosity, sometimes. But never a need. This vocation lets you sample too much, see too much, and because of that, your priorities change."

Bodge was surprised to hear his boss speaking so openly. He had no doubt the Boston story was true. Denholm meanwhile sat nodding ruefully like a man with school fees and a mortgage to pay. The NYPD wasn't renowned for its mistresses of excitement. Most of the men he knew in the department had to rely on a wife to help pay the bills.

As they came off the Brooklyn Bridge his admiration for Palmer had somehow renewed itself, which paradoxically caused Bodge to trust him even less. 'A good spy', he'd read somewhere in the literature, 'can cry real tears with you at your mother's funeral then slide a stiletto between your shoulder blades at the wake'.

The smog of the city hung around the buildings like it was up to no good. It turned Manhattan into a pencil sketch that had been trodden under foot. Bodge had never seen his city look so threatening — so much less of a friend. Palmer slid in and out of traffic as if he'd driven a cab for half his life. He pulled up at the curb, crunched the handbrake and switched off the engine. The car purred, and sighed and fell silent.

The three of them stepped onto the sidewalk, glad to be out of the car at last. Bodge realized where they were. The sign above the door had a slinky cat curled around a martini glass. A drowsy valet in a wool beanie came down the steps to park the car. When Palmer waved him away he turned round and went back inside without saying anything. It wasn't his job to welcome guests, just park their vehicles. In the late-afternoon, not a lot of people came to the Black Cat. The bar was open and they had counter snacks, but the lunch waiters were setting up for dinner and the band was rehearsing a new tune. The late staff didn't come on till six, but there was one man, Mister Lucoz, who was always there; breakfast, lunch, dinner and closing.

He was Maitre D' come manager, and Bodge wondered when he ever slept. He'd known him for years but never saw him anywhere other than in the shadows of the Cat. He was a dark man with the build and profile of a crow. His nose seemed better designed for pecking than for breathing. His formal tail coat curled up at the bottom like tail feathers. Bodge had no idea where he or his accent were from. Even the man's friends called him Mister so it might have been his name.

"Mr. Leon," Lucoz hopped towards Bodge and was about to shake his hand when he saw the bandage. "Oh, dear. We have had an accident?"

"Well I have," said Bodge, not bothering to explain what that accident was.

"I can't recall ever seeing you in the daytime before." It didn't matter much at the Cat as no light got in from outside. Lucoz nodded politely at Bodge's guests but didn't get an introduction.

"Mister, do you remember I was in here with some friends on Friday night?"

"Of course." There was very little Mister Lucoz didn't notice. Bodge and Palmer sat on the stools with their backs to the bar. There were one or two drinkers who appeared to be cemented there like gargoyles. Denholm remained standing. Bodge got straight to the point.

"Did I act, I don't know, strange that night?"

"Strange? Well you are usually quite pickled by the time you reach the Black Cat."

"That's true." Bodge was a little embarrassed to be caught out as a perennial drunk in front of his boss. "I mean stranger than usual."

"You and your friend were so drunk on Friday I must confess I don't recall ever seeing you so...out of it."

"Were we being raucous?"

"On the contrary, you were both extremely...how can I put it? Numb."

"Numb?"

"Like mental retards. Everything seemed to be playing in slow motion. There was no conversing with you. I was surprised at Mr. Lou because he always seemed so in control with his drinking. Only your young friend had any life in him."

"Do you have any idea where we went after we left here?"

"You don't remember?"

"No. I was... on medication..." He looked sideways at Palmer. "...for a cold. I don't think it gelled very well with the alcohol."

"Interesting that you and your friend should be sharing...medication," the manager said with a slight 'I've heard it all before' smile. "Champagne and Aspirin are poor companions."

"We were drinking champagne?"

"A quite expensive one. The young man paid for everything. He and I had to virtually carry you and Mr. Vistarini out to the cab. I strongly recommended you call it a night but the boy insisted you still had life left in you."

"Did you notice where...?"

"Somewhere off Broadway and 41$^{st}$."

"Thanks, Mister.

# 12

## Lake Lac

Hong sipped her last gin. That afternoon she'd smoked her final pipe. She worked out that in two or three days her head would begin to clear. There were two ways to escape and she'd chosen the wrong one. She'd opted for the type of escape where she didn't actually go anywhere — where all the running and hiding happened inside her. Her body remained imprisoned.

She was smart. He wouldn't have chosen her if she weren't. She decided the combination of a barely used brain and endless hours of free time had to be enough to extricate her from her shitty situation.

"Hey ugly. Have another one?"

Lan wasn't an ally at all. She was a friend, a dear friend, but she wasn't on Hong's side. Friends rarely helped. Their advice invariably solved the immediate but made the long-term even more unbearable.

"No, I'm not feeling so great. I think I'm coming down with something."

Lan was in her underwear lying on her back with her pudgy legs akimbo, drunk as a loon. Hong looked down at her from the bed. She'd been her friend since high school. Like Hong, she was loveless. When the selection was made and Hong was escorted to the palace, Lan was the only relic from her past they allowed her to bring along. In a household of maids whose servitude had been passed down through generations, Lan's shortcomings as a servant stood out like the proboscis of a mosquito. As every item, every person in the heady Vietnamese bureaucracy had to be invoiced, Lan was indexed as 'personal assistant/companion to the second consort'. She accompanied Hong everywhere: to all the functions, on all the trips.

But the drinking and smoking had left poor Lan good for nothing else. In the beginning she'd joined Hong in her over indulgences like a friend on a dark night walking her home through a dangerous neighborhood. But soon Lan had learned to run through those dark suburbs alone. Hong felt responsible. She'd turned her friend into an addict and was about to leave her alone in her addiction.

"Come on." said Lan. "You gotta help me finish this bottle, blossom. There's a cellar full to get through before it pickles us."

"Perhaps tomorrow."

"Chicken shit."

Hong wouldn't share her new plans with Lan because confidences were slippery in the grasp of a drunk. Lan had become the gossip columnist for the imperial news network. The cellar maids drank with her and passed on her tattle to the eunuchs. They, in turn, shared their findings with the Chamberlain who decided what was important enough to tell the emperor. Hong was sorry for what she had done to Lan, and one day she would lash her to the rack and wring the evil juices from her. But before then, she would use her friend's innocent leaks of faith to her own end. Two or three more days and Hong could begin to plot her own escape.

As a partial believer in karma and the complicated interplay of omens, Hong knew that a sign would be necessary to confirm her choice of path in this matter. It came almost as soon as the decision was made. With Lan asleep on the parquet, Hong walked from the room clutching her new resolve to her chest. She was returning to her chamber when one of her handmaidens stopped three yards before her.

"What is it, Phoung?"

"Your Highness, it's the girl. She's at the outer gate."

"Girl?"

"The servant from the missionary's villa — Bet. She came yesterday and asked to see you."

"I wasn't told."

"The Great Master said she was probably looking for a job now the Americans have deserted her and moved into town. He told me to send her away and not disturb you."

"And she's back?"

"No, Your Highness."

"What? You said she was here again."

"I said she was here. She's still here. She didn't leave. She spent all night at the gate, waiting."

"That doesn't sound to me like a girl in need of a job. Did she say anything to you?"

"She won't talk to anyone else. Just keeps repeating your name."

Hong had befriended Bet, one of the three Montagnard maids at the neighboring villa during her regular visits there for English lessons. The hill-dwelling Montagnards, more commonly known by the derogatory term *moi* by the Vietnamese, had long been put down and abused by the ruling classes. With what limited influence her position afforded her, she had endeavored to champion their rights whenever possible. Hong hurried down the steps to the ground floor. She walked past the Royal

Guards on either side of the front door, went along the path that wound through the sharpened stakes and barbed wire, and banged on the outer gate. The perimeter guards pushed in the heavy wooden doors and saluted at the sight of the consort.

"Where's the girl?" she asked.

"Over there, Your Highness." They pointed along the perimeter barricade to a bundle leaning against the fence. Hong ran to her. The guards followed.

"We gave her water," said one.

"She wouldn't take food," said the other.

"And she won't speak."

# 13

Medallion Yellow cabs operated out of two terminals. The yellowness of Friday's cab was the only thing that had stuck in Bodge's mind. There were renegade taxis of every hue and shape, but they all had to register under the Medallion legislation. This gave the public a little security and reduced the number of well-to-do passengers who found themselves taken for a ride they hadn't asked for. One or two of these companies used the yellow that was popular in Chicago, but Mr. Hertz's organization was the biggest.

The nearest of their bases to Times Square was on Ninth. That seemed as good a place as any to start. The controller was a cocky Irishman with a sarcastic streak so wicked it was obvious why they'd thrown him out of the old country. He went by the name of Longhurst.

"You're looking for a cabby in New York City with short dark hair and a big nose? Sure, there can't be many of them around." He smiled and looked again at the rear door.

"He had a Brooklyn accent," Bodge added hopefully.

"There then. If that doesn't solve it. You'd be looking for Al."

"Really?"

"Well, it might not give you the exact person, but you'd have narrowed it down to no more than four hundred cab drivers."

Given the squalor of the surroundings, Palmer had opted to sit outside with the heater on and keep an eye on the car. Denholm sat on the corner of the controller's desk. Bodge was wondering why, in the two calls they'd made so far, the detective hadn't once flashed his badge. The cop glared at the man who worked the cab center from seven to seven.

"Mr. Longhurst," he said calmly. Let's go at this another way."

"Two eyebrows? Born of a mother?"

"Mr. Longhurst. Do your drivers keep a record of fares they've taken — addresses — names, anything like that?"

"They're supposed to."

"But?"

"It's hard to keep grabbing the tails of all of them."

"I see. So despite the fact that the new law insists on records, you don't actually check. What about the ones that phone in?"

"Oh, sure, those we have in our ledger. Marjory takes them all down. There's nothing that girl wouldn't take down for a smile."

"Good. So, do you think Marjory would mind if we took a look?"

"Ah. I'm sure she'd be delighted."

With so many cabs on the street, not a lot of people bothered to call in. But Denholm went through the neatly written ledger with Marjory leaning over him. Her earrings jangled and her perfume wafted. Meanwhile, Bodge had the ominous task of going through a large cookie tin full of the twins of every driver photo used on the company ID cards. The original was displayed, by law, in the cab. The spare with the driver's name written on the back was tossed into this old tin.

Thirty minutes later he emerged from the file room with half a dozen possibles but not one he was sure about. Given that he'd been half dead and hadn't seen much more than the driver's nose in the rear view mirror, coupled with the fact he wasn't even certain they had the right company, this was a long shot. Bodge showed Longhurst his catch. The Irishman shuffled through them.

"Well," he said, "these two only work days, and this fellow's having the old sing song in Sing Sing. So that leaves you with these three potentialities."

"Is there any chance of seeing them tonight?" Bodge asked.

"There's a chance of anything in this world if you're patient enough. I'm sure you could sit there behind me and welcome all the smiling faces of the night shift drivers as they clock in."

Denholm joined Bodge on the vinyl sofa behind Longhurst's desk. He'd brought two cups of gray coffee and a pair of sorry looking hotdogs from the all night kiosk.

"This is in lieu of food," he said.

"Thanks." Bodge bit into the dog. As he'd expected it to taste like shit, it wasn't at all a disappointment.

"Detective Deets…"

"Yes, Bodge. I know. It's crap, but just think of it as fuel. Even Agent Palmer refused it and he has an iron clad constitution. We'll get some real food later."

"No, I was about to say, well, we've been to two obvious locations to investigate what happened Friday night. In my statement I mentioned both the Black Cat and the yellow cab."

"Yes?"

"Well, neither Mister Lucoz nor the guy here said anything about anyone else nosing around asking dumb questions."

"You're thinking of your security people?"

"It seems to me they aren't doing a great deal of detective work to find Lou. They didn't even show up this morning to ask about the truck."

"I don't know how they work but I'd suppose they're more concerned about the breach of security at your office."

"You know about that?"

"I'm privy to all the information relevant to this case."

"So who's searching for Lou?"

"We are. And I filed a missing person's. The local police will eventually get around to hunting through the morgue files and the hospital records. They aren't likely to extend to door-knocking and interviewing people on the street. So that leaves us. When are you due back in DC?"

"The boss has decided we might have to spend the week on this. He's rescheduled orientation for next Monday."

"Even that mightn't be enough time. This is a big city crammed full of people who aren't fond of giving up information for free."

They sat there for an hour with nothing to do but get to know one another. Like Bodge, Denholm had failed at marriage and produced no kids. He'd been with the New York police force since he was eighteen and gotten his detective badge when he was a mere twenty-eight. He lived alone and apparently had just the one love — his job. But Bodge got the feeling something had soured that love recently. It wasn't something Denholm Deets felt like talking about.

Drivers came and went, but not the Brooklynite with the nose. It was starting to look like all the men who'd intended to work that night had arrived already. There were only two empty squares on the work roster and Longhurst had long-since been replaced by the night shift supervisor. It was nine and Bodge was wondering whether their time could be better spent elsewhere. He'd availed himself of the office phone to call Lou's till the number rang itself hoarse, and then to talk to Mooney. The only information he'd been able to offer was that a couple of security goons had been hanging around their building all day. That explained where Jansen and Tuck had gotten to. They'd interrogated everyone from the receptionist to the director himself and obviously weren't there with the intention of making friends. They'd left one or two of the secretaries in tears. So Bodge and his team were *it*. The onus was on them to find Lou. They decided it was time to go ferret around his apartment in Little Italy. Maybe someone there would remember something.

They were gathered in front of the supervisor's booth planning the trip across town when the little cabby pushed between them. Bodge recognised the nose and was pretty certain about the face. He nodded to Denholm who stepped in front of the man.

"Excuse me," he said.

"I didn't do nothing," the cabby told him.

"I'm sure you didn't. We were looking for someone who took a fare on Friday night, Saturday morning."

"I take fares every night. What about it?"

"Do you recognize this man?" Denholm gestured toward Bodge. The little cabby looked him up and down and stared up again into his broad face, then shook his head.

"Nah, never seen him before."

"You might want to try a little harder," Bodge pushed. "East Broadway? I know it was you."

"You do? Yeah, maybe," the cabby said at last. He seemed terminally edgy. "You was one of them drunks. Don't tell me. East Broadway, down by the river. Hudson Mansion. Am I right, or am I right?"

"Very good," Bodge told him.

"Got a photographic memory for addresses, me."

"What I'd really like to know is where you picked us up."

"Not sure I can remember that."

"I thought you had a photographic memory," Denholm said.

"It's fuzzy. Maybe if I could get a couple of bucks for a coffee it might clear my mind."

"You don't want to start shaking us down, pal. Especially as I'm carrying one of these." The policeman finally flashed his badge. The driver paled.

"Well, shit. You could of said. I'm always happy to help the cops. I guess I remember after all. I was cruisin' Grand Central, Times Square, around 42$^{nd}$. Some of the guys stay away from the joints late at night. There's drunks I won't pick up and drunks I will. But I got instincts. Yeah, instincts. I figured you two was so far gone you wouldn't give me no grief. And your little buddy was straight."

"You mean he was sober?"

"As a nun."

"And he gave you directions to our places?"

"He had 'em writ down in a book."

"Really?"

"Yeah. And he give me twice as much as I asked for. I was well pleased. I didn't even have to run the meter."

"Where exactly were we when you first saw us?

"Some joint on 41$^{st.}$ and 8$^{th.}$ called Bouncers. You and your buddy was laid out on the sidewalk like the trash. Man, you was so out of it. Me and the kid almost broke our balls gettin' you in the back seat. What you weigh? 250? 280?"

"230," Bodge said, recalling his last weighing two years earlier.

"Yeah? Felt like 280. But I was in the money so I didn't give a shit."

"Did the boy say anything to you, apart from the addresses?"

"Just said you two was celebratin' somethin' and got a little over enthusiastic."

"And he just walked off?"

"Vanished, just like that. No idea where he went. I looked in the mirror and the street was deserted."

"So you dropped me off and took my friend to his place?"

"That's right. He didn't have no idea where he was. 'You're home, buddy' I told him, and he gets out of the cab and stands there swayin' left and right. He was going through his pockets like he was looking for somethin'. I asked him what he'd lost but he didn't say nothin'. I looked in the back of the cab in case it was a wallet I'd get accused of thievin' but there weren't nothin' there. When I looked up he was at the door ringin' the doorbell. So I figures he's lost his key. Nothing I could do about that so I drove off and left him there."

"And you're sure you left him at the right address?" Palmer asked.

"Hey, I know this town like my own wife's you-know-what. Don't you even suggest I don't know where I left him."

Despite its name, Bouncers wasn't a basketball store. It was a clip joint that called itself a "Revue Bar". There were gaudy colored photographs of voluptuous women out front. They wore elegant clothes that looked like they might just fall off if you breathed on them. Sitting beside the main door was a skinny old lady in the type of booth you'd see in front of a movie theatre. Bodge, Palmer and Denholm ignored her and went straight for the door.

"Hey. You guys think I'm sitting here for my health?" she growled.

"We aren't here for the show," Bodge told her.

"If you don't pay, you ain't getting through that door." She looked at the big fella's hands in the pockets of his slacks. "And if that's a piece you got there, I got a bigger one down here under my knitting. So don't you go getting any ideas."

Denholm was about to step forward but Palmer put up his hand. He strode to the booth, gave her his smarmiest of smiles and leaned on the counter.

"I'm sorry, miss. How are you doing today? You have nothing to fear from us. We're government agents." He flashed her his badge too quickly for her to get a look at it and she flashed him her two remaining teeth.

"That supposed to impress me?"

"I hoped it might, yes."

"Well it don't. Y'ain't getting a free show, badge or no."

"Miss, we just want to ask one or two questions. That's all."

"Ten bucks."

"I assure you we have no interest in seeing the show."

"You said that. Ten bucks is the going rate for questions."

"Those are expensive questions. I trust that would get us answers as well?"

"If the questions ain't too hard."

"Then perhaps we could speak to someone in authority."

"Perhaps you could. How about the owner and the manager?"

"That would be just charming. Are they free?"

"No, they cost ten bucks, and they're sitting right here in front of you."

"*You're* the owner?" Bodge asked.

"Put them eyebrows down, boy. You got anything against senior citizens?"

"No, ma'am."

Palmer removed two fives from a well-endowed billfold. He slid one of them under the glass. "Five for the questions. Five for the answers," he said. She took up the note and sniffed at it.

"Shoot."

"Were you here on Friday night?"

"No. You wanna slide me that other five now?"

"Do you suppose we could talk to someone who was here on Friday night?"

"No."

"I get a feeling you aren't trying very hard to earn the other five."

"It's you that's asking questions with 'no' answers."

"What question do you suggest might help us with our inquiries?"

"Ask me why nobody can tell you what happened on Friday."

"Consider it asked."

"Cause, Mr. Clark Gable smile, there wasn't nobody here on Friday night on account of us not being open. If you'd taken the trouble to read that big friggin sign up there behind you, you'd know that we open Sunday to Thursday. Some cops you are."

"Exactly what kind of clip joint closes at weekends?" Denholm asked.

She glared at him as if she could smell his occupation. "One that can't afford to pay the weekend donations the cops charge around here, that's what kind. One that can't compete with the bread the girls can make at other joints on Fridays and Saturdays. And this is a Revue, not a clip joint, thank you." She turned to Palmer, "Now, Sweetie, what other services do I have to perform for you to earn that other five?"

The three of them sat opposite Bouncers in the black Buick.

"So, you weren't in Bouncers," Palmer said. "That means you walked or got dragged here from somewhere else. Does any of this look familiar to you, Bodge?"

Bodge shook his head as he scanned the street opposite. He focused on the lights and posters in front of the clip joint, imagining himself arriving in a cab, finding it was shut, driving on. But nothing came. Only the neon coffee cup in the window of the quaint little café four doors down stirred any recognition in him. But it was a promotion display for the new Nescafé Coffee brand and the money-grabbing Europeans had saturated the city with their expensive advertising. They were everywhere. Who was likely to refuse a free neon sign?

"No, sorry."

"I don't know," said Palmer looking across at the dowdy little revue bar. "Why would anyone come twenty blocks to sleazy holes like this?"

"There are those who get off on seedy bars when they're ten sheets to the wind," Bodge thought out loud and put another nail in his reputation.

"I'm sure. But it was young Eddie's suggestion. Lou and yourself were beyond rational thought. Why would a good-looking young boy with money want to come and hang out in clip joints off 42$^{nd}$?"

"Slumming," Denholm offered. "Little Lord Fauntleroy mixing with dirty whores. I see it all the time."

Palmer grimaced. "Something here doesn't make sense."

# 14

On the drive to Little Italy, Bodge was still mad that the cabby had just dumped his friend on the sidewalk. It wasn't one of the worst neighborhoods but you never could tell in this city. With the old families moving out to the suburbs and all kinds of reprobates moving in, there wasn't that old village atmosphere any more where everyone looked after their neighbors. In this modern Manhattan where money was doing most of the talking, people were content to look after themselves.

It was after ten but they figured that wasn't too late for one last call before they turned in for the night. Bodge had known Lou's building supervisor for five years and she had a crush on him. Twenty years earlier before the bourbon had vandalized her, she'd been a looker. She had old black and white photographs of her beautiful self all around the walls of her apartment. Whatever it was that set her off in this tailspin must have been drastic, because she carried an extra hundred pounds and looked like she'd run face first into a lot of brick walls.

"Bodge, honey. Come in. And who are your friends, babe?"

It suddenly occurred to Bodge he didn't know Palmer's Christian name, or indeed whether he had one. The A on his name card could have been an article.

"This is Marion," said Bodge. Without missing a beat, the older man stepped forward to take the woman's hand.

"Delighted, miss."

"Likewise," she replied with a little curtsy. Although her cheeks provided ample camouflage Bodge thought he noticed a blush. "You won't believe this but in England, Marion's a woman's name," she said.

Palmer smiled. "So I've heard."

"And this," Bodge continued, "is Denholm."

"Howdy."

"Hi there, Denholm. And you can all call me Michelle. Let's go sit on the lounge suite, shall we?" They got the impression this was a rare occurrence of gentlemen callers in the life of Mrs. Harris. She jogged around from sofa to easy chair to footstool removing magazines and paper bags and fluffing up cushions. The apartment smelled of bug spray and vomit.

"There," she said. "*Asseyez-vous.*"

There followed an embarrassing few minutes when they refused, but were painstakingly brow-beaten into agreeing to tea. During the exchange Mrs. Harris slipped in and out of her fake English accent. She finally retired to the kitchen where she clattered around for some fifteen minutes before re-emerging with a new layer of makeup, a fresh scent of alcohol on her breath, and a huge tray. The latter contained a slightly chipped bone china teapot, four non-matching cups, and a plate piled high with chunky shortbread biscuits. She took on the role of mother and poured for her guests with all the formality of afternoon tea at Buckingham Palace.

"I know you must all feel terribly concerned about Mr. Vistarini. Sugar, Marion?"

"Not for me, thank you. Yes, there doesn't seem to be any trace of him. We're all very worried."

"Denholm?"

"Three, thanks."

"Someone's got a sweet tooth. Bodge?"

"One will be fine. Mrs. Ha… Michelle, when was the last time you actually saw Lou?"

"Well, I suppose it must have been Thursday. Yes, Thursday evening. He came home to change and I was watering the plants out front. In fact he said he was off for dinner with you, Bodge."

"That's right. He was. So, you're saying you didn't see him at all on Friday?"

"Friday? No."

"Do you recall…?" She handed Palmer his cup. "Very kind of you. Do you recall being woken early on Saturday morning? Around 1 or 2AM?"

"Saturday, you say?"

"Yes. Perhaps somebody ringing your doorbell?"

"No, darling. Not at all. I really would remember something like that. I'm a heavy sleeper, but once I'm roused it's the devil of a job for me to get back to sleep."

"Are there any other residents on the ground floor?"

"No, Marion. They all live upstairs. There's only me down here."

"So if there were a ring at the door…?"

"I'd be the one to answer it."

Bodge made the mistake of tasting his tea. It was remarkable that with so much loving care invested in its manufacture, it could still taste like cat's pee. He leaned forward on the couch.

"Michelle, to tell the truth, we don't have a lot of faith in the police finding him." Denholm remained dead pan.

"Goodness. Are they involved?" she asked.

"The authorities have been notified, but I'm sure you understand the force is badly undermanned these days, and in truth, there's no evidence of any crime. They wouldn't do anything unless they were presented with proof of a wrongdoing. We were wondering — would you mind terribly if we took a look upstairs? There might be some clue as to where Lou could have gone."

"Well, I was up there myself on Monday, just briefly, after Mr. Mooney called. I didn't do any poking around, mind."

"We're sure you didn't," Palmer reassured her. "But we do think it's vital we take a look."

"You're right, of course. In fact it's strictly forbidden to let strangers into resident's apartments, but this is a special case, and I'm sure you'll vouch for the good character of Marion and Denholm, won't you, Bodge?"

"Absolutely."

"Then I think we should get ourselves upstairs." The three men reached forward with relief to put their almost-full cups on the table. "Just as soon as we've all finished our tea."

Lou's room was impeccably neat, as if he'd been expecting guests that didn't show up. This was the first thing that worried Bodge. Lou was an organized man, but Bodge had been to this apartment hundreds of times and never seen it so fussy. There was nothing lying around: no breakfast things from Friday morning, no trash. Even the bath towels and face cloths in the bathroom smelled of washing powder.

"Is your friend Lou normally this attentive to detail?" Palmer whispered to Bodge out of earshot of the super.

"No. it's like the place has been overrun by hotel chamber maids. There isn't even any dirty laundry in the basket."

"Either he tidied up because he knew he'd be going away…"

"Or someone's done a thorough job of cleaning up evidence. I bet there isn't a fingerprint in the entire place." That being as it may, the two able-bodied men used clean handkerchiefs to handle everything. Mrs. Harris was very impressed at their efficiency, but Palmer knew they could be even more efficient without her breathing down their necks.

"Michelle, my sweet."

"Yes, honey?"

"I'm afraid we might be some time. Perhaps you'd prefer to go down and take a little rest."

"Well, I…"

"And I'm sure this has all been very disturbing for you, too. Perhaps you'd benefit from a little drink to steady your nerves. Do you have any alcohol in your apartment?"

"Are fish waterproof?" Bodge asked Denholm under his breath.

"There may be a little something down there, Marion. I tell you, being here in poor Mr. Vistarini's rooms is starting to get to me. Perhaps you're right. I'll wait for you all downstairs."

Once the idea of booze was in her mind there was nothing human that could keep her from its pursuit. She closed the door and left them there to their work. Palmer had a way of dismissing menials that made them think it was a favor. Bodge was impressed.

"Perhaps you'd benefit from a little drink to steady your nerves?" he mocked.

"Marion?"

"I needed a name in a hurry."

"And that was the first one that came to your mind?"

"It's my father's name," Bodge confessed.

"Then I guess I should consider myself honored."

"Look, let's get organized," Denholm told them. "I'll go through the kitchen and bathroom. Bodge, you take the bedroom. Maid Marion, this room's yours. Fine tooth comb the whole place. Imagine you live here. Where would you keep your secrets hidden?"

Bodge stood in the doorway of the bedroom. He looked around the room and wondered whether it had any secrets to share with him. On one of their many unutilized training programs, the instructor had told his CIA operatives to always begin a search in the most obvious place because basically people were obvious creatures. Bodge went to the bed and lifted the mattress. The instructor had been right. Half way back were three glossy journals. Bodge had little doubt they were girlie magazines kept there out of the eyesight of his prying landlady. And if Lou felt he needed to hide them, Bodge figured these were perhaps a little steamier than the loose bikinis and nothing-visible nudes you could buy behind Penn Station. If he knew Lou at all, they were pornographic.

He held up the mattress with one hand and pulled out the magazines with the other. The cover of the first wasn't what he'd expected. It was written in Italian. The title in large blue letters read, 'Signori' superimposed over a photo of a good-looking chap with a cigarette. Small sub-headings sat across its smoke. Bodge wondered whether Lou had taken a sudden interest in his grooming.

He opened the magazine at a random page and when his eyes focused, something sharp and cold seemed to puncture his lung. The magazine shook itself from his hands and he let go of the mattress. In those few seconds the world seemed to be pulled inside out. Although he'd done nothing wrong he was consumed by fear.

"You'll have to do better than that."

Bodge, caught like a rat under a flashlight beam, froze and looked up towards the bedroom door. Palmer stood there with a handkerchief wrapped around the handle. "Bodge? Are you okay? …Bodge?"

Bodge snapped out of his trance.

"Yeah. Yeah, I'm okay. It's…the mattress was a little heavier than I expected. I'm still a bit weak from yesterday's incident. I came over faint there for a second. I'm okay now."

"You sure? You want me to give you a hand?"

"No. No. Sorry. What was it you said?"

"I was remarking on that rumpled quilt you've left there. I'd forgotten to mention we need to put everything back exactly as it was found. It would probably help if nobody knows we've been here."

"I can remember how everything was."

Palmer returned to the bathroom and Bodge searched for a breath. His heart was pumping.

"Oh, Lou. No."

Bodge had only seconds to consider all the consequences of what he was to do next. His actions there and then could change the future — and the past. His discovery had already altered one person in his mind, maybe two. He wasn't sure just how much more damage it could do. The magazines were pornographic right enough, but none of the performers were female.

# 15

Bodge woke still dazed from a fitful night of shallow dozing. He wasn't sure where he was at first till he saw the curtains he'd bought and his art nouveau wall piece hanging foolishly from a nail. Then, all the other facts came clattering one into the back of the next till he had more information than he needed. He looked at the clock beside the bed. It was set for seven but there was still half an hour before it could do any alarming. Palmer would pick him up at seven-thirty. They'd eat breakfast then spend another day looking for Lou. Palmer, the ever-present, the shadow. Bodge lay still and tried to remember how different he and Lou and life had been only a few days earlier before Palmer turned up. Everything had been so uncomplicated then. Now look at it all.

He rose from the bed, lifted the mattress a few inches and dragged out the magazines. It would be crazy to take them with him today but even crazier to leave them behind. He found an unused manila envelope in his desk drawer, a large internal mail type. It was big enough for all three magazines. He wanted to tape the flap shut but his stupid clumsy hands couldn't find the end of the roll. Instead he folded the package into the inside pocket of his top coat. It was October and although the Indian summer had extended into September that year, the temperature was dropping fast. He didn't feel the cold and usually settled for a jacket, but his heavy wool coat wouldn't look out of place on the city streets.

Later, in the car while Denholm drove, Palmer asked Bodge if he'd remembered the photographs.

"The ph...? Oh, yeah." He reached into his hip pocket and handed his boss three photos of Bodge and Lou together. All three were of the two smiling men in a bar or a restaurant raising a glass to the cameraman.

"You two seem very close."

"You know, that's how it occurred to me when I went through my pictures. It's funny. I guess we take each other for granted. At the time it always felt as if we were hanging out together until some better life came along. When something's too familiar you tend not to notice its good points. Lou is (he almost said 'was') a nice guy. In all this time together we haven't once fought; not even a word in anger that I can recall."

"You spend a lot of time together?"

"Some weeks we go for a drink, usually go for a meal on Fridays. There were one or two fishing trips. Sometimes when we both had a date, he'd come over to my place and I'd order in, or we'd go to his and he'd cook."

"He cooks well?"

"He's the best. Always Italian, but delicious."

"And baseball?"

"No. Lou isn't into sport. He'd sit through a game if I was really interested, but he doesn't really know much about baseball."

"How does he spend his nights, his weekends, when you aren't around?"

"That's just it. All these years and I can't say I really know what he likes to do. Either that or he really doesn't do anything at all. He'd come in on Monday mornings and I'd ask him how he spent the weekend. He'd say things like, 'Just sitting around' or 'Read a couple of things'".

"So it's quite conceivable that you're his only social life."

"I guess." Although in Bodge's hip pocket was a suggestion otherwise. If Lou could keep that a secret from his best friend, who knows what else he was up to? "But he has so much energy. I can't see him sitting around."

"He doesn't have a steady girl?" Every new question got Bodge thinking at a new level. One he'd never thought he'd have to sink to.

"He's had plenty but he gets bored with them soon enough. They'd be too keen on him or not keen enough; too chatty or too quiet. He usually finds a reason to get rid of them."

"Something like you, in fact."

It was an accurate observation which Palmer had every right to make but it still made Bodge feel resentful at his prying. There was something else now too. Bodge might not have been anything at all like Lou. A deep rooted prejudice seemed to be bubbling beneath the surface, one he hadn't realized he held. But Bodge kept to the track.

"I wonder whether we've talked about 'that perfect woman' so often, we subconsciously stopped giving the imperfect ones a shot." Bodge was certainly talking about himself now. "Lou's, how can I put it? He's a confused person. He has questions about everything."

"Meaning of life questions?"

"Meaning of life and all it contains. He doesn't really know what he's looking for, professionally or socially. I understand that now. He's wanted to get out of that office for as long as me, but doesn't really have any idea what he'd do instead."

The car drove into the forecourt of St. Vincent's hospital on Seventh.

"Do you suppose that might be relevant?"

"To his disappearance?"

"You, his friend, get an overseas posting at last and he sees himself stuck in the office all by himself. I can see that being terribly depressing. Can't you?"

"I hadn't thought about it. I can't really imagine Lou being depressed, but I guess he must get that way like any of us. I don't know. He seemed especially happy on our nights out last week. I suppose it could have been a show. But it was almost as if my victory was his victory. He'd been freed vicariously. Who can say? Perhaps I don't really know him at all."

Denholm didn't drive into the car park, just pulled off to one side and idled there reading the sports section. Palmer produced a sheet of paper from his pocket.

"Okay, Bodge. This is what I propose. I have here a list of hospitals and doctor's offices within a two mile radius of Lou's apartment. The one we're in right now is the closest. You and I will work our way down it and find out whether any place admitted Lou on Saturday morning. Nothing official. Just claim to be a relative — find a sympathetic nurse. We can take half the list each. Denholm has agreed to visit the neighbourhood police precinct houses and see if there were any reports on Friday or Saturday. We can meet up for lunch at La Casa around one and compare notes; decide if we need to spend the afternoon on it as well. Before we go our separate ways, have you given any thought to what we may have learned yesterday?"

Denholm put down his paper to pay attention.

"I do have a sort of mental list of main points."

"Let's hear it."

"Okay, in reverse order. One, we're assuming that Lou disappeared from his apartment, which is fair enough as we have no other starting point. But there's no proof anyone let him in. As nobody saw Lou after that, the cab driver is at the end of the line. He may have lied about taking Lou home. I think we'll have to go have another chat with our cabby sometime. Two, early on Friday evening young Eddie had us both believing he couldn't hold his booze. But it appears he was stone cold sober — and organized. It was as if he had something planned for us. Or, perhaps he had something planned for Lou and I was incidental."

"Because?"

"Because I got home unscathed and Lou didn't." This was one theory that made more sense to Bodge with the package burning in his pocket. "Three, it appears we were in the area around Bouncers for a hell of a long time, but we still don't know where we went. Given our conditions when the cabby picked us up, we couldn't have traveled far. I think we need to get a second opinion as to whether the joint was open on Friday or not.?

"Good point. I'll check with the licensing section," Denholm agreed.

"Four, if Friday night was all planned, then it has to connect back to our office and your letter. If the letter wasn't just a lucky excuse to get introduced to Lou and myself, then somebody's taking a very personal interest in the mission. That increases the likelihood that my truck encounter in DC wasn't an accident. It also suggests the security surrounding this supposedly covert operation in Vietnam has been compromised. Although I don't doubt you're concerned about my friend Lou, it seems more likely to me you're going to all this trouble so you can find out how your project will be affected."

Palmer was delighted. "Excellent. Excellent, Bodge. You see why I wanted you on this mission?"

"To compile lists of questions?"

"Without questions there can be no answers. Let's hope, by the end of the day we both know better where we stand. I'll see you two later." He climbed out of the car, slammed the door and jogged off across the forecourt in yet another two-hundred-buck suit. He and Denholm had refused the offer to sleep at Bodge's the previous night. Denholm presumably had somewhere of his own. Palmer said he had access to a place in town. Whatever that place was, it apparently had a wardrobe of clothes to fit him.

The day was a frustrating waste of time when it came to getting information. It wasn't like the various institutions were deliberately holding back. It was just that the wheels of administration everywhere in New York ground so slowly even the simplest questions took forever to find answers to. At his first opportunity, Bodge ditched the magazines. He felt like himself as a teenager hiding a Health and Efficiency naturist brochure from his parents. Out back of Lenox Hill Hospital he found the furnace. There was nobody minding it so he pulled down the checking flap in the door and slotted the brown envelope though it like mail to the devil. It was a weight off his mind.

At lunch the only news they had to share was that Bouncers didn't have a license to operate at weekends. That, Denholm informed Bodge, was the police way of saying the old lady hadn't offered enough for them to turn a blind eye to her staying open. The afternoon wasn't any better. When he met with Palmer and Denholm at Smokey Joe's that evening, no-one had a shred of information about Lou. There was no joy from the hospitals, the doctors or the police. There had been no accidents or arrests on Saturday morning involving anyone whose identity remained unknown. Lou had merely vanished from the face of the earth.

Smokey Joe's was a bar with a juke box, warped wood paneling and only one light bulb. The owner claimed that made the place atmospheric but what it really made it was dark. Bodge and Palmer had a Millers each. They drank from the bottle because it was impossible to see just how dirty the glasses were. Denholm had a lemon squash. He didn't drink.

The only redeeming feature of Smokey Joe's, the only reason they'd arranged to meet there at all, was that it was a short walk from Bouncers. Being Thursday, there was a good chance the place would be open and they could get past St. Peter's grandmother, thus christened by Bodge. They still needed to find Bodge and Lou's destination on their night out and the clip joint was the only lead they had.

Bouncers was even more horrible than any of them could have imagined. They'd run the gauntlet past the owner who sniffed their money before giving change, and told them she'd known they wouldn't be able to resist a peek inside. They walked along a narrow cave of papier-mâché rocks toward the source of the music.

They'd been expecting a cabaret affair with tables and sexy cocktail waitresses; the usual type of dive. But they emerged from their tunnel into a small damp room with a lighted stage on one side. Eight rows of cinema seats faced the stage and beyond them was a bar. Given the setting, it was a surprisingly splendid bar with mirrors and lines of exotic spirit bottles. The barman was a bald Chinese man in a white undershirt that stretched over a pregnant dome of a stomach.

On the stage was a bewigged woman in her late forties luminous with makeup. She was prancing back and forth barely in time to the tune of "Jezebel". It whined from an old gramophone through an amplification trumpet and made Frankie Lane sound like a chipmunk. She wore a two-piece summer suit apparently made of orange crepe paper that crunched as she walked. She perked up noticeably when the three well-heeled newcomers appeared at the back of the room. Bodge and his party doubled the audience and halved its average age.

There were no stools on the customer side of the bar but four behind it. Bodge assumed they were supposed to take their drinks to the cinema seats although none of the three old men had one. The Chinese looked up from the chaotic script of his newspaper as they approached him. He didn't bother to stand up.

"How much is a beer?" Denholm asked.

"Beer? Sure." Before they could stop him, the barman had popped the cap from a small bottle of Budweiser and banged it down on the bar.

"No. I didn't say I wanted one. I just asked how much."

"I open already. You gotta pay."

"I don't…"

"You look for trouble?" he reached under the bar where all of them were certain he kept an arsenal of threatening weapons. This house scam had obviously worked in the past. The customers paid up rather than get shot. For obvious reasons, few would complain to the police. But Denholm already had his badge in his hand and he held it up for the barman to see.

"Shit." The man felt around on the floor for the cap and pressed it back onto the opened bottle. "Why you no say so?"

"Just out of interest," Palmer asked, "how much would that beer have cost me?"

"Beer? Four dollar."

"Goodness me. Then you really would have had to shoot us."

To their dismay, the lady on the stage was still walking up and down in stiletto heels like a housewife at the supermarket. But now her paper skirt had come adrift from her thick thighs and she was unbuttoning the jacket. Bodge hoped they could get away before they had to witness anything unpleasant.

Denholm leaned across the bar and smiled at the barman who ignored him.

"Were you here last Friday night?"

"Without looking up the barman said, "Sorry, I no speak English."

"You're from China?" Palmer asked.

"No."

"Where then?"

"Hong Kong."

At that point, the special ops man launched into an impressive barrage of what Bodge assumed to be Cantonese. The barman blossomed at the sound. Suddenly the two were good friends engaged in a light-hearted private conversation. Bodge and Denholm had little choice but to watch the show.

Beneath the crepe the lady wore a stained set of pink panties and brassiere with tassels. They could see her counting the rhythm out loud.

It was approximately twenty beats between each removal, although she obviously had difficulty counting and prancing at the same time. The three old men were transfixed as if they'd spent the past seventy years in a cloth bag and had just been released for this feast of flesh.

The brassiere clip was in the front. On the count of twenty-one she unfastened it to unleash her modest top. Her breasts were slightly shriveled and appeared to be magnetically opposed to one another. When she noticed Bodge looking at her, she ran her tongue over her lips and wiggled those breasts seductively for him. He was saved by Palmer and the Chinaman who passed him and headed for a curtained exit to the right of the stage. Bodge followed but Denholm stood his ground. Bodge hoped it was just his duty to watch their backs rather than a desire to see the end of the show.

Behind the stage was a dressing room as long and narrow as the aisle on a Greyhound bus. A second "dancer" was wedged at the far end of it. She was as gloriously painted as the first but didn't share her gifts of youth and beauty. At first Bodge supposed the owner had slipped out of her booth and was doubling as an entertainer. But Fifi was much more pleasant than her boss. She was amiable and helpful and talking to her was like chatting with a well-loved aunt. Except Bodge's aunt was less likely to be applying lipstick to her nipples as she spoke.

She knew the area well and was able to give them the names of other dives around that Bodge and Lou might have visited. She even knew of a supper club for the upper classes that was tucked down behind a department store. And there was no doubt that Bouncers had been closed. Both Fifi and the Chinaman swore to it. Bodge and Palmer collected Denholm on their way out. He was leaning on the bar with his back to the stage. The lady had shed her remaining vestment and was showing the enrapt audience what other uses there were for fresh fruit. They didn't notice the newcomers leave. There was no world for them beyond the banana.

Again, Bodge was attracted by the neon Nescafé cup in the window of the café three doors along. He suggested they have a final drink there before calling it a night. They were all beat and frustrated and not at all in the mood for hanging around in dives. The café was surprisingly bohemian and out of place in that particular area. But there was nothing familiar about it to Bodge. Jazz music played from a phonograph behind the counter.

It was a nice, cozy place just asking to get knocked over by any drunk or addict that passed by. The music system alone was worth a good hundred dollars. There was a stringy youth working behind the counter. He wore denim even though his accent didn't suggest he was a farmer. His hair wasn't long enough to call him a beatnik, but Bodge was sure it still annoyed the boy's parents.

"How you doing, fellas?" he smiled and walked over to their table. There weren't any other customers to look after.

"Three coffees, thanks," Bodge said.

"Sure. What type?"

"Coffee's got types?" Denholm asked.

"Sure does," the boy put him straight. He brought over the menu to prove it. Alongside tea and soft drinks there were no fewer than five different brands of percolated coffee listed there. They were all new to Bodge. He caught the numbers written beside them and knew straight away why the place was deserted.

"Do you get to keep the table and chairs for these prices?" he asked smiling at Palmer. His boss looked out at the dark street through the grimy window.

"Come on guys. These coffees are hard to come by."

"Why doesn't that surprise me?" Bodge asked. "You got any of that exotic European coffee advertised on the sign in the window there?"

"That's instant."

"Do you?"

"Yes."

"And what type of investment are we talking here?"

"Twenty-five cents…each."

"Holy Mackerel."

"Come on, Bodge," Palmer calmed him. "It's a nice enough place, good music, and I'm sure the coffee will be delicious. Am I right, son?"

"It's hard to screw up a cup of instant."

"See? Let's live dangerously. Three of your finest instant coffees please, young man."

"Yes, sir." He was about to walk away when Bodge asked,

"You have anything to eat here?" They hadn't eaten since lunch and his mind was convincing him he was hungry.

"Brownies and packaged fruit cake."

"No food?"

"Not if you don't call brownies and fruit cake food. No."

"When's your busiest time, son?" Denholm asked. "Assuming you have one."

"Don't know. Early evening, I guess. Office people on their ways home. Then again after the bars shut."

"And they can all afford these fancy prices?"

"Some. Yeah. There are a lot of connoisseurs around who'd travel for a great coffee. These are rare. They're like the Hope Diamond of coffees."

"I believe that. 'Except you don't piss the Hope Diamond down the john at the end of the night."

"Look. I don't know, you know?" the boy said without actually saying anything. "You should talk to the owner. I just say what he tells me."

"We know. Don't worry about it," Bodge smiled. "And bring me a slice of that fruit cake."

"Coming up."

"I don't know," Denholm said half to himself. "I smell something odd here and it sure isn't coffee."

# 16

**Ban Methuot**

The inspector of schools, M. Petit sat in the vestibule of Le Residence mopping the sweat from his neck with a large white handkerchief. Even with the front and rear doors wide open, there was no breeze. It had been some kind of insanity that transported French fashion to the Far East. In that sticky 90 degree heat he wore a tie and a sodden white jacket. It was expected of callers on official business. He was a slender, rather pretty young man: the type who would age like an old woman. Locals often remembered his blond hair but not his face.

Although Petit was unsure as to what Administrator Dupré did to deserve his inflated salary, he'd been a hard man to make an appointment with. It had been over a week since he'd put in his request for an audience, and the reply had only arrived that morning during his breakfast. He'd hurriedly cancelled two school visits in order to be here by eleven. But the grandfather clock had just chimed the three-quarter hour and still nobody had seen him. He didn't even get a glass of water for his troubles. So he sat, and sweated and cursed under his breath. The smells of cooking, of partridge and venison, were wafting through the large hall. Petit was sure whatever little time he had left would be interrupted by the luncheon gong.

"Ah, so you're M. Petit. I've seen you around."

He looked up to see a slim woman in fine white silks. If the day weren't so stifling, she might have come direct from the tennis court with her short skirt and white sneakers. There was something sporty about her. He stood and bowed. She walked over to him and laughed. "I'm not the empress, you know?" He found her accent rather rough.

She took his hand and, after a cursory flick of her wrist, kept hold of it.

"You're Mme. Dupré?"

"I know. Pity isn't it. Goodness me, you're sweating like a hog. What on earth are you wearing a coat for on a day like this?"

"I was told it was mandatory."

"Really?" She snorted rudely. "Golly. You must be a teacher with such language." She still had hold of his fingers although he was slowly sliding from her grasp.

"Yes. I am," he smiled. "Or rather, I was. Right now I'm the inspector of schools."

"And what did you teach, dear M. Petit?"

"French and English literature."

"English? How I'd love to speak English. I don't suppose you could tutor me, could you?"

She'd said the word "tutor" in a way he'd never heard it said in his life. It made him feel suddenly uneasy. She may have even winked although it was quite hard to be sure there in the shadows of the vestibule.

"I'm sure we could come to some arrangement."

"That's what I'd hoped. I really must help you out of that jacket." Before he could protest or remove it himself, she was behind him. Her fingers seemed to explore his damp chest as she peeled back the lapels. Her pert breasts nuzzled impudently into his back. He felt like a victim of some sort of sexual attack but still missed a heartbeat when the Administrator himself appeared across the hall.

"M. Dupré? I am M. Petit," he babbled. It was a foolish introduction as they'd met before at the official reception. Dupré made out his wife in the shadows.

"Monique? What are you doing, my dear?"

She stepped out from behind Petit with his jacket in her hand. "I'm removing his clothing. You don't mind, do you? The poor inspector was dripping."

"No. No, that's fine. Come in here, lad. Come in." He turned back into his office. Petit looked back at his jacket and into Mme. Dupré's elfin face.

"You can get it," she said. "Any time you want it."

He sighed and walked unsteadily to the office. There had been no misunderstanding. He had been propositioned by the governor's wife. He was relieved to find himself in the light, spacious room that Dupré had adopted as his work room. Fans of various sizes blew gales back and forth across the room. Every stack of documents was anchored down with a paperweight. The portraits flapped on the walls. Dupré sat at an enormous desk and gestured for the guest to sit opposite. It felt significant to Petit that there had been no handshake.

"I've been meaning to have a word with you," said Dupré, forgetting it was the teacher who'd called for the meeting. "I haven't yet got around to your last report. Don't know when I shall. Perhaps you could just tell me from memory how many of our Montagnard villages still don't have schools?"

"You mean buildings?"

"What else would I mean?" Petit could think of a number of things; teachers, books, equipment, all those sundries that turned a place into a school.

"In that case, about twenty."

"Good. So I imagine that many could be put up before the end of the dry season."

"The buildings aren't so hard."

"Splendid."

"But we would need a serious teacher training program and work on the curriculum in order to staff them."

"Surely that's what we have you for, isn't it?"

"The schedule I'm expected to follow is full of inspections. There's no time to train or write."

"Right. Well, in that case, forget teachers. Let's focus on the buildings. Our policy is to have a school in every village."

"Whether they teach anything or not?"

"I doubt anyone in Paris would blame us for that. If the savages don't have anyone bright enough to teach it's hardly our fault, is it now?'

"They're certainly bright enough. It's just—"

"Don't let it worry you. Twenty more schools. Splendid. I'll pass the news on when I'm next in Saigon. There was nothing else was there?" He turned a page of his ledger as if the chapter on Petit were over.

"There is one more thing," Petit said. Dupré looked at his watch. "It's very important."

"Very well."

"I've had a report about a woman vanishing from her home."

"What? My goodness. Have you informed the Sureté?"

"Yes. But they need authorization from you to pursue the case."

"From me? Why in blazes would they need that?"

"Because the accused kidnapper is a foreign national."

"Heavens above. Who was the victim?"

"The younger sister of one of our administrators."

"But that's disgraceful. Who...? One of our administrators? You don't mean one of our village administrators?"

"Yes, I do." The look of relief came over Dupré as clearly as if a pot of white paint had been emptied onto his head.

"So she's *Moi.*"

"Montagnard, that's right. But that shouldn't..."

"M. Petit. Don't you think our police aren't busy enough with crimes against our own citizens?"

"With respect, Governor Dupré, it's a French administration that's running the country under French law. The Montagnard are fighting in our army against the Viet Minh and laboring in French plantations. Don't you think as a show of faith we could demonstrate that French law isn't blind to injustices against them?"

"Petit. Petit, my young friend. Can you imagine what a precedent this would set?"

"I can imagine a very good one."

"Son, every laborer and servant and whore in the country would try their hand at bringing charges against us if they thought there were a few *piastres* to be made out of it."

"If the law finds them in the right, I don't—"

"Enough. I think you should go home and cool off. The heat has obviously affected your mind. Have a cool beer and rethink your master plan for our little colony. I believe it's lunch time." He stood and closed the ledger. "Good day M. Petit. Get working on those schools, now. Don't forget, twenty by April."

# 17

In Little Italy Bodge stood in the shadows of the elementary school opposite Lou's apartment. It was after two. It wasn't that he expected Lou to sneak back in the middle of the night. He just wanted to see how things looked early in the morning — imagine Lou passed out on his stoop — get a better idea of possibilities. And he wanted to do this without his minders breathing down his neck.

Nothing spectacular happened for a half hour. Old Italian ladies with shopping baskets merged in and out of the lamplight, sleepwalking to imaginary late-night food stores. Or maybe they knew things Bodge didn't. There was the sound of yelling from first this upstairs window then some other. He couldn't imagine being in a relationship where yelling was compulsory. But, in fact, he could no longer imagine himself in a relationship. Then there were the rats. It was astounding how they took over the city after nightfall. He hadn't done a lot of staring at streets. He imagined them finding Lou on his doorstep and eating him alive. More and more he was seeing his friend dead.

Suddenly, the light in Mrs. Harris' hallway came on and lit the pretty stained glass in the front door. It was just after two. The door opened and an ancient man with arthritic legs shuffled out and down the steps. Hanging over his arm was a white poodle that appeared to have been filleted. He carried it down to the curb and lowered it to the road. He didn't take his hand away until the wobbling animal found its balance. It shuddered a little then started to shit. No squat or anything. When it was through, the man picked it up and carried it back up to the stoop. Neither the man nor the dog seemed remotely aware of what had just happened.

Bodge jogged over the street and up the steps before the man could close the door. Now, most of the neurotics in New York would have had a heart attack if something like Bodge ran up to them at two in the morning, but the old man just turned round in response to the "excuse me", and smiled.

"How you doing young fella?"

"Hi. You walking your dog?"

"Just emptying him out."

"I don't suppose this is a regular thing by any chance."

"Sure is. Same time every morning the little fucker's yapping at the end of the bed. Why? You with the city council?"

"No. I was just wondering whether you might have seen anything odd on Saturday about this time."

"Saturday. Saturday. Oh, hell yes. That was the night both me and the dog shit ourselves."

"What happened?"

"I was coming down like I always do. But just as I'm about to turn on the light, somebody goes and rings the doorbell."

"Did you see who it was?"

"No. But all the residents here have keys. I wasn't about to open the door to a stranger at two in the morning. There's a bad element moving in to these streets. I put on the light to scare him away. He didn't ring again."

"And you didn't go outside?"

"Didn't need to by then. Trigger here has a finely tuned bowel. He knows how long it takes to get to the street. With us getting sidetracked there in the hall, poor Trigger's mechanism had already started. Little fucker embarrassed himself. I had to clean it all up before the old lush came round."

"Did you hear a car pull away?"

"Did I? You know I may have now you ask. It was a couple of minutes later."

"Great. Thanks a lot."

"No problem. You're that friend of Vistarini. I've seen you around before. They found him yet?"

"No."

"Too bad. Night."

He shut the door on Bodge and left him standing there. It now appeared very likely the taxi driver had told the truth about bringing Lou home. So somehow he had to trace his friend's movements from the doorstep on which he now stood. He'd rung the bell and not been allowed in. What would he have done then? He decided to give his surveillance one more shot.

An hour later he was drowsing against the wall of the school. His toes and fingers were numb from the cold. If it hadn't been for the squeaking of the perambulator wheels, he would probably have missed the old lady completely. She was a coffee-brown woman dressed in layers of clothes like an Eskimo. She dragged the baby carriage behind her piled high with every type of junk he could imagine. This hill of garbage was topped with an old cane chair whose legs held everything in place. It was a miracle of trash engineering.

This was exactly what Bodge had been waiting for: people like Coffee-Brown who owned the early morning streets. These were the spies who saw and heard secrets in the sleeping city. He wouldn't confront her there on the poorly lit sidewalk. He'd follow her from a distance and see where she stayed, perhaps meet her gutter comrades, see who'd been about the previous Friday.

She walked slowly stopping at trash cans and piles of garbage that stood on street corners like neighborhood pyres. Residents could never tell when the refuse collectors were likely to come by, so some weeks the trash piled up and gave the streets a certain smell. A blind man could tell if he was in Chinatown, Little Italy or Jewish Williamsburg just by the stench. But there was gold in them there hills of junk for people like Coffee Brown. She browsed. She tasted. She tried on crushed hats and holey sweaters and heel-less shoes. And all the while, Bodge stood uncomfortably back in the doorways and alleyways she'd passed.

It was another hour before she reached her final destination. Her route hadn't been a straight line. She'd worked her way up and down blocks like a mailman, and Bodge had labored after her, believing she'd never let up. He marveled at how happy she seemed, adding the spoils to her towering chariot. But finally she ended up at a boarded-over building only two blocks from Lou's place. The basement had been converted to an all night center whose lights were blazing even at 4AM.

Coffee Brown walked past the entrance and wheeled her booty down an alleyway beside the building. At its dark end she creaked open a tall gate and pushed the carriage inside. It appeared to Bodge to be the rear entrance to this same center. He walked back to the front and read the plaque screwed to the wall at the foot of the steps.

"Salvation Army - Bowery Shelter", what Lou would call a "bum depot".

Bodge walked down the steps, through an open door and into a well-lighted room. It was fitted out like a cafeteria with clothed tables, and chairs that mostly matched. Against one wall was a long trestle with cups and plates of cookies. A large black coffee pot with cloth wrapped round its handle sat on a stove over a low flame. Although it was likely well stewed, the coffee smelt good to Bodge.

But he wasn't about to steal vital nutrients from the city's vagrants wherever they might be. There had to be someone on duty. The Salvation Army wasn't about to let bums save themselves. There was only one door at the rear of the room. It opened into a large dark space set out with rows of bunks. Half of them were occupied and the place stank of body odor and stale liquor.

"Shut that fucking door, you asshole," came a voice.

Bodge pulled the door shut behind him and immediately felt uneasy there in a dark place with the vermin of New York's night world. Someone on the far side of the room had noticed him. A huge figure picked its way toward him through the sleeping bodies. In the light that sawed through the cracks in the ill-fitting doorway Bodge could make out the features of a well-built Negro even taller than himself. He stopped in front of Bodge and spoke in a deep educated southern accent,

"I'd personally say you've come to the wrong place."

"No, I think I'm right," Bodge answered.

"Are you with the police?"

"Not exactly."

"Yous two gonna spoon there all fuckin' night?" shouted the same, unsettled houseguest.

"Shut up, Slim," the big man said calmly into the darkness. "You want quality, you go and book yourself a room at the Carlton." But the Negro put a powerful hand on Bodge's shoulder and steered him back into the reception room.

"Do you look after this place alone?" Bodge asked. His host walked to the trestle and started fixing coffee for both of them.

"At night, after supper, there's just me. You want to tell me who you are?"

"Sorry, yes. My name's Robert Leon." He reached into his hip pocket for his badge then remembered he'd made a decision earlier not to bring it. "In the daylight hours I work with the Central Intelligence Agency."

"I reckon I've heard of them. Cream? Sugar?"

"Just as it comes from the pot, thanks."

"And what are you after dark?"

"I guess you could say I'm here doing some research."

"About?"

"I'm looking for a lost friend."

"And you think your friend might be in a place like this?" They sat at one of the tables. The man was solid like a pro linebacker. If he hadn't been so exhausted, Bodge might have bothered to ask him if he'd ever played.

"No. But I was hoping some of your…guests might have seen something. Last we knew, my friend was drunk and passed out on his front stoop two blocks from here."

"When was that?"

"Last Saturday morning around 2AM."

"No offence, but I imagine your friend isn't the type of drunk we cater for here."

"I understand that. But I'm sure your people would notice a guy passed out beside the street. I just saw a woman with a baby carriage walking in front of his apartment."

"Vivien Leigh."

"Viv—?"

"Don't ask. Yeah. She sees a lot. She even sees a lot that isn't there. I just have doubts that Vivien and our usual clientele would be comfortable talking to someone like yourself."

"What am I like?"

"Establishment, crew cut, manners, white, money, badge. Take your pick."

"It had never occurred to me I belonged to so many unpopular subdivisions."

"Don't worry about it. I've been here since they opened this place and a lot of them don't trust me, either. And I'm from an inferior race."

"Look, all I want to do is get some information about a friend. I'm not here to start a war."

"You'd be too late anyhow. The war's been going on for quite a while. You just happened to arrive at the front line." Bodge was too tired for a lecture. He knew the place now and could come back when he had some energy. He stood.

"Thanks for the coffee. I needed it."

The night man looked up at him, "I'll ask around. You got a number?"

Bodge pulled a card from his jacket pocket, then remembered a small black and white photo he'd brought from his apartment. He handed it to the night man.

"This your friend?"

"Yeah."

He went to a shelf beside the unplugged TV where he kept his bifocals in an ornate case. He put them on and read one of the cards. There was just Bodge's name and two numbers, one in New York and the other in DC.

"I'll be at the New York number, I guess, until Sunday," Bodge told him. The night man had turned over the photograph and was studying Lou's face. Bodge knew. He knew straight away that something had happened in the man's head. The slight inflection of an eyebrow, a dilation of the pupils, nothing spectacular but enough to tell Bodge the figure in the photograph had triggered a memory in the night man's mind.

"What is it?" he asked.

"What?"

"You know, don't you?" Bodge said. "You know what happened to him."

"Yeah. I know."

"Is he dead?" He wanted to get that out of the way.

"Yes." It was the answer Bodge expected but he still couldn't prevent the chill from squirming up inside him. "I'm sorry. But you got the times wrong. That screwed me up."

Palmer sat on the sofa with his legs crossed. Denholm occupied the easy chair beside a stack of magazines. Bodge had covered four miles walking up and down his living room rug as he told the story. The two men had listened in silence.

When Palmer was sure Bodge had finished, he stood and walked to the dining table. He perched his backside on its edge and folded his arms. Bodge, exhausted, took his place on the sofa. Palmer looked at Bodge and shook his head minutely.

"I can't pretend to be happy that you took all this on by yourself, Bodge. You knew all along you'd be going out to Lou's after we left you last night."

"There was nothing three of us could have done better than one."

"Perhaps you've forgotten that someone's trying to kill you as well."

"We can't be sure of that."

"Right. There's really only one way to find out for sure. Make it easy for them. Hang around on street corners and vagrant centers. Is that what you'd planned? Bodge, I'm disappointed in you. Really."

Bodge was tempted to blurt out all his own disappointments and doubts, but he held on to them. They were still his only weapon.

# 18

It was Saturday morning and Bodge was once more on the train to DC. The previous 24 hours had sped by like the insignificant stations beyond his carriage window. Bodge had found himself relegated from first baseman to the dugout almost as soon as he'd finished telling Palmer and Denholm his findings. With agency pressure, the police force had acted amazingly quickly. The efficiency of the dealings had left Bodge breathless, and also a little afraid. Denholm coordinated things from Bodge's apartment phone, and passed on news as it came in.

A numbered grave on Hart Island had been located and Lou's body exhumed. It was swiftly returned to the city morgue where a formal autopsy began. Meanwhile, a very serious shakedown of residents at the Bowery shelter turned up Lou's clothing. Some of it was being worn by one, Mr. Smith, a career low-life and drunk who claimed to have "found the stuff beside the road." By whatever means, the interrogators subsequently learned that at the time of his finding them, the clothes had been on a dead body. His explanation of events had sounded logical to him and he couldn't understand what the agents were so het up about.

"The guy was dead, right? What the hell use did he have for clothes?"

So, Mr. Smith had dragged the body into a step-down, stripped Lou of his outer clothes, and, very charitably he thought, given the guy his own rags. Mr. Smith was taken into custody as a suspect in the murder of Louis Vistarini. There were however one or two major inconsistencies about his story. He swore that he saw the man arrive in a blue car at about four and that the guy collapsed straight away. The driver didn't stop to help. But then again, Smith was wearing his pants back to front.

The night man at the shelter hadn't seen the body until after six. The police arrived at his apartment with it on the back of a truck. It was picked up on what the cops called the morning sweep up. An average of five homeless people died on the streets every night in Manhattan. Some succumbed to diseases or the ravages of booze. Others died from exposure or just couldn't think of a good reason to stay alive any more. The police would get a call and send the wagon to pick them up. There would be a cursory attempt at identifying them at centers like the Bowery but they wouldn't be kept on ice too long. They'd soon find themselves on the barge to Hart Island, the pauper's graveyard.

While they were at it, the police brought in the doctor who'd signed the death certificate. The agency was interested to know what kind of MD would fail to notice clean fingernails and unblemished skin on a dead street bum. The answer turned out to be an MD who didn't actually go to look at the body. The medical student on duty that night filled out the certificate on his way to the mortuary. Based on the sight and smell of the body, and unvarying experiences, he'd covered all bases by writing 'cardiac arrest' and 'liver failure'. The next day he'd dropped by the doctor's place to get it signed. It was a formality.

It had been the following day when word got back from the coroner's office. Lou's body showed no evidence of violence apart from some minor bleeding and bruising around the mouth. There were no traces of the usual effects of common poisons. According to the forensics man, the medical student might have been right. All the indications were that Lou had indeed died of a coronary brought on by an overdose of alcohol.

Denholm had given the news to Bodge in such a way as to suggest that was the end of it. Mystery solved. Life goes on. Palmer sat with Bodge and commiserated for a while, but before he left he suggested Bodge make his way back to DC sometime over the weekend. They could resume the orientation on Monday. Bodge had nodded, walked Palmer to the door, and smiled politely when the man told him again how sorry he was about Lou.

"Still," he'd said, "I imagine it's better to know for sure what happened than to be forever wondering. You did a fine job of detection, Bodge. I haven't forgiven you for going it alone but it was a fine job. Relax this weekend. Get it out of your system. Things will seem fairer in a couple of days."

Bodge didn't know what that meant. He closed the door and went to sit in his favorite TV reclining chair where he waited for the sun to go down. He couldn't imagine what he'd do in New York over the weekend. The Giants were over in Brooklyn playing the Dodgers, but baseball, so often the only really important thing in his life, had suddenly started to feel like…well, a game. He had no more interest in trivialities. He packed a few more things, took a cab to Penn Station, and caught a late train.

The hell it was all over. Bodge hadn't the slightest doubt in his mind that Lou had been killed. Men in their thirties in passable shape didn't just keel over. Of course, there were ways to murder a man that made death look natural. Hadn't they taught him about that? Why had the agency settled so complacently on the most obvious of causes? He wondered in the rush how many tests they'd done, how many other possibilities they'd investigated.

Everything had gone too fast. It was as if they wanted it out of the way. Permission to exhume a body in two hours? Coroners dropping everything else on their schedule? It was the crime investigation version of bus station burgers. No preparation, no slow grill, no thought at all. Ten seconds and its hot and in your hand. He was leaving New York behind him, but not Lou. The magazines had to be connected, and young Eddie. What the hell did all that have to do with a heart attack? It was time, he decided, to play it clever. He'd only get his answers by listening, by being on Palmer' side. If they wanted him to be a big dumb desk-jockey, that's what he'd be. Something would eventually have to give.

The train, the beat of the wheels on the tracks, two days and nights awake...Bodge put his head against the window and finally got some sleep.

## 19

**Ban Methuot.**

The guest list for the November Confucius Festival dinner at Le Residence was a who's who of VIPs in the district. The French had every cultural holiday — their own, Vietnamese and Chinese marked on the calendar as suitable excuses for dinner parties. They'd somehow squeezed thirty six people around the impressive teak table, not one of whom would have given the others a cursory glance at any other place or time. Being an expatriate in a small town threw odd people together. They were as ill matched as the symbols of the zodiac.

Among the guests were General LePenn, commander of French forces in the West, one or two of the wealthier plantation owners including M. Yves DeWolff, Mayor Thrin — the token Vietnamese, Doctor Moncur, Captain Henry — the Director of Police, there was the Tax Inspector, the Inspector of Schools, and the Health and Sanitation Examiner. All but the general and School Inspector Petit had brought along their wives. General LePenn's wife lived in Auxerre. Petit's lived in his imagination. Naturally, hosting the event were the Duprés. Administrator Dupré sat at the head of the table like Louis XIV, barking orders at the white-clad *Moi* servants and enthralling those near him with stories of history's great clerical mishaps.

His wife sat at the far end, ruddy and silly from too much wine. The couple had another tiff that afternoon. It was sparked by a change in the seating plan. M. Dupré had been alerted by many of the expatriate spouses to the inappropriateness of his wife studying alone with a single man. As a result he'd insisted on hiring a chaperone to accompany her to her English lessons and report back on his wife's. He also began to consider the possibility that his wife, being a beautiful and vibrant young woman, might have been inadvertently attracting unwanted advances from young men. In an attempt to remove such temptation he'd shuffled school inspector Petit's name plate to a spot beside the Vietnamese. Dupré knew the boy didn't object to contact with natives.

His wife, in a fit of rage, moved it back. As she knew it would annoy her husband, she also moved the outgoing missionaries up to her left flank to set up a small English language colony at her end of the table. She argued that a dinner party would be an ideal place to practice her syntax. The Americans had spent the past month in their city house and were on their way home. Dupré had cleverly invited them to this large noisy gathering in part as an official farewell, but mainly to drown them out. Why on earth the church would send a couple who couldn't speak French to a French colony was beyond him. Like most of the Anglos they had the arrogance to expect everyone else to learn their language. But this was Annam. It was only good manners to speak French here. So, with one end of the table jabbering away in English, and the other listening politely to the host, it was left to the large middle section to maintain that happy buzz French parties were so renowned for.

To his astonishment, at his end of the table, M. Petit found himself with a foot on his lap. He was unsure as to what to do with it. He was a shy man, and when it came to carnal knowledge he was very much a freshman. During his three lessons with Mme. Dupré, all the spoken innuendoes and unspoken language of the body had come from her. He wasn't so naïve as to let them pass unnoticed. He felt that if the chaperone hadn't been sitting across his study with her knitting, his student would have spread him across the desk and had her way with him there and then. For his own part he'd smiled and blushed a good deal, and done his utmost to cover his obvious excitement.

But his emotions were mixed. A few places along from him sat a man he suspected of being a kidnapper perhaps a murderer. On his last visit to the M'nong village, headman Tuwun had told him everything. The Montagnard had begged him to pursue justice for his sister. But the police and the administrator didn't consider the locals to be worthy of white man's laws and he didn't know where to turn next. And now, as if he weren't confused enough, in a room full of people, he had the first lady's foot on his lap. As far as he could tell it was an unclothed leg that rolled there from side to side. The hostess had twice invited him to investigate. She tried a third time.

"You go to South before, M. Petit?" She asked in her awful English.

"No," he replied.

"The Delta is so dull," interjected Mrs. Cornfelt, the wife of the reverend.

Mme. Dupré ignored her. "You must go down, M. Petit." She looked at his quivering hand. "You must go down touch ze Delta."

The wine had fired his body and his loins and he was suddenly overcome with the adventurous spirit of an early French explorer. He dropped his spoon into his crème caramel and dove his hand beneath the apron of the tablecloth. It immediately found the warmth of her inner calf. Mme. Dupré smiled and raised her glass.

"To ze Delta, M. Petit. To ze Delta."

The missionaries raised their glasses also. "To the Delta," they said, although Mrs. Cornfelt had seen nothing interesting enough in those flat plains to warrant this young woman's fervor. "The French are so easily aroused," she whispered to her husband.

# 20

Bodge pulled into the parking lot behind the Casually Yours showroom. Given the number of people working above the store, he was surprised how few cars there were on the lot.

The first thing he'd done when he arrived back in DC was check into a motel out in Chevy Chase. It was the type of place that didn't insist on seeing an ID; cash up front, nothing much to steal or damage in the room. His convertible was a deathtrap on wheels he'd rented from the garage opposite. The owner figured a month in advance was more than the heap was worth so he didn't bother with details either. As far as Washington was concerned, Bodge wasn't there. He was untraceable. There was a fine line between being careful and being paranoid, but he rather liked the idea of being a live paranoiac.

He was a different Bodge to the soft man who'd first arrived in DC a week earlier. That Bodge had trusted everyone. This suspicious Bodge wouldn't have been surprised if his own mother was caught turning tricks from the back room of the Women's Institute. This Bodge had lived six years of intrigue in a week. This Bodge looked twice at everyone he passed and had a .44 Smith and Wesson Magnum taped under the dash. He couldn't get away from the fact the CIA owned him, but now he was watching for whatever they had planned for him.

In a way he never would have expected, one of his mysteries unraveled all by itself even before he made it into the building. He was walking across the lot toward the side alleyway when he noticed a rear end protruding from the trunk of a Chrysler. The woman wore a tight skirt and was digging away deep inside the trunk. It was a full, but nicely pear-shaped ass — worth a second look. The stockings beneath the skirt were seamed and the skinny heels on her shoes wobbled under all the strain.

If he'd still been his old Bodge he might even have offered to give her a hand to find whatever it was she'd lost. But he wasn't that Bodge any more. He walked on by, and wouldn't have given it another thought if he hadn't heard his name called.

"Agent Leon. I can't believe you'd ignore a girl in distress." He recognized the voice from somewhere, but not the accent. He stopped and looked back. She stood there now with her arm on the open trunk lid. She wore a cashmere sweater packed with an impressive bosom. Her hair was short, black, and fell chicly over one eye like a Vogue cover for girls with a fuller figure. Her smile was framed in lipstick and ostensibly friendly. That was what probably threw him.

"I don't…" he began.

"Don't what? Don't get it? Don't know who I am? Don't what? Come on, say something. You do remember me, don't you?"

Then he did. Amazing as it seemed, he did remember some other incarnation of this woman. While he was off changing his Bodge, she'd turned into a whole new Stephanie.

"Barely," he said at last. A broad smile came to his lips.

"You wanna give me a hand with these?" She produced a dozen box files from the depths of the trunk. He took a few steps forward but still didn't believe his eyes. She was a hundred pounds lighter. The ugly floral dress, the greasy yellow hair, the mid-west accent, they were all gone. This wasn't something a beauty salon could achieve in a week at any cost.

"You creep," he smiled.

"Hey, watch your language, buddy."

"This is what you were both talking about."

"Talking about when? You gonna take some of these or what?"

"That was all a set-up last Tuesday."

She laughed. "We wanted to see if it'd fool anyone, and you being the observant type…"

"Well, you sure got me."

She slammed the trunk shut and locked it. They started off across the lot. "We intended to run with it for the whole week, fine-tune the hate/hate relationship. But then you went and spoiled all the fun with your truck-busting rodeo show."

"I'm sorry. I can't imagine how miserable I might have been after a week of you."

He looked her up and down as they walked. "Damn you're…"

"Hot?"

"You're good. You really are." He laughed again. "I'm…Hell, I'm impressed." They were both laughing when they reached the side door to the building.

Palmer looked up from his file when the two grinning agents came into the room.

"Well, I see you've met the other Stephanie," he smiled. "I take it you prefer this one."

"I dread to think what she might turn herself into next."

"Good, isn't she?"

"I'm in awe." Bodge and Stephanie sat on either side of the boss.

"As long as you're able to play Pa Kettle to her Ma, I don't imagine anyone in Vietnam will doubt for a second you're who you say you are. I'm sorry we put you through that little charade."

"I'm sorry I said all those things about you two under my breath."

"You still planning to put in for an early retirement?"

"No, I guess I'll stick it out."

"Good man."

"Swell," Stephanie agreed.

So it was, the first domino to have fallen, had been stood back up. It didn't vindicate Palmer, not at all, but it caused Bodge to go back over all the events in New York and cast the man in a slightly different role, one without the cloud of guilt over his head.

The week went well. They were like three college pals working on an assignment together. On the Tuesday they worked through the protocols — learned what they could and couldn't do as agents on foreign soil. They were there to observe, listen and provide information, both factual and surmised. They were to do all this whilst fulfilling their primary role, that of missionaries. There was to be no hiding in closets or breaking into locked rooms. Nothing they did could endanger their cover.

On the Thursday, Bodge and Stephanie had their first public outing as the Reverend and Mrs. Rodgers. Although thoughts of Lou didn't once leave Bodge's mind, for the first time since he'd started his relationship with the operations unit, he actually felt positive about things. He even believed he might be up to the challenge. He liked his new partner and had a feeling they'd do a splendid job together.

They'd driven their own cars to Bodge's motel. The plan was to change into their alter-identities and travel to the meeting on public transport. Bodge unlocked the door to his room and stood back.

"So, they still make gentlemen," Stephanie said, walking into the room. "Nice place." She admired the green and orange décor and the carpet stains.

"It suits."

"Why would you want to stay all the way out here in this dive?"

He closed the door. "It occurred to me, the fewer people who knew where I was, the better."

"So that's why you led our caravan on that merry diversion via Pennsylvania. You still think there's someone after you?" She put her overnight bag on one of the twin beds and sat beside it, crossing her legs a little uncomfortably.

"Better to be safe than sorry."

"You don't think your friend's death was natural, do you?"

"What makes you say that?"

"Finding his body doesn't seem to have relaxed you any. And, I'm like you. I don't believe in coincidences."

"I'm a naturally suspicious type of Bodge."

"Where'd you get the nickname?"

"England."

"What's it mean?"

"Same as botch, really. We were training for Overlord. I was billeted with a pack of Royal Engineer officers. A more sarcastic bunch of thugs you wouldn't hope to meet. I guess I must have screwed up here and there. Little things like climbing up to the passenger seat to drive a truck. You can imagine how it is for a young Tennessean in an alien land."

"Sure."

"In England in those days, if you didn't have a nickname you weren't alive. They were scraping the barrel for some of the boys. There must have been whole battalions of gingers and loftys and chalkies. I was kind of proud to have a name all to myself." Bodge was never really comfortable talking about himself. He didn't consider his history to be much of a topic. He changed it whenever he could.

"You got a nickname?"

"No." She looked up at him. "You got a girl, Bodge?"

The question caught him off guard, especially coming from a woman who was slowly unbuttoning her blouse. That was honestly the first moment it occurred to him he was alone in a motel room with a woman and all of the implications that came with it. Until then he'd seen this as an assignment.

"There...there's a bathroom over there if you wanted to get changed." But, of course she knew that.

"No, I'm okay. So, do you?"

"I was married for a while." A bad case of the nerves came over him. She'd removed her blouse and stood up to unfasten the clasp on her skirt. He hurried to the dressing table and reached for the bottle.

"You want some water?"

"Bodge, is that rouge on your cheeks or are you actually blushing?" He had his back to her but over his shoulder, reflected in the mirror, he could see her skirt and slip collapse to the floor. She stood there with her hands on her hips and a smile on her face. There was a lot of her and most of it was in the right places. He wasn't sure whether his sudden erection was something he should be boasting about. She could, after all, just have been getting changed.

He held the neck of the bottle away from the glass so it wouldn't rattle with the shaking of his hands. He knew this was crazy. He'd been alone with women before. But something about her abilities, her confidence, made him feel like a school kid. He heard the ping of her bra and glanced briefly in the mirror as she unhooked the straps from her shoulders.

"Bodge," she said. He looked down to study the water in his glass. It was splashing around in there something terrible. "I hope you don't mind..."

"No. You go ahead." His voice rattled.

"What I was gonna say is, I hope you don't mind me suggesting something."

He couldn't turn around without suggesting something himself. "What's that?"

"I think it would help if we had sexual intercourse."

His blood stopped circulating.

"You do?"

"Yeah. I mean, well, we're gonna be sleeping together for two years so it'll probably happen eventually anyway." He heard the snap of elastic but didn't dare look in the mirror. "So I figure, what the hell, let's get it over with. We'll be sick of it soon enough and then we can start acting like real married people. What do you say?"

"Well, yeah. I suppose we could do that."

"All right." There was the groan of bedsprings. "I hope you don't mind girls with fuller figures." Bodge turned around with a half empty glass in each hand. She looked down at his crotch. "Wow. I guess you don't."

Reverend and Mrs. Rogers sat on the seat behind the bus driver. They both had quivering smiles at the corners of their mouths. It was quite remarkable how well the sexual intercourse experiment had gone. Stephanie was bigger now and unmade-up. Her greasy yellow wig was like a urinal mop slung over her head. They were trussed up in shapeless raincoats. Bodge wore a tie that was an acre too wide. His glasses made his eyes look like fried eggs. They were two people you wouldn't give a second thought to except to mention how nice it was that "even folks like that can find a life partner".

They got off the bus at a stop almost directly in front of the National Press Building and joined other couples and journalists and VIPs in suits feeding into the auditorium. Bodge was surprised how many people were showing an interest and wondered if any of these other couples were with special operations. He and Stephanie sat at the back as there was nothing much to see. General deLattre, a long-necked stork of a man, sat on a low stage at the front beside a neatly dressed woman. Even before she opened her mouth to introduce their speaker, Bodge knew she was French.

To a ripple of applause, deLattre stood and began to read line by line from his script and pause occasionally for the interpreter to translate. This was the man who had, for the previous six months, orchestrated the gradual taming of the Viet Minh. Before he came along the French had been suffering one embarrassing defeat after another. He was in town to drum up moral and financial support for his beleaguered French troops. He'd spent the day telling stories to Congress and had planned this public press conference in the evening in order to spread his fiction to a wider audience.

It was only natural that the Reverend and his wife, as missionaries on their way to the region, should attend a talk from such an esteemed expert on Vietnamese affairs. The General spoke passionately of the "civil war" in Vietnam. A civil war was a much easier conflict to find funding for than a war against colonists, which was actually what it was. He outlined the atrocities committed by the Reds; the tortures, the rapes, the religious genocide, and by the time he was through, there wasn't a man or woman in that auditorium (bar two) who wouldn't have gladly mortgaged their homes to fund the French campaign.

He'd had a similar effect on Congress so his military budget for the next two years was secure. In fact it was increased significantly to meet the growing threat of communist aggression. This was the perfect time in America's capital to find funding for such a project. All a person had to do was mention the words 'anti-communism' a few dozen times and he'd be driving away with a truck-load of greenbacks.

"Do you believe it all?" Stephanie asked. They were seated at the rear of the "whites only" section of the bus. "The way they treat their own people over there? The atrocities?"

"I don't doubt it happened," Bodge decided at last. "With a pinch of salt. Don't forget his funding goes up a percentage point for every thousand torture victims he can pull out of his chapeau."

"Does it worry you?"

"That we're headed off as ministers of the church, to a country where Christians have their ears ripped off with pliers? Sure. How about you?"

"I don't believe even the reds would assault American citizens." Bodge rolled his eyes. "No, really. It would be a disaster for them if we entered this war in force. Our money's already sending bombs down on their heads. I figure they'd sooner the buttons were being pressed by the inept French than the smart Yankees."

"You believe we're that smart?"

"Absolutely. If we entered the conflict in Vietnam it'd all be over in six months. We're Americans, Bodge. Look at the war in Europe and the Pacific. We get the job done."

# 21

Bodge was himself once more when he arrived at Casually Yours the following day. Purely to hone their image as a married couple, Stephanie had spent the night at Bodge's motel. They both agreed they needed a lot more practice to get things perfect. As it was, Bodge was exhausted. Pushing the two beds together hadn't given either of them a good night of sleep.

Stephanie had left first in Bodge's sedan to give the garage opposite a few more minutes to change the oil in her Chrysler. She had some business to take care of and Bodge wasn't in a hurry. He had a slow shower and shave and strolled on over to the garage.

"Hi."

"Hi there. How's my car?"

"It serves its purpose well enough. Thanks."

"Guess you almost lost it for me last night."

"How do you mean?"

"There was some guy hanging around."

A familiar shudder came over Bodge.

"Hanging around?"

"Yeah, probably nothing, but he could of been up to no good. We was working late, and my boy, Dave, he sees this guy over here in the shadows between you and your…girlfriend's cars. He was probably up for stealing something out of 'em. We come running over with wrenches swinging and he was gone like a fart in a tornado. Lucky we could see your room from the workshop."

"Yeah. That was lucky. Did you see what he looked like?"

"Hard to say. Big guy. I thought it might of been you at first. Dark clothes. He was wearing some kind of a hat, a helmet maybe."

"Thanks for intervening."

"Shit. It's my car."

Bodge had thought about it on his journey in to the briefing. Like Stephanie he was starting to think there was no such thing as a coincidence any more.

"You're late," Palmer said very matter-of-factly when Bodge arrived at Casually Yours as if being late was no big deal.

"Where's my wife?"

"She'll be at records all day. They're putting together a paper history for you two. Besides, she's seen what we're going to look at here. How are you two getting along?" If he'd looked up from his slides he would have seen the color in Bodge's cheeks.

"Pretty good. We were convincingly bland at deLattre's talk last evening."

"Did you learn anything there?"

"That with the right interpreter, a blatant lie can be transformed into a subtle one."

Palmer laughed. He was slotting the last of a box of slides into the carousel.

"There. Get the light, would you?"

Bodge went to the wall and flicked the switch. The windowless room vanished into blackness. There was a slight whir and the face of a distinguished looking Asian filled the screen. He was in his late thirties and wore a ceremonial jacket and wrap-around sun glasses. Bodge returned to his seat and looked up at the face.

"Today you'll be meeting all the actors, from the stars all the way down to the extras," Palmer said as he attempted to line up the photo with the screen. "You'll have a chance to see their faces again and again until they start to appear in your dreams. Who do you suppose this surly looking fellow might be?"

"Bao Dai."

"Ten points. Excellent. Emperor Bao Dai himself. The poor man is such a political football he probably has laces on the back of his head. He's been kicked around by the pre-war French, the Japanese, and now the French again. It's always wise to have a monarch in your pocket if you're trying to control a people. Warranted or not, Royalty does have the effect of bringing together its citizens. It would surprise me if the communists didn't have a long term plan to bring Bao Dai in as advisor to the Party."

There were several shots of the emperor at parties, hunting, on state trips to Europe. Then there were other members of the royal household and the chamberlain council. Bodge looked, studied, memorized and took notes. He'd remember them for as long as necessary. He knew he could. When they stopped serving a purpose in his memory, he'd erase them. But then a slide appeared with a face he doubted he could ever forget. It was the studio portrait of a girl in her mid twenties. She stared off into a space above the cameraman's shoulder and had just the faintest curl of a smile on her lips. Her eyes sparkled in black contrast to her porcelain skin.

"Oh, man."

"Down, Bodge. Down."

"Who is *she*?"

"You have excellent taste, Robert Leon. Obviously the same taste as Bao Dai. She is Her Highness Mademoiselle Nguyen Von Hong, second consort to the emperor. Let us hope you don't run into her when you're there."

"Why on earth not?"

"Because, if any of the imperial eunuchs were to catch you drooling at her like you are now, you could immediately give up any hope of siring children."

There were two more slides of the second consort. In one she was a respectful step behind the first consort who in turn was three steps behind the Empress. She walked with her head slightly bowed and Bodge read a hundred emotions into her expression. She seemed to be embarrassed, sad even, to be where she was, being who she was.

The third slide caused Bodge's heart to thump.

"I probably shouldn't be showing you this one," Palmer laughed. Von Hong, in a one-piece bathing suit, lounged beside a swimming pool with two other contestants in the Miss Mekhong Delta beauty pageant. But the competition was over and the second consort already wore the sash of victory across her chest. The runners up were boys in wigs compared to her. She was the most amazing looking woman Bodge had ever seen. Everything about her captivated him. Oh, she wouldn't have made the qualifying rounds of Miss Tennessee. She didn't have the curves or the chutzpah or the lacquered hair style of her American cousins. But she was Bodge's ideal beauty, slightly self-conscious, smiling, not from happiness but because the cameraman had ordered her to, modest about her exquisiteness. He groaned when Palmer clicked to the next slide and she wasn't on it. He could remember little of the following dozen actors. The consort had rinsed him out like color from a painter's rag. It was the feeling he and Lou, in their debates on love, had doubted existed. But now he'd experienced its allure there was no Lou to call up and boast to.

The slide show progressed into its fourth box. Somewhere along the way they'd paused for lunch. They'd been through the royals, the French, and the minor celebrities of Ban Methuot. Bodge had regained his composure and was again committing the faces to lower echelons in his memory.

Palmer had saved the communists to last. The first face in box five was one Bodge had seen on TV, in government anti-Red alerts. Senator McCarthy himself had held that same photo in front of the cameras there in DC and told the viewers that this was their nightmare. This frail old man was the embodiment of the red terror, the most barbaric of Asian communists. Yet to look at him, you'd never know.

"Now," McCarthy had said, "you can understand our dilemma. They blend in. There is no physical sign to show us who's a commie and who isn't. There's not a horn in sight. It could be the man who does your laundry, your favorite movie actor, even your own lover."

Ho Chi Minh's face was living proof that there were communists under your bed. But the more Palmer spoke about him, the more Bodge felt his host harbored not a small pocket of admiration for the Viet Minh leader.

"Our own government's doctrine," Palmer said "is as clear as day. Communists are bad — end of argument. Colonialists are ill-advised and should, in this enlightened age, be phased out. Nationalists are our friends and must be encouraged, and (he said in a quieter voice) eventually dominated by us."

"One small hiccup in this master plan is our refusal to accept that someone like Uncle Ho could be a communist *and* a nationalist. But that really messes up the categories. Because you have your general coming along claiming the French are just there to protect the nationalists in their civil war with the communists. And let's not forget this so-called nationalist force was actually set up by the French to protect its colonial interests."

Bodge laughed. "So, whose side are you on?"

"Side? We're on whatever side our government policy tells us to be on. Never forget that."

The show went on in spite of two bulbs burning out in the projector and one slide of the Viet Minh commander in the Delta actually catching fire. But Bodge was starting to find the communist boxes hard going. Either his visual memory store was full, or Vietnamese faces got more and more similar as one worked down through the ranks. He felt a kind of relief when the knock came at the door and one of the neat lady secretaries came in.

"Sorry, Mr. Palmer, you're wanted on the phone." To Bodge's ear it sounded as if that were not true.

"Can't you plug it through to this extension?" Palmer asked.

"The Director would prefer to speak to you on the main line, at reception."

"Damned ridiculous. Who does he think's going to be listening in? All right. Sorry, Bodge."

Palmer left the room and Bodge leaned across to the slide box marked "number one". As he replaced three pictures in the tray, he looked back over his shoulder to the door like a schoolboy hiding exam answers in his desk. He slid forward the manual control and Mademoiselle Nguyen Von Hong hung from the ceiling by her feet like a beautiful bat. He turned over the slides and found her again, upright this time and every bit as remarkable as his first viewing. He walked to the screen with his heart thumping, feeling slightly ridiculous. No picture had ever had this effect on him. He was close now to her tranquil smile, could look into her eyes, black as polished coal.

Palmer' voice came to the door, talking hurriedly to someone outside, barking orders further afield. Bodge rushed to the carousel and scooped out the three slides of the concubine. The door opened and he had no choice but to drop them onto the pocket of his jacket. Palmer was visibly upset but he tried to keep his voice calm.

"Bodge, I need you to come with me."

"Okay, I'll just shut down the—"

"No. I need you to come with me this second." Bodge grabbed his bag and stuffed his papers into it as he walked to the door. Beyond the doorway stood a tall man with charcoal hair.

"Bodge, this is Agent Ramos," Palmer said. "You will go with him and do exactly as he tells you."

"What's happened?"

"I'm truly not sure. But as soon as I know, I'll tell you. In the meantime you'll have to put your faith in us. I'll need your car key."

"But I—"

"And that faith begins now. Get him out of here."

"Yes, sir. Agent Leon?" Agent Ramos took Bodge by the arm and led him with surprising strength to the exit. The guards waved them through without a bag or body check. Ramos' urgency was contagious and Bodge found himself taking the steps three at a time. A Casually Yours van was parked out front of the building with the passenger door open. Ramos and Bodge headed straight for it. Bodge felt uneasy as if the whole of Special Operations was on edge and he was the cause.

A large black Lincoln, traveling at speed crossed over from the far lane and skidded to a stop with its headlights flush against those of the van. Ramos reached for his gun holster but then had second thoughts as two men jumped from the car. Bodge recognized Jansen and Tuck as they marched quickly over to stand toe to toe with him and Ramos. Bodge hadn't yet forgiven them for the way they'd handled the investigation of his friend's disappearance, but everything now was happening so fast he had no time to think.

"Going somewhere in a hurry, Bodge?" Jansen asked, tapping Bodge's lapel with a rolled sheet of paper.

"Agent Leon and I have to be somewhere urgently," Ramos told them, and attempted to dance around the two Security men.

"I'm sure you do," Jansen smiled. "But I'm afraid we have to reroute Agent Leon here."

"We have an emergency on our hands. You can talk to him some other time."

"Oh, I wish we could. You see, we have an emergency on our hands also. And I have an intra-agency warrant here that gives our emergency priority over yours. I'm so sorry."

Ramos looked nervously along the street then grabbed the paper out of Jansen's hand. He scanned down it and read the signature. "Then, I insist on accompanying Agent Leon."

"You insist, do you? But what about your emergency? You shouldn't let a little thing like this interrupt you."

"Like you say, your emergency takes precedence over ours. Agent Leon has the right to representation at an interview."

"What makes you think the agent's coming for an interview?" Tuck asked.

"You don't take out a warrant and break city traffic ordinances if you intend to go and have a coffee and a donut for old time's sake."

"Would someone care to tell me what in tarnation is going on here?" Bodge asked in frustration.

"Be patient, Bodge," Jansen smiled again. "All will be revealed soon enough. But you don't want Agent Ramos here to waste his valuable time holding your hand, do you now?" Ramos squeezed Bodge's arm.

"I think he should be there," Bodge said unsurely.

"These Special Ops guys, Fred. Always want someone there backing them up. Very well, let's go for a drive."

"Wait," Ramos insisted. "I have to let my people know where I'm going."

"Sure. You can do that. But I'm afraid you'll miss the bus because our departure is imminent. Let's go, Bodge."

# 22

Ramos and Bodge had been sitting alone in the room for over half an hour. It was some kind of low-budget boardroom. There were eight chairs round a scratched table and another thirty round the yellow walls like in a dentist's waiting room. The minute they were left alone, Ramos had gestured for Bodge to keep his mouth shut. He too assumed a place like this to have electronic ears everywhere. So, Bodge, in his increasingly dense fog of confusion, sat in silence.

A door opened. Jansen, Tuck, carrying a thick file, a woman with a notepad, and a man in a long brown coat carrying a tape recorder paraded in single file into the room like a Confirmation procession. The technician set up the tape and stayed there to operate it. As usual, Jansen did most of the talking. For the benefit of the tape, he gave the date, named the people present, and introduced Bodge as the interviewee. Jansen was obviously enjoying himself which made Bodge increasingly testy.

"Could you state your name and your position."

"My name is Robert William Leon, and I'm sitting down." The stenographer looked up and smiled, but she was the only one who saw it as funny.

"Agent Leon," Jansen said slowly, "this is going to be a very very long interview if you insist on making immature statements like that. I would recommend you respond with the seriousness this situation deserves."

"Well, Agent Jansen. Perhaps if you'd be so kind as to tell me just how serious this situation is, I shall adjust my immature statements to match it."

"It's you that needs to be answering questions, not me."

Ramos intervened. "Bodge, I think we should let the Security agents get their questions out of the way so we can get out of here."

"Very well," Bodge agreed. "But I would like it to go on record that even muggers in the Bronx hear the charges against them before they're interrogated."

"So, you expect to have charges brought against you?" Jansen asked.

"My name is Robert William Leon and I am a grade three official of the Central Intelligence Agency. My badge number is D23."

"At last," Jansen sighed. "Are you, or have you ever been a member of the Communist Party?"

Bodge snorted a laugh through his nose. "Come on, guys. That's what this is about?"

"Bodge, just answer," Ramos said calmly.

"No."

"Are you now," Jansen continued, "or have you ever been a homosexual?" A number of conflicting emotions ran through Bodge's mind. He was beginning to see where the interview was going but he was amazed they'd ask *him* such a question. He looked at Ramos for support but got nothing.

"No."

"Are you aware that your partner, Louis Vistarini, was a practicing homosexual?"

"That's ridiculous."

"Just answer the question."

"If Lou was homosexual, Willie Mays is a...a geranium."

"So you were not aware?"

"There's nothing to be aware of. I knew the man for seven years. Don't you think I'd know if he was a queer or not?" Bodge felt a painful wrenching, a conflict within him. He'd seen the magazines in Lou's apartment. There was enough of a doubt in his mind to stop him from being wholehearted in his defense of his friend. But he had to make it look like he had absolute faith. These men had interviewed enough liars in their careers.

"He never married," Tuck said.

"There are plenty of single men in the world."

"You, for example," Jansen added.

"Hey. What in blazes is that supposed to mean?"

"You and Louey were very close."

"You son of a bitch." Bodge got to his feet. "If you want this tape-recorder shoved up your—" Ramos stood also and grabbed his arm. He nodded toward the lady even though she'd probably heard a lot worse. Bodge sat and considered his performance. It might have been a little more than was called for. But he'd visualized how Jansen might have acted in the same situation.

"A slight overreaction, Leon," Jansen goaded further. "I thought you people were trained not to show emotions in interrogations."

"I'm new at the job."

"So it seems. Now, perhaps you could, in a calmer state, think back over the time you knew your friend, and try to recall incidents, statements, any peculiarities, that may have caused you to doubt Mr. Vistarini's masculinity."

"You mean, did I walk in on him wearing a tutu and dancing the Sugar Plum Fairy on his coffee break?"

"Agent Leon. I've warned you about your frivolity."

"Frivolity? The man's only been dead a week and you're painting him pink before the body's cold. Based on what?"

Agent Tuck looked up from his file. "We have irrefutable physical evidence."

"Bullshit. Show me."

"We aren't obliged, or at liberty to do so."

"You'll just have to take our word for it that there's no doubt on this earth that Miss Vistarini was a faggot," Jansen said.

"...and as such," Tuck interrupted with one eye on the recorder, "a threat to the security of our agency and to our country. You see, Agent Leon—"

Jansen cut back in, "You get pictures of some government queer cavorting around with his boyfriend, and he'll do or say just about anything to stop that picture getting around. Get the idea? The communists have a list of all the nancy boys in positions of responsibility, and they're just waiting for the day they can milk our government dry of information."

"Is that why you did nothing to investigate his disappearance?"

"What?"

"Was it because you suspected him of being homosexual that you ignored the case?"

Jansen looked at the tape. "We pursued the disappearance of Agent Vistarini with vigor."

"Really?"

Tuck took up the defense, "Besides, we didn't get our evidence until after the body was recovered."

Bodge wondered whether there were more magazines. Did they do a more thorough search after they found the body and come up with others?

"Well, if you've dragged me down here to get evidence against Lou, you've wasted a warrant. I doubt anyone knew him better that I did. We drank together. We double-dated. We talked about women."

"If that's true, it was a front," Tuck insisted.

"Then it went all the way through to the back yard. I don't know what evidence you think you have, but I guarantee it was planted. Lou was framed."

Jansen laughed and was really spoiling for a crack in the snout. "Some types of evidence you can't fake, Leon. But thank you for your assistance today." He clicked off the recorder and leaned even further across the table to Bodge. "We've got a picture of him getting his dick licked. How do you fake that? Your buddy was a queer... and you know what? I bet a month's salary you are too. What do you have to say about that, fairy?"

The nose was close enough, and the agent sure as hell deserved it. So, quicker than Jansen could react, Bodge shot forward and planted a kiss on that big schnoz of his. It took all of Tuck's strength to stop his partner taking off across the table. Bodge smiled, stood calmly, and asked whether they might be excused.

"I'm gonna find my proof, Leon," Jansen yelled after him. "And you'll be out of this agency and in jail faster than a run in a stocking. You hear me, you queerboy?"

## 23

**Ban Methuot**

Hong was shown into General LePenn's large office at the southern garrison. He looked up at her over the rim of his glasses and was immediately warmed by her calmness and natural beauty. He smiled a sincere greeting.

"Your Highness," he said, rising from his seat. "This is most unexpected."

He'd seen her with the Emperor on many occasions but had never spoken to her. He had no idea whether her French would be fluent enough to catch his accent. So he was delighted that her reply was grammatically correct and only lightly accented. "I have a habit of doing the unexpected, General."

"Please take a seat. The Emperor isn't with you?"

"He's off massacring innocent wildlife."

"What can I do for you?"

"I know you're busy so I'll come to the point. One of the Montagnard servants in the missionary's house was killed by a Frenchman. I would like you to do something about it."

The violence in her words was intentional. She was looking for an indication that she'd touched a nerve. But this old general had been through too many campaigns to give up his emotions cheaply. He raised his fluffy white eyebrows and assumed an expression of mocking superiority.

"Mademoiselle, surely this is a matter for the gendarmerie."

"The police have chosen not to pursue this matter."

"I assume they have good cause."

"They are choosing to protect one of their own."

"So may I ask who you're accusing?"

"You."

The general laughed with a little too much enthusiasm.

"Me?"

"More directly, the men under your command. A general is responsible for the actions of his men, is he not?"

"And why do you suppose I would want to murder a *Moi*?"

"I don't think that was your intention. I believe your men just got a little too rough."

"And what exactly was my intention?"

"I believe the point was to kidnap the two girls from the missionary's house. But one of them fought. Your soldier hit her to bring her into line and the blow killed her."

"You were there of course to see all of this?"

"No."

"Then how do you know it happened?"

"There was a witness to the beating. A third girl."

"So she could identify the insignia of the soldiers she is accusing?"

"There was no insignia. The men weren't in uniform."

General LePenn smiled annoyingly. At that moment Hong would gladly have walked around his expensive desk and slapped him. But it was to her advantage to remain calm.

"But you have irrefutable proof that these men were soldiers? Perhaps they confessed to the girl?"

He knew. Now she was certain.

"They wore civilian clothes," she said. " — all but their boots. They each wore military issue footwear."

"It hadn't occurred to me the *Moi* would know a boot from a chamber pot."

"You'd be surprised General. You see she had plenty of time to study them. She was on the floor at their feet being raped at the time. She's fifteen."

The general paled noticeably. His armor was down. He looked at his papers and took hold of his pen. "Of course, that is very regrettable. I find rape in wartime particularly repulsive."

"I shall pass on your repulsion to the girl. I believe you have a daughter of around the same age."

"Perhaps you should speak with the police."

"I did. But, as you're aware, the Montagnard are under military authority, as are French soldiers."

"As I say, there's no evidence…"

"No. But I'm a little disappointed you'd dismiss the accusation so readily. If it were my army, I'd be keen to launch an investigation to clear my men."

"I think you should leave military affairs to those who understand them, my dear. During a war it's important to maintain morale. If the men thought their own superiors were accusing them of a crime it would certainly upset them."

"Upset them? I see. Much better to condone rape and kidnap than to upset the men. The new lady missionary was right. I think I should do what she recommends."

"And what would that be?"

"She believes that as the girls were servants at her house, there's an argument for involving the Americans. She believes the embassy would be happy to launch an inquiry."

It was immediately apparent the general was full to the brim of talk of an American presence. "The damned Americans will not be involved in my region."

"I'm afraid, if the Emperor invites them, you won't have any say in the matter."

He looked at her now with sad resignation. She'd arrived as pretty and delicate as a glass bauble on a Christmas tree, but she turned out to be made of iron. The Emperor's young whore had defeated him. It seemed an appropriate insult to compound the series of humiliations he'd suffered this awful year. There were no greater depths for him to plumb.

"He sent you to tell me this?"

"Would it make any difference?"

"Very well. I shall begin an informal inquiry and let your household know of the results."

"You're too kind."

"You may leave now."

Her smile was so sweet it broke his old heart. "You seem to forget, General. I am a member of the Royal Household — not a servant. Whether you believe in the institution of royalty or not is irrelevant. It exists. Whatever you think of my role within it, I exist also. So, as long as we are all on our respective rungs of this hierarchy, you would do well to treat us with respect." She looked around the room calmly. "I think I shall leave now."

She stood, returned her chair to its original position, and walked elegantly out of the door. She knew there would be no inquiry just as she knew the general was responsible in some way for the murder and kidnapping. The only question now was its purpose. She was pleased to have this distraction from her own scheme. If it panned out as she hoped, it could occupy her through the rainy season, until her escape.

# 24

Bodge had been in the safe-house in Delaware for a little over a month. Once they'd walked out of the gay inquisition, Ramos had engineered two cab changes before arriving at a car parked at a pre-designated spot. From there, they'd driven out to this isolated wooden house. Ramos' silence during the trip had been exasperating. Bodge knew something serious had happened, but once the agent had told him he wasn't at liberty to discuss anything, he'd shut up like a Cape Cod clam. The only joy he allowed Bodge, after three volleys of asking, was to agree he'd do what he could to get him a copy of the photo Jansen had been so proud of. In the mean time, Bodge was to lay low and wait for instructions. Under no circumstances was he to leave this house. Ramos assured him all would be made clear to him in due course.

But there he was a month later and not a damned thing had been made clear. The old house had been readied for him. There was a stack of wood beside the potbelly stove in the living room, and enough food in the larder to wait out an atomic holocaust. There was a typed sheet of instructions on the table. He was to read them, commit them to memory, and burn them in the stove. But, as there was no note from Palmer, he was completely in the dark as to why he was there.

Although the house was set away from the road, Bodge was not to walk around outside in daylight. He most certainly could not leave the compound or talk with neighbors (not that he ever saw any). There was no phone so he could only wait for someone to come to him. Wisely, there was also no booze in the larder so he wouldn't turn into a lush during his stay. There was a small but efficient generator out back, a radio set to keep him in touch with the world, and a small tape recorder with a dozen Vietnamese language tapes. That was his world. For the first couple of days he didn't get into a routine. He truly believed someone would come by with news. But nobody did.

He started to listen to the tapes on the third day and work his way through the text. When the sun went down, he'd go into the field behind the house and exercise. He started by marching, and that slowly turned into a clumsy kind of jogging. After a week he was doing something pretty close to a run.

He was able to use the old swing frame for chin-ups, and bench-press an antique truck axle. Even when the snows finally came he was out in the yard exercising away his frustrations.

News on the radio was like something happening in a different world and time. The communists rejected a prisoner exchange in Korea, England's King George IV died of lung cancer, a guy called Emmet Ashford became the first Negro baseball umpire, and they started to use three-colored traffic lights and "Don't Walk" signs in New York.

He still couldn't figure why Palmer hadn't been in touch. The man knew Bodge had to be going nuts alone there in the house. The solitude started to eat into him toward the middle of the second week. It was then the fixation took root. In the pocket of his jacket he still had the three slides of Her Highness Nguyen Von Hong. He hooked up a bedsheet screen in his bedroom, extended the electric light flex by four yards so the bulb could sit on the table, and set up a cone of broken mirror glass around it.

Although the focus was never quite right, he was able to get a big enough image of the concubine on his wall to have someone his own size to talk to. He wasn't sure what their relationship was, although it had to be unhealthy. She was a picture, goddamit. But this wasn't like a smuggled girly magazine. That wasn't the way he felt about her. He liked what he saw in the slide but it wasn't sexual. Not in the beginning anyway. He talked to her and she stared vacantly over his shoulder.

"Honey, you probably won't believe this, but a few weeks ago I was a clerk." He was swinging on the back legs of a chair propped up against the bed. "Yes, I was a well-paid government, secret clerk, but a clerk nonetheless. And I volunteered my stupid ass out of that sweet job and into this — this crock of shit I find myself in today. Excuse my French." She thought that was funny and he noticed her smile. With the mention of *French*, it occurred to Bodge that Her Royal Highness probably had no idea what he was talking about. She'd been educated in Francophile schools. That would be her foreign language. From that moment he only spoke to her in French.

"You see, a friend of mine got himself killed, probably because they found out (he didn't mean to say *found out* but obviously something deep inside him had already convicted Lou.)…they suspected he was homosexual. I'm still not sure how I feel about that. The thought of guys getting it on with each other turns my belly. I can't pretend it doesn't. But Lou was my friend and, well, if that's what his chromosomes had him do I don't think it's right to deny him my support. Do you? (She didn't.) Someone then tried to kill me, perhaps for the same reason. It looks like my country can be very unforgiving if it thinks you're a pervert."

"I have a boss who lies to me, people following me, and now something's happened so serious they can't even tell me what it is. They hide me away with no phone and nobody to talk to but you. For all I know the entire government's been overthrown by communists and no one knows I'm here. What do you think of that?"

That thought stayed with him as he ran laps around the perimeter of the field that evening — his breath froze in the air in front of his face. While the canned stew boiled on the stove, he wondered where he'd be if anything had happened to Ramos and Palmer. What if there really was no one who knew he was there? How long should he stay here?

It was about seven at night when the light from headlights on full-beam flooded through the living room window. Bodge had been listening to a tape through headphones so he hadn't heard the car pull up. His momentary relief at being contacted quickly reverted to panic. Something about that month had fine-tuned his instinct for self-protection. "Assume the worst," he told himself.

He quietly unwrapped himself from the blanket and ran to the alcove by the front door out of eyeshot of the window. He heard footsteps on the gravel, then silence. The thump on the front door made him jump out of his skin. He ignored the first knock. The second was followed by a gruff voice,

"Hello. Someone in there? This is the police. Open up." Bodge edged along the wall to the bedroom door and slipped inside.

"Just a minute," he shouted. "I'm not dressed." He tiptoed to the bedroom window and looked through a crack in the curtain. The Delaware Troopers' Ford Cruiser was glimmering in the moonlight. "Be right with you." He put on his thick lenses and shuffled to the door.

On the step, two troopers with matching moustaches stood with their hands on their hips.

"Evening."

"Could I ask you to identify yourself please, sir?" the taller cop said.

Bodge wasn't sure what to say. The only ID he had on him were his CIA identity card and his driving license. But Ramos had instructed him not to give his real name to anyone unless they came from Special Operations.

"Rogers," he said, hoping they wouldn't ask for proof.

"Robert Rogers?"

"That's right."

"Okay, this is for you." He handed Bodge a thick, sealed package with 'FYO ROBERT ROGERS' printed on the front. The two officers looked at him then down at the package as if they expected him to show them what was in it. But Bodge just held it at his side.

"Thanks," he said.

"You aren't going to open it?" the shorter cop asked with a hint of disappointment in his voice.

"Was there something else?"

"Well, yeah," the tall cop said. "They told us we're supposed to take you out to Washington National."

"What, now?"

"That's what he said."

"Who's 'he'?"

"Some detective from New York. Said you should be there by 21:30."

That was two-and-a-half hours away.

"Any idea where I'm going?" Bodge asked.

"If you open the damned package, maybe we'll all know," the cop said. He seemed embarrassed as if he'd just realized anyone important enough to get a police escort to the airport had to be someone. He added, "Sir." and even managed a smile.

"You want to wait inside?"

"Thanks. We'll be in the car."

Bodge took the package to the kitchen table and opened one end with a meat knife. He shook the contents onto the table and found himself looking at a pile of fake IDs: passport, driving license, registration of ordination as a minister, all in the name of the Reverent Robert Rodgers. There was an air ticket via Los Angeles and Hong Kong to Saigon, a thick wad of hundred dollar bills, a stiff sealed envelope and a note which he unfolded. He was expecting it to be from Palmer or Ramos but it wasn't. The initials at the end were *DD*.

The fact that the New York detective didn't use his full name suggested he was interfering in something that didn't concern him. But his involvement did explain the courier service.

*'Hello, Bodge,*

*I'm sure you were expecting this to be from our mutual friend. All being well he'll meet you at your final destination and explain the changes in plan. There's a warrant out for the arrest of Mr. Leon and things could get nasty if he's caught. Everything should be explained in Saigon.*

*Good luck, DD.'*

# Bleeding in Black and White

It was a careful note, nothing given away if the cops got nosy. But that was all there was. Bodge didn't know what to think. A warrant? What the hell had he done? Who was after him? They were sending him half way round the world without explaining a damn thing.

He slit open the stiff envelope hoping for more information but the contents chewed him up and spat him out like a cow's lunch. Inside was a single eight inch by six inch black and white photograph. It showed some kind of club. There was a sofa and soft easy chairs. On the sofa sat an overweight, elderly man with thick gray hair. One arm was draped around the shoulder of a boy in his late teens. The boy wore heavy mascara and a sequined top, but nothing else. The old man grasped the boy's penis in his free hand oblivious of the camera. At the other end of the couch sat Lou. His shirt was open and his pants were down around his ankles. He was smiling and holding up his glass to someone just out of shot. Kneeling on the ground before him with his lips around Lou's erection, was a naked man whose muscles glistened with sweat. The room seemed dark, but the flash of the camera had left no doubt as to Lou's identity.

Bodge turned over the photograph. On the back, someone had written, "Time isn't on our side." It made no sense. None of it made any sense. Even with such blatant evidence, Bodge still didn't believe he could spend that many years with another man, and not have an inkling of his tendencies. He hadn't studied the psychology of these people, hadn't investigated their illness, but he was sure it wasn't just a quirk. He didn't believe a man could suppress desires and hide them from his friends. There had to be physical manifestations. When it had passed over his desk at Trans-National he'd browsed through the Eightieth Congressional Sex Pervert bill. It was suggested these people were more to be pitied than condemned because in many it was a pathological condition, very much like the kleptomaniac who had no choice but to go out and steal. But, if that were so, why hadn't Lou come to him for help? And was it really such an awful affliction that someone would want to kill him?

Bodge's first instinct was to destroy the photograph, but some unheard voice told him not to. There had to be a reason they'd gone to the trouble to give him a copy. With the cops still waiting outside, he carefully unglued the back and front covers of the bedside Bible, inserted the photo and his CIA card, and resealed them with horse glue he'd found under the sink. This would have to wait.

He sat in the back of the cruiser without saying a word. The troopers weren't that talkative either. They dropped him in front of the Northwest door at Washington National at eight-thirty — plenty of time for their passenger to catch his flight. He said thanks, they said no problem, and they watched him swing open the door and walk inside. Their chore was complete. They were long gone by the time he reached the ticket desk. He was there just long enough to change his flight, turn around, and head back to the taxi stand.

There wasn't a great deal he could do at night, but he sure as hell wasn't about to leave DC without a few answers. A week of orientation? Was this how you got treated at special ops? No, they couldn't do that to a curious guy.

# 25

## Ban Methuot

"Get off."

"I'm sorry."

Petit rolled off the Administrator's wife. She lay on sheets that were sodden with sweat and semen, but sadly not with the juices of her own orgasm. A fee had been arranged for the chaperone's absence and silence and she sat on the front veranda with her knitting. It wasn't proving to be money well spent.

"Do you want me to use my finger again?" he asked sheepishly.

"No, I do not want you to use your finger. I have perfectly good fingers of my own. All I ask is for your cock to remain in me long enough so I might join you in that final pleasure."

"I'm sorry. It's just that you're so glorious. You fill me with a passion I have no control over."

"Obviously." She rolled her eyes to the ceiling and considered the other scant possibilities amongst the sorry assembly of Ban Methuot men. The community of wives was so close-knit she knew a dip in the husband pool would be social suicide. The General's wife was ten thousand miles away, but he was nearing sixty and looked seventy. It appeared she'd have no choice but to find herself a well-hung native. She had no taste for the oriental man but she assumed in the dark she could put any French head on him. Perhaps even a Montagnard would suffice. She'd seen enough impressive torsos on her travels. All they'd need was a good scrubbing with carbolic soap and…Oh, what was the point?

"Petit?"

"Yes, my love?"

"It's time for a new lesson."

"I'll do my best."

"Have you ever observed how a cat drinks milk?"

# 26

Bodge arrived in Saigon in early March in a fog of jet lag and frustration. The place was hotter than Hell. He wasn't surprised there was nobody to meet him at the airport. It was bizarre to be there in the orient but no more disorienting than his last few weeks in the States. As the old taxi with all its windows wide open took him through the rustic stick-and-straw suburbs of the town, he went over the previous forty eight hours in his mind.

On the night he left Washington National and went in search of answers, he'd found only more mysteries and confusion. He'd come up against a brick wall and had been left with no choice in his course of actions. It wouldn't have surprised him to find the Casually Yours warehouse closed for the night. He'd been prepared to wait till morning to speak to Palmer, to Ramos, to anyone who could give him an indication as to what the hell had happened and why they'd abandoned him in a safe house.

What he hadn't been prepared for was finding the building boarded over and padlocked. He'd asked the waitress at the Little Tavern down the street. She told him she'd heard the company had gone bust. "They shut the place down, ooh, a month back. We've been deserted since then. We relied on their custom."

A month? The same time they'd shipped him off to Delaware. What could possibly have happened to throw a government agency into such a panic? There wasn't so much as a night watchman to ask. Bodge used the restaurant pay phone to call the two numbers he had for Casually Yours, but all he got was the hum of a disconnected phone line. He didn't have private numbers for Palmer or Denholm. He bought a meatball hero and phoned police headquarters. No one had heard of a detective called Denholm Deets.

His last and most heartbreaking attempt was to his old pal Mooney, the man he'd gone through the agency with, side by side. He got his home number from the operator and listened to the phone ring a dozen times. Mooney and his wife turned in early. The supervisor picked up on the thirteenth ring.

"Mooney residence."

"Stan?"

There was a long silence before,

"Bodge?"

"Yeah."

"Where are you?" Bodge interpreted the edge in Mooney's voice as annoyance at being woken.

"Listen, Stan, there's a lot of strange stuff going on. We have to talk."

Mooney hesitated again.

"You know, Bodge. This isn't a good time. What do you say you give me an address and a number I can call you back at."

"You gotta make this a good time, Mooney. I'm in the shit. I need your help. I need some phone numbers and names."

"Gee, Bodge. I'm at home, man. I don't know."

Something was wrong. Bodge was certain now. This wasn't the Mooney he'd known all those years. He could tell from the tone something had happened.

"Mooney? What's up?"

"Look, Bodge. Can you tell me where you're staying? I'll call you back in an hour."

"I'm not staying anywhere. If you're thinking of calling me back, you need a number, not an address. Do you want to tell me what the problem is?"

Another pause.

"Okay. Okay, I'll tell you. You're the problem, buster. You make me sick is the problem."

Bodge's heart thumped.

"Mooney?"

"A lot of folks are on your tail, boy, and, tell you the truth I hope they catch you. I don't know what I'd do if I laid my hands on you."

"Stan, I don't know what it is you think I've done, but I—"

"Don't. Don't even start. I know, Bodge. I know what you've done."

"Mooney, I—"

"Bastard."

Bodge half dropped, half slammed down the hand set. The waitress and the only customer looked over. Bodge's hands were shaking and he stood staring at the phone as if it had joined the ranks of the enemy. In the month he'd been at the safe house, the universe had turned upside down. He'd gone from good guy to villain without so much as squeezing a trigger. What in hell's name was going on? The uneaten meatball hero was still in his hand but food didn't seem that important any more.

The bus journey to Chevy Chase had been tense with apprehension and paranoia. Bodge had a billfold thick with hundreds but he didn't dare check into a decent hotel downtown. He couldn't say why that was. Something about Moony's attitude told him he was likely a wanted man.

He needed to stay out of bright lights for a while. The motel he'd stayed at before was a cash-over-the-counter, no ID joint with a receptionist roster that turned over more frequently than the guest list. He paid the fee and walked to the room. There was just the one station wagon parked in front. The sounds of a family bickering came through the window and calmed Bodge's paranoia.

He threw his hold all and raincoat on the bed and sat beside them. There wasn't a lot in the bag — mostly the props from the last night he'd spent there; Bible, glasses, clothes that were now several more sizes too big for him. That night here in this room had been the last taste of normality he could recall, yet it had hardly been a normal night. Him and Stephanie — Reverend and Mrs. Rogers. That was probably the last time he'd had any control over his life. He unfastened the clasps of his bag and took out the Bible with its awful secret hidden in the back cover. "What have you gotten me into, Lou?"

He was about to reread Denholm's letter to see if there were any missing clues, when a thump on his door rattled the glasses beside the bed. He leapt to his feet and instinctively looked around for first a gun, then an exit. There was another thump, loud but not urgent. The door was so flimsy a serious assassin or bounty hunter could have booted it down.

"Who's there?" Bodge yelled from the bathroom where he inspected the small window above the toilet.

"It's me, man. Ernie."

"Ernie, who?"

"Ernie, from Ernie's garage across the way."

Bodge recognized the voice and recalled the car he'd rented from the guy. It occurred to him he probably hadn't ever gotten it back. He opened the door to a short, balding black man in overalls. He was wiping oil from his hands on a rag. He looked up at Bodge.

"Yeah. I thought it was you. Good eye for faces, me."

"Look. I'm real sorry about your car. But this isn't..."

"You kidding? I did better on that deal than I shoulda."

"Eh?"

"Yeah. Your guy give me twice what it was worth. Better'n I deserve considering."

"Considering what?"

"You kidding me? Considering it blew up, is what."

Bodge's stomach dropped. "The car I rented from you?"

"How come you sound like you don't know?"

"I…er, went overseas. Just got back. What happened?"

"I was hoping you could tell me. It's been sitting heavy on me since that day — that day you brought your girlfriend's Chrysler over for the oil change. I was listening to the radio later and I hear about this beige Skylark convertible that blew up just down Normanston. Well, there's plenty of Skylark's so I just kinda filed it away in my brain. Then, next thing you know my place is crawling with Feds. They tell me it was my car that exploded and they grill me about all kinds of stuff. I was sure they're gonna run me in for renting out death-traps. But I just tell them about you and your girlfriend and that guy I seen hanging about and they say 'thanks', call me 'sir', and — poof — they vanish."

"The next day this friend of yours comes by and hands over a mess of money and tells me I don't need to go mouthing off about any of this — specially if I wanna stay in the rental business. I don't need telling twice."

"What did he look like?"

"Big wetback in a fancy suit."

"Did he say anything about the woman — my friend?"

"Not a word. But, like I say, I been feeling bad about it all. I can't help wondering if it was my fault. Did she die?"

And that was the question that had stuck with Bodge halfway round the world. In sticky airports and on rickety air planes that vibrated the hope out of him. First Lou, now Stephanie, and it should have been him. Why? He had to get himself right way up in the world. If he was suddenly such a villain why wasn't his placement in Vietnam cancelled? Why did he have a ticket and fake ID? The only thing he could figure was that Palmer wanted him out of the country. It was a long way to travel for an answer but he'd run out of options in the States. The following day with no check-in luggage, rhyme or reason, he'd boarded the flight to Hong Kong and Vietnam.

Compared to the hustle of the British Colony, Saigon was a beautifully exotic place. Even on a stifling summer's day it retained its elegance like a fine boned duchess in a sauna. It seemed able to disguise its role as a city of invaders in a country of war. As he neared the center, the boulevards opened out like broad carpets umbrella'd by the leaves of young tamarind trees. He passed expensive looking shops and open-air cafes and cinemas. Well-heeled Europeans in light-hued clothes walked along the neat sidewalks. There was nothing of the tentative tourist about them. They shopped and dined with the sophistication and confidence of owners. This was their city.

The lovely Vietnamese women on their sturdy bicycles gliding alongside his cab caused his heart to miss beats. If they asked him in thirty years for the most memorable moments in his life, he knew this sight on his first day in Vietnam would be prominent on the list. With the tails of their white silk *ao dai* floating behind them, they seemed to Bodge like gorgeous herons hovering on the wind. Their half faces below wide straw hats focused on the roadway ahead, not looking left or right, lips pursed in concentration. He looked for Mlle. Hong knowing well the Emperor's concubine wouldn't be on a bicycle in the mid-day heat. But even without her, being in this flock was as near to calmness as Bodge had been for years.

His driver brought him to a hotel whose ground floor was a gash that opened onto the street. If it weren't for the word HÔTEL painted vertically down the central post, Bodge would have taken it to be a small bus terminal. But he wanted to remain anonymous until he could find Palmer and this type of establishment was exactly what he'd had in mind. Four very young girls with eerie powdered faces sat around the lone coffee table that floated in the center of the foyer like an island. They wore colored pajamas and managed to make their chunky wooden chairs look comfortable by curling themselves like cats. They didn't make eye contact with Bodge as he walked past but they commented and giggled behind his back.

The manager was an elderly gentleman who perched on a high stool behind the reception desk. He didn't smile, speak, or respond to Bodge's "hello". He just slid the registration card and pen over the counter. The card was written in French and Chinese. Bodge wondered if there was a second card for locals or whether Vietnamese knew better than to stay there. Bodge slid the completed form back to the manager who calculated on his fingers the room rates for the number of days requested. He wrote a surprisingly low figure on the card and held out his palm for Bodge to pay up.

Money received, the old man slapped a key down in front of his guest. It was attached to an enormous slab of plywood with the number 13 painted on it. It was then the manager uttered his first word.

"Femme?" He nodded towards the girls on their coffee table island.

"Barely," thought Bodge, but he smiled and declined, using a phrase he'd memorized from his Vietnamese text. The old man raised one eyebrow just a fraction which suggested to Bodge he was surprised to hear a foreign devil speaking his language. But he obviously wasn't that impressed.

# 27

Despite the low price and the off-putting lobby, room thirteen was surprisingly livable. The ceiling fan blew up a gale and there was an endless supply of tea in solid thermos flasks. The bed sheets were candy striped and if he stood on a chair, Bodge could see the far bank of the Saigon River over the corrugated roofs. One entire wall was a tropical island lovingly painted in orange and red. As no other rooms he saw had murals, he imagined a long-term guest locked up in this one for months with nothing else to occupy his mind.

Bodge stared at those still palms as he formulated a plan of his own. He decided he'd go to the American embassy and let them know where he was staying. He could leave a message in case anyone wanted to get in touch with him. That was the plan. He'd wait for Palmer, get his answers, then go home to sort things out. He couldn't start to sort his life out until he knew what those things were.

Nothing in his plan included Ban Methuot. In his mind, the mission was over. Vietnam was, what? A holiday? R and R from the rigors of being a fugitive? And here was a weekend, the perfect start to an exotic foreign vacation. His plan began with doing nothing at all for two days until the embassy opened on Monday. Whilst doing nothing, he might even watch a few pretty girls glide back and forth on their bicycles.

A Saturday of girl-watching went pretty well. It was a hobby he'd probably never tire of. He wondered whether he'd been Asian in a former life because he was enchanted by the gentleness of even the plainest girls. He ate a two cent bowl of noodles at the market, then made a coffee last for four hours at one of the classy places overlooking Place Charles De Gaulle. He learned there that sooner or later, everybody worth seeing, and every service and commodity available in the city, would pass in front of that café. The suburban Vietnamese came to discreetly ogle the Europeans without being caught doing so. The Europeans came to be seen by one another. The food sellers wheeled their carts, and the broom sellers pedaled their tricycles. The quack medicine dealers, the masseurs, the dentists and the hairdressers all passed by with card posters of their services drawn in cartoons for even the most ignorant of Westerners to understand. And, without fail, the pretty girls came gliding.

But, nothing had prepared him for Sunday. It was, without doubt, for Saigon that the expression "Sunday best" had been invented. Given the effort that went into their grooming, he couldn't imagine how any woman ever got to sleep from Saturday through Sunday morning . The maids and menials were dressed in their sparkly pajamas and walking arm in arm with their best friends. They dared to peak from the shadows of their coolie hats at the peculiar red devil in the café. Even their lips confessed a dab of lipstick.

The girls of the middle and upper classes weren't able to wear their sensible hats no matter how cruelly the sun beat on them. For how could they show off their hairstyles beneath a straw bonnet? And what a parade of hairstyles it was. Even on the boardwalk at Coney Island, Bodge had never seen so many curls, licks, bangs, sweeps, buns, or strategically placed blooms. As one church released its flock, and another opened its doors, Christian fashion models mingled with Buddhists, Cao-Daists and atheists and it was impossible to tell one from the other. Each sect had as many brightly twinkling stars.

Bodge was in seventh day heaven. He nursed his ice tea until the paper straw had almost dissolved and would have stayed till evening if the elderly man hadn't called him away. He'd run to the café, pointed at Bodge, gestured urgently for him to follow and headed off. He looked back over his shoulder several times to be sure Bodge was following. When the big American rose and headed after him the man stopped and put his hands on his knees panting heavily.

Bodge was no more than ten paces from the roadside café when it split in two. What had been inside blew out. Bodge was thrown five yards onto the street. The glass from the window, splinters of table, crockery shards, fingers and hair blasted past him. His senses froze for several seconds. He was deaf and dumb. He could smell and taste nothing. Only his eyes continued to function. They held his last vision like a still camera. He saw the Sunday parade as in a photograph, heads all turned to the café, mouths all rounded into neat zeros.

Then, at a click, all his senses returned like beasts. The screams deafened him. The stench of smoke and burned flesh choked him. The taste of his own blood was sickeningly sweet. He'd had the wind knocked out of him but he couldn't see any wounds on his body. He turned his head towards the carnage: legs, half-heads, rags of skin. And, before he lost consciousness, his mind deliberately painted over the whole scene. What had been color was converted to black and white, unemotional black and white. The blood that lay in pools now clumsily spilt coffee and it was all right. He smiled and drifted away.

## 28

At the silent man hotel, neither the powdered girls nor the old manager seemed surprised at Bodge's condition. He'd slept off a concussion at the military hospital. His head was bandaged from its thump on the street and a peel of skin was missing from his nose, but he'd been let off more lightly than most. If the old man hadn't called him, his parts would have been loaded into the army truck with those of the other restaurant patrons — the old man who was nowhere to be seen when Bodge came around. It was no coincidence. His life had been saved by the stranger and he had no way to thank him or find out why.

The silent man put the key in front of Bodge and went back to his newspaper. Bodge was in his room long enough to change his clothes, and retrieve his papers from beneath the loose tile under the bed. He took a rickshaw to the US Embassy compound, showed his passport to a lone marine at the gate, and went round to the consular section. He was the only customer so he had to ring a bell on the counter to get attention.

The girl who eventually arrived looked to Bodge not much older than thirteen. She was flat-chested and pimply.

"Gee," she said with a big bright Lana Turner smile. "What ran over you?"

"About two pounds of TNT."

"The café bomb? You're crazy to be out in public. Coffee drinking's getting to be a dangerous pastime these days. What can we do for you?"

"I'd like to, I don't know, report in or something. Let the Embassy know I'm here in Saigon."

"Are you on Embassy business?"

"Not exactly."

"Is that like 'no'?"

"Yes."

"Then why should we want to know you're in town?"

"I'm here as a missionary."

She seemed disappointed. "Oh, well this is the Embassy."

He tried to match her smile, "I'm aware of that. I saw the sign outside."

"What you need is the Evangelical Missions Bureau."

"There's such a place?"

"Didn't they give you orientation?"

"I skipped the last week."

"You don't strike me as being serious enough to be a missionary."

"You don't strike me as being old or polite enough to be a diplomat. So I guess first impressions aren't really worth a damn." He was sure she'd be offended but she seemed to like him more after that.

"Here. I'll show you where it is." She pulled a hand-drawn freebee map from a drawer and put a cross out by Vuon Chuoi market.

"Thanks. So, there isn't some way I can get my name on record here at the Embassy? In case someone comes looking for me?"

"I guess you could rob a bank or shoot the Prime Minister."

"Right. You've been too kind. Have a good day now."

"You too."

The cyclo was still waiting outside in the noonday heat. Bodge pointed to the cross on his map but he might as well have been showing him spaghetti stains on a napkin. Map reading wasn't a prerequisite for peddling a trishaw in Vietnam. So, Bodge navigated with "left's" and "right's" and somehow got them to an old French villa in the Vuon Chuoi district. The sign on the front gate was so small he wouldn't have noticed it if he hadn't been searching; *Evangelical Missions Bureau.*

He paced up the three main steps and into an empty foyer. There were padlocked doors to either side of him and a staircase ahead.

"Hello," he called. "Hello, anyone there?"

He heard mumbling from above and the sound of a door opening. A middle-aged and extremely white woman in *pince-nez* poked her head down from the top of the staircase. Bodge was astonished to see what she had on. Ninety degrees Fahrenheit and she wore a fluffy pink cardigan.

"Can I help you?" she asked.

"Ehrr. They told me at the embassy I might want to come and see you."

"And why's that, honey?"

"I'm on your program."

"You don't say? Heck, you wouldn't be the Reverend Rogers now, would you?" She had that down home southern music on her voice that made Bodge suddenly miss his family.

"I sure would." It was contagious.

"The Lord be praised. You get yourself up here."

Her spectacles must have been for reading, because he was three yards away before she noticed the bandage on his head. "Heaven help us, what happened to you?"

"Little old bomb," he smiled.

"Oh, Lord. Oh, Lord." She fussed around him like a fly round cotton candy. "But that's just awful. What an introduction God has given you to this beautiful country."

"It really isn't as bad as it looks," he said.

He finally reached the top landing and she threw open the door to the office. He was hit by a burst of air as cold as an Alaskan southerly. Bodge stood in the doorway. "Ma'am, this I would never have expected in Indochina."

"It's a wicked and sinful luxury but we'd better close the door before it all gets away. Come on in and take a seat." She closed the door. Two large air conditioners stood by the wall. Bodge had been to expensive stores that had these wonders of modern technology, but not even the head of the CIA boasted one. He sat on a rattan couch that creaked under his weight.

"You must be just dying for a cup of iced tea."

"Now you mention it, I guess I am dying at that."

There were several desks up here in the chilly room all giving the appearance of having owners. But there were just the two of them in the room.

"How many of you work here?" he asked.

"Five, full-time," she said, pouring tea from what looked like a New England antique teapot into a tall glass of ice.

"I thought I heard voices before."

"You probably did." She pointed to the closed door at the end of the office. "There's yet another meeting. You rescued me from it."

"Do they have snow in there as well?" His sweat was crystallizing.

"Reverend, I tell you, you never know what's going to arrive next from this church group or that. I swear we've even got air planes and a helicopter waiting for customs clearance. The soldiers of Christ are digging deep for this mission. I guess the devil must have been a communist."

"I guess so.

"Here's your tea, Reverend."

"Thank you…"

"Goodness, how rude of me. Margaret Johnston. I'm the all round dog's body in these parts. They kick me this way and that and I never howl. You want anything done, just call Maggy J."

"I'll remember that, thanks."

She joined him on the couch. "You're much younger than I expected."

"There are times I'm amazed I've made it to this age."

"Alleluia to that. But I imagine you're anxious to get yourself off into the jungle. You strike me as a man hungry for souls."

"Well, yes I am, Maggy. Famished. But I'm afraid I'm going to need a few weeks of attending the hospital until my head's healed."

"I'm sure poor Mrs. Rogers is worried half to death. Why don't I see if I can get word to her? Tell her you're all right."

"Mrs...?" Obviously news of the mission's cancellation hadn't made it to the Bureau. Here was a difficult moment. As he'd missed the larger part of his orientation, he wasn't to know whether this office was an out-and-out CIA set up, or whether it was an actual missions bureau that, unbeknownst to itself, hosted the occasional spy. He hit center field.

"That's very kind of you. But I think I can manage. I was planning to talk to her myself. I was actually wondering whether anyone had been asking after me."

"The Cornfelts had been keen to meet you, of course."

"The Cornfelts?"

"Sure. The couple you're replacing in Ban Methuot."

"Ah, yes. The Cornfelts. And where are they right now?"

"I'm afraid they left the country just yesterday. Lovely couple, and such caring people. Would you believe they went to all the trouble of taking a couple of girls back with them. Arranged scholarships and everything. I tell you, a person would have to be totally selfless to take on a responsibility like that. Don't you agree?"

"The Cornfelts are saints indeed. They've set an admirable precedent. Maybe I'll even take a couple of girls back when I go."

"Well, praise the Lord for this new generation of big-hearted revivalists."

"And, apart from the Cornfelts?"

"How do you mean, Reverend?"

"Asking after me?"

"No-one else I can recall. But your allowance has come through."

"My allowance has...Oh, thank God."

"I could wire down a note to the French Administrator's office and you can withdraw it through, what they call a *banque*." She made the word sound like a bedspring coming loose. "Unless you want some of it here. For your hospital expenses and all."

"I don't suppose I could get all of it now, Maggy J?"

The roll of greenbacks he'd been given in Delaware was down to a cheroot of twenties. He'd resorted to luxury in his Hong Kong layover.

He realized he'd need spending money if he had to stick around in Saigon much longer.

"All of it? Heavens to Betsy. That's three months of allowance."

"I have a lot of supplies to buy. And The Lord knows how long I'll have to stick around here in Saigon until my wife gets here."

"Mrs. Rogers is coming back? Whatever for?"

"Coming back?"

"She only left four weeks ago. Surely she wouldn't want to make that journey again so soon." She noticed the Reverend's jowls droop suddenly. "Why, whatever's wrong?"

"Are you telling me my wife's in Ban Methuot?"

"Of course, silly. Just what type of painkillers are they giving you for that head wound, Reverend?"

# 29

**Lac Lake**

"You want to play cards, Ugly?"

Eleven of the morning and already Lan was slurring. So, now was as good a time as any. Hong put aside her letter and sat on the cushions on the floor.

"Why not?"

"You bring your gold and silver, my princess?" Hong rattled her cloth pouch of French Francs and Lan fished into her pocket for her own. They were Vietnamese and the thought of playing cards merely for the fun of it would have made no more sense to them than shooting themselves in the ear because they liked the sound of bullets. Theirs was a gambling race and Hong enjoyed to bet as much as anyone. Today she'd be making one of the biggest gambles of her life.

Gin rummy was the game of the season and Lan had once been a tough adversary. But the opium had slowed her mind and the alcohol was making her clumsy. In spite of that, today, Lan was sure to win. They played for an hour before the topic turned to politics. Hong had waited for Lan to bring it up as she often did. She was scooping her latest winnings toward her lap.

"I am a tornado today," Lan boasted. "I sweep up all the money in my path and leave little consorts shivering in my wake."

"I think you must have put something in my rice porridge this morning. I'm playing like a fool," Hong lamented.

"Don't berate yourself, my darling. Even Uncle Ho himself wouldn't beat me on today's showing."

Hong laughed. "You don't for one minute think Uncle Ho plays rummy?"

"Why not? He's Vietnamese, isn't he?"

"It's a decadent bourgeois pastime. The first thing he'll do is close down all the gambling dens. He'll burn every playing card in the country and arrest all the players."

"You're scaring me again. I can't imagine how depressing life would be if he ever took over."

"Does it really worry you?"

"It's too horrid to imagine, especially with us in the Royal household. It's the upper classes they'll wipe out first, you know? Our names are probably already on some list."

Hong put down her cards. "Lan, if I tell you something, do you promise to keep it to yourself?"

"Why would you even need to ask?" She took on a visage of wounded indignation.

"This is very important, but I'll tell you because it might just save your life." Lan's eyes grew wide. Hong came to sit beside her and pulled her close enough to whisper in her ear.

"What is it?"

"If it happens. If the communists do take over, you should go to see my father."

"Why?"

"Lan, nobody outside my family knows this, but my father heads a nationalist movement in Saigon."

Lan laughed. She knew the skinny bumbling little man. He certainly wasn't the archetypal freedom fighter. "He makes ice cream."

"Yes. And who would ever suspect someone like him? You certainly didn't. His factory would be the last place the authorities would look for sympathizers. Am I right?"

"But...but he's not even a communist."

"If you were a communist in the South, would you tell anyone?"

Lan pulled away from her and looked in her unblinking eyes. "Hong, you're serious."

"As the sun is hot. If you go to him, he can protect you."

"How?"

"He's very close to...certain people."

"Ho?"

"I can't say."

"No?"

Hong took hold of her hand. "Lan, I'm breaking my vow to my father by telling you this. But I want you to be safe if it ever happens."

"I can't believe it."

"I swear on my life."

"I need a drink."

"What you need is a strong coffee." Hong stood and looked down at her best traitor. "You stay here. I'll make you one of my specials." She walked across the room to the door with her fists clenched. She prayed to the Virgin Mother that what she'd just done hadn't committed her father to a firing squad. But she had to trust her instincts. Everybody's secret fear of the communists might keep him safe from government retribution when...She'd weighed everything as carefully as she could. It was all in the hands of the gods, now. Her sisters were safely out of the country with the missionaries. There was just one final stage and she'd be free.

# 30

A week had passed. The stitches were out and Bodge was off the medication. He had regular headaches and his hearing came and went. They expected him to take morphine to forget about it. An addiction on top of everything else was more than he needed.

His stay in Saigon had become one long series of routines. From the hospital he'd take a cyclo to the Post and Telecommunication Office trying to get a call through to Ban Methuot. But, as the clerk explained, as soon as they went to the trouble of repairing the phone lines, communist sympathizers would cut them down again. There was a wireless telegraph at the office of the French Administrator. The relay stations were all at protected army bases so they were less likely to be destroyed but Bodge had sent three telegrams and had received no reply. That, the clerk was at a loss to explain.

Bodge had become certain that Stephanie was alive. As there was a wife waiting for him in Ban Methuot, the odds were looking pretty good that she was there. She'd escaped the car blast and for some reason, she'd been allowed to leave while he was in seclusion. He hadn't thought it prudent to ask Maggy J for a description of his own wife. "A friendly enough person," was the best he could get out of her.

In spite of the frustrations of mobility and communication, Bodge's life took a turn for the better. He'd relieved the Evangelical Mission of half his allowance and proceeded to spend it. He bought himself some decent clothes, left the silent-man hotel and checked into the Majestic on Rue Catinat. As his purpose in Saigon was to have people know he was there, he decided nothing was to be gained by slumming. He'd been cured of his fondness for roadside cafés and had taken to eating three quality meals a day in the hotel's first class restaurant. There were armed guards all over, protecting the idle rich from flying ordnance and blinkering them from the ever-approaching war.

Afternoons, Bodge would work on his Vietnamese and do whatever exercises didn't trouble his head. The only books on sale in town were in French so he ventured off into whole different waters to those at his desk in New York. He developed a fondness (if not a complete understanding) for Camus and was reminded that outside government reports and tape transcripts, the French language could be a beautiful thing.

In the evenings he'd join the expatriates at the hotel bar. There were any number of reasons why booze could have turned into a problem for him so he was never seen there with anything stronger than orangeade.

That suited his missionary image as well. It was only his good nature that breached the "teetotal yank missionary" prejudice. The bar was a popular watering hole for journalists who'd been bomb-threatened out of their favourite haunts. Bodge learned a lot there that he'd never have picked up from the official French news service. It was there he'd first heard rumors of slave labor on the plantations, unreported French losses in unheard-of battles, and far-fetched accounts of the sluttish wife of the French Administrator in his own Ban Methuot.

It was there too that he met Raphael, the pilot of the Royal airplane. Raphael had no time for the lecherous journalists and the obnoxious profiteers that loitered in the bar. When he stayed at the Majestic, he spent his evenings reading at a small table in the corner of the restaurant where he had his own keep-bottle of cognac. Raphael, Bodge learned, had a Montagnard wife and had built a home for his new family at Dalat. Whenever the Emperor was at his Dalat palace, Raphael spent glorious uninterrupted days with a family he apparently loved very much. But in Saigon and Hanoi and Hue, he sat moping in hotel restaurants.

Even though Bodge had heard all the stories of this grumpy ex-French Airforce Commodore, he went to great lengths to introduce himself one evening. In fact he had two high cards in his hand. Firstly, the sixty-year-old Parisian was a devout Christian who believed in the ethic of missionary work. Secondly, Bodge showed a marked interest in the plight of the Montagnard at the hands of the French colonists. The correspondents were surprised to see how the pilot had taken to Bodge. They chatted together in French there at the corner table like old comrades. They saw Bodge as some social messiah who could calm even the most savage of beasts.

But Bodge had deeper motives for this humanitarian effort. He knew he'd eventually be able to work the conversation around to a matter of extreme importance. He was sure they'd soon be gossiping about the royal entourage, and, ultimately, of Von Hong. In fact, it happened in only their second meeting. Raphael and Bodge were eating together. The conversation had found its way to Ban Methuot.

"But you know Grand E, Raphael's nickname for the Emperor, has a hunting lodge not far from Ban Methuot?"

"I didn't know."

"It's at a place called Lac."

"I believe the Mission has a place up there too."

"I thought your house was in Ban Methuot."

Bodge laughed. "Ban Methuot is the base of the mission. From what I've learned, the three bedroom villa on the lake is for roughing it during the weekend. It's a hardship post. I've been learning a lot about the Mission's holdings around the country."

"Well then, you and Grand E are probably neighbors. I hear there isn't a lot of real estate up there. I'm sure you'll meet him. He's there as we speak. Been there a couple of months already. He's mad on hunting. They're gouging a private hunting track for him all the way to Dalat. Exclusive for royal use."

"He's up there by himself?"

"He has one of his mistresses with him. Sorry. I mean his concubine. It's the French who have mistresses because we can't get away with inviting them to move in with the wife. This consort is all legal and above board. And I can understand why he's not in a hurry to come down from the lake."

"Why?"

"Ah. She's perfection. She's the type only money and power can get for a man. Naturally, he's besotted by her. I can't say I blame him."

"And..." Bodge tried to maintain an air of indifference. "...is she besotted with him?"

"Hmm. She isn't likely to come to me in the cockpit and say, 'Raphael, the Grand E is a shit.' But I believe in my heart that she despises him."

"When are you next planning to go to Ban Methuot?"

"I have to wait, as always, for word from the Grand E. But I know they have to return for the ceremony next month."

"The consort too?"

Raphael smiled. "See? I knew I'd get you worked up with my talk of the beautiful concubine. Don't forget you have a wife waiting for you in Ban Methuot."

Bodge, appropriately, blushed. "Of course, I didn't mean..."

"Don't worry, Reverend. I'm only joking with you. I don't think Grand E would leave the second consort alone in the jungle. But he's just as crazy about his guns as he is about her. I'm sure he'll be back up there as soon as he can get away. You'll have to meet him."

"And her," Bodge thought. He saw her picture-slide on the wall in the safe house. He imagined her in color. He wondered whether the lake at Lac was too cold for her to go on midnight swims.

"And I tell you what," Raphael continued. "If you can get that head fixed up in a hurry, I might even take you up with me. If they don't give me some Royal hanger-on, I usually do one trip by myself. If we aren't shot down by some hotshot with a rifle, you'll enjoy the flight."

"You're too kind."

# 31

It was midnight in Petit's little house and he had drunk himself into a trance in front of the silently turning long-playing record. The knock on the front door surprised him. Few people bothered to knock. The Administrator's wife had found a new paramour so he had few late night visitors these days. He staggered a little on his way to the door and leaned on the wall to open it.

The woman stood there in a long dark rain poncho even though there hadn't been any rain for months. She wore a conical hat and it wasn't until she looked up into his face that he recognized her.

"Y-your royal highness. I…"

Von Hong hurried past him into the house and motioned for him to shut the door.

"Monsieur Petit, I have to trust you to tell nobody of this visit. I have to be back at the lake before the Emperor wakes up. This was my last chance to see you."

# 32

Still there was no news from Ban Methuot, and no sign of Palmer. The suspense was gnawing at Bodge so he decided on a brief visit to the highlands before the monsoons kicked in. He'd use his head damage as an excuse to come back to Saigon, then hurry back to the States. Any obligation he may have felt to the agency had long since evaporated. They'd treated him shoddily and he no longer felt he owed them his time to spy on French soldiers in a country most Americans couldn't identify on a map. It seemed vaguely ridiculous. No, his effort now would be spent on clearing his name and erasing it from whatever hit list it was on. Stephanie was the only person who could explain things. Raphael had heard from the Grand E and he was to collect the royal entourage from Ban Methuot in two days. Bodge could go with him. In spite of all the intrigue in his life, there was nothing Bodge could do to persuade his thoughts away from the second consort. In two days, just briefly, they'd be on the same patch of earth. He might even see her. They might meet, talk, shake hands?

Here was Bodge, early thirties, living his belated high school crush. He was nothing special, he knew that. He'd be just like one of the faceless fans that hung around the houses of Grace Kelly and Rita Hayworth, hoping for a glimpse. If she bothered to recall him at all, she'd recall a large clumsy white man with a head bandage. She wouldn't even be able to answer questions about the shape of his ears or the cut of his smile. But Mlle. Nguyen Von Hong was stuck to his heart like an annoying growth. In many ways, he hoped she'd be a disappointment in real life.

## Ban Methuot

There was no airport. The landing strip was for military transports and royalty only. All civilians and supplies had to be carried by road in the long caravans that didn't always arrive in one piece. The Royal B24 Liberator Transport churned through the dust and stopped six meters from the end of the strip. Raphael performed a neat pirouette and parked the clumsy craft beside the only structure there. It was the type of wooden lean-to folks back home would use to store hay.

There was nobody there to meet them — a marked absence of security. It seemed to Bodge that everything hung on French faith that the Viet Minh wouldn't ever be acquiring aircraft from the Chinese.

"No Grand E," Bodge said stretching his legs on the runway.

"Oh, they come whenever they feel like it," said Raphael. He'd taken a long-handled mop from the shed and was cleaning the dust from the fuselage. "I might end up stuck here a day or two while they decide what to wear for the journey. That's happened before."

Bodge's heart lost some buoyancy at that news. "How far is the town?"

"About four miles. But don't you go expecting New York, my friend. It's more like Dodge City."

"It's still a long way to walk."

"Don't worry. Whenever they hear the plane, they volunteer someone to come out to meet us. They don't know whether I have any royal personages on board. The etiquette is quite well mapped out. I'd probably lose my head if the Grand E found me taking on passengers without his permission. So, let's get your stuff off and into the shed just in case. If the royal jeeps arrive first we can bullshit that you came out from Ban Methuot to meet the Emperor."

In fact, the first vehicle to arrive was a most unlikely white Citroen. Bodge was sure its manufacturers had never once imagined a day when it would be forging along tropical jungle tracks. Inspector of schools, Petit parked in the shade of the lean-to and walked over to the two men with a tired smile.

"Good afternoon, M. Blanc." Bodge noticed the young man was extremely respectful to the old pilot and was doubtless intimidated by him. Raphael shook the offered hand briefly and nodded. "The Administrator has a meeting. There was no-one else at the office so I came. I take it there were no (he glanced at Bodge and smiled) *royal* passengers on board today."

"No. But the Empress asked me if I'd give the Reverend Rogers here a ride."

Petit reached out his hand to Bodge and the two men greeted each other with respectful enthusiasm. Bodge had to act like a friend-to-all evangelist and Petit was apparently hungry for company. "Oh, good. Then you must be the husband of our new missionary." Bodge felt like the First Lady. It was odd to be referred to in such a way but he put it down to a quirk of the man's English. "You speak some French?"

"Ha. He could embarrass deLattre himself," Raphael laughed.

"I know a little," Bodge said modestly.

"Excellent. Excellent. I am Jacques Petit, Director of Schools for this region. We all met your wife. She's made quite an impression already."

"A good one I hope."

Petit chose not to respond to the comment. "I believe you'll find her out at your lake villa as we speak. She spends a lot of time out there."

Bodge looked over the young man's shoulder to see a cloud of dust out on the hill road. Two jeeps were competing to find the most inappropriate gear for the decline. Petit and Raphael followed his gaze.

"Aha," said the pilot. "Looks like Grand E is in a hurry to get to the city."

Conversation on the air strip ceased as the men watched the cars wind their ways down to the plateau. The front jeep had been bizarrely modified so that the rear seats were perched on a high step. The couple on it sat tall and stiff beneath a canopy like Rajahs on an elephant. The man held a heavy hunting rifle and looked all the time toward the foliage of the jungle. Beside him sat a woman whose head was mummified in gauze. Bodge assumed this was to keep the dust out of her throat and eyes. He recognized the Emperor. The wrapped woman had to be Hong.

His breathing became shallow and he squeezed his fingers into fists. The couple wore Western clothes; he a white linen jacket and open neck shirt with a cravat, she a pink floral frock. Long opera gloves shielded her arms from the sun. As the jeeps neared the strip, the watchers stepped back so as not to be showered in dust. The wobble in Bodge's legs threatened to collapse him. As soon as the driver had killed the engine and almost pulled the handbrake from its moorings, he jumped out to help the Emperor from his podium.

Bodge could see nothing but the woman. She remained on her seat and slowly began to unwrap the gauze. It was excruciating. It reminded him of the way his mother always told him not to tear the Christmas paper when he opened his presents. First one layer, with the outline of her nose and cheek bones. Then a second turn with the shadows of her eyes, the dull red of her lips. And, all at once the cloth came away and Bodge experienced his café bomb in reverse. He was sucked towards her beauty as if it were a vacuum. She shook her hair loose, wiped her sweat with a fine silk scarf, and blew her nose loudly.

Nobody had come to help. She gave the impression she needed nobody's assistance. She leapt down from her perch like a gymnast and Bodge could see her dirty white pumps and her fine ankles. Now he cursed his luck that he wasn't standing between her and the plane. He could hardly put himself in a more noticeable spot without looking ridiculous. She walked directly to the portable steps that led up to the hatchway. Her movement was elegant but youthful. Her back was straight as a bamboo and her breasts stood proudly high on her chest. She didn't just ignore Bodge. She ignored everybody. She seemed to be on the boil. Something had riled her. But Bodge was encouraged by her fury. It could only have been directed at the Emperor.

Although it hadn't been much of a chance it was soon gone. She was out of sight on the plane and he came around from his trance. His attention was drawn to Raphael who was standing behind the Emperor pointing at Bodge. The Emperor rudely crooked his finger and wiggled it for Bodge to come to him. He felt some empathy for the concubine as he walked over.

"Sir?" Bodge's bow was just a nod that somehow involved his shoulders. He knew immediately it was neither deep nor respectful enough.

"Blanc tells me you're the new missionary out here." The Emperor's French was fast and colloquial as if he were trying to catch the American out.

Bodge's reply was just as fluent. "Robert Rogers, Your Royal Highness. At your service. I hope we'll be able to do some good while we're here."

"Well, at least you can speak. That's more than your predecessors could manage."

Although he hadn't yet learned the appropriate language to use with royalty, Bodge attempted to show off his Vietnamese. "What good is living in a foreign country if you can't speak to anyone?"

In spite of himself, the Emperor smiled. "If I didn't know better, I'd say that might have been Vietnamese."

"I'll do some work on the pronunciation, Your Highness."

"Where are you off to?"

"I believe my wife is in the villa at Lac Lake. I'd like to see her."

"Right. Take my jeep. It's going that way. Sit in the front with the driver."

"That's very kind of you."

"What was your name, again?"

"Robert Rogers."

"I hope you aren't just talk, Reverend Rogers." He shook Bodge's big hand and walked to the plane. Raphael smiled, slapped Bodge on the back, and followed. Bodge felt a pang of guilt. He *was* all talk.

All this, Hong watched from the window. She saw the big man retrieve his bags from the lean to and walk to the jeep. The driver and the teacher loaded the bags for him. Already he'd charmed the French and the Emperor. He would do. He would do nicely.

## Lac Lake

The scene in the living room of the lake villa was reminiscent of one from an Inspector Poirot novel. The missionary's wife sat with her arm around a lightly sobbing Montagnard servant girl. Opposite was Captain Henry: the Inspector of Police. Then there was Administrator Dupré and his interpreter, the regional Vietnamese Montagnard coordinator called Duc from the Montagnard Liaison Center, and Captain Faboir from the French Military.

Dupré looked at the American woman with distaste — another foreigner who hadn't bothered to learn French. And a troublemaker to boot. In a little over a month she'd managed to create more havoc than her predecessor had achieved in two years. Neither he nor Faboir wished to be there, but they really had no choice. She'd filled in all the correct forms with her complaint and gone through all the correct channels. It was their legal obligation to attend. And all for what? A couple of *Moi* girls ran off. Another has a bit of a fling with a soldier and squeals to the concubine. It was all a terrible nuisance.

All the accusations and debated points, English, French, Vietnamese and M'nong, had passed through interpreter Tran. They heard the girl's account of what had happened and the Vietnamese coordinator's report of the death and of how the other servant had vanished completely. Captain Faboir complained that there was no call for him to be there as the Western foreigners, if they existed at all, could have been from anywhere. General LePenn had briefed him thoroughly before leaving for France. It soon became apparent to Stephanie that she didn't have many allies in that room. Mlle. Hong had anticipated as much. But this show was necessary to push the complaint within the responsibility of the French Administration, and to show whoever was responsible they wouldn't have an easy ride.

"Look," said the policeman. "Obviously these men — these men that only this emotionally unstable girl saw — are not from around these parts. All our soldiers are accounted for. If they exist, they're probably travelers long gone from the province."

When the translation reached her, Mrs. Rogers laughed. "Are there really so many European tourists wandering around the jungles of war-torn Western Annam? I'm surprised nobody else saw them."

"Of course, without investigating we can't be sure they weren't seen by somebody else," said Henry with unhidden aggression in his voice. "But, until then, it would appear this was an isolated incident."

The sound of the royal jeeps returning along the lake road intruded upon the tense atmosphere in the room. Stephanie glared at the Vietnamese coordinator. He'd already had a royal visit this week so he was in a spot. "*No.*" He said. It was one of the few Vietnamese words the Frenchmen in attendance had bothered to learn.

The Inspector looked at him in disbelief. Were his ears deceiving him or did this clerk just contradict him? "I beg your pardon?"

Duc looked again at the American woman, then at Tran. He spoke a basic French that was good enough to do his job. But the buffer of having Tran there, expressing Duc's thoughts more eloquently than he could himself, gave him the confidence he needed to drop his bombshell.

"This wasn't an isolated case."

"What do you mean?" Dupré asked.

"Sir, in the last three weeks, thirteen Montagnard women have vanished."

"What?" Dupré sat up.

"Probably went off to earn better money in Madame Ving's brothel," Captain Henry joked but didn't elicit any laughter.

"No," Duc continued. "They were all married women. Most had children. Either they didn't return from the fields or they disappeared from their homes at night. The two other girls from this house were also married."

"Why hasn't anyone reported this?" Dupré yelled. They were momentarily distracted by the sound of a jeep pulling up at the outer gate, and the guards shouting.

"We reported each incident to the police," Duc continued. "You can check the files."

"Well?" He turned to Henry.

"It may be true. But these are *Moi* matters. If there's a *Moi* dispute, we refer it to the army."

"So, Captain Faboir," Dupré asked. "Did you already know about these cases?"

"I didn't hear anything personally about it, Administrator. I'd have to check the files to see whether we received a complaint."

"Then I suggest you do so immediately, Captain. We can't just lose thirteen *Moi*. Saigon would view that as gross negligence. I won't have any *Moi* from my district vanishing. Do you understand me?"

"I'll look into it."

"And I expect…"

The atmosphere in the room was suddenly changed by the arrival of a new guest. Standing in the doorway with an armed guard at his back, was a large man with a scabby nose. Every face in the room turned toward him, nobody knowing what to say.

Stephanie was a little stunned at first but she leapt to her feet and went to Bodge. She was in her Mrs. Rogers disguise so there was nothing athletic about her approach.

"Bobby. Bobby," she cried. "I've been so worried about you. Thank the Lord. Thank the Lord."

"Good afternoon," the man said with a friendly smile and impeccable French.

"May I know who you are, sir?" Dupré asked.

"Certainly, I'm Reverend Rogers," said the new missionary as his wife took his hand. Bodge looked around at the confused faces. "I believe this is one of my houses."

"We were led to believe you wouldn't be coming," said the administrator.

"Ah, yes. Well that is a very long story,' Bodge said, and hoped he wouldn't be asked to tell it. He hadn't yet made it up after all.

# 33

"And what's he like?" Monique asked, jabbing at the fish on her plate.

"Like? What are all missionaries like? Single-minded, superior, boring. But, at least, this one can speak. I have to confess I was impressed with his French. He's the first yank I've met who could string together a sentence." Dupré threw back the remaining wine from his goblet and refilled it. The traumas at the Lac villa had left him with no choice but to get pickled over supper. With the wine and the candlelight and Debussy on the phonograph, he considered this a particularly romantic setting. His young, virtually untouched bride sat opposite him with her slinky housecoat fairly clinging to her breasts.

"No, I mean, physically. Petit said he was absolutely a giant."

"I'd hardly call him a giant."

"Fat?"

"No."

"So what then?"

"Honestly, what does it matter what a missionary looks like? I admit I was expecting him to be completely different."

"Really? Well, as nobody here seems to want to tell me how he looks, I'm not actually in a position to share your surprise, am I now?" She attacked a Vietnamese turnip with her knife.

"It's just that his wife is so…matronly. She's fat and greasy-haired, and simple looking."

"Whereas he…?" She wielded her knife like a conductor.

"Whereas he's more attractive, and…It's hard to say."

"Try."

"Well, it was more like he was her brother than her lover. She hadn't seen him for months yet she hesitated to greet him. And then it was as if her embrace was more for our benefit than his. I get the feeling they aren't a very physical pair. But I imagine religion has that effect on people. It encourages you to look beyond the outer coating and fall in love with the soul within, or so I'm told. That inevitably draws some peculiar people together. Not like us."

Monique looked up. "And what kind of people are we?"

"Oh, there were probably some personality traits that contributed, but ultimately it was the physical that drew us together."

"It was?"

He smiled, his cheeks burning from the wine and the memory. "Don't pretend our evenings in the back of my car didn't influence your decision to become mine."

She kept her smile to herself. "You're probably right."

## Lac Lake

It was early and Bodge lay naked beside his fake wife looking through the open window, overwhelmed by the silence. Outside, lofty cranes untangled themselves from the reeds with small-fry in their beaks and flew off to their nests. Bats, no bigger than inkblots, dived back and forth across the bloated moon and, one by one, the drunken moths were drawn into the oil lamps on the balcony and cremated as penance for their addiction to light. In the distance, lightning slithered a warning across the horizon. All this happened in complete silence.

"Not sleeping?" Stephanie asked.

"Can't stop my head from thinking."

"It's what they do, heads."

"It drives me nuts when I don't have answers. I'd kind of hoped I'd get here and you'd solve all my mysteries for me."

"Sorry about that."

"Could you go over it again?"

"What?"

"What happened."

"Bodge it's three in the—"

"Just once more and I promise I won't ask you again. Every little detail."

She sighed and eased herself up on her elbows. "You're annoying. You know that?"

"It's just—"

"Okay. Okay. I'm driving your piece of shit convertible into the city. It's seven something and I have to be at records by eight to start getting the visas and passports sorted. I get the urge for a coffee so I stop at Chucky Chicken. I go by the restroom and do a number one cause my lady's parts were still aching from all the—"

"That's more information than I need."

"You asked for details. I get a hot coffee and a donut that cost me eighteen cents for the two and I'm on my way back out to the car when the thing blows sky high. I even had time to think how pretty the explosion looked before the blast sent me flying backward ass over tit across the parking lot. Next thing I know I'm surrounded by a flock of nurses asking me how I feel. I've got a bump on my head the size of Boston so I ask for pain killers and they pump me full of something that knocks me out again.

"When I come round I'm better able to grasp what happened. It occurs to me I must have put enough in the collection plate that Sunday cause, by rights, I should have been in little bits at that stage. Then it hits me that I was in your car and it should have been you in little bits, not me. So I staggered to the phone and called the Casually Yours people.

"Then things went kind of fast. The cop at the end of my bed was replaced by a guy in a necktie who wouldn't tell me zip. Then Palmer arrives and asks me when I'll be well enough to travel."

"When was that?"

"The evening of the explosion."

"So I'd already been through the homosexual inquisition and was at the safe house. Did he tell you anything?"

"Just that they suspected there was a time bomb — probably planted under the seat of your car — that you were safe and that there were serious concerns about security. He hinted there was probably something a lot deeper going on but he couldn't tell me about it. In fact, he didn't seem to have a clue. He wanted me out of DC as quickly as possible so within twenty-four hours I was on a flight. Said he'd be here soon to explain stuff. He gave me the impression you mightn't make it here."

"So why did he send me tickets?"

"Beats me."

"Something happened to keep me in limbo for another month."

"So it seems."

"And the only one who can explain all this is Palmer."

"Wherever the hell he is."

**Bangkok**

Some said the human depression that had squatted on Southeast Asia for the past six months somehow worked its way up into the heavens. They said it made the gods so sad they began to cry, and that was why the rains came early. There had to be an ethereal reason, because the meteorologists couldn't explain it. It was unprecedented. After a week of thunder and lightning that promoted the forthcoming spectacular like a move trailer, the skies finally opened and sent a torrent of water onto the dry earth.

Thailand's capital had been a city of canals. But in the built up areas they'd started to fill in the water courses to make streets. A modern city had to have streets. But the rain didn't respect the dreams of the city planners. With nowhere to escape, water flooded whole suburbs, damaged property and dragged all kinds of vermin up out of the sewers.

This, the first rainy season for the new luxury Santhi Hotel, showed the owners their folly in building slightly below street level. The reception area was a pond. Plants drowned in their pots. The expensive furniture stood in great sculptures, piled one piece on top of the next.

The bellboy's trousers were rolled up above his knees. He waded to the night manager's desk.

"Got any stamps, Khot?"

The night manager was a third-year student from Chulalongkorn University and one of the few people around who could speak English. The owners insisted on English-speaking staff. Khot was reclining on top of the desk like some Roman Emperor reading a magazine. He reached down to the drawer.

"How many do you want?"

"America. It's pretty heavy so I'd say about eight baht. Better make it ten."

The young manager tore the stamps from the sheet and exchanged them for the banknote. He put it in the money tin, locked it, and put the key underneath the tin. "Who's up writing letters this time of the morning?"

"Him, the suit guy, 310. He's drunk as a fart."

"Again? I hope he doesn't trash the room."

"Nah, he's not the violent type. He's probably just—"

The internal phone rang on the desk behind Khot. The light on the console showed them this was the third floor hall phone. Being a very modern hotel, each floor had its own telephone. "I wonder if I could get electrocuted using this thing with all the water around. Hello? Yes, speaking. What can I—? What? Right, I'm coming up. Don't touch anything."

The bellboy noticed how the color had suddenly drained from the young man's face. "What is it?"

"That was the woman from 308," he said, grabbing the master keys. He jumped down into the water and splashed across to the stairwell. "She said there's been a shooting in the room next door. It woke everyone up. That's your guy with the suit."

"But he's on his own in there."

"Then it sounds like he's done himself in."

# 34

## Lac Lake to Ban Methuot

The rains that lashed the continent quickly filled the paddies and swelled the rivers. The lake at Lac rose four feet in a week and Bodge seemed to understand the confusion of the birds whose migratory patterns had been thrown into chaos by the premature loss of summer.

Bodge and Stephanie decided to move to the Ban Methuot house before the road became difficult to pass. They shuttered the villa and took Bet, the servant, into town in the Land Rover. Their town house was a two-story French chateau with a steeply sloping tile roof and trails of morning glory clinging to the walls. There was an outhouse for the servants and a backyard where vegetables presently lay submerged in water. The border of the property was marked with a white, picket fence clogged with ivy like a vegetarian's smile.

Over the porch was a hand-carved sign with *House of the Pearly Gates* engraved in gothic script.

"See? I knew I'd get here eventually," Stephanie smiled.

"Should I use the key or wait for St. Peter to answer the door?" Bodge asked. They laughed.

"That's the last sacrilege I want to hear from you, Reverend."

There was indeed something heavenly and unreal about the interior. On their way there they'd passed shanties where water and mud formed the floor and urchins sat in puddles. They'd seen families foraging through the bins out back of the Expatriate Club, and Montagnard begging from soldiers. But they were living in a small medieval castle. Their place was expensively furnished and oils of European landscapes took up most available wall space.

"Actually, I like it," Stephanie said, exploring the drawers and cupboards. "It's brazen."

"I wonder if my Aunt Helen in Arizona knows her missions' contribution has gone toward a Queen Anne occasional table. It's obscene."

"You're right. Let's sell all this stuff, give the money to the poor, and live a Spartan existence."

"Hey, I didn't say I couldn't learn to live with it. I just had some perverted idea about how the poor missionaries were suffering. I thought they were in the bush living on insects."

"You having second thoughts about leaving, Bodge?"

154

"No, but if I can't get away, I don't feel quite so bad about staying."

They'd reached the top landing where a large comfortable chair stood at the window. The house was on the edge of town just a short walk from the French jail. From this window the exercise yard was visible behind barbed wire that topped the walls. The rear gardens of a dozen or so Vietnamese huts abutted the perimeter wall, and at the end of the row stood a peculiar building.

"Stephanie, what does that look like to you?" She came to join him at the window. Directly ahead was what looked like a small motel. It was painted in gory pink. A slim bamboo flag pole rose from its roof, but it certainly wasn't a flag that stood there at its top.

"Isn't it a leg?" she asked.

"Sure looks like one." At the top of the pole was a shapely store-mannequin leg. It wore a red high-heeled shoe whose stiletto pointed to heaven.

"Probably a shoe store," she laughed, and went back to her ferreting.

"If you're right it appears our predecessor had a fetish for shoes." Bodge sat in the chair and had a mental picture of Reverend Cornfelt looking down like God at all the sinners in Ban Methuot.

"Now this is beautiful," said Stephanie sliding down the curved shutter of a writing desk. Bodge went over to see. "I love these things." She started to feel inside the drawers and under the lid.

"You hoping the Cornfelts left their life savings in there?" Bodge asked, walking into the master bedroom.

"These things are a spy's delight. They always have secret compartments and hidden drawers. I'll find one."

Bodge was exploring the main bedroom and its on-suite bathroom. A large *yow* tree weighted down by the rain cut out the light through the window. There came the faintest of clicks from behind him.

"Gotcha." Stephanie had found her compartment.

"Anything in there?" he asked.

"Only this," she said, producing a clunky German Lugar.

"Wow. Is it loaded?"

From the way she handled and inspected the weapon, Bodge could tell his new wife had been around guns. He was starting to believe she was much better at this covert life than he was.

"Yup."

"You suppose the Cornfelts ever used it?"

"The missions are strict about us not using guns. I doubt they even knew it was here."

"Rules or not, it makes me feel better to have something lethal to fight off the Viet Minh. I couldn't see me beating them back with my Bible." He held his ever-present holy book before him and fought off an imaginary invasion. "Until now, we were the only two people in the entire country who weren't armed." He saw her raise her eyebrows and whistle. "We weren't armed, were we Stephanie? Steph?"

It rained all through the night which may have partly explained why they had no callers. None of the neighbors dropped by with fruit baskets or asked if they were settling in okay. Bodge got the idea this would really be an ideal spot to vanish from the world for a couple of years. If he didn't make any waves he was sure he'd be ignored by just about everyone. Perhaps that was what Palmer had in mind.

But that theory took a setback the following morning. It was still raining when Stephanie went off to get some shopping done at the market. She hadn't been gone a minute when Bodge heard a stranger's voice downstairs. In the large living room he found Bet attempting to make herself understood by a pretty but overly decorated young woman with wild, deep blond hair. She looked up at Bodge, smiled, and abandoned Bet completely.

"Monsieur Rogers." she said, reaching out for his hand and not releasing it. "I'm so glad to meet you at last."

"Enchanted, Madam." He could feel the large rings on her wedding finger.

"I'm Madame Dupré, the wife of the Administrator. I believe you met my husband."

"Yes."

"He was very impressed with your French. I must say I find you impressive as well."

Her hand was slowly kneading his and through it he could feel her excitement. He suddenly believed the rumors he'd heard in Saigon. She buzzed with sensuality. It was as if she were wired for the mating season. The way she eyed him up and down. The way her tongue flicked her top lip. The way her hips ground slightly as she stood. Bodge had no doubt Mme. Dupré was advertising. He could remember very few meetings in his life that made him realize so clearly that he was just a man.

"Ehrr, do sit down, Madame," Bodge said with a flutter in his voice.

"Thank you so much, but I can't stay. I just came by to pay my respects to you both. Is your wife here?"

Bodge couldn't understand how they hadn't met on the front path. "No. She's gone to the market."

She still had him snared between her fingers. She looked at the small plaster on his head and then, deliberately, to his thigh. "I heard about your terrible misadventure in Saigon. I hope it hasn't impaired your normal functions."

"I'm getting better, thank you."

"I do hope so. We expect a lot from you."

"You do?"

"Ban Methuot has so many people... in need."

"So I heard." He didn't like this woman.

Finally, she released him from her hand but still held his crotch with her eyes. "I hope to be seeing much more of you," she said and licked some stray lipstick from her front tooth. She smiled, turned, and sashayed out the front door. It didn't occur to Bodge to show her out. He was still a little stunned. He was certain he'd just been violated in some way but couldn't put a name to it.

# 35

Over the next few days, the Rogers put together a short term plan to give the town some evidence that they weren't just there on holiday. As soon as there was a break in the weather, they would drive out to the villages on the Cornfelts' list and introduce themselves to the Montagnard. They decided it would be circumspect to offer Bible readings there in the living room also, but they would be in English to avoid the likelihood of anyone turning up. There was a Vietnamese Catholic priest in town to take care of Ban Methuot souls. They felt they could get away with doing their evangelical business in the surrounding countryside.

"Steph?"

"Yes, honey?"

The missionaries were once again lying naked side by side bathed in sweat. The empty Cabernet bottle and the bedside corkscrew the only evidence of their nightly tipples.

"This, what we do…what we are?"

Stephanie waited patiently for more but heard only the distant toads toasting the end of another storm.

"I think I'll need a little more if you expect a response."

"I'm sorry. I mean, how would you classify our relationship?"

"I'm not sure what you mean."

"I mean, what role does emotion play in what we have here?"

"Did you want me to answer for both of us?"

"No, just you will be fine."

"You're asking, 'Am I crazy in love with you?'"

"That's a start."

"No!"

"You don't want some time to think about it?"

"Are you relieved? Disappointed? Do you think someone like me should be grateful to have a man interested in her?"

"Stop that, now. You're being mean… to both of us. You know that isn't what I think at all. I'm just trying to understand the way I'm feeling and it would help if I knew what was going through your mind."

"You don't handle mystique too well, do you, Bodge? You always expect there to be an answer."

"Is that unreasonable?"

"It's unromantic. Situations tend to lose their magic when you start to analyze them. Relationships are a good example of that. The most incredible romance I've ever had was in Guatemala with a guy who didn't speak a word of English. I had no idea what he was thinking. I was so in love with that man."

"You don't think — sorry — you don't think that's a little bit two-dimensional?"

"What's wrong with shallow? That third dimension is terribly overrated. To really be infatuated with someone it helps not to know them at all. Look at you and the concubine."

A feeling of guilt descended upon him and Bodge could only fight his way out of it through indignation.

"Don't be ridiculous. I've never met the woman."

"Yet you instantly know which particular concubine I'm talking about."

"I...I can't s..." Bodge was caught out — a guilty paramour exposed in the marital bed. He'd barely mentioned Hong. He'd perhaps inquired about Stephanie's meetings to discuss the case of the missing Montagnard women but he'd been careful not to ask too many questions about the concubine. How could she know? They were unfathomable, these women.

"Stop changing the subject. I'm asking about you and me."

"You and me? We work together and we fuck, Bodge. We're friends who fuck. We admire certain things about each other but we don't get too carried away."

"How do you know I'm not carried away?"

"Oh, Bodge. See what I mean? This communication thing's a real bummer in relationships."

"Really. How do you know I'm not in love with you?"

She laughed and rolled onto her back. He watched as her breasts caught up with her and settled. "You men. You always confuse physical feeling with emotion."

"So, tell me."

She tipped her head to his side of the pillow and let the back of her hand creep across his thigh. "When you thought I'd died in the car bombing what did you feel?"

"I was devastated."

"How sweet. And how long did that devastation last?"

"How long?"

"Yeah. How long was it before you could fight your way back into your routine? How broken up were you? Was your own life suddenly not worth living? Did you consider suicide, Bodge?"

He thought it was a joke question so he laughed. But it became quite clear from the way she clamped her hand onto his balls that she was deadly serious.

"Ow! I didn't know you so well then."

"And you still don't. If you did, you'd know that devastation's the very least I expect from a man I bothered to love — wrist slashing, heart crushing, life ending devotion. That isn't something you pick up gradually. It's a thing that slaps you from the first moment you meet. Palmer told me about your reaction to the concubine's photos. That's the way I want a man to feel about me."

"Will you stop bringing Von Hong into—?"

"I don't want to train him. I want him to be convinced from the outset that he isn't going to find any better. If that doesn't happen, that's fine. But don't expect compromise from me. I like you, Bodge, and we get along well together. Sex works for us. But you aren't offering enough. Get over it."

She released her grip on his balls and his conscience and turned her back to him. The interview was over. He put his hand on her shoulder and kissed her neck. Love was a word that had lost its worth. Its devaluation over the years had rendered it appropriate for so much meaningless flotsam. He loved Stephanie, he knew he did. But how much more than he loved Lou's cooking or his expensive hi-fi he couldn't say. She was right. He would never end his own life to mourn her death.

With his arm around Stephanie, he dreamed of Hong that night as he had on many other occasions. When Bet knocked on their door to tell them they had a visitor he was still in the company of the consort and had difficulty leaving her to go to the door. He grabbed his robe from the door hook and walked drowsily to the staircase. And such was the cohesion between the sleeping and the waking worlds, it didn't immediately seem a surprise to him to see Hong standing in the middle of the living room. It wasn't until she moved toward him and spoke that a panic took over him.

"Monsieur Rogers," she said in beautiful melodic French. "I'm terribly sorry to trouble you so early."

"Your Royal Highness," he replied, cemented to the fourth step. He nodded pathetically.

"You seem to know who I am. That shows great initiative on your part." She walked to the bottom step and held out her hand to him. It was a probe extending through some other dimensional tunnel from the world of fantasy to the world of reality. He looked at it for the longest time until it occurred to him he was expected to take hold of it. But as soon as he did, he realized he could never go back to his own world. The warmth of her fingers sent a shudder all the way to his heart.

"Your Royal Highness."

"I believe we've already established that, Monsieur Rogers."

"Yes, of course. You're right. What, ehr, what can I do for you?"

"I take it Madame Rogers didn't inform you of the meeting we have scheduled this morning."

"We have a meeting? I mean, perhaps she did. I have a terrible memory, and so many meetings."

"I understand. If I may sit?"

"Sit? Oh, I'm sorry. Yes, please do."

She sat on the large soft Liberty Print sofa that had been imported from London to make visitors to 'heaven' feel they were sinking into a flower-patterned cloud. To Bodge, she looked positively angelic amid the green petals. He ventured down to ground level and realized he was in the presence of royalty and he was wearing nothing but a bathrobe.

"Reverend," she said with the slightest of smiles on her lips. "You seem a little flustered. I hope my visit hasn't caused you any discomfort." Bodge stood behind a waist-high aspidistra to disguise his dishabille.

"No, no. I guess I'm not exposed to that many royal personages in New York." Of course he was supposed to have said Tennessee.

"Then you should relax. Royalty isn't really all it's cracked up to be. I'm flesh and bones, just like you."

"Hardly."

"I beg your pardon?"

Bodge's discomfort was interrupted by a ring at the front door. Bet sped past them and headed for the door, bending uncomfortably at the waist the whole way. School Director Petit handed her his umbrella as he walked in.

"Hope I'm not late," he said, bowing deferentially toward the consort. This made Bodge feel even more awkward in that he'd forgotten all he'd learned in his protocol class. And, at that moment, Stephanie, dressed impeccably in a wrap-around skirt and silk blouse strode down the staircase like an operatic diva. It appeared there was just the one attendee who hadn't been expecting this meeting. As they sat around the expensive lounge suite, Bodge whispered into his wife's ear.

"Didn't you forget to tell me about this?"

"No, I thought it would be a lovely surprise for you," she replied.

# Bleeding in Black and White

Bet, still doubled over like a shelf-hinge ran in with a tray of water glasses and a full pitcher, deposited them on the coffee table and was about to flee the scene when Hong told her to stop.

"My friend," she said in the girl's own language. "If you don't mind, I'd like you to attend this meeting as well." The teenager almost fell to the floor in shock. "Please," Hong added. Bet sat on a wooden chair by the table. "This will be our final meeting before the long process of official paperwork begins," Hong went on. "And I believe I have some good news for you all."

# 36

As a result of the pledges made that morning, Bodge found himself inextricably trapped in Ban Methuot. There were fewer and fewer convoys passing through, now. As they decreased, the chances of Bodge escaping lessened. But even if he'd been able to secure himself a place on one of the trucks, his promise to the second consort prevented him from leaving town until their work was done.

"I don't get the feeling we've started our stay here particularly low-key," he said to Stephanie as they ate one of her home made dinners that night.

"I couldn't really refuse the Emperor's consort, could I now?"

"She is something, isn't she?"

"Is that a sparkle I see in your eyes, Reverend Rogers?"

"Sorry, Mrs. Rogers."

"But I agree. She came to see me almost as soon as I arrived here. I know we aren't supposed to get ourselves tied up in domestic issues. But I enjoy a good fight and I didn't think it would hurt to be on friendly terms with our royal neighbors. Plus she isn't the easiest woman to refuse."

"You like her?"

"I like what I see. But I think that lady has more layers than I could ever start to unpeel. You keep away from her, Bodge. It sounds to me you're in enough shit already without that. You hear me?"

"Yes, ma'am."

If disaster hadn't struck as cruelly as it did, Bodge may well have avoided trouble right through to the dry season. But, although he had no idea at the time, the ill winds that had been gathering were all converging on Robert Bodge Leon.

It was a Friday. The rain had taken to coming on in the early evening and lulling the inhabitants of Ban Methuot to sleep. Apart from those with access to the Administration's generator, there was no electricity. Most families were guided by the setting and rising sun as to when to go to bed and when to rise. The Roger's chateau was outside the electricity quadrant so the house was a shimmering grotto of oil lamps.

Since the meeting the previous week, school's Inspector Petit had been the only regular visitor at the Rogers' house. Mademoiselle Hong had mysteriously disappeared so all their arrangements had been put on hold until they could find her. But Petit enjoyed discussing American literature with Stephanie and preferred the company of this couple to that of the French expatriates at the clubhouse. His English was very turn-of-the-century classic and Stephanie found herself adopting the same style when they spoke.

"Mr. Petit," Stephanie said. The three of them were in the dining room still sitting at the table enjoying an after-dinner port. "There is a mystery my husband and I can't seem to solve. Perhaps you could help?"

"I'll try, of course."

"Behind our house is a garish pink building with a leg sticking out of the roof." Even in the dim lamplight she could see him blush.

"That," he said, "is the House of the Eight-and-a-half Women." Bodge and Stephanie laughed.

"You might have to explain that," said Bodge.

"It is what I've read to be called a bawdy house. The owner is one Madame Vin, whom I'm told was once a very famous singer in Hanoi. She modeled her establishment on a grand bordello in Saigon named the House of the Five Hundred Girls. It's just that it's harder to get girls out here in the wilderness, especially with the French military ban on troops visiting the place."

"They don't let soldiers go to a brothel?" Stephanie asked with an astonished look on her face.

"The present Western commander, General LePenn, expressly forbids it. He's convinced the place is riddled with sexually transmitted diseases."

"And, is it?" Bodge asked.

"I'm sure I wouldn't know such a thing. Madame Vin does give her girls regular checks, so I hear."

"You've not been there yourself?"

A look came over Petit's face that suggested he was deciding whether or not to lie. He was, after all, in the company of workers of the Lord. "I may by chance have wandered in there on occasions."

Bodge smiled at Stephanie. "And what happened, when you wandered in there by chance?"

"I took the opportunity to look around, naturally. A teacher has to be a student of life."

"What did you see?"

"They have an area for smoking."

"Opium?"

"That's right. Then there's a section for flirting with young ladies."

"And short time rooms?" Stephanie asked.

Petit looked down at his empty plate. "I believe so."

"I'd always been led to believe that smoking opium and…flirting weren't the most compatible of pastimes. I've been told that opium quells the passions," Stephanie said with a studious expression.

"For which the girls are occasionally grateful — I should imagine." He took a large gulp of his port. This wasn't the type of topic he ever expected to be discussing with missionaries.

"Which leaves only one question then," Stephanie pushed onward. "I can understand that women would prefer to work in establishments such as this if there were a regular flow of randy servicemen to…service. So, as Ban Methuot has banned its soldiers from attending, Mme. Vin can find only eight girls. But I'm at a loss to understand where she might find a half woman."

"There is, so I believe," Petit offered, "a gentleman working at Madam Vin's who is of the belief he's actually a woman. He's afflicted with feminine mannerisms and dresses exactly as the women there."

"And does he pass as a woman?"

"He's probably the most beautiful person there. Most of the fights that occur at the house result from unsuspecting male suitors reaching the winning tape only to discover…"

"And have you reached that particular tape, M. Petit?" Stephanie asked.

"Madam Rogers, what type do you take me for?"

"An adventurous student of life: a man who revels in new experiences."

"I assure you, my dear lady, I am totally masculine."

"So you only sample the women there?"

"Absolutely."

Caught. Hoist by his own petard. The regional inspector of schools had just confessed to whoring to a Baptist wife in the House of the Pearly Gates. He was plainly devastated. "I mean…"

"Oh, for goodness sake, don't worry, M. Petit. We're all grown ups here."

"But you're—"

"We're of the modern breed of evangelists who don't crucify a man for being weak. But you will have to suffer a penance for your sin."

"I…? In what way?"

"Once we finish our desserts, you will take my husband to the House of the Eight-and-a-half Women."

"What?" Bodge arched his eyebrows at the same time.

"And you will introduce him to Madame Vin and the eight girls and the one gentleman who would that he were."

"But you are…he is…"

"M. Petit. Pray tell me, would a mechanic expect to repair an engine without lifting the hood to look inside?"

"No, but…"

"Then, how can a missionary expect to mend broken souls without tinkering around the depths of the low lives of society?"

Petit looked astounded. "And Mr. Rogers. You would agree to go into such a place?"

Bodge looked almost angelic. "Mrs. Rogers has always been my spiritual leader. She has often guideth'd me directly into the still waters. But she's invariably right. If she wants me to go to a whore house, to a whore house I shall go."

"Then, in that case, I shall visit your lavatory and prepare to do my missionary duty." Petit stood, bowed like a knight entrusted with a holy grail quest and walked off to the bathroom.

Bodge swung back on his chair and laughed. "Are you trying to get me laid?"

"Don't be vulgar. Of course not. Some of the best secrets are overheard in brothels. We adopt one or two of the girls into our holy family and we'll learn more about the war and the French administration in a few months than we could from two years of dinner parties at Le Residence. You don't really believe the military guys don't make dates outside bordello hours, do you now?"

"Your engine's always running, isn't it." His admiration for her grew stronger every day. She was constantly considering what was best for the mission, whereas Bodge hadn't even begun to. "You're certainly the real thing, Mrs. Rogers."

"I know."

Petit returned with his shirt newly tucked and his hair wetly slicked. Bodge rose to join him on their crusade.

"And I don't want you back before eleven," Stephanie said. She came round the table and gave Bodge a peck on the cheek.

"No, dear." Bodge smiled again and followed Petit out of the door.

# 37

From Reverend Cornfelt's observatory the pink house seemed very close. But in fact they had to circumnavigate the prison to get there as there was no access from this side. The gardens and fields were already flooded. The rain had settled into a semi-permanent drizzle that was pleasantly refreshing after one of Stephanie's home-cooked meals. Her first action in her new role had been to fire the guards, the gardener, and the fussy Vietnamese chef. Bodge and Petit walked in silence around the high whitewashed wall and were briefly challenged by the Montagnard guard in front of the gate.

They continued through a maze of small unlit huts that Petit negotiated quite expertly. The hovels were still decorated with bleached offerings and washed out pictures left over from the Tet Festival. There were small altars to household spirits here and there, even in front of the Catholic dwellings. Poor Vietnamese liked to cover all the bases.

The outside of the brothel had no moonlight to reflect its pinkness so it sat black against a black sky. Its leggy masthead was invisible, but the red curtains seemed to flicker as if a dangerous fire was raging out of control inside. To Bodge's surprise, a gramophone recording of Robert Johnson's music wafted out from the strip curtain that dangled in the doorway. As they neared it, he found that the music carried scents of incense and opium smoke and sweet perfume. It was an erotic cocktail that he found unnerving.

The area inside the doorway was lit with beeswax lamps wrapped in red silk. The town apparently had inspectors for everything except fire risk. There wasn't a receptionist. A first time visitor would have to try one of the three doors like an Alice arriving in Wonderland. But Petit knew his way around. The left-hand doors opened into a dark cavern of a room laid out with floor-level cots. Time had slowed in there. Even the smoke rising from the pipes seemed suspended as if in a photograph.

Out of nowhere a small Vietnamese man in black satin pajamas appeared beside them.

"Welcome, gentlemen," he whispered. Even his words seemed to stop on the air in front of his mouth. "This way please."

"Thank you," Petit said. "I'm just introducing a new friend to your establishment."

The Vietnamese was obviously overwhelmed by such polite French so he said again, "Welcome, gentlemen. This way please."

"We'll be back," said Petit, and led Bodge back out through the doors. "I realize a man such as yourself wouldn't be interested in artificial stimulation. Just thought I should give you the full tour." He opened the center doors onto a corridor of rooms that appeared to Bodge to be a prison block for very small offenders. "These, I believe, are short-time rooms to which a man can bring the girls for...well, I'm sure you understand."

"I can imagine," Bodge smiled. Being a missionary was going to be quite an enlightening experience.

"You're sure you want to meet the staff?" Petit asked.

"Absolutely."

"Then, follow me." Petit opened the final set of doors to reveal a huge lounge decorated like a somewhat tacky Chinese palace. The girls were dressed in *ao dai* but without the silk trousers. Their shoes were exact copies of the one that kicked heavenward from the roof, and their hair-dos sprouted magnificent blooms. Two hostesses were occupied with guests on the well-stuffed sofas, but the others appeared to be free and desperate. Spotting the two brave punters who'd ventured out in the rain, they stampeded toward the doors.

"Jackie, Jackie, Jackie," they twittered around Petit.

"They appear to know you," Bodge laughed.

"I...I've brought guests here before. These girls have incredible memories for names."

They were soon overwhelmed by a pungently sweet-smelling posy of heads. Bodge felt a hand reach for his crotch and immediately begin to undo the fly buttons there. His arms were held fast and he couldn't step away without crushing another flower. Petit saw what was happening and was enraged.

"No. No," he shouted. "Don't. Don't touch him. He is the new reverend. He is a man of God. He hasn't come for that. Unhand him."

The blossom in front of Bodge did unhand him, but not before discovering that the new reverend was well loved by his Lord and already semi-happy to be there. It was news that found its way around the garden in a rapid Vietnamese whisper. Bodge caught the drift of it but Petit had no idea. The reverend wasn't sure how to react. Perhaps he could argue that modern evangelism allowed its disciples to become aroused in the presence of half-naked whores.

"Hello, Big Reverend," said a demure young flower, her fingers locked in a Chinese salutation. A second girl branded a deliberately deep sign of the cross into her left breast with a finger — twice.

"We've come to see Madame Vin," said Petit, slapping hands away from his crotch.

"She's in the usual place," said one girl who was hanging unshakably from his arm. Bodge, still silent and aroused, followed his guide to the rear of the room. Madame Vin sat in a small cubby which reminded Bodge of the one in front of Bouncers in New York. She had a window that overlooked the service area and a slot for payment. She had her head down and was counting money when Petit rapped on the glass.

"Ahh," she shouted and erupted into an unnaturally large smile. The makeup cracked at the corners of her mouth. This was apparently her first smile of the evening. "Ma Cherie, M. Petit." She came out of her aquarium and hugged the Frenchman. "My girls were speaking of you just yesterday. They were saying how…"

"Actually," Petit interrupted, "I'm here to introduce you to the new Evangelical Missionary, Reverend Rogers."

She looked over Petit's shoulder and gave her second smile to Bodge. It was more delightful in the subdued lighting of the lounge. She glided over to him in her elaborate silks like a small upholstered battleship. She took his large damp hand between her small dry ones.

"M. Roger. I am so pleased to meet you. I am delighted you have honored us with your presence. You do speak French I hope?"

"Yes, I do," Bodge affirmed. "I'm pleased to meet the owner of such a colorful establishment."

"Ahh," she screamed. "But you speak it so beautifully, too."

"As do you."

"Ahh, you flatterer." She giggled like a young girl. Madame Vin had all the modest charms of a professional man-pleaser. "You know, I've always been of the belief that our two faiths should become more intimate."

"And, may I learn what your faith is, Madame Vin?"

"You certainly may, but I feel you probably know already. Ours are the two oldest doctrines, M. Roger: the worship of God and the worship of the body."

"There are those who would claim the two are incompatible."

"Are you not married, M. Roger?"

"Yes, I am."

"And do you not love her?"

"Passionately."

"And how do you show your love to her?"

"I read her poetry."

"Now, don't be coy, M. Roger. You know what I'm talking about. The worship of her vagina. Do you not worship your wife's vagina?"

"I probably wouldn't say 'worship'."

"Whenever you visit that temple between her legs, you are making an offering to God." The girls put their hands over their mouths and chuckled.

"I doubt Mrs. Rogers would see it that way," Bodge smiled.

"Really? But does she not shout, 'Oh God, Oh God' whenever you make your offerings?"

The girls now screamed with laughter and Petit hid a smile behind his palm. Bodge had no choice but to join in the mirth. "Madame Vin, allow me to buy you a drink so we can discuss this merger in more detail."

"Goodness, a man of God in the house of the devil drinking fire water from hell…"

"…With the daughters of Ho Chi Minh," came a mellow voice from one of the seats. The girls laughed again. A tall, incredibly beautiful woman there smiled but didn't divert her gaze from the elderly sales representative at her side. This, Bodge suspected, was the final half. He gazed down on the incredible sight of this elegant halfway creature before turning back to the hostess.

"The modern church believes you have to step into the ring with the devil before you can knock him out."

"You can step into my ring," said one of the girls.

"You see?" said Madame Vin. "You see these sinners? What can we do to bring them back to the path of righteousness?"

"I could probably find them a job in a post office," Bodge said. "A bank?"

"Oh, I've tried, M. Roger. But these girls have heads like broccoli, they only know three numbers. Isn't that right, Truc?"

Truc was probably the prettiest of the real women. "Yes, Madam. Hand job 15 piastres, sucking, 50 piastres, fucking, 100 piastres." The girls all applauded her recitation.

"You see, Reverend? What good would these numbers do her in a bank?"

"I'm sure it would lead to an increase in deposits."

At last, Madam Vin laughed. Cracks appeared all over. "Touché, and what a fitting adversary for my clever tongue. Come sit, Man of God, and tell me your life history. Feel free to wine and dine as many of my girls as you wish and I shall give you a first night discount. Maybe I'll even let you throw dice for the bill." She escorted Bodge and Petit to an empty copse of armchairs. "Truc, take off that funeral music and put on something with fire. Let's invite the devil for this bout."

During the few seconds of silence while Truc found some hotter music and placed the record on the gramophone, a long, agonized woman's scream sliced through the damp night and down the spines of the girls in the bordello. Madame Vin knew that neither of the men had noticed it because they were men, and only women were attuned to violence against their own.

# 38

Bodge's John Bull watch warned him that morning had arrived. Petit had long since returned from one of the tiny rooms where he'd helped Truc with her French. Bodge had thrown the dice for the bill (already he'd been submerged in vice and booze so gambling seemed like a modest sin to add to the list) and lost. As a result, the bill was doubled. Madame Vin reminded him what an insignificant fraction of his allowance it was, considering the number of potential converts he'd managed to get drunk. Everyone there had a much more positive view of the church as a result. Bodge was certain that most of Ban Methuot knew how obscene his mission budget was.

He'd only drunk modestly, and goodheartedly refused all the advances from the girls. As only one person there came anywhere close to his type, and she was a man, the temptations hadn't been hard to resist. Yet, somewhere, lurking behind his common sense like a city mugger in a dark alleyway, was a desire to self-destruct. Stephanie was a woman with stronger instincts for survival than anyone he knew. So Bodge was sure she understood he had the potential to foul up their mission. He wondered why she'd thrown him into the fire and brimstone at Madame Vin's. Perhaps she was tired. Perhaps she wanted to go home to a quiet retirement on a beach somewhere.

"The French refuse to drink this. They say it's real whisky diluted in horse piss," Madame Vin said as she handed him his change and a complimentary bottle of malt whisky.

"For me? Thank you."

"I would like to meet your wife, Robert."

"I'm sure she'd like to meet you too."

"She must be a very remarkable woman."

"That she is."

"And I know she loves you very much."

"How do you know that?"

"Because she trusts you alone in a room full of sexual goddesses such as myself."

"Obviously she didn't realize just how alluring you were."

At the double door she kissed Bodge on both cheeks. In the revealing light of the red reception area her makeup looked like the surface of some ancient planet. The trails of time beneath its crust told of its eons of history. But her eyes, trapped in their craters of mascara still glistened with the passion of a young temptress who had broken many hearts.

"Make sure my best customer gets home safely, please."

Petit was hung around Bodge's arm like a raincoat. "Isn't true," the Frenchman slurred. "Only I show visit people come." His English had fallen into a butter churn.

"Come, M. Petit," Bodge said. "The air will do us both good."

The girls waved goodbye while Bodge carried Petit into the slow drizzle of the early morning. Bodge wasn't about to lug him all the way across town. The pickled Frenchman would be the first overnight guest at the Pearly Gates.

His sense of direction was usually good, but the maze of shanties had Bodge turned this way and that until he somehow found himself arriving at his house from the rear. They pushed through the gap in the privet hedge and were suddenly at the edge of a large rectangular pond that had once been a vegetable allotment. The rear of the house stood before them with just the flicker of a downstairs lamp beckoning them forward. Yet, neither man moved. There was something foreboding about the silence that neither man could explain in words. Something was wrong. On the back porch, they removed their soaked shoes and opened the unlocked French doors. In the doorway Bodge found himself wiping his bare feet on the mat so as not to slip on the tiles. Petit followed suit. But the mat was already damp. They walked into the house and were confronted by the bitter smell of uncooked meat. It was eerily quiet. Bodge's first reaction was to head upstairs to see if Stephanie was okay, but they did a quick sweep of downstairs before climbing the stairs. Still they hadn't spoken. Bodge was tense, but he took the lamp from the living room table and led the way. On the top landing he stopped and held up his hand for Petit to stop also. Together they held their breaths to listen. There was the slow tapping of water drops onto the outside sills, and the loud ticking of the clocks. The teak steps behind them were uncreaking their knots, and that was all.

Bodge ignored the closed guestroom door and headed directly for the master bedroom where he hoped in his heart to find Stephanie sleeping soundly. Although she was normally in the habit of sleeping with the door and windows open, that door was shut also. He decided that bursting in to find her asleep and having to answer for himself was better than knocking and giving an intruder time to get out through the window. He counted down from three on his fingers and crashed through the unlocked door. Petit followed close behind.

Two more steps and they would have tripped over it, or worse, kicked it across the room. Bodge fell to his knees and dropped the lamp at his side. For Petit, after a night of excesses, such a discovery was too much. He turned behind the door and emptied his stomach. That stench quickly mixed with others: with blood, with flesh, and with the remnants of indescribable violence. It was a scene that would doubtless return to haunt both men far into old age.

# 39

There had been loose tongues at the Residence dinner table. Mme Dupré was sulking again at the shortage of men. "There don't even seem to be any soldiers in the town these days."

M. Dupré had looked up forlornly from his soup. He'd become attuned now to his wife's interest in other men, and, although he had no evidence, he had more than a sneaking suspicion that her desires had gone beyond her imagination. His jealousy was all consuming. Recently, she'd been talking about attending the English Bible classes at the home of the new missionaries. He was certain the arrival of this Bible thumping John Wayne had prompted an awakening of her single soul. Now she was missing soldiers.

"The rains have come early," he said sulkily. "The men's leave has been brought forward so they can go home and relax with their wives and children away from the rigors of war."

"Well, have they all gone?"

"No."

"How many?"

Dupré wondered how many she thought she might need but resisted saying so. He'd looked over at Tran who sat blandly in one corner of the room. He'd been drafted in at meal times to solve problems with the serving Montagnard. He sat as still and expressionless as the table candelabra.

"A large number," Dupré confessed.

"God. Our throats will be slashed by the Reds as we sleep." She held her throat. "How could you let them all go?"

"Relax, dearest. They haven't all gone. The garrison's to the north and south are still partially manned."

"And to the east? Isn't there a track through the mountains that passes Lac Lake and the emperor's lodge? What's to stop them coming that way?"

"It isn't in their nature. Too many mountains. The Vietnamese have a real fear of the highlands. They believe the water is tainted and the spirits are evil there."

"How can you be so sure?"

"Monique, my little flower, allow me to educate you as to the intricacies of war in the tropics. Basically, the rainy season is a hiatus in Indochinese conflicts. The armies rest, re-arm, keep dry, return to their villages and make babies to fight in the next war. Nobody attacks anyone in the monsoons. Even the skeleton guard at Pleiku and Dak Song will be untroubled at least until August. Believe me, if there were a need to safeguard the Lac pass, General LePenn would have reinforced it before he left."

"Hell! Even the General's gone? Who's running the show now then?"

"I imagine Captain Faboir."

"God help me. My life's in the hands of a mere captain."

"Trust me. We're as safe as the French Empire." He looked at her eating like some farm animal; uncultured, uncivilized, and with the sudden return of her "monthly condition", once again untouchable.

# 40

Bodge and Petit lay in parallel cots at the *clinique*. Dr. Moncur had decided they'd benefit from a strong sedative each to counteract the trauma. Bodge had certainly been shocked and repulsed, but he wouldn't have considered himself traumatized. He'd been in control enough to notice several details the police missed.

He thought back to his arrival in the master bedroom. In the dim glow of lamplight, the scene had almost turned itself to gray without his help. Stephanie's hand had greeted its guests from the center of the rug with its fingers beckoning. With its nerves and veins and arteries still attached, but its arm missing, it looked like an electrical attachment that had been ripped from an appliance. The rest of the room resembled the floor of an abattoir. Her parts were scattered. Her sensible nightdress in shreds. Bet's body lay at the end of the bed still in one piece but with its neck torn open and clotted with blood.

At first, Bodge assumed they'd been hacked to death with a sword or an axe, but then he'd heard the gurgle from the bathroom. He walked, stunned, through the carnage to see what was there. The tiger had still been alive then; huge, a beautiful animal. It filled the tiled floor space like a marvelous fur quilt and looked up at Bodge with sad, almost pleading eyes. From its neck protruded the end of a long silver corkscrew. The trail of its blood ran from the wound and down its white bib.

Bodge had been able to see the events quite clearly, as if he'd been there in the room when they happened. The tiger had arrived as if from nowhere and pounced. It locked its fangs around Stephanie's neck. With the only weapon she had at hand, she'd buried the bedside corkscrew into its throat. Enraged, the enormous animal had shaken her like a dog with a rag. It had broken her in its fearful jaws, and, once certain its prey was dead, had begun its feast. Bet had come to help the woman who had shown her kindness and been dispatched for her trouble.

Slowly, the tiger's own life's blood was oozing from it until, dazed, disoriented, it staggered into the bathroom and collapsed. Bodge had knelt beside the beast and stroked its head without fear of its power. It had only seconds to live and he realized there was no blame. The animal had hunted successfully but was felled in battle by a worthy adversary. It deserved its proud death.

There had been chaos then. Police came and military. Montagnard guards were placed all round the house to keep back sightseers. Bodge, remembering his role, had adopted the same vacuous trance as Petit beside him there on the downstairs couch. Police sympathized and squeezed his shoulder and whispered together and nodded in his direction. No, Bodge wasn't traumatized, but he was distraught for his lover and a girl who had already known so much sadness in her life. And he felt sorrow for himself. The curse was continuing. There could be no connection between this death and those in the US. He was the only common thread that strung the victims together. *He* killed people. He infected them with his black luck. And the thought that ran through his mind there in his tainted house was whether he dared befriend anyone else: whether he was condemned to maintaining a distance from people for fear of loving them and, accordingly, of killing them.

And, of course, he observed. He observed the officers coming and going in their wet boots, making trails that hadn't been there. He observed two small slivers of flesh, one very close to Bet's room beside the kitchen. He observed the large gouge that had been taken out of the wooden porch. He observed the sleek gray trunk of the Yao tree whose leaves fanned at Stephanie's window. Before Dr. Moncur drove the two stunned witnesses to the *clinique*, Captain Henry had made a summation of events for their benefit. Bodge knew it was incorrect.

"I'm so sorry, Monsieur," he said. "But it is one of the reasons we try to insist that foreign nationals hire guards at all times. The tigers are drawn to the towns when hunger sets in. Your house was an easy target. But, if it makes you feel any better, I believe your wife wouldn't have felt a thing. It was swift."

Bodge had smiled politely. He imagined Stephanie's horror with the tiger's teeth clamped on her neck. She would instinctively have sensed the finality, even as she stabbed it pathetically with the last of her strength. He looked up at the policeman.

"How did it get in?" he asked.

"How? Probably through the door and up the stairs."

It was as if the "how" didn't matter to him. It was as if a five hundred pound tiger could walk through a garden of mud and climb a flight of stairs without leaving a trail. It had been there and had killed the missionary's wife — that was all there was to be said. Perhaps that was why Captain Henry had been banished to this remote outpost of the colony to do his policing.

# 41

Bodge left the *clinique* in the morning. He was in danger of drowning in the syrupy wishes of goodwill. People he'd never seen before began to fulfill their neighborly obligations beginning at six thirty. It was as sincere as you'd expect from foreigners who were perhaps truly shocked by the tragedy, but who knew neither the American victim nor her husband. *"How must he feel?" "They'd been together for so many years." "I've heard they were inseparable."* So, the wives came, and representatives of various offices, to offer their condolences and take a look at the survivor. There was only one visitor he hoped to see but she too had vanished from his life without word. Bodge had to get away.

Still drowsy from the drugs, he dragged his feet through the puddles, along the main street of the town in the direction of his house. He pretended not to hear the cyclos and the kids selling hand-rolled cigarettes. He went through the market and took time to browse; the cured pig snouts, the ducks' heads in batter, the rancid butter and pastries with their extra crust of flies. None of this affected him because he'd just seen a lover torn to shreds. The Vietnamese shopkeepers ignored him, as always, but he could tell they knew who he was and what had transpired the previous night. News was like a monsoon wind in Ban Methuot. It blew through the town so suddenly you couldn't turn your face from it.

At his house, he unlocked the front door and walked inside. The place was spotless. It reminded him of Lou's apartment in New York after its secret invasion. There were fresh orchids in jars he didn't remember, and the air was pungent with the scents from small baskets of potpourri placed here and there around the room. He imagined the Ban Methuot wives club with their handkerchiefs wrapped round their faces, dusting and primping and looking through drawers, pretending to be erasing unhappy memories from the house. He knew their effort was as much to make themselves feel better as him. He wanted each and every one of them thrown in irons. He collected the baskets and threw them into the trash can. He knew upstairs would have been scrubbed and carbolic'ed. There was probably a generously donated rug and a new mattress untainted by the congealed blood of a massacred woman.

A note on the entrance table was from Mme. Dupré, the wife of the Administrator. It said how sorry she was and informed him there were spare rooms at the Residence if he couldn't bear to stay in this house with all its memories. Bodge wanted space and time to himself. He had a lot of thinking to do. If, by some warp of time, he were to find himself back at his desk, he vowed he'd never complain again about having nothing to tax his mind. His life was so turned around he didn't know which way was forward. He didn't really believe he'd done anything to warrant all this upheaval. He'd certainly made no mistakes as far as he could…He put his hand to his cheek and felt the wetness. The tears had begun to flow without wishing to trouble him, but once discovered there was no ignoring them. He stood in the center of the room and sobbed until his throat hurt. He put his hand across his eyes and bawled until they were dry.

What he did next might have counted as his first mistake. In fact it was the worst thing he could have done. The bottle of Jim Beam he'd been given by Madame Vin was sitting on the drinks cabinet. Without thinking, he poured a large shot into a tumbler. He didn't bother to open a soda. He threw back the drink, poured a second and walked upstairs. Thus began his slide.

It started, like all defeats, with a period of over-confidence. To unjumble all the memories, he had to go back to the beginning. In the movies they always said, "I know I've missed something. I know the answer's right here in front of me." But this was no movie and if there were something obvious he would have found it by now.

There had been no convoys for a week so his chances of getting away were remote. Still if the rain held off for a few days, he might catch a ride with someone coming through town. As he thought, he paced the landing. The upstairs doors were shut. He didn't bother to look in the master bedroom because he knew what to expect. He could already smell the bleach from the bathroom. He opened the bureau and found a pad of lined paper and a pen. These he took to the soft leather chair. On his pad he wrote four questions;

*Was L homosexual?????*
*What happened to Casual Carpets and PJ?????*
*Who attempted to kill me with the car bomb and WHY??*
*Why was I hustled out of the office (and the country)????*
Then, as an afterthought, he added a fifth,
*Can tigers climb trees?????*

He looked up for the reservoir of answers to impossible questions and found himself gazing out of the large window. The leg atop Madame Vin's stood out against a cloud the shade of a heavy bruise. The first drop of the latest round of rains splattered onto the glass pane. It was the prelude to an onslaught — large globs that seemed to have a score to settle with the window. Monsoon rain had attitude. It thudded onto the roof and against the walls, and day and dusk suddenly changed places.

And, behind him, the bedroom door handle turned slowly and the door opened.

# 42

**Saigon**

"It's raining, or haven't you noticed?" The emperor stood in his tennis whites and a blazer, frustrated again by a sudden downpour.

Hong sewed in her favorite chair and didn't look up. She was angry that he'd forced her to return unexpectedly to the capital and was not expecting to return with her next week. Everything depended upon her being in Ban Methuot. "But *you're* going."

"I know *I'm* going. But there's good reason for me to be going. There's good hunting to be had in the rains. The animals are confused. It's why I had the new hunting trail graveled — enough of it anyway — so I could hunt in the rains."

"I want to be with you," she pouted but still didn't look up.

He was afraid she was about to cry. He threw his racquet onto the sofa and walked across to her. She rarely expressed a desire for him, but when she did he found her irresistible. He knelt in front of her.

"And I want you with me. I'm just afraid you'll be bored at the lodge. Think of all those long days without me there."

"I'll have Lan."

The Emperor closed his eyes in disgust. "Do you really have to keep her around? Look what she's become."

"She's my friend."

"She'll lead you into bad ways."

Hong laughed. "My Emperor, it's the other way round. She didn't smoke or drink before I taught her how."

"But you had the character and strength of will to pull yourself out. She's a country girl."

"I hope you have nothing against country girls, sir. For, I trust you remember — I'm one too."

He leaned forward and kissed her lips gently. She allowed it even though there was a servant standing in the doorway. "You are many things, some of which I haven't yet worked out, but you are certainly a lady."

"So I may come?"

He laughed "Yes, yes, I suppose so. And bring your addict with you."

"I should like to transfer money to the Administrator's office in Ban Methuot."

"What on earth do you need money for in the jungle?"

"I should like to commission an extension for the lodge."

"In the wet season?"

"If you can hunt, I'm sure they can build. The tradesmen will be grateful for the work."

"What do you have in mind?"

"It's a surprise, in honor of your next birthday and the thirtieth anniversary of your coronation."

He looked into her devious eyes. He hadn't learned to read them but he was sure he saw excitement about this project. She was softening to him gradually. One day he might even hope she could love him. How could he do or say anything to endanger that possibility? And what was money to him? If it made her happy she could have it all.

"Talk with the head of the treasury."

She put her arms around his neck and smiled. "And they say you're a tyrant."

"Who? Who says that?"

"All the girls who've been beneath your sheets."

"Ah, then it might just be true."

# 43

Monique Dupré stood in the doorway of the master bedroom rubbing sleep from her eyes like a small child or, more accurately, a stage actress pretending to be eleven. When he heard the creak of the door, Bodge had looked back over his shoulder. His shocked eyes were met with the sight of the Administrator's wife in her frilly pink underwear coming out of the bedroom; the bedroom of his very recently departed wife. She looked surprised but by no means startled to see Bodge sitting there in the armchair. She made only a cursory attempt to cover her brassiere with her forearm.

"M. Roger," she said. "You're here." Because of who she was and who he was supposed to be, even though she was an enjoyable sight, Bodge averted his eyes. "I was certain you'd be at the *clinique* all day. I'm sorry, I…"

"Mme. Dupré," Bodge said, staring at his knees. "Wouldn't it perhaps be more appropriate if you got dressed before we continued this conversation?"

"What? Oh, yes. Of course." But she didn't hurry back into the room. "We were cleaning your house early this morning, I'm sure you noticed. It appears I was overcome with fatigue. I do apologize for surprising you like this."

Once she was certain Bodge wouldn't be looking at her again, she went into the room and shouted from there. "It was very rude of me to use your bed. I'm sure I don't know what came over me. I didn't want to crinkle my robe so I hung it in your wardrobe. I noticed…"

She walked back into the landing area, still buttoning her bodice, only to find that Bodge had gone. She walked down the staircase and discovered him standing in the center of the living room. "There you are. I was saying I noticed the wardrobe only contains your wife's clothes. I thought that was a little odd."

"I dress in the guest room. My clothes are there. My wife likes…liked to have her own wardrobe."

"I see. For a moment there I thought…Oh, never mind. Silly idea." She looked dramatically at the grandfather clock. "Goodness, it can't be that time already."

Bodge took a step toward the door. "It was very kind of you to come by."

"Nonsense. We're all foreigners in a heathen country, M. Roger. We have to offer what support and solace we can to our own kind in times such as this. Are you certain you don't want to come and stay at the Residence?"

"Yes, I am. Thank you."

"Then I'll just have to pay you visits here."

"That really isn't necessary."

"Of course it is. You've just lost your loved one. The last thing you should do is mope around here alone. You need company."

"I'd far prefer to mope around alone, at least for a few weeks. But, thank you for the offer."

A tear miraculously appeared at the corner of her eye, as if on cue, and rolled down her red cheek. "You poor, poor man. How must you be feeling? Forgive me."

Before he could forgive her, she had him locked in a sisterly embrace. It was what the people back home would have called a hug, but in this case it felt like some erotic slow dance. Her orangey breasts were crushed against his stomach and the scent of oil rose from her hair. He stood with his arms loosely by his sides and thought of Kilpatrick's Sliced Bread and what a marvelous, time-saving invention it was for the average North American housewife. Thankfully, the thought diverted him from an erection.

At last, Monique pulled away and did nothing to disguise her frown of disappointment. There was no doubt in Bodge's mind that this was a dangerous minx. A good-looking and lethal one at that. If he could get her out of the door he'd bolt it. He wondered what there could possibly have been in his missed orientation program to numb a field agent against circumstances such as these. She was armed with some kind of libidinous kryptonite that made him feel ashamed and weak.

"Well then, I shall go." she said. "If there's nothing else I can do for you..."

"Absolutely nothing. Thank you so much. The Lord blesses you for your kindness."

"Does he? I'm pleased."

She walked to the door and allowed him to open it for her. She shook his hand, gave a vaguely cryptic smile, and rocked her backside down the front path with his pilfered umbrella up against the storm.

For the next twenty-four hours, Bodge was able to keep himself isolated. In the beginning, despite his posted note; 'In mourning. No visitors.' people had hammered on his front door. He'd heard the voices of Petit and Monique and Captain Henry calling up to him from the front stoop. He'd heard coins tapping on the glass doors at the rear, so loudly he was sure the glass would shatter. The rains fell incessantly and, eventually, drowned the enthusiasm of his callers.

On the afternoon of whatever day it was, he was sitting, as usual, in Cornfelt's leather chair looking at the gray view between the rain trails. The drips were the races at Belmont. He had his life savings on a small dribble in the left hand lane. He'd been watching it for several hours so perhaps it was a series of drips. Perhaps his concentration was shot. Since returning from the *clinique*, the depression had seeped into him. He'd countered it with booze, but his misery was stronger. He'd worked his way through everything in the drinks cabinet and various unidentified bottles from the cellar.

He'd lied to himself about his reaction to Stephanie's death, pretended he wasn't wounded. Instead of openly mourning, he let it work its way through him like mildew. In the beginning he was depressed because people wouldn't leave him alone. When they left him alone he started to be depressed because nobody cared. In his effort to drink himself happy, he hadn't had time to sleep. He'd eaten what was available in cans but had gradually lost the ability to negotiate their opening. He was depressed because he was tired and hungry. And he was angry now, and that made him more depressed. His weakness made him angry, and anger made his depression total and irreconcilable. He decided that his misery couldn't be complete without someone to share it with. He needed company, desperately.

He had to smash the lock on his back doors because he couldn't remember where he'd put the key. It felt grand to be out in the rain, the black sky curling around him like a hypnotic python. He set off, walking, crawling, staggering, falling often, in search of friendship. He'd forgotten totally that his friendship killed people.

# 44

There were moments.

Dark. Dark, but cozy and wrapped in smells and smoke and ignorance. Fireflies here and there, or candles. A low table with dried fruit, tiny tea cups. An ache in his side as if he'd been lying for hours — days — forever. A mesh net around him, darned in one place. The gathering like a fairy's star. No sound but for a single cough, not his own. No movement. No ideas. Emptied of thoughts and purged of worries and responsibilities. This was the numbness he'd sought. He smiled and reached for the shadow of the fairy star, and slept.

A long-fingered hand stroking his face. A voice deep as an unwanted old memory.

Laughter and sweat. Tears and perfumed beers and sweet opium, caramel fragrance, hashish. Yes, more. Hot moths. Coverless books. Chocolate concubines. The bitter taste of tin. The embarrassment of vomit, of trying to light an empty pipe, of his own smell, of forgetting his name. Seeing stars in the day sky, being able to take handfuls of darkness and mould it into shapes. Yes, more.

A scream. A fight. A flight.

Light. A faint smell of bleach and perfumed oil. A chandelier like a firework frozen in crystal above him. An electric chandelier in a house with no electricity. A dull wooziness in his head, long phrases of frightening daydreams — daymares. One of them of flesh beside him, taut, intense flesh. Two people in his wife's bed and he recognizes neither. They melt together, and thrash and pummel and stop, wet with sweat. Yes, more. Not his voice. Reach. Reach for the flesh and restart the process. Yes, more. When it's over, throw up again.

And again.

And again.

The slam of a door. The slam of a head. Still light when his eyes open. To the chandelier. Bodge was alone and naked and in pain. He needed a drink the way winos on the Bowery needed booze to keep breathing. His mouth was Nevada after the A bombs. He edged his way off the bed and swayed to the bathroom. Wondered why there was no tiger skin on the floor, wondered who the beast was in the mirror. A horror. How many days of growth on its face? How many pipe rings of opium around its eyes, and blood tendrils of liquor in its cheeks?

He gulped water from the tap, careful not to look again into the glass. This was no time to pull himself together. He needed a drink. The door to the hallway was gone. It threw him into a panic till he realized — of course, he was in the bathroom. He stumbled back to the bed. There, on the bedside table, a bottle, a full bottle, open and ready. He sat on the floor propped up against the bed and worked on that bottle — worked on it like an artisan. It mattered not a jot what was in it.

He drank.

And sat.

He was still sitting there, in the dark now, when he heard the front door. Beyond the open bedroom doorway was the staircase, and he saw a halo of lamplight rising from the ground floor. Monique's face behind the flame was almost saintly. Evil and saintly. She came into the bedroom and knelt beside him.

"I see you're wearing my favorite suit," she smiled. Bodge looked down and noticed he was still naked. Realized he could understand French. She put the lamp on the table and reached for his penis. He watched her play as if he were in a fifty cent dirty picture house. Watched himself become aroused but felt nothing. "My darling husband is in Pleiku for the night. I can enjoy this till morning," she said. "But you smell. Come and take a shower."

Without question or protest, Bodge rose on numb legs and she helped him into the bathroom. He had become exactly what she wanted. The opium had worked its way out of his system but she'd been able to keep him topped up with alcohol, and today she had a new devil for him. It had arrived via the *Sureté* for the attention of the Administrator. A marvelous new drug, highly addictive. Her husband informed her it was technically called Lysergic Acid Diethylamide. Unless someone came up with a more fashionable name, it would be known as LSD. A stash of it had been confiscated from French troops who'd apparently bought it in

Saigon from a journalist. It had been left with the Administrate keeping.

As Monique had access to the safe, there wasn't a great de... of the stuff left. She found the effects particularly arousing, and decided to add it to her slave's cocktail of intoxicants. It was a decision that would prove to be her undoing. For an hour, Bodge tumbled around in its current like a fool in a Technicolor Electrolux washer and spin drier. But when he came out of it, he was ironed out and folded into an angry paranoia. While Monique slept off her high, he showered again, dressed, and sat in the leather chair, working his way through the last of the bourbon.

He extinguished the lamp flame, found the Luger, and went to the bedside. She was to blame. This one. She had no right to live.

# 45

Madame Vin recalled that there had been three shots in all. Why should she come forward with such information? Gunshots were common enough, and she had no idea at the time where they'd come from. The first had woken her. The second and third came a minute or so later. There'd been no screams, police whistles, or sounds of fleeing. She looked at the luminous dials of her alarm clock. It was 3 AM exactly. That's how she remembered. One shot for each hour. She yawned, and swore, and fought her way back into her dream. Women like Madame Vin needed all the beauty sleep they could get.

Indeed, there was no mystery reported for the first three office hours the following morning. Nobody at the Residence was surprised that Madame Dupré hadn't come downstairs for her breakfast. She often slept late. As Monsieur Dupré was in Pleiku, the breakfast things were still there untouched at eleven fifteen. The servants cleared them away and prepared the table for lunch.

The acting administrator, one Monsieur Desailly, a pale-faced career clerk in his late fifties, had come in from the district office to man the fort while the Administrator was away. It was in the regulations that there had to be someone of level four or above in situ at all times. But without phone lines or telegraph, there had been no urgent business that called for his attention. He dealt with a minor inquiry from Duc, the Montagnard coordinator, and gave permission for the plumbing engineer to re-chlorinate the water tank. He then sat at Dupré's desk and worked on a three-month old crossword in Le Figaro.

The butler came and asked his advice on whether they should awaken Mme. Dupré for lunch. Desailly thought it wise to knock and see whether she was unwell. As the butler was leaving the office, a guard passed him in the doorway. He saluted and informed the acting administrator that an armed jeep had just arrived from Pleiku and a garrison lieutenant would like to speak to Administrator Dupré.

Desailly wasn't surprised, given the difficulties of communication, that wires had somehow gotten crossed. What did surprise him was that the captain hadn't noticed the Administrator's convoy on his way south. There was only one road. He walked out to the covered front porch where the jeep stood dripping like a large muddy hippo. The lieutenant, a large-chested Breton, obviously didn't know Dupré by sight.

"Administrator?" he saluted. "We're here to escort you to the Northern garrison."

"No, Lieutenant. I'm not Dupré," Desailly told him. "He left already,"

"Left? For where?"

"Why, for Pleiku. The convoy left yesterday morning. He should have arrived by now."

"Sir, the convoy arrived yesterday as planned."

"Well, then."

"But the Administrator wasn't with it."

"Of course he was. I saw him off myself."

"I understand he left with the convoy, but it appears, on the way, he ordered his driver to take him to a Montagnard village off the main road. The rest of the convoy was instructed to carry on without him. They were told he'd catch up. But he never did. We assumed he'd returned here."

"He left the convoy? But that's...that's..."

"Crazy, sir."

"Exactly."

"The Administrator suggested the rains would prevent an ambush. The Viet Minh wouldn't expect anyone to be traveling in the monsoon."

"That's awful. He didn't come back here."

"Are you sure?"

"Am I sure? Don't be ridiculous. Of course I'd know whether the Administrator returned or not. What village did he go to?"

"R13. We stopped off there on our way down."

"And?"

"They didn't see anything."

"Or, so they say." Desailly shook his head. "Lieutenant, I want you to go to the southern garrison. You tell them what you've told me and get them to pull together as many men and vehicles as possible. Tell the acting commander there we need to launch a search of the area around R13 immediately."

"With respect, sir. That would be an army decision."

"With no respect, Lieutenant. There are no senior military people in the region and the Government representative has vanished. If your army has a better idea, let me hear it now. If not, get your ass over to the garrison."

The army man paused for a second, then nodded. "Yes, sir."

"I'll go see Captain Henry of the Gendarmérie. This is awful. Just awful."

The lieutenant climbed into his dirty jeep and looked up at the sky. "The roads are in a terrible state. Most of the bridges are out. If these rains keep up, the rivers will be too deep to ford and we'll be cut off."

"Then get a move on, son."

"Sir."

As the jeep splashed off through the puddles, Desailly headed for his own truck. There was no key in the ignition and the driver was nowhere to be found. The man hadn't expected to work while his boss was in the office. Desailly yelled at the top of his voice. His shouting brought out everyone but the driver. Soon, the servants and the Administration staff, caught up in the new atmosphere of panic, were running back and forth in search of the errant driver. As Desailly stood waiting in the drizzle, a Montagnard chamber maid walked nervously up to him and bowed.

"What is it?"

"Mme. Dupré," she said.

"What about her?"

"She no here."

"No where?"

"No in room. No in bed. No sleep in bed."

"Ee, gods. What on earth's going on here? They're both missing?" The driver appeared from down the road, still buttoning his uniform shirt. "Lord! What have I done to deserve a day like this? What have I done?"

# 46

By mid-afternoon, every vehicle from the Ban Methuot garrison had left to scour the countryside for the missing Administrator. Many had spent their time getting stuck in mud or slithering off the road into trees. Only five men remained at the base.

In the town, Inspector Henry and his men had the task of locating the Administrator's wife. Henry and his sergeant had begun by visiting the expatriate wives in their homes. His first two interviewees said they had no idea where Madame Dupré might be, although both were lying through their teeth. Henry wasn't much of a policemen, but he could tell the women were holding something back, something important. They didn't seem nearly concerned enough that Mme. Monique had vanished.

It wasn't until his third house call that he got an answer. He was at the house of Mme. Moncur, wife of the doctor. She was in her sixties, prickly as a cactus and had no love for what she called the ladies of the expatriate wife pack. She was particularly hostile towards the Administrator's wife who she considered a tramp in fine lace. Although most of the women agreed, this was far too honest for small town domestic politicians so they kept their distance from Mme. Moncur.

"You don't seem very surprised that Mme. Dupré is missing," Henry said. He sipped his ice lemon while his Vietnamese sergeant, Officer Nga, stood in full uniform and thirsty behind the couch.

"I'm not."

"Then, perhaps you might know where she is?"

She laughed. "How many single men are there around Ban Methuot, Inspector?"

"Madame! I hope you aren't insinuating…" He cast a glance at his sergeant.

"No, Henry. I'm not. It's an outright statement. The woman's a whore. I'm surprised she hasn't bedded you, yet. Or perhaps…"

He let out a sort of growl and glared at the old woman. There had been advances, but Henry, given his position, was forced to play the small town community deaf and blind game. "Unlike yourself I'm not one for rumors Mme. Moncur. I'm a policeman. I rely on hard evidence."

"You'll no doubt find hard evidence between Mme. Dupré's lovely thighs this very minute."

"Mme. Moncur, I'm surprised at you. I don't feel this type of talk is appropriate when referring to the wife of our Administrator."

"Well, then stop asking me questions. More lemonade?"

"No. Thank you. If you have any specific information as to Mme. Dupré's exact location, I would appreciate such information."

"Why is it always the police are the last to know?"

"To know what?"

"About the *rescue* of the American missionary from the whore house."

"Rescue? What rescue? He was held captive? What are you saying?"

"He was held captive by his grief and his sudden dependency on opium to get him through it. It wouldn't have done him any harm. I'd have let him stay there till he'd worked it out of his system. I certainly wouldn't have gone in there with the morality cavalry blowing its trumpets. But our great leader's wife went in with her salvation army to save his soul...for herself."

"You weren't with them?"

"Goodness, no. I know what the motivation was for the rescue."

"And what was that?"

"Come on, Inspector. Don't pretend you're as naïve as you look. The she-cat sent all the other wives away and stuck around the house to... nurse him back to health."

"You surely can't believe she..."

"A big muscly American — still young enough to mate — suddenly unattached."

"But, his wife has only recently died."

"Opium and alcohol have their own ways of interpreting the mourning process. Trust me."

It was a difficult call for Henry to make. He didn't want to show up at the Missionary's house and disturb Madame Dupré *in flagrante delecto*. But he also needed to eliminate that particular lead before looking elsewhere. So, he did what all good investigators do. He sent his sergeant.

After knocking at the door for several minutes and getting no reply, Sgt. Nga walked around to the back. He knew the layout of the grounds well as he'd accompanied Henry on the day of the tiger attack. He was a wise old policeman who, were it not for the French hierarchy, would have been a chief inspector by now. Instead, he languished in the depths of the lower ranks, constantly held back by French officers who feared his potential. Henry knew that Nga probably had other views about Mrs. Rogers' death, so he hadn't asked.

At the back of the house, Nga knew he was in trouble. He walked into the type of tension that surrounds places where bad things have happened. He'd found himself in them often in his career. The rear door was open again, but this time the glass was smashed. He took his pistol from its holster. Being a sergeant, he'd normally have a couple of young recruits in front of him in situations like this to catch bullets, but Henry had insisted he come alone, 'so as not to cause the wife of the Administrator undue embarrassment'. Right now he was more concerned about causing himself undue death.

He stood on the rear step and looked in at the shadowy interior. There was no shortage of footprints this time leading into and out of the house. Before taking a deep breath and going in, he glanced back at the yard. It was like a paddy field with rotting plants poking limply from the water. Something… something he couldn't put his finger on, was different about that yard. It hadn't looked like this the last time he saw it. But that would have to wait.

Despite all the mess, he removed his boots. He didn't want to be clunking around on the tiles. He skirted around the muddy footprints and walked silently into the house. Something or some body had rampaged through the lower floor like an elephant in heat. Fine antiques were shattered, expensive oils were slashed, and the beautiful old grandfather clock Nga had looked upon with envy during his last visit was smashed irreparably.

He picked his way through the debris, still careful not to make a sound. There were traces of liquid that could have been oil or paint or blood. It was hard to tell against the dark floor, but in such a situation, a man's mind invariably chooses the darkest possibility. He felt sure that every step he took would be his last. He edged his way up the staircase with his pistol shaking between his fists. If he'd held it in just one hand it would probably have leapt from his grasp.

The last time he'd gone up this staircase, he'd witnessed the awful mess that was left of the missionary's wife. He doubted any sight could better that for sheer terror, but on that day he'd been told what to expect. He hadn't been alone. He'd known the danger had passed. This time he didn't. The top landing was in no less of a mess than downstairs. As his head rose above the floorboards, he could see into the master bedroom. He could see the bed. A woman's legs were stretched out on it. After all the noise it took to wreck the house, he doubted she was sleeping.

Still silent, hopefully unnoticed, he cleared the final step and walked to the bedroom. His gun was thrust so far forward it seemed he could barely reach it. He followed it through the doorway. The sight on the bed took his old breath away. The thought of there being some maniac alone with him in the house suddenly took flight like a flock of bats. Mme. Dupré, as naked as the Venus, was laid out on the silk sheet like a banquet. Her breasts looked so delicious it was several seconds before Nga's eyes passed beyond them to the large gaping hole in her forehead. Incredibly, her face smiled politely as if to be apologizing for the mess.

For Nga, this was a sight more disturbing than that of his previous corpse. Then, he'd been able to go home and describe to his wife every gory detail. But how could he return this evening and tell her he'd been stimulated by the sight of the dead wife of the Administrator?

He looked in the bathroom, the guest room, and the storage alcove, but his instincts already told him he'd seen the worst. It was his duty now to drive to the Sureté and break the news which would launch a stampede of officials and experts and gawkers. So, before he did so, he sat in the bedroom on the pink cloth-coated dressing table stool and stared at his corpse in its last moments of privacy. He enjoyed the silence of the house whose horror had been frozen in time.

Finally, he went downstairs and paused in the rear doorway to put on his boots. He looked again at the flooded yard. What was it? What had changed? Something was missing. Surrounding the garden was a tall wooden fence. The previous tenants had segregated the vegetable patches into varieties — peas here, tomatoes there, squash and beans. And they'd imprisoned each species behind smaller fences like zoo animals. The fence slats were sawn to a point and protruded defiantly from the water, but not all. That was it. One entire line of fencing was gone. But if it had merely fallen down, surely it would now be floating on the surface.

Nga still hadn't gotten around to putting on his boots. He was wondering, with all the valuables inside the unlocked house, why anyone would bother to steal a length of fence. He waded through the tepid water to the place he was sure the fence had been, and felt around carefully with his naked feet. Sure enough, he found the fence flat on the mud. What, he wondered, could be holding it down? He moved sideways along the fencing until his foot touched something large and soft. He reached down with his hands and was left with no doubt as to what he'd found.

The body under the water was heavy and appeared to be held fast there. It was as if it were somehow nailed to the ground. He found a belt around its waist and heaved with all his might until suddenly it was surrendered by its tether. It bobbed to the surface sending Nga backwards, splashing into the water. He didn't hurry to get up. He sat and looked at the man who floated there face-down in front of him, a foolish smile smeared across his face.

# 47

The local Vietnamese photographer Henry used for crime-scene photos seemed to be taking a lot more snaps of the first victim than he normally did, certainly far more than he took of the second. At least, Nga noticed, Henry was doing it right this time. Even the inspector hadn't been able to put a natural death label on this one. The house was cordoned off, front and back, and only he, Nga, and the photographer had gone into the place.

They bagged samples of this and that, Nga took notes, and Henry said 'shit' with grim regularity. A more confident man would have been able to admit how far out of his league he was on this one.

"Shit. Look at that."

The camera snapped. They were still standing knee deep in water having discovered at last what had nailed the second victim. It turned out he had become impaled on a metal stake once used to anchor a bird feeder. Henry was rarely one to voice his suspicions until the final report, but in this case he obviously needed support from his sergeant.

"This is the way I see it, Nga. Something causes him to leave the house in a hurry. He exits through the back door into a flooded garden. He falls forward over the fence and onto the metal stake." He glanced briefly at Nga who denied him a nod even though he agreed with the assessment. But it was clear a good deal more investigation needed to be done before they could establish who had killed whom. It was time to bring in experts. "Very well. I think we're finished here," Henry said to Nga. "Arrange for the bodies to be collected. I have to somehow get a report to the Gendarmérie in Saigon. That will be another challenge in itself."

"Yes, sir."

## Lac Lake

Hong had returned the previous evening with everything worked out. All she needed now was to regroup her troupe and the first matter on the agenda— the intrigue of the missing women in Ban Methuot — could be addressed. Then she could begin healing her own life. The American knight was to be the unwitting star of both spectacles and she hadn't seen him or his so-called wife since she'd arrived back in the Highlands. She was certain the couple would spend weekends at the lake house during the wet season. It was tradition for the missionaries to hibernate till the summer, but their villa was still locked and boarded.

She had met with Chama, the matriarch of the M'nong tribe the night before. It was the culmination of the plan that had been hatched in the missionary's living room. Hong had shown her to one of the guest rooms to allow her time to get cleaned up from her journey. To Hong it felt like a great and inappropriate honor to have the grand old lady travel to see her. But Chama had insisted. This way, the consort wouldn't be implicated in their plan. She shouldn't be seen at any Montagnard villages until this thing was resolved.

They met in the emperor's study — a library full of books he'd barely thumbed through — a room he rarely visited. Chama was a splendidly large woman dressed in an ornate sarong and tiers of beads that lay across her mountainous naked breasts. Her hair was cropped short and her earlobes stretched to accommodate five-inch disks of polished sao wood. She was a glorious sight.

"We've found them," was the first thing she said. She spoke Vietnamese well. They sat opposite one another at the desk, Hong on the guest chair.

"Excellent. I expected as much." Hong knew Chama's own people had been out into the countryside offering rewards for information. "Where are they?"

"On DeWolff's estate."

"But that's ridiculous. Why would he do such a thing?"

Chama's smile was like the entrance to a coal cellar. The mountain people appreciated the beauty of gumminess and often removed the front teeth of young girls in order to better appreciate it. "Don't you know the best place to hide twenty four women is in the last place you'd expect to find them?"

"But their husbands work on the estate."

"Yes, but they work on the plantation. It's a huge place. The women are in an old stockade at the farm. The Montagnard aren't allowed there. It's the domain of the French overseers and their families. You'd need an army to get in."

"I'm hoping we'll have one. This news makes things a lot easier."

"What's your plan?"

Hong laughed. "I'm afraid Plan A has suffered a setback. I'm working on Plan B."

"What went wrong?"

"It depended on the cooperation of the evangelical missionary and her husband. Unfortunately I haven't seen a sight of them since I got back. I was…What's wrong?"

Chama's expression switched back and forth between shock and guilt. "You don't know?"

"Know what?"

Chama tapped her big fingers on the varnished desktop and raised her eyebrows. "The Americans? They're dead."

# 48

Dr. Moncur was neither a coroner nor a surgeon. But, as the senior medical officer in Ban Methuot, he was often consulted on forensic matters. In the dry season he would insist bodies be shipped to the capital where they had the personnel and equipment to do the job properly. But, in the rainy season he'd been called on several times to perform unqualified autopsies while the bodies were still fresh. The two he'd just performed were undoubtedly the most important he'd ever done.

The woman had been shot in the head. One bullet had finished her instantaneously. It had passed through her brain so there was no doubt. They found the bullet in the pillow. The army corporal who came to consult with Moncur was no expert, but he'd served in the second war in Europe. He recognized the bore of the bullet as being compatible with the Luger they'd discovered in the mud near the body in the yard. The water in the male's lungs told Moncur he had still been alive when he went face-down onto the metal spike. He died from drowning. It would certainly have been an agonizing death.

At the Sûreté there was a necessary but uneasy coalition of police and military. In the absence of an Administrator, deputy Desailly was also spending a good deal of time at the police station. He had to have answers. By now, news of the disaster had probably reached Saigon via the Pleiku garrison. They would, no doubt, fly someone down on military transport to conduct an official inquiry. Desailly wanted all the facts at his fingertips. He asked Henry for his appraisal as to what had happened.

"Right now, I'm not certain," he confessed. "A crime of passion? Viet Minh assassins? Don't forget the man's mind was deranged from the loss of his wife. He was capable of anything. It's an awful mess. This monsoon blew in on a nightmare. I wish I'd drawn home-leave so some other fool could suffer all this."

"Me too."

**Lac Lake**

When Lan woke from one more of her regular naps Hong was out sitting on the balcony looking down the hillside in the direction of the missionary's house. But she was looking towards it, not at it. Everything had collapsed in her world. It had all gone so well until now, perhaps too well. She knew she'd been due for a setback, but surely she hadn't deserved one so final.

"What are you doing, ugly?" Lan slurred as if her tongue had grown too large for her mouth. Hong didn't answer. Lan slapped the sleep from her own face as she walked outside. "Goodness, girl. You look as gray as the day. What's up?"

"The Rogers are dead."

"That's terrible." Lan sniffed and spat a gob of mucous over the edge of the balcony. "What's a roger?"

Hong lost her temper. "You know? You disgust me," she said. "If you could take some control over yourself just for a few seconds, show yourself some respect, perhaps you might start to notice what's going on around you."

At first, Lan didn't move or speak. Hong could almost hear her breath in the icy silence. Then she turned and walked quickly back inside. There was a slam from the boudoir door that seemed to vibrate through the lodge. Hong sighed. She'd completed her rout. Her hope was ended and now she'd alienated the only friend she had.

A wind blew a chill through the warm monsoon air. Down the hill the orchids on the Cornfelt's balcony swung back and forth on their wires in formation. They hung inside the porch roof dying of thirst. They were a yard from the pouring rain and there was nothing they could do about it. Hong understood what that feeling was like.

The front gate guards insisted they accompany the consort down the track. She insisted they didn't. There was something in her tone that told them she could make their lives very unpleasant if they disobeyed her. So, they watched the pale blue umbrella glide down the snaking trail in the direction of the foreigners' villa. They watched it round the deserted guard post at the lake's edge and skirt the high water line to the porch. There, it disappeared from their view.

On the balcony, Hong rested her open umbrella on the wooden deck and climbed onto the heavy table to unhook the first of the thirsty orchids. They'd been so beautiful when they had love and care. Mrs. Cornfelt wasn't that good with people but she'd been a mother to her orchids. She'd had them delivered from all over Indochina. Leaving them behind had been a trauma, but what future was there for orchids in North Carolina? When she'd come for her English lessons, Hong had made a point of visiting the balcony orchids every time. They were temperamental plants and she was afraid they'd never forgive the human race for torturing them like…

A sound.

# Bleeding in Black and White

She froze. Some object — some round, hard object had fallen to the ground and rolled. It had bumped into something and stopped, then silence. But it wasn't a sound from the porch. It had come from inside the villa. The shutters were closed, the doors locked, but the sound had most certainly come from inside. Her first reaction wasn't fear. It was anger. She knew what was happening and she didn't like it. Some opportunist was squatting in the empty house. Someone was taking advantage of the Rogers' absence — now their demise — and was stealing from them. She should certainly have gone back to the lodge and summoned the guards, but she was so angry, so wrapped up in the frustration of her crumbled plans, that her personal safety was not at the forefront of her mind. She needed a whipping post.

The handles of the solid double doors that opened onto the deck were fastened together with a heavy padlock. The metal chain looped twice through the handles and, at first glance, the doors seemed impenetrable without a key. Yet, something about their alignment was wrong. The left side was an inch lower than the right. In fact, it was so low it rested directly on the wooden floor. Hong looked carefully at the hinges and understood immediately. On the left side, they'd been cut through with a hacksaw blade. Although the door had been pulled back into its frame and appeared closed, the sawn hinge halves didn't match up.

A six-inch nail had been driven into the wood as a barely visible handle. When she grabbed it and tugged, the whole unit gave way like a Chinese screen. The center chain rattled and the door creaked and she knew her arrival wasn't going to be a secret. As she was inserting herself through the gap she went over the possibilities in her mind, Viet Minh, bandits, escaped Montagnard slaves. She reached inside her *ao dai* to the secret pocket she'd sewn there, and pulled out the skewer she carried with her always. It wasn't for show. She knew how to use it and had done so, once with devastating effect.

With all the shutters closed, the only light to disturb the black interior came from the gap she'd just created. Her prey had the advantage of eyes accustomed to the dark so, once she was inside, she leaned against the doors and heaved them as far open as they would go. Now she could see much of the living area. She knew the house well. It was single story but with wings on either side of this large living room. One housed the servant's quarters and the kitchen with its extensive larder. The other contained the bedrooms and Mrs. Cornfelt's study.

"Don't be afraid," she called, perhaps to herself and took two steps forward. "We aren't here to harm or punish you. I won't tell my men to come in from outside. You may take whatever you can carry, but you must leave. This isn't your house. We've promised to look after it for the owners... Do you hear me?" To be sure, she repeated her warning in pidgin French.

She noticed the tremor in her voice. The adrenaline had run out. This had never been a good idea, but it had taken this far to realize just how foolish it was. She edged backward. Her skewer was up in front of her face like the deadly horn of a unicorn. Her senses tingled just a fraction of a second too late. She heard the crash beside her and felt an arm around her throat. A strong hand grabbed her wrist. It shook her weapon loose almost without effort. The intruder's mouth was against her ear. She could feel the warm breath that spit the French words into her ear.

"If you scream, you'll be sorry."

Almost before the phrase was completely out, she let out a shrill, deafening scream.

The guards at the gate of the emperor's lodge looked at one another, just briefly. There had been something vaguely human about the scream, but this was the jungle. The monkeys and the cockatoos, and the wild pigs spent much of their time impersonating the agony of human suffering. Neither of the two men bothered to mention his doubts to the other for fear of sounding foolish. They'd been caught out too many times by the tricks of the jungle. But both secretly prayed it had been the sound of a monkey, or a bird, or a pig — anything but a concubine.

# 49

A high-ranking representative of the French Administration in Saigon named Billotte, the head of the national Gendarmerie, Chief Inspector Lacouture with his assistant, and Mr. Copeland from the United States Embassy arrived on a Westland-Sikorsky S51 military helicopter that put them down directly in front of the Ban Methuot Sureté building. Travel in the monsoons would have been a lot easier if everyone had a helicopter. The sound of the rotor passing overhead was the first indication to Desailly that his message had made it through.

He hurried across town in his truck to greet the delegates. The two senior Frenchmen in the party seemed extremely angry about things and were intent on taking out that anger on anyone in Ban Methuot who had the decency to have remained alive for their visit. Desailly was at the front of the queue when it came to pecking order, but he bore the scars of a life of beak wounds so it mattered little to him. For Inspector Henry, however, it was a completely different matter. He'd reached the stage in his colonial life where he'd been the big mango for a while, and he wasn't used to having anyone criticize him or his methods. It was extremely degrading therefore when Lacouture announced, almost the second he stepped down from the helicopter, that he would be conducting a private inquiry with his own assistant, beginning immediately. They didn't even take Henry on their trek but left him bubbling in his own bile at the police station while Sgt. Nga showed them around.

It wasn't until mid afternoon that the visitors and the locals were able to sit around the meeting table at the Sureté. It was a building that had been white at some stage, but the paint had grayed and the vines had climbed its walls to give it the appearance of some ancient tomb about to crumble. They sat in the open back alcove where rain fell from the overhanging roof like a tinsel curtain. Lacouture called on Desailly for a thorough briefing of everything he knew about the events leading up to the murders. A shorthand stenographer from Saigon took notes. Although he spoke French with an awful accent, Mr. Copeland seemed to grasp most of what was going on.

When the summary was over, Lacouture asked his first question to the table. "Is there any doubt in anyone's mind that the American and Mme. Dupré were having an affair?"

Henry nominated himself spokesman. "She was naked in his bed. She'd recently been seeded. Of course there's no way of telling whether the semen was that of Monsieur Rogers. But it must be assumed he was…"

"Exactly," Lacouture interrupted. "In fact this strikes me as an investigation fraught with assumptions, Monsieur Henry. (Henry was speared through the heart that his superior would use a title other than his rank) Guns fired in the middle of the night and you couldn't find one witness?"

"This is the Wild West, Superintendent," said Desailly as a sort of tentative support for the local policeman. "I'm sorry to say gunfire isn't that unusual. I'm sure everyone just turned over and went back to sleep."

"I'd very much like to ask about Mr. Rogers, if I may," said Copeland. After an hour of listening to the French, this was his first interjection, but still it seemed to annoy everyone in the room. "I believe he was very upset about the death of his wife."

"Of course," Henry answered.

"And you believe he could have been temporarily insane enough to have committed murder?"

"Yes."

"You don't need to think about that?"

"No," Henry answered quite emphatically. "I've often seen the combination of grief and intoxicants turn a man mad. Plus, he's American. What can I say?"

Far from being insulted, Copeland laughed as if it were the funniest thing he'd heard. "But you have no evidence," he said at last.

"We have the murder weapon."

"Which has no fingerprints."

"It was submerged in the mud beside the body."

"I see. And how do you explain…?"

The Chief Inspector believed he'd let the American play long enough. "Mr. Copeland. I have to remind you, you were invited as an observer."

"I'm so terribly sorry. It's just that one of our respected citizens has been accused of murder, and is not in a position to stand up for himself. Naturally the Embassy is concerned."

"I appreciate that, just as I hope you appreciate the fact that this is my investigation. If you don't mind."

Copeland nodded and Lacouture directed his attention to the local policeman. "Henry, according to your report, you have formulated a hypothesis. It is your opinion that Administrator Dupre arrived unexpectedly at the missionary's house and that, in a fit of rage, the American shot at him then killed his lover?"

"It is, sir."

Lacouture read from the report, "Rogers presumably chased Dupre into the garden and fired shots at him. Dupre collapsed onto the stake and drowned. The American then returned to the house and shot his lover before fleeing."

"Yes, that is one hypothesis."

"But, unfortunately, the hypothesis you chose to send to various departments in Saigon."

"Why is that 'unfortunate', sir?"

Copeland laughed and interrupted once more, "You can't honestly believe that, can you, Henry?"

Henry took a deep breath and called on his deepest voice. "That is exactly what I believe."

"Well, M. Henry, I'm not a policeman…"

"Then you should trust one who is."

"…I'm not a policeman, but I do know horse shit when I see it."

Henry squeezed his mouth into a hurt smile and looked to his superior for support. "Sir, I believe we could get through this debriefing a lot faster without civilians in the room. (The Government representative looked up and raised one eyebrow) I mean foreign civilians, naturally M. Billotte. Pardon me."

"M. Copeland," Lacouture said calmly. "Henry is right, of course. You have no jurisdiction over this investigation. In fact I can't say I actually know what your position is at your embassy. The Ambassador was quite vague on your qualifications. (Henry's smile widened) But, Henry, whether the gentleman is qualified to assess your report or not, I have to say I agree totally with his appraisal."

"What?" The smile was gone in a blink.

"It is indeed the shit of a horse, and I'm sorry you sent it to other agencies to read before I had a chance to censor it."

The air had been punched out of the inspector. "I…I'm sorry you see it like that."

"So you should be. Your investigation ignored several facts and skirted around evidence that didn't fit your hypothesis. For example, the Administrator aborts an important trip north, and sneaks back into Ban Methuot in the dead of night, presumably to catch his wife in the act of being unfaithful to him."

"There's no evidence to that effect," said Henry, half to himself.

"Why else would he instruct his driver to park off the road in the rain for the entire afternoon? There they sat in silence until the sun went down and started back in the dark. Dupré was apparently topping himself up with cognac for most of that time." Lacouture called across to his assistant. "What do we have after that, Jacques?"

The young man read the driver's quotation from his notebook. *"Without any explanation, the Administrator got me to drop him off round back of the jail. We got there around two. He told me to go back to my place and wait there till I heard otherwise. I wasn't to tell anyone he was back."*

"There," Lacouture said. "Doesn't that strike you as just a little strange? Are these not the actions of a jealous husband?"

"Perhaps so, sir," Henry conceded. "He disturbs his wife in bed with the American who becomes enraged, chases him out of the house and shoots at him."

"And misses."

"But causes him to stumble over the submerged fence and impale himself on the stake."

"And then Rogers returns to shoot the wife?"

"To keep her quiet."

"The wife who has remained calm and naked on the bed in spite of all this drama that's taking place in the garden?"

"She…she might have been drunk."

"As might you, Monsieur Henry. And a drunken administrator probably would need little help in stumbling over a fence and impaling himself. It would appear you have been more intent on preserving the reputation of your administrator and his wife than in actually conducting an investigation. I believe the only way we will be able to solve this mystery is to find the American."

"Are you discounting him as a suspect, then?" asked Desailly.

"Not at all," the senior policeman smiled.

"But it does make him an accessory rather than a suspect," Mr. Copeland put in.

"No, Monsieur," Lacouture waggled his finger. "He is certainly still a suspect. We are most anxious to locate Mr. Rogers and involve him in our ongoing inquiries. But, Henry, I'm expunging your report from the records. When we do find him, we shall begin with a blank page, but he still has a great deal of explaining to do. In the meantime, if he hasn't fallen to the enemy, there seems to be only one logical place for Mr. Rogers to be."

"The Lac villa," Henry came alive. "It was the first place we looked, obviously."

"Yes, I believe your men did walk around and bang on the doors. But this time we'll be taking the keys with us and looking through the building. If nobody has anything else to say, I suggest we get over there before it gets dark. Fortunately, we have a helicopter so the roads won't present us with any problems."

# 50

**Lac Lake**

"I confess it threw me out of my stride when you burst into tears," Hong said, a slight laugh in her voice.

"I only burst into tears because you screamed." Bodge's own voice was still fluttering. "You frightened me. I distinctly told you not to scream, didn't I?"

Bodge and Hong were down by the lake hidden within the folds of an inlet overgrown with thick vegetation. The rain had let up and there was a rare glimpse of blue sky through the clouds. They'd brought down a razor and a pair of scissors from the villa and Hong was slowly removing the werewolf beard from Bodge's face. He'd tried to do it himself but his hands still had their involuntary shakes and he was afraid of taking off his nose. He'd told her it was just the booze, but he knew there was more to his wobbles than that.

"I'm not the type of woman who does what she's told," she said, squinting as she hacked at the rough growth.

"So it seems."

An hour earlier in the villa, once she'd realized who had hold of her and was over the shock, they'd sat on the rattan couch talking in whispers. Bodge could see no need for secrecy and was certainly not sufficiently in control of his wits to make anything up. So he told her the lot, from Mrs. Rogers' horrible death, through his rapid emotional decline, to his seduction at the hands of Mme. Dupré. He told her how coming out of the LSD high had made him extremely ill, but that it also snapped him out of his temporary insanity. Everything had suddenly seemed clear.

His subconscious had toyed with the idea of shooting Monique, but fortunately his common sense had returned to stop such a foolish notion. Instead, he left the Lugar on the pillow beside her. It was a symbol intended to frighten her. He hoped she'd get the message. He'd taken the jeep, driven along the hairy mountain trail to the lake and hidden the vehicle in thick bush half a mile from the villa. And here he'd been ever since. People had come, knocked, tested the chains, walked around, but, before Hong, none had been smart enough to work out his way of getting in and out. He'd hidden in the dark through the day and let himself out at night to breathe fresh air and swim in the lake.

It hadn't occurred to him he might be in any trouble. He'd just wanted privacy. If anything, he was hiding from Mme. Dupré and the curse. It was naturally a shock to hear from Hong that she and he had died back there in Ban Methuot.

"How did you...? Ouch."

"Sorry."

"How did you hear all this?" he asked.

"That you were dead?"

"Yup."

"From Lady Chama, the M'nong leader.

"And how did she find out?"

"The M'nong have an efficient news network."

"They must have. No telegraph or phones, traveling on foot. Did she give you any details?"

"No, just that you killed your lover and were shot dead yourself."

"I suppose it could have been a rumor. One of those Chinese whispers that gets the facts muddled up."

"She seemed quite certain — There, that'll do. I'm not a professional but there isn't a lot of blood."

"There can't be many men who get a shave and haircut from the royal consort. Thanks. How do I look?"

"Ugly."

He laughed. "I shouldn't have asked."

He went down to the water and washed his face. Hong looked at him. A big buffalo of a man, but gentle. And she, one of the white herons that sit on the buffaloes' backs and hitch a slow ride through the paddies. She could weigh no more than a few feathers compared to him. There was something about his bulk that gave her a feeling of security. He would hate her for what she planned to do but she was sure it wouldn't damage him. He was good and solid and unbreakable.

Bodge lingered at the water's edge. He'd been making schoolboy errors in his French. Before every statement, every question, he'd had to consider his words, be certain he wasn't about to make a fool of himself. He was trying so hard to impress her he hadn't once been Bodge, or perhaps he'd been Bodge at the age of eleven. No woman he'd ever met had made him feel like this.

Although Hong had immediately felt an overwhelming surge of relief that he was alive, she was also sad. She was seeing a man who had come to the end of his rope and had all but lost his grip of it. It threw her. In order for things to work, she couldn't have any fondness for him, or sympathy, or personal interest.

He turned back from the water to see Hong sitting like a swirl of vanilla ice cream in her white *ao dai*. She'd released her long hair from its clasp and was using his scissors to trim the ends. He so wished he had an easel, a set of oils, and even a smidgen of ability so he could capture that beautiful sight.

"Mr. Rogers," she said, concentrating on her ends. "I understand that you've been through an awful few days and I'm certain you could benefit from a little rest."

Bodge sat cross-legged in front of her. "But?"

"But I wonder whether a diversion might help you through all this. If you think it might, perhaps you could help me with something."

He would have considered dismantling the Royal Palace brick by brick with his bare hands and rebuilding it upside down if she'd asked. "Our Montagnard project?"

"Yes."

"You've learned something new?"

"Yes. Quite a lot, actually. You'll recall we were mystified at first as to why only married women were going missing. It didn't seem logical. There's no market for the trafficking of older women. But it turned out they had one thing in common. Their husbands are all under contract at the plantation of DeWolff."

"That doesn't sound like a coincidence." Bodge bit his lip to keep in any further inanities. Something about the name of DeWolff registered in the depths of his mind.

"According to the agreement between the French and the local Montagnard elders," Hong continued. "the men can be farmed out to the planters for no longer than two months at a time. If they don't volunteer for a second tour, the owners are obliged to let them go."

"Reluctantly," Bodge thought aloud.

"They don't want them to leave at all. Why should they train new men when the ones they have are already experienced? And, in fact, what with military conscription, there aren't really many able-bodied men left in the villages to replace them. As slavery has been outlawed in Vietnam, the plantation owners have to constantly come up with new tricks to keep the men there."

"Like kidnapping their wives."

"So it seems."

"Excuse me for asking, but why wouldn't the plantation people just kill the women and pretend to have them held someplace?"

"For some reason I haven't yet worked out, the army was involved in the kidnappings. I believe the General had some say in the wellbeing of the women."

"Do you know where they are?"

"Now we do, yes. They're on the plantation."

"Then I imagine they're well guarded."

"Yes, but we've put together a plan."

"…that involves me?"

"I have no right to ask. You're a man of the cloth and I know that this may conflict with your principles."

A man of God? It hadn't occurred to Bodge recently that anyone would still consider him a man of the cloth. He also wondered whether he had any principles left. While Hong went over her plan, he felt his respect and admiration for her grow. She was an awesome woman, one he'd be loath to get on the wrong side of. He was certain if he were the Emperor he wouldn't leave her on the bench as second string pitcher.

Before she could finish outlining her plans, she paused and looked to the sky. He heard the sound a few seconds later — the rotor of a helicopter. From his brief orientation, Bodge knew there were fewer than half-a-dozen in the entire country. This one was coming toward them from across the lake. Its noise engulfed the heavenly place like the voice of Satan.

"Under cover, quick," she said, and they scurried into the thick bush.

The clumsy Westland-Sikorsky with a hospital cross on its side, flew almost directly over their heads, along the bank, and landed beside the villa. Bodge and Hong were lying side by side in the damp leaves. When the engine finally went quiet, Bodge could hear her breathing, see her chest rise and fall beneath the silk.

"Something must be wrong," she whispered. "They would never have access to a helicopter just for a casual visit. Are you quite sure you didn't do anything wrong?"

"Not to anyone but myself."

"Then we need to find out what they've come for. Wait here."

"What? Where are you going?"

She stood, brushed herself down and refastened her hair. "My umbrella's still on the veranda. If they go inside they'll know someone's been staying at the villa. I have to regain control."

"What can you tell them?"

"Right now, I don't have any idea. But, by the time I reach the house, I hope I'll have some nice lies all ready. Stay out of sight."

She walked elegantly along the hog trail that cut up through the vegetation and vanished from view. Bodge had a smile on his face the size of Texas. He put his hands behind his head oblivious to the leaves that soaked his clothes. "Oh, man," he said. "What a gal."

When Hong reached the steps leading up to the rear balcony of the villa, she could see the heads of five men. They appeared to be gathered around a very noisy bunch of keys arguing about which one might open the padlock. She recognized two of the visitors. Her arrival took them by surprise. They looked around at the sound of her heels on the wooden steps.

Henry took a step forward and bowed his head respectfully. "Madame Hong. I wouldn't have expected to find you here in the rainy season."

"Captain Henry," she nodded back.

Henry introduced the Chief Inspector and his assistant, Mr. Copeland, and finally, Billotte from the Saigon Administration.

"Yes," said Billotte. "We are acquainted." He too nodded briefly but it sounded to Henry as if their acquaintance hadn't been a cordial one.

"What brings you gentlemen here?" Hong asked, putting a bucket of water on the deck at her feet. The bucket had been conveniently waiting for her beside the lake along with her story.

"Government business," said Lacouture. "But perhaps we could begin by asking you that same question." He left his assistant alone to hunt for the key.

"If you must," she said. "I come every day to water Mrs. Rogers' orchids."

"Such a long walk. Wouldn't it be easier to move them up to your own lodge?" Lacouture asked.

"Why goodness me, Chief Inspector. Surely that would entail breaking the law. They belong to Mrs. Rogers. Why should I steal them?"

"Then you obviously haven't heard," Henry cut in to Lacouture's annoyance.

"Heard what, Inspector?"

"Poor Mrs. Roger's was killed by a tiger several days ago."

Hong flopped back onto one of the patio chairs and looked to all assembled there like a woman about to pass out. "Oh, but how terrible."

"Were you close?" Lacouture asked.

"We'd only known one another a few weeks, but we became friends right away. I'd hoped we could become closer."

"So, you know her husband, also."

Hong resented this attack from a man she'd never met. "No. She arrived before him. I left before he came. Of course she talked about him."

"That is the Royal Lodge I can see on the hill?"

"Yes."

"So, if anyone had been here the last few days, you, or someone up there would have noticed."

"That's correct."

"And did you?"

"Did I what?"

Lacouture bared his teeth at her like a wolf. "Did you notice anyone here?"

"You mean, apart from Mr. Rogers?"

"He was here?"

"Yes."

"But you said you've never seen him."

"And I have not. But the guards remembered him from the day he arrived. They informed me he came by the villa one or two days ago, very early in the morning. I was still asleep at that hour. He drove up to the front gate in his jeep, was inside for most of the morning, then left with a suitcase."

There came a cheer from the men at the door. Finally the correct key had been found. Fortunately, they only bothered to pull open the right-hand door, assuming the left to be stuck. Lacouture was more interested in completing his interrogation.

"Did they mention which direction he drove?"

"I wasn't interested in such information. I can ask if you wish."

"You do that, Miss."

"Actually, it's *Your Royal Highness*."

"What is?"

"My title. If I were a sheep herder it might be appropriate to call me *Miss*. But I'm not."

There was a long moment of silence before, "I apologize."

While the men from Saigon looked around the villa, Hong pumped Henry for information outside on the veranda. He'd been barred from the search and it was looking increasingly like he was about to be barred from his job. He was naturally very bitter about it and was only too happy to tell Hong everything he knew, both Lacouture's version of what happened at the Ban Methuot house, and what he considered to be the true one.

The sun was sinking behind the mauve mountains when the men finally came out of the villa with cane baskets full of "evidence".

"There seem to be an awful lot of empty cans for one man," Lacouture said to Hong. "Are you certain he was alone when he came?"

"No," she answered curtly.

"But you said…"

"I said that my guards told me he was alone. That hardly makes it *my* certainty, does it now?"

Mr. Copeland seemed to be enjoying the hostilities far more than Lacouture, but he pointed out that it would be better for them to return before nightfall.

Lacouture continued to stare at Hong who smiled prettily back. "I shall return tomorrow and talk to your guards," he said.

"Yes, I give you my permission."

Lacouture stormed down the steps to the waiting helicopter. Before joining him, Copeland went to Hong and smiled. "Your Royal Highness," he said. "I'm so sorry we didn't have a chance to talk." He handed her a name card. "My name is Copeland, from the American Embassy. If Mr. Rogers should happen to return, I'd be so grateful if you could give him my card. I would very much like to speak with him."

"Of course."

"I'm sorry everyone has been so businesslike. I'm sure this has all been very upsetting for you. Please accept my apologies."

"That's very nice of you," she nodded slowly. He clicked his heels, military fashion, and hurried down the steps to join the others in the cramped helicopter. It lifted unsteadily and filled the lake basin with its ugly noise, sending birds into a panic and raising a chorus of jungle animals. Hong watched it head off into a spectacular sunset. She really believed there would be a temporary respite from the monsoons at last.

# 51

The armed guards waved down the black jeep and trailer that had just come slithering along the mud driveway. A huge slab of granite stood beside the road with the words; *Plantation DeWolff*, carved out of it with great precision.

One of the guards was French. He sauntered over to the jeep, half-heartedly saluted the driver and glared at the woman beside him.

"What's your business?" he asked.

Bodge in his best black suit and white shirt was impressed. There couldn't be many employers in the colonies who still had money to throw away on imported gorillas.

"My name, sir," he said, "is the Reverend Robert Rogers, and this lady is Sister Natalia of the Redemption Missions." Sister Natalia was a huge black woman squirming uncomfortably in a yellow floral frock. She hid behind thick, black rimmed sunglasses. "And we are here on the business of the Lord. Today is the Sabbath and we've come to give the gift of religion to the heathens."

"Are they expecting you?" the gorilla asked. He'd apparently been taught half-a-dozen guard phrases.

"Would I be here if they weren't?"

It was all too difficult for the guard. He walked around the back of the jeep and lifted the tarpaulin that covered the low trailer hitched behind. It was packed with shiny black Bibles and framed pictures of Jesus bleeding on the cross. He replaced the tarp and went round to the passenger's side where he gestured for Sister Natalia to get in the back. She did so slowly and with a great deal of grunting. He took her place in the front and ordered Bodge to drive.

For the past few days, Bodge had been holed up in one of the emperor's hides up in the hills beyond the lodge. Hong had provided him with enough supplies to sustain him but had given him none of her time. The first actual conversation they'd had was when she came to pick him up in the jeep that morning. She had a neat black suit for him and a clean white shirt. Given their size, they had to have been made to measure. They went over her plan once more and took him to meet his ally for the first time.

Now, an hour later, here they were driving through endless acres of coffee orchards and rubber groves. The drive, even at some speed, took fifteen minutes and Bodge began to understand just how important it was for the French Government to protect its interests in Indo-china. The sale of produce from this single plantation could have fed and clothed Paris for a year. By the time they reached the magnificent Villa DeWolff, Bodge had become entranced by mile upon mile of crisscrossed rows of neatly pruned trees.

"You wait here," the gorilla said.

"Guard phrase number five", Bodge noted, watching the man run to the house. Bodge climbed down, picked up his Bible from the seat and smiled at his honored guest. "Better you stay in the car."

"Okay, Boss."

He walked toward the enormous building. A very black West African girl in a maid's uniform came running down the steps to head him off. "Welcome, Sir," she said with a big smile. "Please come into the guest room." She had the build of a weightlifter so Bodge felt he had no choice but to follow. She sat him in a glorious room of marble and teak and gilt cornices that made him feel like a tourist on an historical visit to Avignon. He composed himself. The encounter that was to follow would be the life or death of today's plan and perhaps of himself. He had to get it just right.

He wasn't alone in the room for long. He heard the footsteps and barkings of an angry man. DeWolff appeared in the doorway with his arms open like John the Baptist. He was a short man with freckles and ginger hair, rather too comical to be a convincing despot, Bodge thought. The man's reaction to his arrival caught Bodge by surprise.

"Monsieur Rogers," he said. "What an honor. What a great, great honor to have you in my house." He took Bodge's hands like a child welcoming home its father. "I heard you'd arrived in Ban Methuot. I was honestly planning to come to see you. And here you are, saving me the trouble. Come. Let's get out of this dowdy room. Come, my friend, to my study. I know you'll like it there."

DeWolff led Bodge by the arm along a hallway flanked with European tapestries, and steered him into a scale replica of the Royal study at le Palais de Papes. Bodge knew it well as he'd visited the place after the war.

"You have an impressive house, M. DeWolff," Bodge said before being lowered onto an antique Louis XV chaise longues.

"And you have a marvelous grasp of our language," DeWolff replied.

Things were running far too smoothly for Bodge's comfort. He'd expected some opposition to his arrival, some objections to his proposal. He had a complicated speech worked out, but it didn't look like it would be getting an airing.

"Port?" the host asked, pouring from a decanter.

"Thank you. I don't drink on Sundays. Which actually brings me to the reason for my visit."

"Yes?"

"I was hoping I'd be able to conduct a sermon today, for your heathen workers."

"What a splendid idea. Marvelous. You know I was trying to get your predecessor to do exactly that. Couldn't get him interested. This is just splendid." He called out for a man called Manx. An overseer in a sweat stained uniform arrived at the door. He was bow-legged and built like the Arc de Triomphe.

"M. DeWolff?"

"Manx, this is Reverend Rogers. He's kindly agreed to preach to our menials. Would you be so kind as to get the Montagnard assembled in the cutting shed?"

"All of them?" the man asked.

"Every last man of them. It's Sunday. We're going to introduce them to the one true God."

"You know it's their only day off?"

Bodge caught a glimpse of the tyrant in DeWolff's eyes. He was fighting to remain civil with his henchman. "All the better. All the better. This is the beginning of a relationship with the Reverend here that I'm certain will blossom like a glorious frangipani in the months to come. Go to it, now."

The overseer shrugged and slouched out of the room. Bodge assumed a smile that wasn't remotely indicative of his feelings. Everything he'd heard about DeWolff warned him the man was a snake. All this kindness curdled in Bodge. Something stank.

"I must confess," Bodge said. "I wasn't expecting such a hospitable welcome."

DeWolff sat opposite with a goblet of port the size of a fish bowl. "And I must confess I wasn't expecting you to be back at work so soon, considering."

"Considering?"

"Your terrible loss, of course."

"I see. My wife would have wanted me to continue with our mission."

"Word reached me that you'd suffered a tragic decline, a slide into Hell, as it were. (There; the low punch Bodge had been waiting for.) But, it could have happened to any of us I suppose."

"I…I'm not sure I know what you mean." Bodge looked down at the Bible on his lap.

"Oh, I'm sure you do. And I'm sure the flock at your home church in Mississippi, or whatever awful place you come from, would understand also."

"My church?"

DeWolff reached into a drawer in the small cabinet beside his chair, and produced a brown envelope. Bodge noticed there were other envelopes in the same drawer.

"You see?" DeWolff said, producing a dozen or so black and white photographs. "I'm something of an amateur cameraman. I also collect pictures of beautiful things. And I'm sure you'll agree, (he crossed over and dropped the photographs onto Bodge's lap) that these are very beautiful things. It appears you and General LePenn have similar tastes."

Bodge thumbed through them. His first reaction was to laugh, but he managed to turn his smile into a gash of anguish. The pictures showed Bodge in one of the back rooms at Madam Vin's. He was naked, but clearly unconscious. With him in the room was the tall, beautiful half-girl. While the comatose victim slept, she, or he, stripped naked to leave no doubt as to his gender, and performed several unlikely acts with and to the body. Bodge was certain, even though he could argue unconsciousness, the series would be devastating to a real missionary. He knew men in his home town who would kill themselves rather than have such pictures exposed.

But on this day, and to this particular missionary, all they achieved was to galvanize Bodge's dislike of this man and his empire. He was more intent than ever to ensure the day's plan was a success.

"Oh, God help me," he said. "No, it can't be." He buried his head in his hands and wept. "Please. You can't be so heartless."

"Disgraceful, isn't it? DeWolff smiled. "But perhaps people would eventually be able to forgive you — the psychological stress and all."

"No. They could never understand such…such depravity. My career, my life would be over."

"Really? I'm sorry to hear that. And I always believed Christians were a forgiving lot." He laughed as he retrieved the pictures.

"You…you animal," Bodge sobbed. "How could you do this?"

"How? With clever planning and *piastres* invested in the right places. I was afraid for a while I'd put my money on the wrong horse. I was sure you'd blasted our beloved first couple into the beyond, but it appears you've talked yourself out of that particular scandal. Or, how else could you be back at work?"

"I had nothing to do with that," Bodge pleaded.

"I believe you, Reverend. And I'm delighted. I have much more use for you out of jail."

"Me? I have nothing. What could you possibly…?"

"Tsk, Tsk. So modest. You have nothing? Don't insult me, M. Rogers. You have an income far exceeding anyone in Ban Methuot. You have cars and, quite soon, your very own airplane. And most importantly, you virtually have diplomatic access to the shipping of goods in and out of the United States. I can't begin to tell you how useful all that could be to my enterprise."

"Do you have no shame? Why, that's blackmail."

DeWolff clapped his hands. "Bravo. Bravo, you sad and pathetic man. Welcome to the start of our ongoing relationship."

"And, if I don't cooperate?"

"I can't begin to imagine what reaction there would be in Washington to these pictures, can you? I hear there's a terrible to-do about homosexuality in your country."

"You're an evil man, DeWolff."

"Now, if you're ready, you have a captive audience for your first sermon."

"You can't possibly expect me to preach now. Not after…"

"Force yourself, Father. I've been trying to push Christian values into these aboriginals for years. It might even make them more grateful for what they get here. And, consider it penance. You have a lot of making up to do."

# 52

The cutting shed was a vast roof. There were no walls. The floor was packed dirt and some three hundred Montagnard men sat cross-legged in rows as neat as the rubber trees. Six overseers with rifles were seated on chairs around the periphery. They didn't seem any more pleased at losing their one day off than the Montagnard.

When the caravan of DeWolff, Bodge, Sister Natalia, and Overseer Manx marched into the hall, a slight mumble worked its way through those assembled there. Some at the rear straightened their backs to get a better look. The mood seemed to suddenly change. DeWolff held up his hands for silence.

"Gentlemen, thank you for coming to this, your first Sunday Mass," he said. He spoke in colloquial French because he refused to stoop to the barbaric *petit negre* pidgin of these common folk. As a result, very few of the men ever knew what he was saying. Incredibly, only one of the overseers spoke a Montagnard language and he'd failed to return from his Saturday night in town. That, of course, was no accident. They would eventually come to find him tied and gagged in the jungle behind the market. "I give you, Reverend Rogers of the Evangelical Missions."

Even when Bodge took a step forward, all eyes were still on Sister Natalia, better known to them as Great Matriarch Chama. Not one man could imagine what she was doing up there in front of them dressed like a French flower pot.

"My brothers," Bodge said. His voice was strong and sincere. It was the type of voice he'd listened to endless Sunday after Sunday since his third birthday. "We are gathered together here today under the watchful eye of the Lord our God... Sister?"

Chama remained where she was, behind Bodge's shoulder like a subservient interpreter. The M'nong language had become a lingua franca at the plantation. The words she spoke appeared to DeWolff and the overseers to be a translation of the preacher's sermon. But they were not. She began with,

"Brothers of the tribes, I want you to react to my words as if I'm translating from the cross worshipper, here. Don't act surprised or angry or excited. Just stay as blank as the mist."

There followed a half hour of Bodge spouting a fiery tirade against the evil of sin and what terrible things would become of sinners in the afterlife. All the while, Chama was laying out her instructions. Once she'd signaled to Bodge they were ready, Reverend Rogers instructed all the men to get to their feet. Because he didn't know the words in French, he started to sing, 'We Shall Overcome' in English. He clapped his hands and the Montagnard clapped theirs. In fact they appeared to be overcome with some inexplicable religious fervor. Bodge went to Sister Natalia and wrapped his arms around her. The Montagnard began to hug one-another and chant to some unseen God above them.

There was such an overwhelming atmosphere of love and happiness, the overseers couldn't help but smile at the childlike innocence of their charges. They'd never seen them so cheerful. Even so, they were edgy in the beginning when the first men came to shake their hands. But they couldn't begrudge them. They clutched their guns in their left hands and shook with their right. But more and more came. They crowded around the overseers smiling and singing, till one guard couldn't see the next. Bodge went to Overseer Manx and locked him in a loving embrace. It was then Chama issued forth with the screeching ancient battle cry of the M'nong.

The overseers were subdued in seconds without a shot being fired. The only injury was sustained by Manx who came off second best in a brief wrestling match with the reverend. It occurred to Bodge it was the first actual hand to hand fighting he'd been involved in since he joined Operations — or even, since college. DeWolff, in shock, was about to flee but Chama quickly put herself between him and escape, and held her knife to his testicles.

They went first to the house, where fourteen domestic servants seemed only too happy to be restrained and gagged. Mrs. DeWolff on the other hand was so appalled to see a gang of black thugs in her clean house that she fainted on the spot. The layer of Bibles and bleeding Jesus's in the trailer behind the jeep was only a foot deep. Below it were some fifty carbines all oiled and loaded and ready to fire.

Bodge and the Montagnard approached the overseers' compound silently from three different directions. Only two more men were found there and they were woken from deep sleeps and hog-tied. The local wives and whores of the expatriates were rounded up by the armed Montagnard and marched off to the stockade. They found the kidnapped Montagnard women exactly where they were told they'd be — in the cellar of a barn fifty yards behind the compound. There was no guard. Although many of the captives were scared and unused to daylight, most were in good health. It turned out that General LePenn had insisted on that. The stronger ones went to help their husbands gather their belongings and begin the long walk home to their villages.

All the while, Bodge took photographs with DeWolff's own Brownie. The slavery on that particular plantation was over. It had been a swift and bloodless coup, and in spite of all the weaponry, not a shot had been fired. Even the overseers had to admit it had been cleverly done. There remained only one last matter for Bodge to deal with. DeWolff, tied hand and foot, was sitting on the antique chaise longues — naked in front of his house, tears streaming from his eyes as the workers paraded in front of him laughing at his predicament. Hong climbed down from one of the Royal Lodge land rovers and walked over to Bodge.

"Any problems getting past the guards at the gate? he asked."

"No, we caught them a little by surprise."

"And Ban Methuot?" he asked.

She looked at her watch. "I think our visitors from Saigon will find this far more interesting than hunting for you. The letters should be arriving at the Residence, the garrison, and the Montagnard liaison office about half an hour from now. That gives us time to get out of here."

"Wait. They have a helicopter, you know."

"I'm afraid it's going to have a mechanical fault."

He laughed. "I see. Is there anything you haven't taken care of?"

"And the photos?"

He swung round to show her the camera. "I have the whole show documented. We can leave this for the Saigon people. And I have some souvenirs of a number of local celebrities. Our eminent plantation owner here has been running a blackmail racket. It includes one or two high ranking army officers — one general included. That should be enough to ensure military cooperation, don't you think?"

"Perfect."

They walked together through the house, Hong astounded by the opulence. It made them even more pleased to have caused DeWolff's comeuppance. At the end of the tour they stood smiling at each other in the shadow of the doorway. She seemed to glow with an aura of victory — a common pride in a job well done. There was something magical about the moment. Bodge was certain she felt it too but couldn't put it into words.

"Hong?" Bodge said.

"Yes?"

"I...I think you've done a marvelous thing here."

"I couldn't have done it without you," she blushed slightly. It was barely noticeable but it made her look vulnerable for once and gloriously feminine. To his own surprise, Bodge leaned forward to kiss her. He was about to close his eyes as he got closer. Like a boxer she took a step back and gave herself room to swing her fist. It landed at the corner of his mouth with a crack they could have heard in Hanoi.

"Hey!" he cried, reeling backward. He immediately tasted blood on his tongue.

"Perhaps you thought you were back at a high school dance in Tennessee, for a second. Don't you dare dishonor me like that again, Reverend." She threw back her hair and walked out into the sunlight.

Bodge, stunned, worked his jaw to see if it was broken. He knew his lip was split. It hurt when he started to laugh.

"Wow. What a gal."

# 53

Bodge drove, Chama sat beside him, and Hong sulked in the back. They passed the guard post where one Frenchman and two Vietnamese sat roped to the fence.

"Three more men who underestimated a woman," said Hong, still fuming. In fact, the atmosphere didn't improve until two kilometers later when Lady Chama suddenly ripped off the French sack and began adorning her naked breasts with beads from her handbag. It was hard to stay moody at such a sight. As if she realized she owed these two people a debt of gratitude, without expression on her large face, Chama told them a story. She was fluent in five Montagnard dialects and Vietnamese but her French was a rough pidgin that removed all subtlety from her tale.

"I know where you tiger he come from," she began. Bodge eased his foot onto the brake and pulled the jeep to one side of the mud track. He killed the engine and turned to look at her.

"Where?"

"Tell you true, I'm not think. I'm know." Her hands began to organize the beads around her necklace and her deep voice related the story. "Not normal for whitey to order tiger that still living. Normal he want skin or tooth or claw, but this whitey he want the whole thing, still breathin'. Goes to a Bahnar village down by Mo-in. Famous they be for huntin' tiger. They find whitey a tiger. Not such biggest one they ever get but he happy enough."

"You know his name?" Bodge asked.

"No. But I know he a soldier man. Big shot soldier man."

"How do you know that?"

"Bahnar say he order little soldier round. When he come to pick up the tiger he order little soldier round. Then he tell Bahnar keep quiet. They tell someone they get dead. That why I no say nothing. But now I owe you big time Mr. Bodge. An I sorry you missus. This a bad thing."

Bodge removed the envelope from his jacket pocket and produced a photo of General LePenn. He held it up to Chama. "Is this the man?"

"No, boss. Him tooth too long. Whitey about same year you."

"Do you think you could get one of the Bahnar to come here and point the man out?"

"If I tell him, he come. But soldier man say he kill all."

"I think there might be a way to protect them once the official inquiry begins. Damn, the army is supposed to be looking after the Montagnard, not threatening them."

"Then I make him come."

They dropped Chama off at the rendezvous point where her nervous bodyguards had been pacing for most of the morning. She kissed Hong and Bodge and chanted short mantras of eternal blessing for them. She made them promise to come for a feast and lots of rice whisky once everything was sorted in Ban Methuot. But something in her mind told her she'd never see these two again. That left Bodge and Hong uncomfortably alone. The consort opted to remain in the back seat. Neither seemed to know what to say. After five minutes Bodge looked in the mirror and touched his fat lip.

"I think I'm going to need stitches."

There was a moment of silence before, "You're lucky I was in a good mood or you'd need new teeth." Even a threat sounded beautiful in her lovely French.

Bodge smiled and winced. "Look, I'm sorry. I didn't mean anything by it. It was just the adrenaline making me overly bold."

"I'd like you to remember who I am."

"I will. But, don't forget you're flesh and blood just like me. Don't forget that royalty is overrated."

She recognized her own words and smiled to herself.

"If I promise to remember who you are," Bodge continued, "may I call you Hong, rather than *Your Esteemed and Respected Majesty*?

"I suppose so. After today's project I believe you've earned that much, Reverend Rogers."

"My friends call me Bodge."

"It's a silly name."

"That may be true. But it's mine, silly or not. So, Hong...?"

"Yes..., Bodge?"

"Are you in love with the Emperor?"

"Mr. Rogers," she pulled herself up stiffly in the seat. "Are you absolutely determined to ruin this day for me?"

"Sorry." He focused his mind on the road for a few seconds while he negotiated a stretch of deep mud. Once he was clear of it he looked again in the mirror. He wasn't certain but he may have noticed a slight smile there. "So, are you?"

"It's none of your business, so just drive."

"Yes, Ma'am." He touched the imaginary brim of his chauffeur's cap. "Did you have a choice?"

"Mr. Rogers!"

"Bodge."

"Mr. Rogers, what do you think gives you the right to ask personal questions of me?"

"Well, the way I see it, I should have been dead many times over. I get the feeling I'm living on borrowed time. Tomorrow, I might be killed by the Montagnard warriors, or shot by police, or soldiers. Knowing he owes a debt to death makes a man impatient for answers to all the questions he has in his head."

She stared at his eyes in the mirror. "I can't recall having met anyone as direct — yet apparently uncomplicated as you. So full of secrets, yet wide open for all to see like the Dowager's sarcophagus." Bodge smiled again. "No," she said. "I had no choice. But he's a good man."

"It doesn't worry you that he changes teams so often?"

"He does not. You understand nothing. He's faithful to his own team, to his own people. You seem to forget isn't a man as such. He's the embodiment of Vietnam's royal traditions. It's his status that's shuffled back and forth between the French and the Viet Minh and the nationalists, not him. It's all symbolic, very much as if each in turn is occupying the royal palace. But the man himself wants only what's good for his subjects."

"And shooting deer at close range is good for his subjects?" It was a cruel comment and Bodge wished he could take it back. It had obviously been seasoned with jealousy.

"How sadly cynical you are, Mr. Rogers. He hides up here for a very good reason, so that he isn't seen on newsreels or in the journals taking dinner with the invaders. This is his protest."

"Okay. I can buy that."

"At last. Now, let us talk of the motivation for the military's attempt on your life. What do you suppose they had to gain?"

"Surely you can see that?"

"If I could, I wouldn't waste my time asking you."

Bodge found a comparatively dry spot on the road and stepped on the brakes again.

"Right," he said. "If I'm going to share my theories with you, I'm not doing it through a rear-view mirror like some servant. Either you sit up here or I'm keeping it all to myself."

Hong's lips reluctantly creased into a smile and she climbed into the front passenger seat beside him. Once they were back on the road, Bodge laid out his interpretation of events.

"I believe it all started with our little conspiracy."

"The official inquiry?"

"That's it. We got it into our heads that we could stir things up enough to get the Vietnamese government and the French administration interested in the murder/rape case of the Montagnard girls."

"And we did."

"Indeed. Between you, me and Petit we were able to raise a big enough stink for the French embassy to promise a military inquiry. Now, if the men in question were conscripts they'd know what trouble they were in and get the hell out — desert. But, what if there was an officer involved? What if the man responsible was hoping to advance his career in the French military? Rape and murder, particularly of a people he had sworn to protect, would have him court marshaled and thrown in the stockade. Such a man would have good enough reason to be very upset."

"You think he'd go to the trouble to kill all four of us?"

"No. And he didn't need to. His motivation wasn't revenge. We've assumed the tiger was brought to the mission house to silence Mrs. Rogers and myself. But that wasn't the point at all."

"Bet?"

"Exactly. She was the only witness — the only person who could have identified the officer and his men. And he didn't even need to kill her. Just the fright she'd get from waking up with a tiger in her room and a few well-placed threats would be enough to ensure her silence. I imagine they'd underestimated the ferocity of a half-starved tiger.

"I saw slivers of meat on the ground floor the day of the attack. The police assumed they were just more remnants from the carnage. But they weren't. The army officer's unit had carried the tiger to the house under the cover of darkness — I imagine, in a wooden crate. They'd laid a trail of meat to Bet's room while she slept and cleaned up their footprints with the mat before releasing the animal at the back door. That door was closed when I arrived and I'm sure I don't know of any wild animals with the wherewithal to wipe their feet and close the door behind them. Once the animal was safely inside, the soldiers had left it to its own devices and fled. But our tiger was a curious beast. For some reason it wanted to begin its hunt upstairs where it found Stephanie's door open. And the rest, we know. I imagine the thunder lulled, Bet heard the commotion and ran up to investigate. That was her undoing."

"So, you're saying our meddling was responsible for those deaths."

"We weren't to know what kind of people we were dealing with. Nobody could have predicted this. Your plan was sound and well-meaning."

"Don't patronize me, Mr. Rogers."

"No, really I'm not. Thanks to you, twenty five women have been rescued. I wouldn't be surprised if most of them could identify the soldiers who kidnapped them. Filling in the gaps and solving the murder at the missionary lodge shouldn't be that difficult. Bet's death will be avenged one way or another."

## 54

"Well, what do we do?" Henry asked. He and the Saigon delegation, minus Copeland, had arrived at the plantation a few minutes before Captain Faboir and a unit of soldiers. Mr. Duc of the Montagnard Liaison Center and acting Administrator Desailly followed them in.

"I don't believe we have a lot of choice, Inspector," Billotte said. "You read the letter. The evidence is all there."

"Monsieur DeWolff is a very influential man in these parts," Henry said, shaking his head.

"Nobody is that important they're above French law," Chief Inspector Lacouture reminded him. "If we let him get away with this, there'll be an international incident. It won't be long before Copeland finds out about what's happened here. In fact I wouldn't be surprised if he got a letter himself. Where's DeWolff?"

"Inside," the Captain told him. "He's ranting quite seriously. He's apparently trying to implicate the army. He says it was all General LePenn's idea."

"Does he have any evidence to substantiate that?"

"No. And there are one or two overseers who are straining at the leash to put the blame on DeWolff for anything and everything."

"Excellent," said Billotte. "So, let's arrest him. If the letter's accurate, we have the names and addresses of several hundred Moi happy to act as witnesses. That should be enough."

"But, what about the plantation?" Desailly asked. It's an important source of revenue. You can't just shut it down."

"Then, let's see if the overseers are willing to take it over," Billotte suggested. I'm sure if they cut the profits and upped the wages they'd be able to find Moi workers without pointing guns at them. We'll see what they can salvage before the rains ruin everything."

Desailly wasn't sure why, but Billotte seemed delighted to have this opportunity to remove DeWolff. He wondered whether the plantation owner had something on the man from Saigon just as he apparently did on half the male population of Ban Methuot.

"Ehrr, there's one other thing," Captain Faboir said.

"What's that?"

"The overseers — they said the American was here."

"Rogers?" Chief Inspector Lacouture asked with a genuine look of surprise on his face. "Doing what?"

"They say he was the ringleader. He gave a sermon, got everyone worked up, and led them to rescue the women. One or two of the Moi witnesses also back up those statements."

"What exactly is that man playing at?" Henry whined. "He's on the run for murder and he organizes something like this. Is he mad?"

Lacouture scratched his head. "If he actually were responsible for a murder, I'd say 'yes'. But this doesn't strike me as the action of any man with a guilty conscience I've ever come across."

"Me neither," Billotte agreed.

"In fact," Lacouture smiled. "He sleeps with the Administrator's wife, the royal consort lies for him, and he overthrows this tyrant. I think I'm starting to admire the fellow."

# 55

When they reached the intersection that would ultimately led them to the lake, Hong told Bodge to keep going straight.

"Are you sure we should be heading toward town?" Bodge asked.

"Yes."

"Isn't it pushing my luck a little to be driving through military checkpoints?"

"We won't be going that far."

"I see? You have yet another plan."

"Yes."

But she didn't tell him what it was. They were half a kilometer from the first checkpoint when she directed him to take a left at a barely discernable trail. It wound around the rim of a wide gully which opened out to rice fields and dull, featureless landscape. Despite its apparent anonymity, the trail was well drained and graveled. It was barely twenty minutes before the airstrip came into view with the B24 Liberator standing beside the lean-to. Bodge looked at his co-conspirator and smiled.

"It's one of the emperor's secret tracks. They're everywhere," she said, not looking at him.

"Is the plane waiting for me?"

"Raphael is expecting the emperor. I have to convince him to take you instead."

"And how do you plan to do that?"

"I have a letter in Bo Dai's hand."

"Which he didn't write."

"It's an easy enough style to copy — standard French calligraphy."

"Remarkable. May I ask why you're going to all this trouble for me?"

"I have reasons."

"Why do I have the feeling there's more you expect of me in return?"

"I have no idea."

Raphael was pleased to see Bodge and cautiously respectful to the consort who he'd never seen out of the company of her master. He opened the officially sealed letter and read slowly. As he doggedly kept himself outside the walls of expatriate gossip and had spent the past week with his Montagnard wife and children awaiting word of his next mission, it was evident that Raphael hadn't heard news of the scandal from Ban Methuot. When he reached one point in the letter, the big pilot put his arms around the American and whispered regrets into his ear. Bodge had to assume he'd just learned of Stephanie's death. When they pulled apart, the eyes of both men were damp with tears. Raphael wiped the back of his arm across his face and read on. He looked up at the consort and smiled.

"Delighted to have you both aboard," he said.

He rushed ahead to ready the plane and Bodge looked at Hong.

"You're coming, too?"

"It's complicated," she replied and climbed aboard the plane.

For the duration of the flight there was no further explanation and Bodge was left to tumble around in his emotions. The desire that he had fashioned in his own mind, merely from viewing three black and white slides of her, had turned to a passion. And the object of that passion had falsified the royal seal and was currently absconding with him in the Emperor's private aircraft. He was aware that she could be executed for less. In one foolhardy moment she had become even more of a fugitive in her country than he — and he loved her for it. His vanity allowed him a flicker of hope that he might in some small way be the motive for her actions.

With no conversation forthcoming from Hong, Bodge spent much of the flight up front with Raphael.

"I've been trying to get a message through to the tower," the Frenchman told him, "but all I get is this." He turned the volume knob and the ugly crackle of static filled the cockpit.

"That's okay. We'll be in Saigon in half an hour, won't we?"

"No."

"Why not?"

"Because we aren't going to Saigon. Her ladyship wants us to touch down in Dalat."

"Dalat? What's there?"

"My house and my missus. Another Royal residence. Saigon tourists. Important thing is it's safe and only twenty five minutes from Ban Methuot in case we have to fly back for the Grand E."

The journey to Dalat took the transporter directly toward one almighty storm. It became spectacular, like a flight through shards of glass. Bodge had never been so close to lightning, yet he wasn't afraid. Everything that had happened to him recently had apparently removed fear for his own life. The aircraft bucked like a mule as it rounded down over the lush pine forests. Even with the airstrip directly in front of them the air currents still conspired to jerk them from side to side.

Without radio contact Blanc hadn't been able to get clearance to land. The storm had absolute control of the air waves. But visibility below the clouds was good and the pilot could be certain there was nothing on the runway to hit. The rain hadn't yet caught up with the complicated storm. Although there were potholes along the dirt strip, there were no puddles. The plane bumped down and Blanc slalomed skillfully around them. The engine was cut, and Bodge slapped the still-smiling pilot on the back for a job well done.

"Be staying in the royal villa, will you?" Raphael asked with a wink. Bodge ignored the question and ducked through to the back. Hong apparently had a closet on the plane. She was now wearing very Western black stretch slacks and a billowy blouse. A huge pair of sunglasses sat on top of her hair like Mickey Mouse ears. Bodge found this transformation disappointing, but chose to say nothing.

Dalat was a sad looking, hurriedly put together resort-of-a-town where Saigon residents kept summer houses and weekenders came to escape the heat of the plains. It had been kitted out in a Sino-Swiss ski resort style that didn't suit it. At three thousand feet, cool breezes would normally skip along the unlaid dust roads. But today, the clouds had it packed in like a tacky oriental vase about to be shipped in the post.

There was something Hollywood Romance about the pony and trap ride from the airstrip. Bodge felt clear, as if all his troubles had been flushed out and only happiness and joy lay ahead. As if to prove it, here he was with his perfect gal in the back of a wagon. It was only missing a Bing Crosby soundtrack. She leaned close to him and pointed out interesting sights. There was the lake where her dog had once drowned chasing a goose. There was the Salon de Thé where the Emperor had once gone in disguise to hear the gossip about himself.

When they finally clomped up the grandiose driveway to the Baliverne, Bodge wanted, more than anything, for her to come in with him. But he didn't have enough teeth to make such a suggestion.

"Don't give your real name," she said as he climbed down and collected his things. "I'll contact you later. Don't go anywhere."

He felt like an employee. "No, Ma'am. I'll register under the name of Leon."

"Someone you know?"

"Someone I used to know."

He explored his room. The only thing he found worthy of note was a foul smell that rose from the Western toilet. He flushed the creature, lowered the seat, and closed the door. All he'd brought from Ban Methuot was his Bible, and his jacket. He threw them on the bed and lay beside them. Before he could even count the blades on the overhead fan, he was asleep.

He was woken by a tremendous clap of thunder that seemed to split the world in half. It was dark. He had no idea where he was, or why. Nothing at all stirred in his head. He lay still and tried to force a thought into his mind — even the briefest memory. It was an eerie moment and one he'd experienced often of late. Then, a flash of lightning gave him a glimpse of the room around him, and everything came back.

He fumbled beside the bed for a lamp. It was the first thing he noticed when he'd arrived — electricity. It had been quite a while since light had been available to him at the flick of a switch. He was worried the storm might have knocked out the power, but one click lit up a humble but effective forty watt bulb. He sat on the edge of the mattress. He felt heavy from his first real sleep in fifty hours. He wondered where Hong was. Why hadn't she been in touch? Was something wrong? Was she in danger? At last, someone to be worried about.

He hurried to the bathroom. He needed to get clean. He stood under the tepid shower and scrubbed the unpleasant odors from his skin. He turned off the water and turned to look at himself in the full-length mirror. He was astounded at how slim he'd become, how his muscles had hardened, his hair had grown. He stepped out of the tub and walked closer to his reflection. Now he could see the wounds, the scars, the insect bites. Lou wouldn't recog...

He sighed. There was no Lou, but that memory sparked a thought. He wrapped a small grayish towel around his middle and went back to the bed where his Bible lay. There was a letter opener on the desk that someone had honed to a sharp edge. He sat on the mattress and used it to score around the inside of the front cover of the holy book. "God of gods, Lord of kings, and a revealer of secrets", he said under his breath, trying to match the quote to either Daniel or Luke.

He peeled back the handwritten Lord's Prayer and removed a rectangle of card from inside. Between it and the thick cover were his Agency ID, and two twenty dollar bills he'd completely forgotten about. Still, hardly enough to get him back to the States. He repeated the process with the back cover. Only one secret was concealed there, and he wasn't that certain he wanted to see it. The photo of Lou and his homosexual friends hadn't lost any of its venom. When Bodge had first seen it, he hadn't been able to look, not with a critical eye. But if there was anything to be learned from it, he needed to go over it in detail. "Use your mind, Leon, not your gut."

The reading glasses in the top pocket of his jacket were for show — but they magnified. He held the picture under the lamplight and scanned the glass slowly across it. "Your mind. Anything odd. Anything at all."

He began, gradually, to notice things in the black and white photo. Lou's pants for example. They were crumpled down by one ankle. They were unquestionably his work slacks and he still wore his black shoes. That told Bodge his friend had stopped off at this…club after work. He would never wear office clothes at the weekend. He hated the style. There was further confirmation of this when Bodge picked out a small pile of material on the couch between the two men. It was striped, and was probably Lou's necktie.

"So Lou, you have a tough day at the office, and decide to stop off at one of your hangouts and get yourself serviced. I suppose I can live with that if that was your thing. But, you know, you aren't a bad looking guy. If there are as many faggots around as they'd have us believe, couldn't you have found yourself a steady boyfriend?"

Bodge felt odd even thinking like this, but he had to look at the situation as it was. He couldn't understand why Lou would subject himself to this public…humiliation. He looked again at the fat old guy beside Lou who seemed just as oblivious to Lou's presence as Lou was to his. "Don't you care who's watching, guys? What kind of place is this?" He scanned the spectacles along the wall behind the men. He decided this was wallpaper, expensive kind, but pretty old. He'd seen something like it before, perhaps at DeWolff's mansion? It seemed too somber to be a house so he settled on the idea of a private member club.

He looked up and cricked his neck. The cracking of bones was an unnecessary skill he'd picked up in Vietnam. He'd already found ways of getting percussion from each of his fingers. He flipped over the photograph and once again read the neat handwriting there.

*'Time is against us.'*

"What does that mean, Denholm? What are you trying to tell me?" Obviously the policeman was being cryptic. He couldn't have been sure the state troopers who delivered it wouldn't go through the package. So there had to be something there. He turned the picture back and reconfirmed to himself there was no clock on the walls. "Time. Time," he repeated. It was a while before he found it. At the extreme left of the photo was the arm of another chair or sofa in shadow. It had barely made it into the shot. Resting on the arm was a hand. All that was visible were three fingers, the face of a wristwatch, and the rolled up cuff of a white shirt. "Does the time on the watch make a difference?" Bodge got so close to the picture he could smell the developer on the paper. He moved the lens back and forth in front of that small detail. But he couldn't make out the time on the dial. Then it hit him.

"The too obvious." Somewhere in his training Bodge had heard a speaker talking on the subject of looking and not seeing. Once you saw the truth, you couldn't imagine how you'd ever missed it — how you'd ever seen anything else. The obvious was staring straight at him. His mouth fell open and he pulled away from the photograph. He shouldn't have been looking at the time, but at the watch itself — the battered John Bull on the wrist of Robert Bodge Leon.

# 56

The tap came at the door, who knows? An hour later? A minute? A few seconds? Bodge had remained hypnotized by the left hand corner of the photograph where he'd suddenly appeared like a late guest. He heard the tapping but didn't relate it to himself. Perhaps it was just part of the timpani the heavy rain was playing against the window. But then the sound got louder and turned into a clear knock and he slipped the photograph between the pages of the Bible and went to answer the door.

"Who is it?"

"Me," it was Hong's voice.

He hesitated. He wasn't sure he wanted to let her in, not now. There were many reasons he didn't want to see her. He just couldn't vocalize any of them. So, he opened the door a crack wide enough to talk, but somehow she sidled in through the gap.

"Don't Americans wear pajamas?" she asked, looking down at the serviette that was his only cover. She, in contrast, was wearing an enormous rubber poncho. The legs of her *ao dai* were splattered with mud. She was wearing too much, he, too little, although it took him a while to realize what she was talking about.

"Sorry," he said, and walked slowly into the bathroom. There was a cotton robe on the hook behind the door. Before putting it on, he took another look at himself in the mirror. Yet another Bodge looked back. Just how many of them had there been since New York? When he came back into the room, the poncho was self-standing like a tent beside the bed and Hong was on a guest chair wiping the mud from her feet. Bodge was aware of how beautiful she looked but was still too dazed to see the situation as erotic.

"I can't offer you anything," he said.

"That's good," she smiled. "I haven't come for refreshment." She was wearing a primrose *ao dai* and her hair lay thick as molasses over her shoulders. Bodge sat on the end of the bed and watched her fussing at her ankles with the handkerchief. The mud didn't seem so important. She was delaying. She had something to say and couldn't bring herself to say it. So he waited till she was ready.

Even without looking up at him, she said, "Mr. Rogers…"

"Bodge."

"Bodge." She finally lifted her head and seemed surprised again at how vulnerable he looked. "Are you okay?"

"Yes thanks."

"Bodge, I'm about to make a request. Unfortunately, it isn't a request you can refuse. I don't want you to get angry. I apologize for having to do this because I think you are basically a good person." She paused for effect but he saw her draw in a deep secret breath to shore her nerves. "I'll begin by telling you what I know."

"Go ahead."

"Your name isn't Rogers. You are not a missionary, and you were not married to that poor lady who was killed by the tiger in Ban Methuot." She waited for some reaction from him but received none. "You are an agent of the Central Intelligence Agency and you have been sent here to spy on the French and on us."

Bodge spoke, not because he was shocked or indeed because he had anything to say. He spoke because he could tell from her face that she was waiting for a comment and he didn't want to disappoint her. "Where did you hear all this?"

The confrontation and exposure were not going the way Hong had envisaged. There were no denials, no innocent chuckles or signs of embarrassment. But she had no choice but to go on with her prepared speech. "We Vietnamese aren't as stupid as you take us for. You aren't the only ones with intelligence networks and spies."

Again he felt obliged to react. "Wow!"

There was nothing on Bodge's face beyond the expression of a man listening to an interesting story. Hong wondered whether she might have grossly underestimated this man, whether he was devilishly clever and already one step ahead of her. There was an element of panic in her next comment.

"If anything happens to me tonight, this information will be released to both the French Administration and the Viet Minh. That process is already in place. Your whole operation — all your other agents in Vietnam, will be compromised."

"What could happen to you?"

"What?"

"You said, if something happens to you. Something like what?"

She couldn't read him, not at all. She had no idea of his tactics, no inkling of what he was thinking. Her only course was to go forward.

"In the next few days, I shall be defecting. I shall travel to America with you. I have a passport in the name of Mrs. Rogers, and a US Embassy signed certificate of our marriage. Naturally, these are counterfeit but I believe they'll pass the most stringent inspections. I have sisters in your country. You can leave me there with them and come back. If you go along with this, I won't expose your operation. "

"Thank you."

Had he actually said, "Thank you"? Did she hear him right? "Don't you have anything else to say?" she asked.

"Well…" He thought about it. "This is actually what we'd call at home, blackmail."

Her heart plunged to her stomach. Something was wrong. "You could put it that way, yes." A full thirty seconds passed while she watched him think. It was as if he were mentally assessing the damage, going through filing cabinets to see what would be lost. When he finally looked at her, he seemed to have come to a conclusion. She felt an eerie shudder tingle at her neck. She honestly had no idea what to expect.

Bodge's mouth turned up into a smile and he laughed. He seemed so very happy. "I might have to borrow some money for the air fare," he said. "I'm broke." And he chuckled again.

"So… so you agree?"

"Oh, lady. You wouldn't believe how happy you've just made me. As soon as I set foot on US soil, I'm out of this life."

"But what about your work, your career?"

"Screw it."

"You aren't angry with me?"

"Hong, are you in a hurry to go anywhere?"

"I don't know. Why?"

"Because if you've got a couple of hours, I have a story that will shock you."

Hong left the hotel at 5:30. She had to unbolt the front door to get out. There was nobody in reception and no guard out front. The rain still fell in torrents and hammered onto the rubber of her cape like the drums of war. But there was nothing foreboding about the sound. It was invigorating. The rain drums beat out a tattoo — a marvelous announcement of her freedom.

She walked barefoot through the slimy mud, her shoes in her hands. And she smiled. For once it wasn't the imitation smile of a diplomat, or the masking smile of a reluctant lover. She smiled because she was truly happy. For the first time, she honestly believed things were going to work out. Her life might turn out to be right. She'd shared the sweet American's horror story, cried real tears at his losses, and agonized with him over the unsolvable mysteries. But, as he spoke, she looked at him and was aware that she actually liked him. Being there with him was good. Before she left, she'd kissed him on both cheeks and watched him blush.

"Thank you," she'd said, and, for once, she meant it. She was thanking him for sharing, for his honesty and trust. She was thanking him for giving without expecting anything in return.

The skinny man had been motionless in the shadows that surrounded the hotel. His black umbrella blended with the sagging canopy of leaves. He shuddered from the cold and damp that had risen up trough his bones. Four hours she'd been in the foreigner's room. Four hours. Unacceptable. She'd have to pay.

## 57

Bodge was woken by the silence. The rain had stopped and something in his subconscious had come looking for the missing sound. The light through the window could barely be called day. It was a gray, Boston-like dullness that made a person want to stay in bed. But Bodge thought it was the loveliest morning he could remember. The room still held her scent. The bed still assumed the shape where she'd lain at a conservative distance, listening to his stories like a teenager. His mind still held her presence, her voice, her smile, and her honest tears. His stomach clenched as he thought of those final nervous kisses on his cheeks. There was no doubt in his mind. Being in love was getting better.

He showered. Even the stink from the toilet had assumed a bouquet, a fruity pungency. The free toothpaste beside the sink tasted of a heather frost. Slowly, a second reason for his elation came to him. The photograph projected itself on his mind and he smiled. He and his pal, Lou had been set up. The little shit Gladstein had got the two of them stoned and taken compromising pictures of them. That's what the security guys had over him. Far from annoying the hell out of him, he felt great about it. He had his friend back. He hadn't misread Lou at all, and one hurdle looked lower. It was jumpable. He just needed to be back there to take the run up.

He dressed in his stale clothes and wondered, in this little town, where he'd find anything new in his size. Suddenly aware of an almighty hunger, he went downstairs to see whether he was too late for breakfast or too early for lunch. It had been a very long time since he'd eaten. To keep off unwanted contact from restaurant guests, he took his Bible and sat it open on the table in front of him. He was too nervous to enjoy the food. That morning, he and Hong, the unthinkable duo, were to leave for Saigon and plan their escape.

Even the glare from the hotel bell-boy didn't succeed in destroying Bodge's mood. Both the footman and the receptionist watched eagle-eyed as he walked to the front door, looked up at the sky, and ventured out. The Vietnamese raised their eyebrows at the peculiar Western habit of taking a stroll for its own benefit whatever the weather. They wouldn't realize for another few hours that he'd just checked out. When you're wanted for a double homicide, running out on a hotel bill seems such a trivial thing. Bodge walked down the broad driveway, looking left and right, his ears primed for sounds from behind him. The skinny man in black wasn't hard to spot. Why would a Vietnamese man in a French suit be admiring bougainvilleas that dripped rainwater onto his head? Bodge passed him and nodded and the man looked away.

Bodge walked in the direction of the royal villa they'd passed the previous afternoon on their way to the Baliverne. It was only ten minutes walk, but the streets were slick with mud and deserted as if people knew the rain would be returning shortly. The clouds were bloated like abandoned milk cows. It wouldn't be long before the next downpour. His shoes filled with puddle water. His trouser cuffs were red with mud.

The skinny man followed twenty yards behind on the opposite side of the narrow street. He wasn't much of a follower. In his black suit he stood out like a shadow puppet against the whitewashed walls. For five minutes, Bodge splashed through the puddles and was just beginning to enjoy the scenery when the unexpected happened. Traveling at an unsuitable speed for the toy town streets, an enormous black Cadillac came hurtling round the bend and headed straight for Bodge.

He'd seen the scene a dozen times. The car slows, the doors open, and Edward G Robinson gets perforated with machine gun fire. So, Bodge ran across the street in front of the car and dived head-first into the thick mimosa bushes. The car's brakes locked and it skidded ten yards past him. He poked his head out to see the skinny man run toward it, slip, and land on his rump. The Cadillac door opened and Hong looked out.

"Bodge, quick!"

The skinny man, his suit ruined, climbed to his feet and undid his jacket. A large pistol, the type one would expect a pirate to use, was tucked into his belt. He reached for it. Bodge broke out through the bushes, ran for all he was worth to the car, and threw himself over Hong's lap into the passenger seat. The man had the gun in front of him now and pointed it directly at Bodge's side of the windshield. Hong slammed her foot on the gas and headed straight for the would-be assassin. He dropped the gun and flattened himself like a charcoal drawing against the wall. The wing mirror took a button off his jacket. Bodge looked back to see him shaking there with fear and anger in the exhaust smoke.

"That was fun," Hong said smiling at the rear view mirror.

"Who in blazes was that?" Bodge asked, twisting himself into a proper sitting position.

"Chamberlain, Drung."

"Chamberlains carry pieces?"

"He's sort of a guardian — one of the Emperor's spies. He keeps an eye on me when I'm here. He's angry because the Emperor is off on a hunting trip and he can't get word to him."

"You don't suppose he might have actually used that gun on me, do you?"

"There's no question about it. It's what he does."

"Shoots people?"

"Protects the Emperor's interests. He read me the riot act when I got back to the villa this morning. He put me under house arrest and said he'd be 'taking care' of my friend. That's you."

"How did you get away fr…Okay, never mind. You aren't the arrestable type. I know. So, should I assume there's been another change of plans with regard to transport to the capital?"

"We'll be driving ourselves."

"That's what I was afraid of. Isn't that a bit dangerous?"

"Yes."

"Splendid. Do you suppose Billy the Kid will be sending out a posse after us?"

"Billy…?"

"The skinny guy you just squidged against the wall."

"He doesn't know where we're going. He wouldn't imagine we'd be crazy enough to drive all the way to Saigon overnight in this weather. But there may be army patrols on the road that report the royal number plate."

"And Viet Minh?"

"You never can tell," she said. Bodge smiled. "Does that worry you?"

"Strangely, no."

Hong smiled and gunned the engine to climb the first of many hills that rolled toward the southern planes.

# 58

The rains caught up with them at Duc Trong, about forty kilometers from Dalat and would be with them all through the night. Bodge and Hong shared the driving. They passed a hundred sentry towers but not one guard bothered to step out into the rain to check their papers. Travelers in the daytime usually had their paperwork in order. The couple had talked about many things, but at around 3AM the conversation came round to leaving Vietnam.

"You do know I don't have a passport, don't you?" Bodge reminded her. "It's back at the house in Ban Methuot."

"I might be able to do something about that. But it'll take time — a week?"

"We can't get it sooner? The longer we wait, the more chance there is of us getting busted."

"No. Unless…"

"What?"

"Unless you had a friend at the US embassy."

"I don't have friends anywhere…present company excepted. You are my friend, aren't you?"

"Not really. I don't trust anybody."

"Couldn't you just pretend to be? Just till we get to America."

"I'll see." She looked at the black shapes passing her window and at her orange reflection from the dash lights in the glass. "Wait! You do have a friend. Copeland. I forgot all about him."

"Who's Copeland?"

"He came to Ban Methuot with the French authorities. I didn't have a chance to mention him. He's from your embassy. He seemed really keen to find you."

"And put me in jail."

"No. I didn't get that feeling about him. He seemed, you know, kind."

"Yes, we have a knack of giving that impression, just before we drop ordnance on you. You really are a sucker for Americans, aren't you?"

Hong had spun around on his seat and was rummaging through the junk on the back seat. He looked sideways at her rump for a second too long and almost drove them into a ditch.

"Steady," she said.

"Your fault. You disturbed the balance."

She returned with her old *ao dai* and pulled something from the secret pocket. "Here."

She took a cigarette lighter from the glove box and held its yellow flame up to the name card. "Marion Copeland, United States Aid Agency."

"What was that?"

"United States Aid…"

"No, I mean the name."

As he spoke, a breeze blew out the flame and she couldn't get it to light again. "I think I'm out of fuel."

"Give it here."

She handed him the card and he ran his fingers over the embossed lettering. Even before he raised it to his nose, he could smell the faint trace of scent. "What did he look like, this Mr. Copeland?"

"Normal, about sixty."

"Gray hair?"

"You know him?"

"How was he dressed?"

"Smart. Nice white suit. Good tailor."

Bodge thumped the wheel with the heels of his hands and whooped. "Yup, I guess I do. You remember me telling you about Palmer?"

"You think it might be the same man?"

"Well, it might just be wishful thinking, but if we make it to Saigon in one piece I believe Mr. Copeland would certainly be worth a visit."

They almost made it to Saigon in one piece. Although they hadn't seen it yet, the sun had risen several hours before. They'd talked their way through two Vietnamese army roadblocks. Being in the Emperor's Cadillac helped. It was quite obvious who Hong was, and Bodge flashed his CIA ID which nobody could read, to prove he was the royal bodyguard. They'd just passed through Phuong Lam, about 100 miles from Saigon when the car hit a submerged boulder and the front axle snapped like a chicken bone. Hong had been driving at the time but Bodge assured her he wouldn't have seen it coming either.

"So, where are we?" he asked.

"Stuck," she said.

"And exhausted," Bodge added. The going had been slow in the rain and neither of them had managed to sleep. "I don't suppose there's a Best Western up ahead."

"Is that a hotel?"

"Yes."

"No."

"Didn't think so."

"But we can't be more than three miles from Din Quan. Do you feel like a walk?"

"Do I have any choice?"

Hong found her old poncho and a spare cape in the back, and put some important bits and pieces into a cloth bag. Bodge still had only his Bible so he offered to carry the satchel. The cream-colored cape barely reached his thighs and made him look like a toadstool. The rain had become a mid-day drizzle and somewhere beyond the low clouds, they got the feeling the sun was attempting to make an entrance. They kept to the road but, in the hour it took them to reach the outskirts of Din Quan, nothing passed them. There wasn't so much as a buffalo in the fields.

"Best Wes-tern. Best...best. Bodge," she said. "We'll have to start speaking to each other in English soon. I'm quite an imbecile in English. I'm sure you'll lose all respect for me."

"Well, if you prefer, we could speak to each other in Vietnamese. Then we'll see who's the imbecile."

She laughed and squeezed his arm. Bodge had become extremely sensitive to her every move and word and touch.

The signpost at the first intersection told them to go straight if they wanted to hit Din Quan town center. Hong walked on but Bodge stood reading the second pointer. "'Ho Tri An', that's a lake."

She stopped. "Good boy."

"Does it connect to a river?"

"Of course."

"Does that river go to Saigon?"

"Yes."

"What are the chances of renting a small boat?"

She smiled and came back to join him. "Poor."

"Damn."

"But for the cost of a night at Madame Vin's we could probably buy one."

The detour took them through suburbs of dowdy shacks where timid people crouched in corners on platforms raised above the flooding. When they reached the grubby shore, there was no clear line as to where the street ended and the lake began. Bodge hid behind a banana leaf fence while Hong negotiated with a fisherman. Inside the hood of her poncho and without makeup she looked anything but the Emperor's concubine. Their conversation sounded more like the staccato of spice market bartering. She yelled and spat and once they'd come to an agreement she slapped the man's palm.

When Bodge emerged, the fisherman suddenly recalled there were one or two extra costs for foreigners. Hong laughed and ignored the hopeful surcharges. She climbed on to her new sampan, Bodge close behind, the fisherman last. The man got a spark from the little diesel engine and took them a hundred yards out and back. Satisfied, Hong handed over the cash and the man left them alone, counting and recounting his good fortune.

Hong bought some food and supplies in the half-submerged village and Bodge played with the steering shaft that angled into the water. By the time she got back he had a pretty good idea how to control the thing.

"So, what do you think?" she asked.

"I knew I'd own a boat some day. Did you get any champagne? We need to christen it."

"What name do you have in mind?"

"Something hopeful, like 'USS Please Don't Sink'"

"All right. 'USS Please Don't Sink' it is."

There was something in the air other than the threat of more rain. On their walk from the car Bodge felt their relationship had transformed into something tense. It was an apprehension as if the inevitable were lurking in the rice fields about to flap out at them. Nothing had been said but Bodge could feel a magnetic field around Hong. Whenever he stepped into it his heart missed a beat. He was certain she could feel it too. At least he put so much hope into her sharing his feeling he knew some of that hope had to infect her. But he'd learned his lesson well enough not to act on his instinct this time.

"I was talking to the villagers," she said at last. "They advised us against going down the river in the dark. There are Viet Minh units all over. They only come out at night but then the waterway pretty much belongs to them. They stop river traffic and scrounge cargo and fish. I think they'd consider you a good catch."

"So what do they suggest we do?"

"They say we should go to the south of the lake and find a safe mooring for the night. We can camp there and head onwards at first light."

Bodge's stomach had been engaged in a lot of unnatural turning and churning since Hong came into his life but now it was rolling like an old mangle. How on earth could he spend the night with her feeling the way he did? "What about…what about mosquitoes?" he asked, even though it wasn't the question at the forefront of his mind.

"All taken care of." She patted her bag.

As there was no longer any urgency they did a relaxed tour of the lake to find a suitable spot. The sun, after a day of struggling to free itself from the clouds, made an appearance just in time to perform a moody sunset. They'd tied up in a small inlet that led nowhere and had no smugglers' paths opening onto its shore. Hong grilled fish on an open fire and Bodge peeled fruit. With his hands shaking as they were he was a menace with the knife.

She'd hung the mosquito net inside the canopy of the sampan. They'd agreed to retreat there as soon as the vampires of the riverbank began their evening quest for blood. Bodge looked up at the green mesh from time to time. There was only one net visible. He was honestly more nervous than he'd been at any stage over the past four months.

The sky behind the black clouds was purple. Bodge and Hong sat beside the fire watching the color bleed into the lake. They swigged from a bottle of apricot rice wine that gave them a heady feeling of peace. Neither of them had spoken since the meal. They listened to the cicadas' final concert, the baby birds calling home their mothers, the rude burping of frogs and the splashing of water rats. Bodge wasn't at all expecting Hong's question.

She spoke in a breathy French whisper. "Bodge, do you like me?"

He had no idea how to answer. 'Like" was such an inappropriate word he was tempted to say, 'no'. "Why do you ask?"

"I've been so…so mercenary. If I were you, I'd hate me for using you, or planning to. But you seem so calm about the whole thing."

He couldn't open the sluice gate and let all his feelings pour out all at once. In fact he wasn't sure he should pour at all. He didn't want to frighten her. He didn't want to lose this tentative grasp of her companionship. He had to turn the tap lightly and dribble a little affection at a time.

"I can't think of anyone I'd sooner be used by," he said, displaying neither affection nor sympathy. Confessing love was an art he really had no skill for.

"That's very gallant of you," she smiled, both of them still looking up at the sky. "I'm really not as awful as I've been behaving. It's just that once I decided to get away, I had no chance but to be a bitch about it. I had to lie a lot."

"You do it very well." He bit his tongue again. "I don't…"

"You do hate me. I was afraid of that."

"No. I don't. In fact, I …"

"I feel safe with you. I certainly wouldn't be alone in the forest with any other man I've met. You're a gentleman. This wine…" She took the bottle from Bodge and swigged from it. "It's making me brave. Can you tell? I don't talk with too many men. I'm usually too afraid of what might happen. But, I'm not at all afraid of you."

Bodge looked at her vanishing in the new blackness. A mosquito was sucking at his neck, but he didn't want to damage his image by smacking at it. She knew he was safe. She knew he wouldn't dream of acting on all those erotic thoughts that were dancing in his mind. She knew that however desperately he wanted to take her in his arms and make love to her — he wouldn't. Damn it.

"I'm getting bitten," she said. "Can we take the wine into the sampan and talk in there?"

She didn't wait for an answer. She poured water onto the campfire and carried the bottle across to the boat. He heard the strike of a match and the modest flame of a candle bathed the interior of the sampan in a grayish light. He watched her lift the skirt of the mosquito net and crawl slowly inside.

"Bodge, are you coming?"

Without another thought, he dispatched the mosquito on his neck to insect heaven and hurried to the boat just in time to see her escaping out of the back of the netting. Beyond the first net at the far end of the sampan, there was a second. It was incredible to him how impenetrable two layers of cotton mesh could be.

# 59

The rainy season in Indochina isn't something you can set a clock by. The season itself usually turns up at roughly the same time every year, but monsoons come and go. A week might go by with skies of blue and not so much as a huff of a cloud. When the little sampan putted along the Saigon River and came to a stop near the Delta Ferry port, the couple that stepped ashore were tanned dark from the sun.

It was an easy disguise for Hong. Her skin had been plastered with foundations and makeup as thick as cake icing from the day she'd entered the royal fold. Pale skin was a symbol of affluence in this nation of farmers, and the matrons had insisted she keep her face out of the sun. But her olive complexion naturally absorbed its rays and made her glow like an ember.

On their journey from Din Quan, she'd hacked her hair short with a knife and left it uncombed. She'd donned a commoner's pajamas and sandals, and now looked no more like a concubine than Bodge looked like Charlie Chaplin. Bodge had washed his only set of clothes in the river and dried them from the sampan mast.

They bade farewell to USS Please Don't Sink and took a cyclo to the hotel of the man who didn't speak. Hong stood back like an obedient short-time prostitute while Bodge signed the card and asked for room thirteen. The old man must have remembered the American because he didn't ask for his passport. As Bodge already had his "femme" the owner had nothing at all to say.

Hong loved the palm tree room and commended Bodge on his choice. This, she agreed, was the perfect place to hide. He closed the door and she set to making up a bed on the floor by the window. They hadn't so much as shaken hands but it was all still a remarkable dream for Bodge. He was certain the alarm clock would sound at any second. He didn't believe he deserved such good fortune but still hanging over him each new day was the curse. Anyone who'd gotten close to him was dead. His love for Hong may very well have hexed her but he didn't have the will to push her away.

As far as they knew the authorities were still looking for Bodge. Hong decided neither of them should be walking around the streets in broad daylight. Bodge wasn't exactly easy to disguise. But he did need to contact the embassy. If Copeland and Palmer really were one and the same there had to be a way of getting word to him without alerting anyone else. Bodge used the hotel phone and called the American Embassy switchboard. A girl who apparently had a clothespin on her nose answered in English.

"United States Embassy. May I help you?"

"Yes. I'd like to speak to your Mr. Copeland."

"Mr. Copeland? Do you know his extension number?"

"Sorry, I don't."

"Are you sure you have the name right?"

"Yes."

He heard the crinkling of paper. "I'm sorry. We don't have anyone here by that name."

"Miss," Bodge said calmly. "I have an embossed name card here in my hand that says you do."

"I'm sorry." And she hung up, just like that.

He called again.

"United States Embassy. May I help you?"

"Miss, if you hang up on me again I shall arrange for your immediate dismissal from your job."

"Who do you thi—?"

"My name is Federal Agent Robert Leon. Make sure you write that down. Robert Leon. I'm here on a fact-finding mission for the State Department. So, I'm very much in a position to fire you. I'm staying at the…(He searched his memory for the name of a hotel) "…Majestic. I expect you to find Mr. Copeland, inform him I've arrived, and arrange for him to meet me at the hotel at 7:30 this evening. I hope that's not too difficult for you."

He hung up. He decided his real name shouldn't mean anything to anyone at the embassy but Palmer. They'd probably contact the Majestic and discover there was nobody by the name of Leon staying there. But, word might just make its way through to his old boss.

At seven, Bodge was already mingling with a group of French bean experts in the foyer of the Majestic.

As they began to trail out, Bodge realized he'd be all alone in the foyer and would stand out quite badly. So, he looked around once more and joined the exodus. He walked two lengths of the street in front, keeping out of the lamplight and watching for people arriving at the hotel. He spent most of his time fending off offers from cyclo drivers;

"We go massage today?"

"You need girl?"

"Boy?"

"Ganja?"

"Mr. Bodge?"

Bodge looked up at the middle-aged man who was slowly peddling his cyclo alongside him. "Yes?"

"You come."

No questions in French or Vietnamese drew another word from the rider. He was a short-legged man who lost contact with the pedals at the base of each orbit. He rode silently for half an hour out of downtown and toward the docks. The last three blocks took them along unlit streets with doorways ideal for lurkers. In front of a small office building the cyclo stopped and the man nodded to an upstairs window where a cloth blind held back a dim light.

As soon as Bodge climbed down from the seat, the tricycle was off and away. Only an eerie silence remained. Bodge walked through the doorless entrance and worked his way up a pitch black stairwell. His only marker was a sliver of light around the upstairs door. He kept his eyes on that and ignored whatever might be crawling there in the shadows of each landing. In front of the door, he knocked. The reply was in Vietnamese.

"Who's there?"

"Robert Leon."

He heard footsteps on a wooden floor and the slide of a bolt. The door was flung open and Palmer stood there with a huge, sincere smile. "Bodge! As I live and breathe." They went into a bear hug with equal enthusiasm. "I was certain on so many occasions that you were dead."

"Me too," Bodge said, not really knowing when to let go. "I have that third adjective for you. I think I'll go with *charmed.*"

They pulled apart. "So it would seem. Come in."

The room was a well-equipped office with electrical gadgets and filing cabinets. It looked like an operations center but without the operators. Bodge and Palmer were alone.

"Coffee?"

"Please."

A pot was percolating on the side cabinet. In the light of the room Bodge could see the changes in the older man. The skin of his jowls was hanging loose. His eyes were red and puffy. He seemed to have aged a decade since Bodge had last seen him. As always he made the coffee without asking how Bodge wanted it.

"You're a hard man to find, Mr. Palmer."

"I'm very sorry. These have been disturbing times." He handed Bodge a steaming mug. "How much do you know about what happened?"

"Nothing — except for the homosexual photos. I'm guessing the security section was given snaps of me sometime after those of Lou. I imagine Tuck and Jansen were delighted."

Palmer sat opposite Bodge. "The timing was perfect. The agency had just launched a very serious witch hunt. They were burning all the gay or alleged gay federal workers at the stake. Some espionage expert had submitted a report to Congress saying that having homosexuals in positions of responsibility was a national security risk. Actually it fitted very neatly into the euphoria that's been spreading around the country since they introduced the Sexual Perverts Bill.

"The way I see it, some foreign power got wind of it and decided to exploit the situation. You wouldn't believe how many tapes and photographs have turned up from anonymous sources; how many witnesses have crawled out of the woodwork."

"And that was why you moved me to the safe house?"

"No. We moved you the day of Stephanie's car explosion. We found the housing for the bomb in your car and realized you were in ongoing danger. That's Operations policy if we think a mission's been compromised. We considered it a serious enough breach to relocate our offices. Security didn't get the photos of you until after you were moved."

"The pictures of me were—?"

"Pretty much the same as those of Lou."

"Damn."

"Jansen was very keen to talk to you. I refused to disclose your whereabouts. I couldn't contact you because I was sure we were under surveillance."

"The Agency tailing the Agency?"

"You'd be surprised how much animosity there is between our two departments. You can imagine the pressure there was on us when they found out that you and Stephanie spent the night together before she died."

Bodge looked uneasy. "I'm..."

"Don't worry, Bodge. I agreed with her it would be a good idea to loosen you up. I would have loved to be in the meeting where they tried to fathom out what a gay man was doing in a motel room with a woman. But it still made you their number one suspect."

"So as far as the Security people were concerned I was wanted as a pervert and a murder suspect."

"They had an agency warrant out on you."

"Did that include 'shoot on sight'?"

"No. You were just to be brought in as a witness. Why?"

"I felt a lot of hostility from Jensen."

"He certainly has a problem. Research in Europe suggests the most violent anti-homosexuals have latent tendencies themselves."

Bodge laughed. "Perhaps he had the hots for me."

"I doubt it. Those big military types like their boys petite."

They sipped at the coffee and smiled.

"I hear you were in Ban Methuot," Bodge said.

"It's the only one of our postings that's collapsed."

"I'm sorry."

"Oh, son. I don't blame you in the least. I was even surprised you bothered to go."

"I believed Stephanie might still be alive. I needed to get answers to all these questions. I hadn't planned to stick around there."

"I'm so sorry about what happened there. I should have read the omens and cancelled that mission. It's been jinxed from the start."

"You don't strike me as the type of person who believes in fate."

"In this case, fate's been knocking on my mind since your truck encounter in DC. I didn't listen to it."

"Do you suppose it's all connected? That and the gay purge?"

"There's no evidence of it. Ramos was still working on it when I left. His investigations hadn't found any links."

"I was hoping that finding you would solve all these mysteries."

"I'm sorry, Bodge. I haven't been of much help to you, have I? What are you planning to do next?"

"I'm going back."

"I'm not sure if that's a good idea, considering."

"I'm not the most popular person here either, you know?"

"Point taken."

"Can you arrange me a passport?"

There was something in Palmer's expression, something about the way he hesitated and looked down at his cup that told Bodge all was not well.

"I'm...not officially connected to the Embassy."

"But you're the head of CIA operations in Vietnam. Surely you could call on a few favors."

"I..."

"What is it?"

"I'm no longer connected to the CIA either. The Ambassador here was just doing a favor for a friend of mine when he let me go to Ban Methuot. I can't tell the embassy who I actually am."

"Why on earth...? Wait. They've got you too, haven't they."

"They scheduled a hearing to discuss my background. I skipped the country before it could happen. I've been suspended indefinitely. That's why you were forgotten for so long at the safe house."

"What have they got on you?"

"A witness: an old lover."

"The bastards. Where do they find these guys? I mean, how much money would it take to get a man to stand up in court and announce he's a faggot?"

Palmer looked into Bodge's eyes and smiled sadly. "In this case, I don't believe money was the issue."

"Why else would he...?" Bodge suddenly felt stupid. Palmer had already answered that question. "Oh!"

"Forgive me, Bodge."

Bodge took a few seconds to look up at the reservoir of answers. When he looked back at Palmer Bodge was shaking his head. "I'm not certain it's something you should be asking forgiveness for. It hasn't had any effect on me. But..."

"What, Bodge?"

"Why are you telling me? Surely, the fewer people who know about this, the better."

"I've had to make some important decisions since I left the States. I tried the obvious one. I had the whisky and the loaded revolver. I decided it was best to put myself out of everybody's misery. It turns out I wasn't as good a shot as I thought I was. Put a darned big hole through a hotel ceiling. After that failed, I only had one course left open to me. Bodge, I've been lying about this all my life. Holding in a lie for so long makes it infectious. It starts to spread, starts to take over your whole life. I'm going to cut it out before I become the lie."

"Admit to it?"

"Yes."

"They wouldn't let you stay on at the Agency."

"I've done my bit. I have money. I don't have to work. And I believe people will eventually come around to accepting us as humans. There are more people like you out there."

"Like me?"

"Ramos told me how you took the news that Lou might be gay. You were enough of a man not to judge him for it."

"Hmm. I'm not sure I didn't. I do have problems with it."

"Which is to be expected. Having doubts and having prejudice are entirely different. People like Jensen would have no doubts whatsoever. It's a hanging offence to him."

"Okay, I need some time to work out exactly how I do feel about this. But, if it makes any difference, I'm glad you decided not to top yourself."

"That's very sweet of you. Listen. I don't have anyone here who can fix you a legal passport. But I do have people in Hong Kong. I can get you there on a naval vessel without having to worry about papers. That should solve one of your problems."

"Well, I…"

"Bodge, you're a wanted man. They'll have your details at the embassy and the airport. You can't just get yourself a passport and fly out as if nothing had happened."

He sighed. "I know."

"There's something you aren't telling me."

"Von Hong."

"The consort?"

"She's decided to defect. She chose me as her courier, I mean, long before she found out I was *persona non grata*. She's set everything up already to protect her family."

"Bodge, no."

"Sorry. It isn't negotiable."

"Are you insane, boy? You can only survive this by keeping a low profile. I would hardly call smuggling the Emperor's minor wife into America 'low profile'. It's madness."

"I have no choice."

"Tell her no. Run off without her." Palmer studied Bodge's face. "This isn't just an act of political kindness, is it?"

"I love her."

"Oh, my goodness." Palmer shook his head and began to laugh. Bodge laughed along with him except his own sounded more manic. "Robert Leon, we are talking 'International Incident' here. The United States could be seen as kidnapping a member of Vietnam's royal family."

"Or rescuing one from the dangers of war. Heads of state are whisked away from armed conflict all the time."

Palmer laughed again and stood. He mussed Bodge's hair like an affectionate uncle. "Does she have travel papers?"

"A US passport in the name of Mrs. Rogers, and a marriage certificate from our embassy."

"Very resourceful. Are you sure she isn't just using you?"

"She was, in the beginning. Or, at least, she tried to. Right now I think there's an even chance she respects me."

"Who could resist you? Okay, if she can get herself to Hong Kong, I'll see what I can do about getting you both into the US. But you'll have to leave first."

"Why?"

"The cruiser to Hong Kong sets sail at eight in the morning. You have to be on it."

# 60

When Bodge got back to the silent man hotel, Hong was in the room trying on her disguise. It amounted to a henna hair rinse and a pair of dark-rimmed eyeglasses. He agreed she did look different. He believed the old Clark Kent Myopia might just be enough to fool the busy Immigration worker at the airport. A lot of Vietnamese women were leaving the country as French wives. It was inevitable the Americans would take over that export trade when the French had gone home.

There was a moment of panic in her eyes when Bodge told her he had to leave the following morning. She decided to attempt to leave on the Air France flight around mid-day. Money still carried a lot of weight at the airline desk and if there were enough of it she thought she could arrange for someone to be bumped. She had enough. All the money for the extension to the royal lodge was in her pack. If she missed that flight, she could bribe in advance for the following day. Whatever happened, she and Bodge would be together in Hong Kong by the end of the week. That seemed to Bodge like an awfully long wait.

They sat together propped up on pillows against the orange palm trees that night before the great escape. For some unfathomable reason, she suddenly had the urge to tell him about her life. He said she could tell him any time but she insisted now was the moment. She whispered it through a background of car horns and cyclo bells from the street below.

"I worked hard when I was young," she began. "My father started a small ice-cream shop and my sisters and I watched how much life he put into his work. Our mother had died giving birth to my youngest sister. Father was determined that all three of us should have the opportunity to study. He got us into the best French lycee. We wanted to repay him, so, when we came home from school we would all work alongside him. It made us very close.

"At school we were all excellent students, but I had something else. Some wicked turn of fate had sculpted my sisters plain and me with some finesse. With the escalation of the war, my father's business took a downturn. Money became scarce. My sisters urged me to enter a local competition. It was the type which would ignore a girl's social and mental inadequacies and give a prize for the shape of her chest and the allure of her smile. My tits and teeth gave us a reprieve from starvation.

"That competition led to others to the point that my body became the main bread-winner for my family. It almost paid for me to enter University the following year, until, on one fateful day, the Emperor sent his talent scouts to the top competition in the Delta. I won the day and lost the life. There was enough money in royal whoring for my father's business to be resurrected and my sisters to go to college. I was the sacrifice.

"It may be true that the Emperor loved me. It isn't important. Some years before, I'd put my first experience of love to one side, reserved for someone who was truly remarkable. It was commandeered by a man who believed he was remarkable, and therefore couldn't have been. I needed desperately to get away from that life — to find my true self. But I had to be sure my father and sisters were safe. I erected a lie that I hope will give my father a chance of survival if the Viet Minh ever wish to purge those families with connections to the royalists. Then I used another deceit to get my sisters out of the country.

"Your predecessors, the Cornfelts were lazy missionaries. They made rare trips to the hilltribe villages and staged a lot of photographs. These they sent back to their mission headquarters claiming incredible feats of humanitarianism in helping the poor and downtrodden. I knew that these were false claims and I threatened to tell their donors exactly what they were using this aid money for. You've seen the furnishings at both houses. One chest of drawers from the Ban Methuot house could have fed a village for a year. So I didn't feel bad about blackmailing them. All they had to do was sponsor my sisters for study in North America. I think they got off lightly actually. They left last month so the stage was clear for my own departure."

"And how long had I been in your escape plan?"

"You were integral from the moment I learned there were spies on their way to my country. That's why I was waiting for you to arrive. That's why I was looking after you."

"What do you mean?"

"The bomb in Saigon."

"That was your man — the old guy?"

"I wanted to be sure you could make it to Ban Methuot."

"Did you have a hand in my ride on the royal airplane?"

"A little. Originally I'd intended to blackmail the two of you with my knowledge of your backgrounds. I was sure your organization would assist me for my silence. My emperor has a terrible habit of leaving top secret documents beside the bed and falling asleep. But I liked your colleague and I appreciated the fact that she was willing to fight for the rights of her servant girl. I knew it was a terrible risk considering you were both supposed to remain incognito — not make any waves. But you were my passport to leaving Vietnam and that became my priority. I have come to like you too so it pleases me greatly that you aren't offended by my subterfuge. I really don't wish to hurt you. I wish I could have known you under different circumstances."

It was a wonderful speech but something about it made Bodge feel uncomfortable. There were elements of a eulogy about it. He'd always been expecting his luck to run out, so he was hearing what he believed was inevitable. But the way she looked at him before curling up on her uncomfortable nest beneath the palms drove that thought from his mind. He had no doubt on that last night in Saigon, that Hong truly loved him as much as he loved her — that their futures were inexorably connected. Yet still he'd said nothing of his feelings. He spent his remaining two hours lying on his bed watching the faint rise and fall of her breaths.

At seven, he kissed her sleeping cheek and took a cyclo to the navy docks. He arrived at Quay Four to find Palmer standing in front of the gate. He had a suitcase and two large brown paper parcels at his feet.

"Morning, Bodge."

"Sir. Are you going somewhere?"

"As a matter of fact I'm on my way to Korea, so I'm going with you. Now you're accounted for there really isn't much point in sticking around in Saigon."

"You came here just for me?"

"Pretty much. You were one of the loose ends I felt bad about leaving dangling." He picked up the suitcase and pointed his chin to the parcels. "Those are yours. No offence, but I prefer my shipmates to have a decent change of clothes."

The US Navy guard at the gate saluted and didn't ask to see paperwork. USS Charleston was moored beside the quay taking on supplies in unmarked crates. They walked up the gangway and a second seaman saluted when they stepped onto the deck. They all seemed to recognize Palmer. The skipper was supervising the loading. He spotted the new arrivals and came over at the double to take Palmer's hand.

"Ant, you old stowaway. Who let you on board?"

"Off with you. You're delighted to have me. Captain Eckhart, this is Bodge."

They shook hands. "Howdy, Bodge. Welcome aboard. I've saved you girls the honeymoon suite down aft. You remember where it is?"

"How could I ever forget? Thanks, Jim."

"My pleasure as always."

Once Bodge and Palmer where settled into the storage area behind the subsidiary engine and had slung their hammocks from the hot pipes they were already desperate for air. They walked to the fantail and watched the crew prepare to set sail. Bodge modeled his new slacks and shirt for their buyer. They fitted him perfectly.

By the time the cruiser sailed into Hong Kong Harbor, Bodge had a clear idea of what needed to be done in the US and a list of allies to help him do it. For the first time, he thought he might have a chance. Once they'd docked, Palmer walked him to the top of the gangway.

"Are you sure you won't come ashore for a few hours and join me in some food that doesn't come out of cans?" Bodge asked.

"Thank you, but no. We'll be shoving off early in the morning. Besides, I don't want to spend the evening watching you and your lady friend making goo goo eyes at each other. So…"

Bodge shook his hand and held on to it. "Boss, I told you in Saigon I'd need time to think about those things you told me in your office. Well, I guess I've thought and I have to say I admire you, really. I can't think of anyone who'd have the balls to do what you've decided to do, to stand up to those hypocrites, stick to your principles. In fact, I think that makes you something of a hero to me. I'd be honored to get together with you when this is all sorted out and have a few drinks to talk over the odd old days."

Palmer's lips quivered slightly then turned up into a smile of gratitude. "Thank you, son," he said. "I would like that very much. In fact, you'll need me around when you get older. No one's going to believe a word of these stories you'll be telling the old-timers in the bar. I know they're all true and I still don't believe 'em."

They hugged and Bodge bounded smiling down the gangplank onto the dock.

There was a fifty-fifty chance Bodge would find Hong at the Ritz waiting for him. But, if she hadn't made it onto Tuesday's flight or Wednesday's, she wouldn't be there till later today. So, he didn't want to get too excited. He knew from experience how erratic airplane bookings could be. He walked to the front desk and smiled at the pretty girl. She wore a neat blazer with the hotel logo on the pocket, and a hairnet. If he hadn't been so anxious about Hong, he would have asked her why.

"Hello," he said. "My name's Rogers. I was wondering whether my wife had checked in yet."

"Ah, Mr. Rogers," she smiled. "We've been expecting you." He felt an overwhelming relief. They'd agreed on this hotel but hadn't made a reservation. It appeared the most difficult part of the journey was over. The girl was leafing through the large ledger on the desk. He assumed she was looking up their room number, but he was wrong. She stopped at an empty page where a brown envelope was wedged into the fold.

"Mr. R. Rogers, is it?" she asked, and held out the letter. He didn't want to take it. He looked at his name in Hong's neat handwriting and knew. The curse had kicked into reverse. Whatever was inside that letter would kill him. "Someone from yesterday's flight dropped it off."

He carried the envelope out into the street and walked till he found a small bench at the edge of a littered park. For an hour he sat there with the envelope unopened beside him on the seat. People passing by looked at it. Ants crawled on it. A breeze attempted to lift and run off with it. But it remained unopened until Bodge could stand it no more.

*'Cher Bodge,'* it began.

*'I'm sorry to do this by letter. On top of all my other faults, I'm a coward. Over the past few days, since we left Dalat, I've come to understand that I can't desert my people in their hour of most need. It would look very bad for the Emperor to have his household running away like rats from a sinking ship. I didn't know how to tell you.*

*I think life in America would have been very happy, and perhaps, sometime in the future, I may still make it. But this is not the time. I shall never forget you, Mr. Rogers and I hope you will not forget me. I believe you will be able to solve all your mysteries and be accepted again by your own people. Good luck. Hong.'*

'Good luck?' That was the best she could do? That was the most suitable sign off she could come up with? 'Good luck?' He crumpled the paper into a ball and threw it onto the ground. A flock of desperate pigeons came down to inspect it. There are two types of disappointment. One comes when the totally unexpected hits you and knocks you flat. The other is one you wait for. You go over it in your mind even to the point of how you'll react when it arrives. But you never get it right. You never completely take into account how much damage sadness can do to you.

Bodge continued to sit on the bench, waiting for the feeling to go away. At one point he rescued the letter and read it again. He folded it neatly and put it into his pocket. But no matter how long he waited, the sadness stayed there with him like an undertaker at a death bed.

## 61

"So, even when we were together in New York you were under suspension?"

"It's been five months, now."

"With pay?"

"Half."

"How do you get by?"

"Anthony's family helps."

'Anthony!' Palmer's first name. At last. He had a Christian name. Anthony and Denholm — the gay old bachelors. Palmer hadn't given anything away on the boat. It had all come together in Bodge's mind on the long flight from Hong Kong. Denholm had been there at LaGuardia to meet his flight. Palmer's Buick was parked in the tow zone with a large 'On official Police Business' card tucked in the front windshield — one of the last perks of a soon to be inactive service with the New York police force. They drove along Grand Central Parkway toward Manhattan. It was a rolling badly-laid road and long stretches of it had no central dividing lines. With its overgrown acacias it didn't give any indication it led to one of the world's most developed metropolises. It was like sneaking into the city on a back road.

The early questions on the drive were all from Denholm about his lover's wellbeing. He seemed to know about the depression and the suicide attempt. It was all Bodge could do to persuade him that Palmer's state of mind had settled and that the man was back in control of himself.

"But, they don't have any actual evidence against either of you," Bodge went on.

"Nothing physical — but enough circumstantial to force us out of our respective jobs. They interviewed neighbors, talked to the building superintendent. You know? We'd naturally been careful but once the virus takes root people's memories tend to turn even the most innocent comments and gestures into blatant queer behavior. You saw the reaction when people thought your pal was homosexual."

"I sure did."

"Look, Bodge. I don't know how you feel about all this, but, if you'd sooner work with someone else on clearing Lou's name I could put you on to a private dick I trust. I can help you out with money. I'd understand. My badge isn't going to do us a lot of good. I'd sooner keep it in my wallet unless it's absolutely necessary."

"Is there really no one in the department who supports you?"

"Are you kidding? You know cops, Bodge. Even if someone did have doubts about people like us being disease-carrying perverts there's no way on God's earth they'd let anyone else know that. Most of the guys I worked with believe I've betrayed them. There are one or two who've kept quiet but I don't dare approach them for help. I guess they're as close as I am to anyone in the force these days."

"But do you think we could call on them if we need official backup?"

"Oh, don't worry about that. I know a guy with the FBI who — shall we say — has a vested interest in busting a few queer myths."

"He's—?"

"Yup!"

"You don't say? Gee. The government service actually is riddled with perversion."

"You'd be surprised."

"So, when you were coordinating Lou's exhumation from my place —?"

"It was all done through him. I didn't have any direct contact with the police."

"Could he get us an appointment with a coroner, do you suppose?"

"Already taken care of."

"There you go. Organization. I think you and I are going to be just fine partners."

"Thanks, man."

As the high-rises of the Upper East Side loomed up in front of him, Bodge felt like an unarmed gladiator on his way into the coliseum. As far as he was concerned this was enemy territory. There was an Agency warrant out on him. The police were probably looking for him, too. Whatever ferreting around they did would have to be discreet and clever.

Their first stop was the Cornell Medical Center morgue where most of the Agency related autopsies were conducted. Denholm's name on the visitor's list got them past a receptionist who didn't seem too interested and down into the basement office of Dr. Lee, the head coroner. His secretary went through the records and found that the doctor himself had performed the autopsy on Lou Vistarini.

Dr. Lee was a small Asian with a troubled expression. He hurried into the office from the dissection room, ignored the big man on a chair in the corner, and the tall man reading a wall chart, and rushed to his desk. The only thing on his mind seemed to be getting the Lucky Strike from his drawer and breathing in some life-saving nicotine. After three puffs, a look of divine enlightenment came over his face and he sat in his chair and smiled. That's when he noticed the visitors.

"Oh, hi. Can I help you?"

Bodge introduced himself as Agent Rogers from Operations. Denholm kept quiet. Bodge said he was following up on the Lou Vistarini case and needed to ask one or two questions. The coroner, with his beloved cigarette dangling from the corner of his mouth, gladly went through the files. He emerged with a thin folder with Lou's name typed at the top.

"Here he is," Lee said. "What specifically do you need to know?"

"Did you find any traces of drugs? Anything that could have knocked him out?"

"Let's see. Stomach contents. Stomach contents. Oh, wait. I recall this case, now. This is the chap that had been buried once and exhumed."

"That's right."

"So, it would have been a few days after he died before I got to see him. Some traces would have dissipated after that long. But, let's see."

Bodge was surprised Dr. Lee could read the file with his eyelids squeezed together to keep out the smoke. "Yes, here we are. There was some chemical and natural residue in the stomach I couldn't identify."

"You don't do tests?"

"We can only test for things we know about. This seemed to be a cocktail of weird and wonderful compounds. Probably something new from overseas. In fact there were only two components that I could positively identify."

"And, what were they?"

"One was an opiate of some kind. The other was an alkaloid of the belladonna family."

"Belladonna's a poison."

"In large doses, yes. But it can also be used as a medicine. In some of its forms it may work as a sedative. I believe it also has hallucinatory effects. It all depends on the dosage and what it was mixed with. It's odd, though."

"What is?"

"Well, opium and belladonna are antagonistic."

"Meaning?"

"Opium is an antidote to belladonna. They should cancel each other out. Taken together…I can't imagine what would happen."

"Disorientation?"

"I'd certainly think so. But again it would depend on what these other traces were. And if alcohol were involved, whoosh." He threw his hand into the air like a rocket taking off.

"You don't think it's anything he'd be likely to administer himself for a medical complaint?"

"Oh, absolutely not. Belladonna can have a disastrous effect on someone with a medical condition — heart problems for example."

"Could this cocktail have been lethal by itself?"

Lee held up the file. "I doubt it. I have here as cause of death; 'Cardiac arrest'. I confess that's often a catch all for a coroner to use if he hasn't got a clue, but in this case I wrote here; 'clear signs of subintimal hemorrhage'."

"And that means?"

"There was a rupture that caused an obstruction in the blood vessel. Mr. Vistarini's heart shut down."

"Is there anything else that could have caused it?"

"I don't know. Shock, sometimes in older people. Respiratory paralysis due to an overdose of stimulants, perhaps."

"Was there any evidence that he might have overdosed? Drink, for example?"

"Like I say, I got him a few days late. If he'd drunk himself to death it would have been hard to tell from the autopsy. His liver didn't look too bad so I didn't consider alcoholic poisoning. There was this, though."

"What?"

Lee produced a photograph he'd taken of the face. Bodge was shocked to see the condition of his friend. His face was a death mask — all humour and kindness and verve had been drained from it. Bodge's stomach heaved. There were bruises and cuts around the mouth.

"Could that have happened when he was being buried?"

"No. This bruising could only have happened when he was still alive." When Bodge last saw his friend in the cab, there were no face wounds. He stared up at his reservoir of explanations and plucked one down.

"Could these wounds have been caused by someone force-feeding him booze, doctor?"

"That's not impossible, son. Not impossible at all. In fact, as far as I could see, one of his teeth was cracked too. Could have been caused by a glass bottle. Only conjecture of course but not impossible."

Bodge breathed deeply and took in a lungful of cigarette smoke. "Dr. Lee, did you happen to send a copy of this to the Security division?"

The doctor looked at the attached note. "Yes. Someone came from there to pick it up."

"So, they knew all this."

"Yup."

"Thank you, doctor. You've been very helpful."

They didn't voice their opinions on what they'd just heard until they were back in the car.

"All right," Denholm said. "So we have a possibility that your friend was force-fed, and the possibility that he died from an alcohol overdose. Where does that leave us?"

"It leaves us with the fact that Lou picked up those cuts and bruises after I left him in the cab. I wasn't at my most observant that night so I guess we could use a second opinion."

# 62

The little guy with the nose was just arriving for his shift when Denholm and Bodge stepped out of the shadows.

"Holy shit. You two scared the daylights out of me." His edgy twitch had become more pronounced. It was either generic or he got nervous in the company of guys in suits.

"How are you doing, bud?" Denholm asked.

"A lot better for not having you two jump out at me. Now what is it?"

"Just a couple more questions."

"You know?" the cabby said, trying to edge past them. "I'd love to gas with you boys, but I really gotta cab to drive."

"That's perfect, then," said Bodge. "Because we're looking to hire one. What do you say we go for a drive?"

Either the guy was a naturally bad driver or something had spooked him badly because they hadn't gone a hundred yards and he'd already screwed up the gears twice.

"Something bothering you?" Denholm asked.

"Me? No, sir. I'm as right as rain, me."

"You know?" said Bodge. "I've kind of been expecting you to ask whether we found my friend."

"Oh, right. Yeah! So, did ya?"

"We found his body."

Even through the rear view mirror they could detect a drastic loss of colour in the cabby's face.

"He's dead?"

"Does that surprise you?"

"Yeah! Well, why…why shouldn't it?"

He was driving so slowly the cabbie behind them started leaning on his horn. Their driver nearly jumped out of his seat.

"Why don't you pull over for a second?" Bodge suggested.

Once they'd come to a stop the two passengers leaned on the back of the front seat.

"And when they found him," Denholm went on, "his mouth was bloodied and he'd broken a tooth."

"As if he'd been beaten up," Bodge added.

"And, as you were the last person to see him alive…"

"Don't you try that one on me," the driver said, swinging around in his seat. "That ain't true."

"But that's what you told us," said Bodge.

"I said he went to his door."

"And nobody let him in. And that's where they found his dead body four hours later in the step down of his own building."

"No, you know? That ain't possible."

"Why not?"

"Look. I can't…"

"It's a murder rap," Denholm reminded him.

"I didn't do nothing."

"So you keep telling us."

"Oh, man. They got my registration. They'll know it was me."

"You're being squeezed to keep quiet?"

"He said he'd find my family. I don't want my family hurt."

"If your information turns out to be reliable we might be able to offer them protection. Ninety nine percent of threats don't lead to anything. It's either that or you're looking at jail time."

There was silence for a full minute but Denholm and Bodge let it ride. The driver's eyes darted back and forth between the two men and out into the street.

"All right. But I didn't do nothing wrong."

"That's for us to decide."

"Okay. Okay. We was almost back at his place when he comes round. I mean the guy you're asking about. He asks me where he is and I tell him. He asks where you are and I say I just dropped you off. He's confused, you know? Not all there. And it's like he remembers something. He says, 'Sons of bitches' or some such thing and tells me we gotta go back."

"Back to where you picked him up?" Bodge asked.

"Yeah. And I got no problem with that long as he's got money to pay me. He was out of it — not firing on all rockets you might say. So I had to check he had enough for the fare. He goes through his wallet and throws me a twenty. So I'm just about to turn back when he decides he wants to make a phone call. Seeing as we're close to his place he says he'll stop off there and call."

"Did he say who to?" Bodge asked.

"Nah. I didn't get half of what he was saying. He staggers over to the door and I guess he can't find his key cause I see him reach up and ring the bell. He's swaying away, you know? Getting mad. Then he makes his way back to the cab and climbs in. Again he wants me to take him back to where I found him so off we go. I didn't see nothing strange in it. A lot of drunks forget stuff in bars and get me to turn round. It must have been about, I don't know, three? And he gets me to cruise up and down 8th real slow and I point out the garbage cans I found him in front of. So we stop there and he just sits and looks around."

"And this is in front of Bouncers?" Bodge asked.

"That's right. We're sitting there twenty minutes, I guess. Just sitting. Then, all of a sudden, my door flies open and this guy leans in and sticks a derringer in my face. I don't mind telling you I shit myself. A couple of other guys are in the back seat and wrestling your buddy out and onto the sidewalk."

"Did you see where they took him?"

"Are you fucking kidding me? Man, I got a gun barrel against my teeth. And the guy holding it gives me a choice. He says I can choose for him to shoot me right there and then, or I can turn blind, deaf and dumb. He says he's got the cab numbers and if I ever remembered what I just seen he wouldn't think twice about coming after me. And, I tell you, I believed him. I had to keep quiet. You can see that, can't ya?"

"And you drove off?"

"Fast as I could."

"Would you recognize the guys if you saw them again?"

"The punk that was in my face, sure. But it was all too fast and dark to get a handle on the others."

"Okay," Denholm said at last. "What's the fare?"

"What? That's it?"

"Sure. You've been very cooperative. Thanks. We'll be in touch."

"What about the threat?"

"Did he look at your drivers license?"

"No, but he got the cab registration."

"And is this the same cab as that night?"

"No. We switch."

"Then you've got nothing to worry about. It was just a threat. They won't come after you."

"You two found me easy enough."

"Yeah, but you forget. We're the good guys. We're a lot smarter."

It was Friday night — long after midnight, and Bodge was into his third hour of surveillance. A hundred yards up ahead, on the other side of the street the normally flashing light out front of Bouncers was dark. Drunks had passed him, looked in the car and decided not to hassle the big guy in the dark fedora. He could have been a cop, or a mobster or just a late night murderer waiting for a victim. It was safer to leave him be.

In all the time he'd been there, only two teenagers had gone into the café down from the clip joint. Bodge thought about Denholm's comment the night they'd gone in there for their twenty-five cent instants. "I smell something odd here and it sure isn't coffee." Who'd own a place like this in such a neighborhood? Why would he want to price himself out of the market unless he wasn't so keen on attracting customers and making money? Bodge tapped his fingers on the dash and considered that last thought.

"Unless he wanted to keep the place empty."

He decided it was time to stretch his legs. He locked the car and strolled along his side of the road. The street smelled of smoke and garbage. When he came level to the café, he looked across into the dim interior. He recognized the same long-haired kid reading a magazine behind the counter. But, it was odd. He was in there by himself. Bodge was sure the other two boys hadn't left. So, where were they?

He continued walking past the dark front of Bouncers and all the way to the corner of the street. All the while he glanced back to be sure he wasn't missing anything. You can only stand on a street corner for so long around 42nd Street without feeling uncomfortable. Bodge turned and headed back toward his car. A cab pulled up in front of the café and two drunks got out. No — they weren't both drunk. One was propping up the other, paying the cab fare, telling the driver to keep the change. But, boy, was his friend smashed. Bodge stopped walking and watched.

The cab drove off and the sober friend half-carried the other to the door of the café. The boy inside saw the new customers arriving and hurried out to give a hand. Between them they got the drunk inside and the door closed. Bodge walked on, trying to keep out of the lamplight, until he reached a spot opposite the window once again. He got there just in time to see the threesome vanish somewhere at the rear of the café. "Bathroom", Bodge thought straight away, but the disappearance of the earlier customers was still on his mind. He decided it was time for a cup of fancy coffee.

The bell over the door tinkled as he went in but he was by himself. He heard a door creak out back and the youth came running out, a flustered look on his face.

"How are you doing?" he asked.

"Just fine," said Bodge, sitting at a table near the window.

"What's your pleasure?" the boy asked, handing Bodge the menu that showed just how much his pleasure would cost him. He didn't seem to recognize Bodge from his previous visit. But, this was a different Bodge altogether.

"Oh, what do you recommend?"

"The Brazilian Gold's really good," the boy said pointing to it in the menu and lingering his finger beneath the cost.

"Sounds good. Give me a cup of that."

Bodge gave the boy a few minutes to get busy behind the counter, and waited till his back was turned before making a dash for the rear of the shop. The boy saw him too late. He'd reached the back door and was halfway through it.

"Hey, mister."

Bodge found himself in an unlit area. Ahead was a second door. He heard the boy calling out as he stepped forward, turned the handle and pushed. The door opened a few inches then hit against what felt like a chain. The door behind him was flung open and the boy came rushing through. In his hand he held a small derringer. "What the hell do you think you're doing?" he shouted.

"What the hell does it look like I'm doing?" Bodge answered. "I'm going to your rest room. Darn thing's locked."

"We don't have a rest room. Get out."

Bodge looked down at the gun and dramatically threw his arms into the air. "Hey, steady. Don't shoot, cowboy. I'd hate for my wife to find out I got killed for going to the bathroom."

Bodge walked back through to the café and the boy seemed to come over embarrassed about his overreaction.

"Look, I'm sorry," he said. "In this neighborhood we get a lot of addicts trying to hold us up. I get a bit jumpy at times."

"I hope I don't look like an addict to you."

"No. Really. I'm sorry. I'll get your coffee."

"What kind of café are you running that doesn't have a bathroom? Isn't there some City Ordinance against that kind of thing?"

"I don't know. You'll have to talk to the owner."

"Look, son. You've really shaken me up with all this gun play. Let's forget the coffee, shall we?"

"Sure."

Bodge knew. He knew everything. Maybe the possibility had been in his mind all along but now he was certain. He walked back down to 42$^{nd}$

to the call box. He removed the 'Out of Order sign from the phone and dialed Denholm's number. The policeman was sleeping off his shift.

"Okay," Bodge said. "It's on. Let's hope your FBI guy isn't just talk."

With all the heat he expected to go down in the next hour, Bodge could hardly stick around on the sidewalk. But he had to be sure the FBI got it right. He had to be sure *he'd* got it right. So, he went back to the car and waited. Those first thirty minutes seemed to tick over without any real urgency. He could imagine all the guilty parties leaving the scene of the crime before anyone else got there.

Then a delivery van went past and parked fifty yards ahead of him. He couldn't imagine who'd want a Bendix tumble drier at that time of the morning. The pressure was off. He knew he was no longer playing cop all by himself. Five minutes later, a black limo came down the street and parked twenty yards after Bouncers — then another. Another five minutes and a well-dressed couple staggered together down the street, a little tipsy, and went into the café. A bum in a long trench coat slouched up to the front of Bouncers and fell into the shadows there. It was like watching a stage production of the covert. If he hadn't been expecting these things, he wondered how much he would have noticed.

Two, maybe three more cars passed him and parked, another bum, another couple joined the first. Then, to some unheard, unseen signal, it all happened at once. All the vehicles discharged their passengers. There were simultaneous invasions of Bouncers and the café, although the groundwork had already made access to both a good deal easier. There was a small explosion and gunfire. There was yelling. Then there was silence.

For the second act, three squad cars arrived on cue with their sirens silent, and the uniformed officers took up posts in front of the two buildings. Although the police had obviously been briefed to act nonchalant, New Yorkers have an uncanny ability to sniff out a fracas. Those three cop cars didn't just park for the hell of it. Curious onlookers started filtering down from 42nd almost immediately. Bodge pulled his hat down over his brow and joined them. For the first half hour there was nothing to see. The flustered police officers were sick and tired of questions they couldn't answer. The crowd started entertaining itself and attracted more and more people.

"Hey," some drunk shouted. "You got a murder in there?"

Then another, "This ain't much of a show. I want my money back."

And a third, "My Gladys here can sing. You want a song?" There was a cheer and Gladys proved her beau a liar. So, when the first of the FBI emerged through the broken front door of Bouncers, the crowd deserted her and surged forward to get a better look. The sight was unusual enough to silence the jokers. The agents had three teenaged boys wrapped in blankets. Their faces were painted like showgirls but their hair was short.

Bodge edged his way to the front. More agents came out with their arms hooked around those of three older men who appeared to be drunk, or high. Bodge knew they were drugged. He doubted any of them would remember this scene in the morning. All three had towels over their heads. Bodge recognized the clothes of the drunk who'd arrived at the café a little earlier. An alleyway or some kind of passage led directly from the back door of the coffee shop to the rear of the clip joint. That was now obvious. For each delivery of characters from Bouncers, there was a van to collect them and whisk them away without comment. Naturally, the press had arrived and the flashing of cameras was turning the event into the end of the Oscars reception.

Next came the villains; the boy from the coffee shop, two goons in cuffs, and an older, distinguished looking man in a dark gray flannel suit and Ivy League tie. Then, last of all, the jackpot. Young Eddie Gladstein didn't seem in the least embarrassed. His confidence astounded Bodge. It was as if he'd been deprived for too long the adoration his amazing performances deserved. This was his curtain call. He smiled like Gary Cooper and would have posed for the cameras if the agents hadn't wrestled him into his van and slammed the door.

The crowd had enjoyed the third act but they knew the show was over. They watched the last of the FBI people carry assorted evidence out to trucks and leave. The police chained the doors of the two establishments, and there was nothing more to see. Soon, Bodge and the cop who'd drawn sentry duty were the only two there.

"Good night, officer," Bodge said, and went to his car. It had been a good night's work, but there was still much to be done. He was about to drive back to Palmer's apartment on Ninth when he heard a tap on his window and turned to see a stocky man in a dark overcoat standing there with a gun.

"Agent Leon?"

# 63

It was late afternoon before all the interrogations and witness statements and official rigmarole were over, but they still had Bodge sitting in an office re-reading drug enforcement posters. He'd identified young Gladstein and the man who'd helped the drunk into the coffee shop earlier that morning. He'd given up his compromising photograph of Lou taken, as it now seemed, in a Bouncers that was set up on weekends to look like a members club. One of the teenagers in the photo had been picked up during the raid and he led the feds to the other. But despite the fact that a procession of agents brought him coffee and sandwiches through the day, none of them left him with answers to his many questions.

Although it had obviously been Denholm who'd told the FBI where Bodge was parked that morning, the detective hadn't made an appearance all day. For a guy like Bodge, it was as frustrating as hell to be kept in the dark. He'd given a statement outlining every damn thing he'd done since Gladstein came into his life and had left himself wide open. He had no idea whether he was still under suspicion, or under arrest, or just helping agents with their inquiries. Nobody seemed to know. The sun was setting behind the Chrysler Building outside the window when the door finally opened and Denholm strolled in with two open bottles of Schlitz in his hands. He gave one to Bodge. There were no emotions reflected in his face.

"You don't drink," Bodge said.

"Time to start."

"Are we celebrating or commiserating?"

"Bodge, you wouldn't believe it." He sat on a chair opposite Bodge and took a long swig of the icy beer. Bodge shook his head.

"Okay, what is it I wouldn't believe?"

"I'm not at liberty to say." He ducked to avoid the flying pencil. "Okay, but don't forget I was just hanging around with the FBI as a witness and technical advisor. I just picked up threads here and there. It would appear some of the gentlemen they arrested at Bouncers had very close ties to the Soviet Bloc."

"What do you know?" Bodge laughed. "There really are Reds under the bed. That should keep the senators happy, knowing the Communist threat is alive and well. Tell me!"

"Well, most of the guys we picked up weren't willing to speak, but there was one who was hoping to get immunity from prosecution for squealing. Naturally, he was led to believe that wouldn't be a problem. This is the way the FBI reads it. It appears the Reds thought they could take advantage of the pervading atmosphere of queer paranoia by setting up a system for blackmailing government employees. The operation at Bouncers has been working for over a year. That's why they didn't grease the palms of the local cops to get a weekend license. There's so much sleazy late night activity in that part of town nobody would give a second thought to guys off their heads being carried in and out of bars.

"They used a cocktail of drugs to keep their victims on their feet but off their heads at the same time. Most of them were so stoned by the time they got to Bouncers they had no idea where they were. Same goes for the trip home. It appears your friend Lou had a particularly high resistance to whatever it was they gave him. They'd never had anyone come back before. It spooked them. The young guy in the café saw Lou parked out front in the same cab and he got his cronies to drag him out. They funneled whisky down his throat till it killed him. I guess the drugs didn't help either. Then they sent him back to his place and dumped him out front. That explains the conflicting witness statement at the Bowery Center."

"So how do I fit in to this story?" Bodge asked.

"Well, they figured that if your buddy could remember where you'd gone, there was a good chance you'd remember too. They didn't want to take that gamble. This was turning into a very lucrative operation. They'd gotten Lou out of picture and you were next."

"And Gladstein was integral in the whole setup. Why would he pick on a couple of nice guys like me and Lou?"

"Well, one that you were single, and I guess they figured you had access to sensitive documents. But I think it was your reports about the French in Indochina that was their main goal. They wanted to get intelligence to the Vietnamese communists. I guess they planned to blackmail you into handing over reports regularly."

"And Lou was an innocent bystander."

"It would seem so."

"But how did this young guy get into a secure office?"

"The same process, really. They set up one of the boys in the mail room and blackmailed him into handing over his security badge. There are new people in and out all the time so nobody questioned it. It wasn't the first time by all accounts. When the spy got there he told everyone he was relief and went through the mail. I doubt whether there was a set plan. He'd see what opportunities presented themselves and play it by ear.

That day was just bad luck for you, Bodge. It was a fluke that Palmer's letter to you arrived on a day Gladstein was there. He was a bit of a prima donna in their clique but undoubtedly talented. He knew you'd be going to DC for training and they got one of their operatives to take you out. Luckily for you the guy wasn't very good at his job."

"Jesus. Did they follow me to Vietnam as well?"

"No. As far as I can see, they lost all trace of you once you were at the safe house in Delaware. That's when they released your photo to discredit you should you try to close their operation."

"So why didn't they just move to another location?"

"They did shut down for two months to see whether you were going to cause any trouble. They figured if you were planning to expose them it would be sooner rather than later. When you didn't show up they decided the coast was clear — business as usual."

"Where does it all leave us?"

"Well, according to our guy here, your organization's in turmoil. You wouldn't believe the trouble this has caused up at Security. That's probably why nobody turned up here today. Half the Security police there are under suspension — including your old pals Tuck and Jensen. They're being accused of going at this whole matter with one eye shut. They ignored a whole lot of evidence — just saw what they wanted to see. Most of the men they accused of being homosexuals are taking out writs against the agents that interrogated them. I wouldn't be surprised if heads roll over this."

"Palmer?"

"I'm trying to get word to him, but something tells me he won't be riding this wave of public sympathy. I guess he's made a decision."

"And you?"

"I'll deny all the accusations against me — join the tidal wave of indignation, probably get a commendation or a cash handout to keep me off the back of the department. I've got family and friends I don't want to hurt and I'm not financially independent like Anthony. I've got several years of salary earning ahead of me. But you know, Bodge? Something like this never really goes away. The guys might slap me on the back and take me for a beer and pretend everything's back to normal, but they'll never really relax around me."

"Will you and Palmer...stay together?"

"Yeah, Bodge. Somehow or other. This isn't a very forgiving country for perverts but he was the only one who supported me when they put me on suspension. We'll find a way. We talked once about befriending a couple of lesbians and moving into adjacent houses in the suburbs."

Bodge wasn't completely convinced it was a joke. It sounded more like something he and Palmer had actually considered. But the image of it threw him into a chuckling fit that pulled Denholm in too.

"That I have to see," Bodge laughed. "I want to be the first guest invited round for Thanksgiving,"

"You'll be very welcome, my friend. I'll get Bertha to do her special cranberry sauce."

They took long swigs of the beer and waited for the laughing fit to subside.

"What about you?" Denholm asked. "Will you stay with the agency? There's no doubt in anyone's mind that you were set up. You're in the clear. There'd probably be other missions out there for a French speaker."

"You know, Dermot. I really can't say I'm too happy about the way they ditched me and Lou when they thought we were different. Those are the times you find out who your friends are. It taught me something about humility. You see, I'm not sure how Lou and I would have reacted if it had been someone else. I'd like to say we would have stood by the guy and given him our support, but I can't swear we wouldn't have closed ranks with all the other bigots and let him fry. At the very least it means I've got a lot of learning to do about life. I need to get away from this city for a while and give myself a few other dimensions."

"Any immediate plans?"

"Think I'll go catch a few fish."

# 64

Bodge knew Lou's father from fishing trips. He lived out on Putnam Lake so he knew a thing or two about fishing. In fact he was the only one of them who did. They were so bad the standing joke was that their fishing trips were a cover for some other illicit activity. It was only when Lou's dad turned up that any of them got fish to eat. The rest of the time they survived on canned corned beef and beer.

Lou senior lived by himself in a shack on the lake. He'd been a successful businessman in Manhattan when Lou was growing up and the apartment that Lou lived in till his death had belonged to the Vistarini family. Some years before Lou's mother passed away, his dad gave the apartment to his son and the parents escaped from the pollution. As Bodge neared the lake, he considered the escape to have been well executed. It was a truly beautiful spot. As soon as the car pulled up, Mr. Vistarini came trotting out to meet it. He was in his seventies, but fit and sporting a crop of healthy white hair. Lou would probably have ended up just like him.

"Bodge? Bodge, is that you? Well, I'll be…"

"Lou, good to see you."

"I hardly recognized you. You been in training for something?"

"Survival. I've got the finals coming up any time now."

They walked around to the back of the shack, Lou Senior's arm around Bodge's shoulder. Three excited Collies skipped around their feet. The back patio reminded Bodge of the villa in Ban Methuot. The glassy lake stretched out to the skyline. He sat in a deckchair and petted the dogs while Lou Senior went inside for three cool beers. When he returned, neither man really knew how to begin. Bodge took the initiative. He grabbed one bottle from the table in front of them, got to his feet and held it up toward the lake.

"Lou, how you doing?" he said.

Mr. Vistarini took up another bottle, stood and held that toward the lake also. "I miss you, son."

With that, the two men drank until both bottles were empty. Bodge stepped forward, picked up the third bottle from the table and took a mouthful from it. He handed the bottle to Lou Senior who did the same. The two then walked to the balcony and Bodge watched the old man pour the remains of Lou's beer into the water.

"There," he said. "I guess that makes more sense than half-a-dozen square heads in pretty uniforms firing blanks in the air. It's just, when we three agreed this was the way we wanted it, I always figured it'd be you and my Lou toasting me on…" The words caught in his throat. He turned and walked into the shack. When he came back out five minutes later he'd regained control and was carrying two more beers.

"I figure he's had enough, don't you, Bodge?" They both laughed and set the dogs off yapping.

"Have you got a bottomless supply in there, Lou?"

"Enough for us, anyway. I haven't touched the stuff since he went."

"You want to talk about it?"

"I've been waiting for you. I knew you'd come. Haven't seen a one of his so-called friends since all this started. I need to get some honesty from someone. They came out to see me, your Agency heavies. They seemed more annoyed that I knew what my boy did for a living, than anything else."

Lou had always ignored the agreement of secrecy when it came to his dad. Bodge admired him for that and wished he'd been better at breaking rules himself from time to time.

"I bet they weren't that sympathetic at your loss, either," Bodge said.

"Bodge, it was as if Lou was the enemy. After all these years I couldn't believe his own people would turn on him like that."

"That was Security, Lou. They're from a different planet. They didn't know him. There wasn't a man or woman in our office who didn't love and respect your son."

"Bodge, they said…They accused Lou of being…"

"I know."

"It's a lie, Bodge. An evil lie."

"I know that, too. Someone framed both of us."

"You too? Can you prove it?"

"It's all taken care of, Lou." Bodge reached behind him for his jacket and pulled the sealed envelope from the inside pocket. He handed it to Lou's dad and watched him tear it open and read through the apology. He looked up with a smile and a tear in his eye.

"That's fine, Bodge. Just fine."

"They let me bring it myself sooner than posting it."

"I wouldn't have wanted it any other way. Thank you boy. You want to tell me how it all happened?"

Bodge told Lou Senior about the night his son died, about the boy, Gladstein, and the blank spot in Bodge's memory. He didn't leave anything out, not the street bum or the pauper's graveyard. Bodge watched as Lou Senior's burden — the doubts, the Agency lies, the unanswered questions — slowly lifted. When it was all out, Lou Senior crossed over to Bodge, put a hand on one side of his head and kissed his hair like a Pope.

"Thank you, Bodge. I can't tell you how much I needed this visit.

Bodge was drained. The inquest was all over.

"So, how's the fishing?"

The afternoon turned to evening while they drank and talked of happier things. Bodge listened to tales of young Lou and the scrapes he'd gotten himself into. He listened with a mixture of envy and regret to the love story of Lou Senior and his pretty Venetian bride.

"May I ask you how she died?" Bodge asked.

"Well, she was diabetic, then the angina caught up with her. Her father had it. That's why we came up here when she first showed signs. Doctor's said it was a combination of those two things that killed her. She was always afraid she might have handed the angina down to Lou. We managed to keep that from her till she passed on."

"Keep what from her?"

"The fact that Lou was suffering from angina."

"Wait. Lou had a heart condition?"

"Sure, Bodge. You had to know that."

"No. He never said a word about it. How could he have passed the medical for the agency?"

"It's a degenerative disease. It comes on in middle age. When he applied, he was fine. He didn't start to feel anything till he reached his thirties."

"But they ask for medical history of the family."

"What they actually ask is, 'Did your father have any signs of angina?' And, of course, I didn't. It's far more common in men. They don't expect it to be passed on from the mother."

"The son-of-a-gun kept it to himself. I knew he was always getting heartburn, taking antacids. But I figured that was just from his Italian cooking. I had no idea. How serious was it?"

"Serious enough to get him out of the Agency."

"Whoa. Hold up, there. Are you telling me Lou was on his way out on medical grounds?"

"He had another six months to go. Full pension."

"So, that's what he meant when he said he had plans."

"The lifestyle you boys were living down there was killing him; sitting all day at a desk, smoking, eating, drinking. It would have gotten too bad for him to work after a while. It wasn't life-threatening or anything. He was on his way up here. The air here would have sorted it out I reckon."

"That old skunk. He was going to leave me there by myself. That explains why he was so delighted I got the posting to Operations. You know, Lou, he told me one day I didn't know a thing about him. It turns out he was right."

"So, I guess he didn't tell you about the houses either?"

"Houses?"

The dogs romped off ahead as Lou senior led Bodge around the lake shore about half a mile. In a clearing they came upon two semi-completed wooden cabins side by side looking out over the water.

"Me and Lou worked on them whenever he came down at weekends. That one was going to be yours, Bodge."

"Mine?"

"He figured once he was out of the service he could finally get himself wed to a local girl and move out here. He said he had to be free of lies and secrets to really give himself to anyone. I think he had a couple of fillies in mind. So, he was building himself a house and he figured he couldn't imagine living next door to anyone else but his old buddy, Bodge. So we started putting this other place together — for you and your wife. It's still yours if you want it. You got a girl, Bodge?"

# Epilogue

Once Bodge had left her at the silent man Hotel, Hong showered and left her few possessions in the room. There was nothing she needed there. She took a cyclo to an apartment building in Da Kao. She'd rented it for three years but never lived there. It was unfurnished and she used it to store things she didn't want anyone else to see, like her suitcases, and her traveling clothes.

She was in the back room changing into a Western suit made of the finest Vietnamese silk. Her heart was flying. The worst was behind her. Only one more leg. Two hours from freedom and the man she'd learned to respect, and love.

She hadn't heard the unlocking of the door or the footsteps behind her.

"Your Royal Highness?"

The voice came from the doorway and seemed to slam into her heart. She turned in shock and hurried to cover her breasts with her shirt. The Chamberlain stood half hidden behind the door in a somber charcoal suit with an apologetic smile on his face.

"What? What are you doing here?" she stammered.

"Forgive me," he said, looking down at the floor. "I have a message from the Exalted One."

"I don't wish to know it. The Emperor no longer has any influence over me."

"With respect, that is not true. His Excellency knows of your plans."

"I don't care." That was a lie. She cared deeply. How could he have found out? How did they know about this place? Her dreams were turning to smoke in front of her. "It's too late to stop me."

The skinny man half raised his eyes. "Perhaps Your Royal Highness would care to go to the window and take a look down into the street?"

She hated him and his officious ways and his phony deference. "Turn your back," she ordered.

"Yes, Your Royal Highness."

She put on her blouse. Her trembling fingers could hardly grip the buttons. She took a deep breath and walked to the small uncurtained window. Parked opposite was an open back truck. The girls seated there looked up at her. One of them waved. She was wearing the cream suit Hong had bought her for her journey to America. The other had on jeans and a T shirt, the uniform of the idle West. These were the sisters Hong had smuggled out of the country. If indeed they'd left, their exodus had been brief. Hong's misery was compounded. Her fate had been settled for her.

"I think you should write a letter to your American friend now," said the chamberlain.

# About the Author

Colin Cotterill was born in London in 1952. He trained as a teacher and worked in Israel, Australia, the US, and Japan before training teachers in Thailand and on the Burmese border. He wrote and produced a forty-programme language teaching series; English By Accident, for Thai national television and spent several years in Laos, initially with UNESCO. Colin became involved in child protection in the region and is still involved in social projects. He set up a book and scholarship programme for his beloved Laos and runs two small schools for the children of Burmese migrants near his home.